THE BOUNTY HUNTER . . . HUNTED . . .

"Seal off the cockpit area." Boba Fett spoke aloud. He was already leaning over the control panel as *Slave I*'s onboard computer executed the command; with a hiss, the hatchway door closed behind him. With a few quick jabs at the controls, he silenced the alarm signals once again.

Even from this distance, where the visible details of his enemy's ship were little more distinct than the stars behind it, he could recognize the vessel.

It's Xizor. The outlines of the Falleen prince's flagship were unmistakable—and intimidating. The ship was known to be one of the deadliest and most thoroughly armored in the galaxy. If *Slave I* had gotten into a full-pitched battle with it, there wouldn't even have been this much of Boba Fett's ship left hanging together.

The mystery of why the *Vendetta* hadn't moved in for the kill was easy enough to determine. *He's holding back,* decided Fett. *Just waiting to see if there's any sign of life.* Prince Xizor was known to be something of a trophy collector; it would be entirely consistent for him to want the hard physical evidence—the corpses—of those he had set out to kill, rather than just blowing them into disconnected atoms drifting in space.

STAR WARS®

THE BOUNTY HUNTER WARS
BOOK THREE

HARD MERCHANDISE

K. W. Jeter

SPECTRA™

BANTAM BOOKS
New York Toronto London Sydney Auckland

STAR WARS: HARD MERCHANDISE
A Bantam Spectra Book / July 1999

ISBN 0-553-57891-X

Published simultaneously in the United States and Canada

Bantam Books are published by Bantam Books, a division of Random
House, Inc. Its trademark, consisting of the words "Bantam Books"
and the portrayal of a rooster, is Registered in U.S. Patent and Trademark Office and in other countries. Marca Registrada. Bantam Books,
1540 Broadway, New York, New York 10036.

PRINTED IN THE UNITED STATES OF AMERICA

OPM   10   9   8   7   6   5   4   3   2   1

*To Mark & Elizabeth Bourne
and Austin Lawhead*

ACKNOWLEDGMENTS

The author would once again like to extend thanks to Sue Rostoni and Michael Stackpole for invaluable assistance, and to Pat LoBrutto for saintly patience. Also, a special thanks to Irwyn Applebaum. *Honi soit qui mal y pense.*

1

Two bounty hunters sat in a bar, talking.

"Things aren't what they used to be," said Zuckuss morosely. As a member of one of the ammonia-breathing species of his homeworld Gand, he had to be careful in establishments such as this. Intoxicants and stimulants that produced feelings of well-being in other creatures often evoked a profound melancholy in him. Even in a high-class place that supposedly catered to all known physiologies—the soothing, programmed play of lights across the columned walls, the shifting spectra that were supposed to relax weary travelers' central nervous systems, struck Zuckuss as crepuscular and depressing as the faded hopes of his youth. *I had ambitions once,* he told himself, leaning over the tall, blue-tinged glass in front of him. *Big ones. Where had they gone?*

"I wouldn't know," said Zuckuss's companion. The droid bounty hunter 4-LOM sat across from him, an untouched drink—perhaps only water—in front of him. A mere formality: the drink had been taken away twice already and replaced with exactly the same thing, so the charges could be rung up on 4-LOM's tab. That was the only way that nonimbibing constructs such as droids could make themselves welcome in any kind of watering hole. "Your attitude," continued 4-LOM, "implies a value judgment on your part. That is, that things were better at one time than they are now. I don't make those kinds of judgments. I merely deal with things as they are."

You would, thought Zuckuss. This was what he got for hooking up with a cold-blooded—cold-circuited, at least—creature like 4-LOM. There were plenty of excitable droids in the galaxy—Zuckuss had run into a few— but the ones that were attracted to the bounty hunter trade all shared the same vibroblade-edged logic and absolute-zero emotional tone. They hunted, and killed when necessary, without even the tiniest acceleration of electrons along their inner connectors.

The bar's soft, dirgelike background music—it was supposed to be soothing as well, with harmonic overtones of almost narcotic languor—made Zuckuss think of his previous partner Bossk. The Trandoshan bounty hunter had been cold-blooded, literally so, but one would never have guessed it from the way he'd carried on.

"Now *that*," said Zuckuss with a slow, emphatic nod, "that was *real* bounty hunting. That had some *passion* to it. Real excitement." He extended the retractable pipette from the lower part of his face mask and sucked up another swallow of the drink, though he knew it would only deepen and darken his mood. "We had some good times together, me and Bossk . . ."

"That wasn't what you said when you agreed to become partners with me once more." 4-LOM's photo-optical receptors kept a slow, careful scan around the bar and its other occupants, even as the droid kept up his end of the conversation. He talked for no reason other than to avoid drawing attention to himself and Zuckuss as they waited for their quarry to make an appearance. "Value judgments aside, the exact record of your statement is that you had had enough of Bossk's way of doing business. Too much danger—if that's what you mean by 'excitement'—and not enough credits. So you wanted a change."

"Don't use my own words against me." Zuckuss knew that he had gotten what he had asked for. And what could be worse than that?

"Mourn the old days if you want," said 4-LOM after a few moments of silence had passed. "We have business to take care of. Please direct your waning attention toward the entrance."

Worse than dealing with Boba Fett, grumbled Zuckuss to himself. At least when you got involved with Fett, you were assured that you were face-mask-to-helmet with the best bounty hunter in the galaxy, someone who had plenty of reason for taking such a high-and-mighty attitude. Where did 4-LOM get off, lording it over him this way? If it hadn't been for some stretches of bad luck, and a few unfortunate strategic decisions, it would have been the droid that had been looking to hook up with him again, rather than the other way around. Though they had been partners before, and for a lot longer than Zuckuss had been hooked up with Bossk, the relationship between them could never be the same. Back then, 4-LOM had even saved Zuckuss's life, when he had been dying from his ammonia-breathing lungs having been exposed to an accidental inhalation of oxygen. The two of them had even made other plans together, of working for the Rebel Alliance in some way . . .

Those plans hadn't worked out, though. Their time as members of the Rebel Alliance—double agents, actually, since they had kept secret their new allegiance to the Rebel cause—had been occupied with one significant operation: an attempt to snatch from Boba Fett the carbonite slab with Han Solo frozen inside it, before Fett could deliver the prize to Jabba the Hutt. The plan, using several other bounty hunters as unwitting dupes, had had disastrous results. It hadn't succeeded, and 4-LOM had needed a complete core-to-sheath rebuild to get back on his feet. *And,* mused Zuckuss, *he wasn't the same after that*. This idealism that had led 4-LOM to join the Rebel Alliance had all but evaporated, replaced by his former cold-spirited greed. Zuckuss supposed that came from hanging out once again with the other bounty hunters; he had felt their mercenary natures rubbing off onto him as well.

Plus there was one factor that both of them hadn't counted on when they had joined the Alliance. A factor that made all the difference in the universe—

Being a Rebel didn't pay.

At least not in credits. And there were still so many tempting targets all through the galaxy, the kind of hard merchandise that a smart, fast bounty hunter could get rich from. Like the one that Zuckuss and 4-LOM had come here to get.

Zuckuss took another sip of his drink. *Triple agents,* he thought. *That must be what we are now*. Neither he nor 4-LOM had ever formally renounced allegiance to the Rebel Alliance, but they had both been taking care of their own business for some time now.

Moodily, he shook his head. He'd have to think about all the rest of those things some other time; right now, there were more pressing matters at hand.

Zuckuss did as he'd been instructed by 4-LOM. The entrance to the bar was the one direction, in back of 4-LOM, that the droid bounty hunter couldn't scan without cranking around his head unit. Bright laughter, some of it as high-pitched and sharp-edged as breaking glass, and a tangled whirl of gossiping conversations sounded in Zuckuss's ears as he lifted his gaze toward the entrance's fluttering circumference. Beyond it, a sloping tunnel led up to the surface of the planet and its night sky filled with a chain of pearllike moons. Smaller and more avid orbs dotted the length of the entrance tunnel; those were the eyes of the tiny ergovore creatures that scuttled and darted in and out of the soft, trembling crevices.

As a way of keeping weapons out of the establishment, metal detector units would have been both useless and insulting; the bar catered to a clientele that not only included independent droids such as 4-LOM, who could pay their way handsomely enough, but also any number of the galaxy's most aristocratic and stiff-necked bloodlines. From the rims of his own large, insectoid eyes, Zuckuss could spot some of the galaxy's richest and most glittering denizens, devoted to spending their vast inherited wealth in as ostentatious a manner as possible. For many of them, their weapons were ceremonial ornaments, dictated by fierce custom and the privileges given to their rank; to have asked them to divest of even the smallest dagger or low-penetration blaster would have been an insult, expiable only by the death of the establishment's proprietor, a stub-fingered Bergamasque named Salla C'airam. The only acceptable alternative, preserving their honor and the bar's decorum, was to ask them to hand over the power sources for their blasters and similar high-tech weapons, thus limiting the damage and potential loss of life to what could be achieved with inert metal. C'airam kept the ergovores in the entrance tunnel hungry enough that their sensitive antennae were at constant quivering alert for the emanations from even the smallest power cell, no matter how well hidden; their flocking and chittering toward any they detected was a sure giveaway of anyone trying to violate the house rules.

All of which meant that the blaster holstered at Zuckuss's hip was useless at the moment; that was an uncomfortable feeling for him. It was little consolation that everyone else in the bar was similarly disarmed. He would have preferred the usual setup that he encountered in the watering holes in which he more often hung out, where everyone including the bartenders was armed to the teeth. *Then you know where you stand*, thought Zuckuss. *This other stuff's too tricky*.

"How much longer?" He leaned forward to ask the question of 4-LOM. "Until the merchandise is supposed to show up?" He didn't have much patience for waiting, either. He hadn't become a bounty hunter in order to sit around waiting.

"His arrival is precisely fixed," replied 4-LOM. "Such precision of movement and timing is nearly the equal of my own; in that, I admire the creature. Especially given that there is a price on his head, a bounty that it is our intention to collect. Many other sentient creatures, given those circumstances, would try to make their comings and goings erratic, to vary them in such a way as to frustrate pursuers in determining their target's patterns of behavior. But he has confidence in the precautions that he has taken, including the limiting of his public recreational activities to this establishment." 4-LOM rested his hands unmoving on the table. "We shall soon determine if the merchandise's confidence is rewarded with a continuing freedom."

There was no point in arguing with a droid such as 4-LOM. One might as well have had a conversation with the tracking systems aboard a standard pursuit ship. Even worse, Zuckuss knew that 4-LOM was correct; there had been a good reason for arriving at this place so far ahead of their quarry, getting set up and letting the minutes pass until the moment of action came. He knew all that; he just didn't care for what he knew.

If only . . . Zuckuss kept an eye on the bar's entrance and allowed his thoughts to slip back into brooding about the past.

If only the old Bounty Hunters Guild hadn't broken up. If only its successor organizations, the short-lived True Guild and Guild Reform Committee factions, hadn't fallen apart with the speed of a core meltdown. Those were big ifs, Zuckuss knew, especially when it was taken into account that the main reason the Guild and everything that came after it had disintegrated so rapidly and thoroughly was the basic greed and irascibility that lay at the center of every bounty hunter's heart—or whatever a droid like 4-LOM had instead.

That was the real reason. Zuckuss took another sip of the drink in front of him. *Boba Fett was just the excuse.* There were plenty of bounty hunters, former members of the vanished Guild, who blamed Fett for everything that had happened. And it was true, up to a point, that Boba Fett's entry into the old Bounty Hunters Guild had been the event that had brought about the organization's disintegration, and that had put every creature in it at the throat of those he had previously called his brothers. But Zuckuss knew that Boba Fett had been no more than the key in the lock that had let free all the forces of avarice and conspiracy that had been bottled up inside the Guild for so long, getting stronger and more malignant all the while. It was amazing that the Bounty Hunters Guild had even endured as long as it had, given the irascible and hungry natures of its members; that was a tribute to the organizational skills of its final leader, the Trandoshan Cradossk. He had probably been the only creature in the galaxy ruthless and clever enough to have kept a lid on the Guild's rank and file.

We did it to ourselves, thought Zuckuss glumly. The drink, and the ones before it, had done nothing to lift his spirits. *Now we have to live with the consequences.* He knocked back the sour dregs at the bottom of the glass.

"You know what?" Zuckuss let his thoughts turn into spoken words. "It's a cold, hard galaxy we live in."

4-LOM gave him a typically unemotional droid glance. "If you say so."

Nothing that the Rebel Alliance could do was likely to change that, either. The Rebels didn't have a chance of winning, anyway, not against the massed strength of the Empire and all of Palpatine's deep, enfolding cunning. In the darker corners of the galaxy, where surreptitiously acquired information was bought and sold, traded in whispers from one furtive creature to the next, rumors had been heard of a gathering of the Imperial forces, somewhere out near a moon called Endor—

like a fist clenching together, into a hammer that would crush the Alliance forever, and end once and for all its crazy dreams of freedom. And now, the galaxy's bounty hunters were without the Guild that had preciously enforced professional relations among its members—the Hunter's Creed had at least kept them from murdering one another outright in the course of pursuing business. Small, upstart organizations had sprung up in the power vacuum created by the old Guild's destruction, but they were still too weak to create order among such naturally violent and greed-driven creatures. Most hunters were still on their own, friendless except for whatever partnerships they could forge with one another. Zuckuss had been partners with different bounty hunters before, even while the Guild had been going through its ugly process of disintegration. He had even been partners with Boba Fett, on more than one occasion—but somehow, he had never come out any the better for it. Typically, Boba Fett wound up getting what he was after, and all the rest were lucky if they were still alive afterward. Doing business with Fett was a recipe for disaster.

Truth to tell, though, Zuckuss's other partnerships hadn't gone much better. Whatever his personal feelings about 4-LOM, he could swallow those easily enough, given that the two of them had actually been putting credits into their pockets since hooking up. They seemed to have complementary skills: Zuckuss operated on instinct, the way most organic creatures were capable of, and 4-LOM possessed the cold logic of a machine. What had made Boba Fett such a fearsome individual in the bounty hunter trade was that he had all of those capabilities, and more, inside a single skin.

"Here he comes—"

Zuckuss's musings were interrupted by the soft-spoken announcement from 4-LOM. Even without facing the entrance, the droid bounty hunter had been able to detect the sudden flamboyant appearance of their quarry, the presently free creature they planned on turning into hard merchandise and a hefty addition to their credit accounts.

"A round for everyone, innkeeper!" The booming voice of Drawmas Sma'Da filled the bar, like the rumble of thunder over the planet's horizon. Zuckuss looked up from his drink and saw the immense, befurred, and caparisoned form of the most notorious gambler and oddsman in five systems, spreading his arms wide. The gemstones studding Sma'Da's pinkly manicured fingers sparkled in a multicolored constellation of wealth and extravagance; his broad, thrown-back shoulders were swathed in the soft fur pelts of a dozen worlds' rarest species. The artfully preserved heads of the animals that had died for his adornment, with black pearls for eyes, dangled over a belly of wobbling girth. "If I'm in a good mood," shouted Sma'Da, "then *all* should be so lucky!"

Luck was a preoccupation with Drawmas Sma'Da. As it was with Zuckuss and every other sentient creature in the galaxy: *If I had his luck,* thought the bounty hunter, *I'd be retired by now.* Sma'Da had been fortunate not only in the placing of his bets, but clever as well, in that he had virtually created an entirely new field of wagering. The flamboyant gambler had been the first to cover wagers on the various ups and downs of the struggle between the Empire and the Rebel Alliance. No military conflict was too small-scale, no political infighting too inconsequential, for Sma'Da to make odds, accept bets— often on either side of the outcome, then pay off and collect when the particular event was over. By now, his "Invisible & Ineluctable Casino," as he called it, stretched from one end of the galaxy to the other, a shadow of the actual war going on between Emperor Palpatine and the Rebels. No matter who won, either on the battlefield or the database of wagers, Drawmas Sma'Da came out ahead: he raked off the house percentage on every bet placed, win or lose. All those profitable little bites mounted up to an impressive pile of credits, one reflected in Sma'Da's own ever-increasing girth.

Two humanoid females, with the kind of large-eyed, mysteriously smiling beauty that made the males of nearly every species weep with frustration, draped themselves on either side of Sma'Da's capacious shoulders, as though they were the ultimate ornaments of his success and wealth. They moved in synch with him, or almost seemed to float without walking, so ineffable was their grace; the tripartite organism of Sma'Da and his consorts moved into the center of the establishment, like a new sun rearranging the orbits of all the lesser planets it found itself among.

The proprietor Salla C'airam, all bowing obsequiousness and fluttering tentaclelike appendages, hurried toward Sma'Da. "How good to see you again, Drawmas! It's always too long between visits!"

Sma'Da had been in the bar just the previous night, Zuckuss knew. The proprietor was carrying on as though he and the gambler had been cruelly separated for years.

A crowd of sycophants, flatterers, favor-seekers, gold diggers, and those who derived some deep spiritual benefit from basking in the radiance of accumulated credits, had already formed around Sma'Da. Signaling to the bar's waiters and serving staff, Salla C'airam led the way to the highly visible table that had been kept in readiness for just such distinguished personages. Sma'Da's jowly face, split by a gold-toothed smile, beamed above the crowd as it shifted, like the swell of an ocean tide, toward the other side of the bar. A banquet equal to both Sma'Da's appetite and credit accounts had already been laid out by the swiftly darting waiters; crystalline decanters, filled with exotic offworld liqueurs and roiling with low-level combustibles, towered above platters of meats spiced with cellular-suspension enhancements.

"There's enough in front of him to feed an Imperial division." Zuckuss kept the gambler and his entourage in sight from the corner of his eye. If the expensive viands had been converted back into credits, the sum would have gone to feed several divisions. He could see Sma'Da's oddly delicate hands, pudgy folds welling around the wide bands of his rings, picking at the delicacies, playfully stuffing the choicer morsels into the smiling mouths of the consorts at either side of him. "Eventually," mused Zuckuss, "he'll implode, from sheer mass and density, like a black hole."

"Unlikely," said 4-LOM. "If creatures could suffer such a fate, that's what would have happened to Jabba the Hutt. His appetite was many times greater than this person's. You saw that for yourself."

"I know." Zuckuss slowly nodded. "I was just trying to *forget* about anything I might have seen at Jabba's palace." As with every other mercenary type in the galaxy, he had spent some time in the employ of the late Huttese crimelord. Jabba had been involved in so many shady dealings throughout the galaxy that it would have been hard for a bounty collector not to hook up with him at some point. Rarely, though, had any of them profited by it; a successful assocation with a creature like Jabba the Hutt was one that you survived intact.

"Anyway," continued 4-LOM, keeping his emotionless voice low, "don't waste time worrying about our target's state of health. He just has to live long enough for us to collect the bounty that's been posted on him."

A burst of laughter and bright, chattering voices came from the crowd at Drawmas Sma'Da's table. All eyes and attention in the bar had been drawn to the gambler from the moment he had entered. Zuckuss felt a bit more secure because of the noise and the general diversion, as though it had made him and 4-LOM briefly invisible. With someone like Sma'Da in the room, no one would be watching them.

"It's ready." 4-LOM made the simple, quiet announcement. The droid bounty hunter leaned forward slightly, passing a small object underneath the table to Zuckuss. "Time to put our plans into action."

Time was always the crucial factor. Despite his complaints, Zuckuss knew exactly why they had had to arrive at the bar so much earlier than their target. Some preparations required precisely measured amounts of time, things readied in silence and stealth, even if right under the inquisitive eyes of a bar full of ignorant onlookers. *They don't need to know,* thought Zuckuss with a measure of satisfaction. *But they will.*

He took the object from 4-LOM's hand, carefully minimizing his actions so that anyone glancing in this direction would have no clue of what might be happening beneath the table. The rest of the preparations were swiftly completed; there was no need for Zuckuss to watch his own hands going about their work. With this kind of equipment, so essential to a bounty hunter's trade, he could have performed the necessary operations with his large eyes completely blindfolded.

"Okay," said Zuckuss after a moment. He leaned back, chancing a quick peek under the table's surface. A tiny blinking red light indicated that his part of the preparations had been completed satisfactorily. "Looks good to me."

4-LOM gave a slight nod, a humanoid gesture that he had picked up somewhere along the way. "Then I suggest you proceed."

It's always up to me, grumbled Zuckuss to himself as he pushed back his chair and stood up. No matter who he had for a partner, somehow he always wound up doing the dirty work.

"Excuse me . . ." The crowd around Drawmas Sma'Da's table had grown even larger and denser, just in the short while that Zuckuss had been getting ready. He shoved and wedged himself through the press of bodies, the din of their excited words and laughter clattering in his earholes. "Pardon me . . . I've got a message for the esteemed Sma'Da . . ."

The blinking dot of red light that Zuckuss had checked under the table with 4-LOM was safely hidden inside his close-fitting, equipment-studded tunic. A couple of quick, sharp blows from the points of his elbows right to a few midsections of the closely packed crowd enabled him to work his way right up to the front of Sma'Da's table. He gave a slight, formal bow as he found himself confronting the gambler over the trays of picked-over delicacies.

"A message?" Drawmas Sma'Da was well known for his alert attention to voices from the crowd. "How interesting. I wasn't expecting any such; these aren't my usual business hours." The gambler's eyes were barely visible through the rounded folds of flesh, pushed upward by his exuberant smile. "But," he continued with an expansive wave of his grease-shiny hands, "I *might* be interested in hearing it. If it's *important* enough."

Sma'Da's words hardly counted as a witticism, but the smiles on the faces of his escorts widened, and his flatterers in the assembled crowd broke into loud, appreciative guffaws.

"Judge its importance for yourself." Zuckuss gazed back into the gambler's fat-swaddled eyes. "The information in it comes from Sullust."

The smile on Sma'Da's own face didn't diminish, but what could be seen of his eyes grew brighter and more avarice-driven, like glints of razor-edged durasteel. " 'Sullust'? That doesn't sound any chimes in my memory." He tilted his head to one side, as coyly as possible for something so massive. "Who is this Sullust you speak of?"

At Zuckuss's back, the laughter and the hubbub of voices had died away. They knew what the name meant— the bar was exactly the sort of crossroads where information about Imperial and Rebel comings and goings would be traded.

"Not *who*," replied Zuckuss, "but *where*. And I think you already know that." Sma'Da had based his entire gambling enterprise upon rumors and secrets, the tiny scraps of information that enabled him to calculate odds with such precision. "Don't you?"

"Perhaps so." Sma'Da's golden smile gleamed even more dazzlingly. "But only a fool turns down an opportunity to learn more. Dear things—" He turned to his female companions on either side of him, one after the other. "Amuse yourselves elsewhere for a little while. I need a moment alone with this *interesting* person." He fluttered his beringed paws at the crowd. "Make way, make way." Pouting, the females detached themselves and floated away. The sycophants and other assorted hangers-on took the cue as well, dispersing while whispering among themselves and keeping watch on the gambler from the corners of their eyes. "There," said Sma'Da as Zuckuss sat down beside him. "Much more private now, wouldn't you say?"

"Adequate." Zuckuss still didn't feel entirely at ease in such public surroundings. Proper bounty hunting, he felt, was best done in remote areas or in the depths of interstellar space, where it would have been just him, the target, and a high-powered weapon pointing in the target's direction. *That'd wipe the smile from this one's face,* Zuckuss thought. He glanced over at the table he'd left; 4-LOM was sitting as placidly as before, not even seeming to be interested at all in the action that was about to come down. Zuckuss turned back toward Sma'Da. "I was pretty sure that a creature in your line of business would be interested in news from Sullust. You're probably already taking in bets on it."

"Oh, I might." The dangling animal heads bobbed as Sma'Da shrugged his broad shoulders. "It's hard, though, to get any of my regular clientele to put down their credits, one way or another. The reports that have circulated, concerning the Imperial buildup near the moon of Endor, have made a great many creatures nervous. It's one thing to bet on a minor battle here or there, a mere skirmish or a Rebel raid on an Imperial armaments depot, that sort of thing; quite another to place a wager on what could very likely be the end of this great game." Sma'Da heaved an immense, fat-quivering sigh. "If that should be the case—if Emperor Palpatine should indeed quash the Rebellion once and for all—how I shall miss these glorious days!" He shook his head, as though already immured in regret over a vanished past. "The Rebel Alliance has brought the radiant aspect of hope to every corner of the galaxy; and where there's hope, there's risk-taking. And then . . ." Sma'Da's smile reappeared, even slyer than before. "There's wagering. And that's always profitable, for someone like me."

The gambler's words gave Zuckuss a measure of cold comfort. *He's no different than me,* thought Zuckuss. Not that he had expected anything different; most of the galaxy's denizens, in Zuckuss's estimation, spent all their time looking out for Number One, namely themselves. If he had ever believed otherwise, he might have been tempted stay with the Rebel Alliance. But he was certain that idealism was a rare trace element in the universe's composition, whereas greed was as ubiquitous as hydrogen atoms.

"I like profits as well," said Zuckuss. One of the waiters had brought another drink, shimmering amethyst in color, and had placed it in front of him; he didn't touch it. "That's why I sought you out."

"Good for you." Sma'Da gave an appreciative nod. "And good for me, if whatever information you've brought with you should turn out useful. The more one knows, the easier it is to make odds. Though mind you"—he peered closer at Zuckuss— "it's hard to take me by surprise on these things, anymore. There's not much I haven't heard about what's been going on near Endor; I have excellent sources for all kinds of gossip and rumor."

"I'm pretty sure this is something you haven't heard before." Zuckuss reached into his tunic.

"Ah." Sma'Da put the tips of his glittering fingers together. "My pulse races with anticipation."

"How's this, then?" Zuckuss pulled out a blaster pistol and set its cold, hard muzzle against Drawmas Sma'Da's forehead. "You're coming with me."

He had the satisfaction of seeing the gambler's eyes

widen for a moment. Then they all but vanished again, from the upwelling pressure of Sma'Da's expansive grin.

"That's very funny. How amusing!" Sma'Da drew his hands apart, enough to clap them together again in appreciation. "Everyone—please observe!" He called out loudly to the crowd in the bar; eager faces swiveled in the direction of the table. "To what lengths creatures go merely to provide me with a few fleeting moments of amusement!" His laughter boomed against the walls, as though to frighten the play of colors against their surface. "Bringing in and waving around a blaster, in the one place it's sure to be useless! Not even a power source for it!"

The laughter was contagious; Zuckuss could hear it sweep through the establishment like a wave breaking over and carrying away the staff as well as the patrons. Their bright, barking noise mounted louder, approaching some critical mass of hilarity. Zuckuss glanced over at 4-LOM, in the center of the establishment's space; the droid bounty hunter was the only one not laughing. 4-LOM sat and waited with machinelike patience, knowing what was to come.

"You poor fool." Drawmas Sma'Da hadn't bothered to pull away from the blaster placed at his brow; he obviously wanted all the onlookers to relish the joke to its full. "Did you think I'd be somehow frightened by a lump of dead metal? Or did you not even notice what happened when you came in here, what little piece of that weapon was taken away from you by our good innkeeper's minions? Really—" With one pudgy hand, he dabbed away the tears that had managed to squeeze past the folds surrounding his eyes. "It's just too good."

"Even better than you think," said Zuckuss. He shifted the blaster slightly away from Sma'Da's head and squeezed the trigger. A coruscating bolt of energy shot out and blew away a section of the bar's ceiling, charred fragments and hot sparks raining down on the upturned faces of the crowd. "This weapon's live."

Sma'Da had instinctively dived when the blaster bolt had scorched past the side of his head. His immense girth had toppled the table, sending a cascade of liquor and the remains of the banquet cascading across the floor. Crockery and crystal decanters shattered, the fragments gleaming like transparent teeth imbedded in the wetly gleaming disorder. A few of the bar's patrons still looked stunned and disbelieving; some of the sharper-witted ones had rushed for the exit and were now scrabbling to get past one another and up the narrow tunnel to the surface.

"Let's go." Zuckuss reached down with his free hand, grabbed Sma'Da's trembling elbow, and pulled the gambler to his feet; he had to lean back to counterbalance Sma'Da's greater weight. "There's some creatures who are ready to pay a nice pile of credits for the privilege of having a talk with you. A *long* talk." And probably not a pleasant one, judging from the panicked look on the other's face and the fear-induced quivering that shook this mass like a small planet's seismic activity.

The bar's proprietor came rushing up, pushing his way past the remaining crowd. "What is the meaning of this?" Salla C'airam was nearly as agitated as the gambler caught in Zuckuss's grip. "It's an outrage? It's impossible! It's—"

"It's business." Zuckuss diverted the blaster's aim for a moment, away from Sma'Da and toward C'airam. That was enough to stop him in his tracks. C'airam's tentacles drew short and wrapped themselves tightly around his body. "You've already got a mess here." Zuckuss used the blaster to point to the sodden, trampled-upon— and expensive—garbage on the floor. "You can either start cleaning it up . . . or you can join it. Your pick."

C'airam's floppy, seemingly boneless appendages settled lower, a sure sign in his species of wanting to avoid a violent confrontation. "I do not know," he spoke with measured sulkiness, "how you managed to get a power source for your weapon into these premises. It's strictly forbidden—"

"Sue me."

"If any of my staff here were involved . . ." The gaze of the proprietor's gelatinous-appearing eyes, nearly as large as Zuckuss's, swept menacingly across the waiters and bartenders. "If I should discover any complicity, any treachery on their part . . ."

"Don't worry about it," said Zuckuss. He pushed the trembling mass of Sma'Da ahead of himself. "They're off the hook." He didn't feel like sharing any of the credit for this job with nonbounty hunters; the little bit of action, the deep, warm feeling of empowerment that came with drawing a live weapon on a fat, blubbering piece of merchandise, had given his spirits a considerable lift. With the gambler's quivering bulk ahead of him, Zuckuss stopped just beside the table at which his partner 4-LOM had remained sitting throughout all the commotion that had taken place. "Speaking of your staff"— Zuckuss turned, swiveling the muzzle of the blaster back toward C'airam— "you've got the usual service droids in your kitchen, don't you?"

C'airam gave a puzzled nod.

"Fine. Go have one of your other staff pull the motivator out of one of 'em. A standard FV50 unit will do nicely." Zuckuss raised the weapon's muzzle a little higher. "I suggest you have them hurry. I might not have the same resources of patience that you do."

On hasty orders from C'airam, one of the bar staff scuttled back into the establishment's kitchen and returned only seconds later with a double-cylindrical object in his hands.

"Thanks." Zuckuss took the motivator from him, and then shooed him away with a wave of the blaster. "Don't move," he warned Sma'Da—needlessly. The gambler, face now shiny with sweat, looked incapable of anything beyond involuntary respiration. Keeping the blaster in one hand, Zuckuss set the motivator down on the table, then swiftly—he had practiced this step before coming to C'airam's bar—unlatched the access panel just below the back of 4-LOM's head unit. "This should do it . . ."

"Don't forget the red feedback-loop clip." Even without a working motivator inside the bounty hunter droid, 4-LOM retained enough low-level auxiliary power to maintain consciousness and interactive communications. "Make sure you've got that in-phase *before* you power up the major thoracic systems."

"I know what I'm doing," Zuckuss replied testily. With just one hand, it took a few moments longer to get the circuits aligned properly. "You'll be up and running in a minute."

4-LOM's immobilized state had been a necessary part of the plan; otherwise, the droid could have taken a more active part in rounding up Drawmas Sma'Da. The most essential item, though, had been making sure that Zuckuss had had an operative blaster pistol to work with. That had meant getting a power source past the establishment's security—impossible—or creating one on the spot. Which was exactly what 4-LOM had figured out how to do in its preparations for this job, even before he had taken Zuckuss on as a partner. With the help of a few highly paid technical consultants, 4-LOM had designed and installed within himself a device capable of stripping out the internal circuit of a standard motivator, the primary mechanism that enabled droid locomotion, and high-grading the resulting simple power source into one both powerful and small enough to be used in a blaster pistol. Like the alchemical wizards on certain remote worlds, who claimed to be able to convert base materials into infinitely more valuable substances, 4-LOM had given himself the ability to change a dull but useful internal component to something very valuable indeed—a blaster power-source, in a locale where none was expected to be.

There were only two drawbacks to the motivator-into-power-source procedure. The first was that the resulting power source would only have enough charge for a few bolts. The second was that without a motivator, 4-LOM would be incapable of any motion, either walking toward the target's table or even lifting an arm with a weapon clutched in its hand. That second problem was the main reason that 4-LOM had decided to take on a partner; pulling this off was obviously a two-creature job. And as far as the first problem was concerned, that new partner was well versed enough in ordinary, nonbounty hunter psychology to know that a few shots would be all that was needed.

"Got it." Zuckuss slammed the access panel cover into place. "Time to get out of here."

"Agreed." 4-LOM pushed its chair back and stood up from the table. The droid reached over and grabbed Sma'Da's elbow. "I would prefer it," 4-LOM told the gambler, "if you did not show any resistance. I have ways of enforcing my preferences."

Sma'Da stared back at the droid bounty hunter with blubbering terror.

"Good," said 4-LOM. "I'm pleased you understand." 4-LOM glanced over at Zuckuss. "You see? I told you this would be an easy job."

Zuckuss nodded. "I've had worse." *Lots worse,* he thought. So far he hadn't actually risked being killed on this one. Though that might change, if he and his partner didn't hurry.

"Both of you—" The proprietor Salla C'airam had recovered enough of his composure that he was able to screech and flap several of his appendages simultaneously. "You're barred from this establishment! Permanently! Don't ever show your faces around here again!"

"Don't worry about that." Zuckuss shoved Sma'Da toward the exit tunnel. He kept everyone in the bar covered with the blaster—there were one or two shots left in its charge, at the most—as he and 4-LOM hustled Sma'Da out. "The drinks were terrible, anyway."

Not until later, when he and 4-LOM were aboard the droid bounty hunter's ship, with Sma'Da safely stowed in a cage belowdecks, did Zuckuss realize that they had stiffed C'airam. Neither he nor 4-LOM had settled their drinks tab before leaving.

Serves him right, thought Zuckuss.

"So where are we taking this merchandise?" Standing in the hatchway of the cockpit, Zuckuss gave a nod to indicate Drawmas Sma'Da below them.

"I've already notified the nearest Imperial outpost." 4-LOM reached across the controls and made slow minor navigational adjustments. "They know we'll be bringing him in. And they'll have the bounty ready to be paid out."

"This was a job for the Empire?" Zuckuss hadn't even bothered to ask before he had agreed to hook up with the other bounty hunter. "Why would Palpatine want him?"

"Let's just say that our merchandise, in his previous role as gambling entrepreneur, was a little too accurate about setting odds for various military encounters between Imperial forces and the Rebel Alliance." 4-LOM didn't glance back as he tweaked the ship's controls. "There's a limit to how many times one creature can predict things like that, using nothing but intelligence and luck. At the rate that Sma'Da was calling the shots, it began to look like he might have had access to some sources of inside information. From inside the Imperial forces, that is."

Zuckuss mulled the other's words over. "It's possible," he said after a moment, "that it could've been just luck. Real good luck."

"If that's the case," replied 4-LOM drily, "then it wasn't good luck for our merchandise at all. It was bad luck—the worst kind, in fact, since it brought him to the attention of Emperor Palpatine. Now he's going to have a lot of explaining to do. It won't be a pleasant process."

Probably not, thought Zuckuss as he left the ship's cockpit area. Even if Drawmas Sma'Da rolled over on any informants he might have had among the Emperor's minions, the techniques that would be used to ensure that the former gambler was telling the truth would leave him a squeezed-out rag. He wouldn't be so fat and jolly when all that was over.

The brief excitement that Zuckuss had felt during the job, when he had pulled out the live blaster and fired it off, shutting off all the onlookers' laughter like flipping a switch, had already faded. He sat down with his back against one of the ship's weapons lockers and defocused his large, insectlike eyes. He couldn't help feeling that even if his bounty hunter career was going better now that he had hooked up with 4-LOM, it somehow wasn't quite as much . . . fun, for lack of a better word. Granted, that kind of amusement had nearly gotten him killed, and on more than one occasion. Still . . .

His thoughts turned to memories as he leaned his head back against the locker. He remembered two other partners in particular; one of them, Boba Fett, could be anywhere in the galaxy now. There was no stopping Fett, or apparently even slowing him down. The last glimpse of Boba Fett that Zuckuss remembered had been through the narrow hatch of an emergency escape pod, just prior to being jettisoned from another ship similar to this one.

There had been another bounty hunter in that escape pod, one that had fumed with a murderous anger the whole time that the pod had been hurtling through space, toward some yet-unknown destination. That had been Bossk; both murder and anger were things that came naturally to Trandoshans. But it had made for cramped quarters inside the little durasteel sphere. Tempers had flared, both his and Bossk's, and they had kept from killing each other only by agreeing, once the escape pod came to rest on the nearest planet, that they would go their separate ways. And so they had.

He was both glad and somehow sorry that his partnership with the cold-blooded, fiery-tempered reptilian Bossk was long over. There was no amount of fun that was worth the risks that came with an association with a creature like that.

Zuckuss shook his head. *At least I'm still alive,* he thought. *That has to count for something.*

He wondered where Bossk was now . . .

2

He didn't need to kill him . . . but he did. Bossk thought it was a good idea, not just to stay in practice for the bounty hunter trade, but also to make sure that no one in the Mos Eisley spaceport knew the circumstances of his arrival.

The broken-down old transport pilot, a shambling wreck with a spine bent nearly double by too many high-g landings, had come gimping up to Bossk, obviously looking for a handout. "Wait a minute," the old man had rasped, digging a yellow-nailed paw through the grey wisps of his beard as his rheumy eyes had peered closer at the figure in front of him. "I know you—"

"You're mistaken." Bossk had taken passage aboard a number of local system freighters, all under assumed names, to reach the remote planet of Tatooine. There had been plenty of times in the past when he had flown his ship *Hound's Tooth* directly here and had made no attempt at concealing his identity. Right now, circumstances were different for him. "Get out of my way." He shoved past the beggar, heading for the perimeter of the spaceport's landing field and the low shapes of the buildings beyond. "You don't know who I am."

"I sure do!" The beggar, dragging one foot-twisted leg behind himself, tagged after Bossk. They crossed the landing field, streaked with blackened char marks from thruster engines. "Bumped into ya out in the Osmani system; that was a *long* while back." He struggled to keep up with the Trandoshan's quick strides. "I was piloting a shuttle between planets—that was the cheapest gig I ever worked—and you lifted one of my passengers right off the ship." The beggar emitted a phlegm-rich, cackling laugh. "Gave me a damn good excuse for blowing my schedule, it did! I owe ya one!"

Bossk halted and turned on his clawed heel. From the corner of his eye, he spotted some of the other passengers that had disembarked with him, now glancing over in this direction as though wondering what the raised voices were all about. "You don't owe me anything," hissed Bossk. "Except a little peace and quiet. Here—" He dug into a belt pouch and pulled out a decicredit coin, then flipped it into the dust beside the beggar's rag-shod feet. "Now you've made a profit on our little encounter. Take my advice as well," growled Bossk, "and try to keep it that way."

The beggar scooped up the coin and followed after Bossk. "But you're a bounty hunter! One of the big ones! Top of the biz—or at least you were."

That brought blood up into Bossk's slit-pupiled gaze; he could feel the muscles tightening underneath the scales of his shoulders. This time, when he stopped and turned around, he reached down and gathered up the front of the beggar's rags in his clenched fists and lifted the insolent creature up on tiptoe. He didn't care if anyone was watching. "What," he said quietly and ominously, "do you mean by that?"

"No offense." A gap-toothed smile showed on the beggar's seamed humanoid face. "It's just that everybody in the galaxy knows what happened to the Bounty Hunters

Guild. It's all gone, ain't it? Maybe there aren't any big-time bounty hunters left." The smile widened, like an overripe fruit splitting open in the heat of Tatooine's double suns. "Except for one."

Bossk knew which one the beggar meant. It didn't improve his temper to be reminded about Boba Fett. "You're pretty free with your little comments, aren't you?" Holding the beggar up close, he could smell the encrusted dirt and sweat on him. "Maybe you should be a little more careful."

"I'm no freer with 'em than anybody else in this dump." Dangling from Bossk's doubled fists, the beggar nodded toward the sun-baked hovels of Mos Eisley. "Everybody around here talks their heads off, however many they've got of 'em. Pretty gossipy bunch, if you ask me."

"Did I?" Bossk felt the points of his claws meeting through the beggar's wadded rags.

"You don't have to, pal. 'Cause I'll tell you the way it is." The beggar appeared completely unafraid. "Place like Mos Eisley, ain't much else to do except talk. Mostly about each other's business. Maybe your business, once they know you're in town. Lots of 'em would be real interested in hearing that a certain bounty hunter named Bossk just arrived. Without a ship of his own, traveling on an ordinary freighter, and"—the beggar leaned his head back to survey Bossk with one squinting eye—"not looking like he was doing too good at the moment."

"I'm doing fine," said Bossk.

"Sure you are, pal." The beggar managed a shrug. "Appearances can be deceiving, right? So maybe you got some real good reason for coming here, all incognito and all. Tricky guy like you, maybe ya got some big plan up your sleeve. So you probably want to stay incognito, right? Is that a good guess, or what?"

Bossk forced his anger down a few degrees. "If you're so smart, why are you a beggar?"

"It suits me. Nice clean outdoor work. You meet lovely

people, too. Besides, it's only a part-time thing for me. It's a good cover for my real business."

"Which is?"

"Finding things out," said the beggar. "In a place like Mos Eisley, somebody like me is just about invisible. It's like being the plaster on the walls. So when creatures don't notice you, don't know you're even there, you can find out some interesting stuff. Stuff about other creatures—like you, Bossk. I didn't just *recognize* you, like pulling something out of my own personal memory bank. I knew you were coming here to Tatooine; I got friends all through this system and out on the freighters. They let me know you were heading this way. We kinda keep an eye on interesting characters like you, when they show up in these parts. Let's face it, nobody comes to a backwater world like this, unless they got a good reason. It's not exactly the center of the universe, you know. So it figures that *you've* got some kind of a reason for coming here." The beggar scratched the side of his head with a dirty fingernail. "Couldn't be any kind of job for Jabba the Hutt—he's dead, must be a coupla weeks now. Ain't nothing worth bothering with out in what used to be his palace. And there's nobody around here with a bounty on his head—and believe me, I'd know if there was." The expression on his grizzled face turned slyer. "So maybe it's just kinda your *personal* business, huh?"

Bossk glared straight into the beggar's eyes. "I'd like to keep it that way."

"I'm sure you would, pal. So that's why I was thinking, soon as I recognized you, when you came off that transport. Thinking about some way you and I could do business, like. You've had partners before—shoot, bounty hunters are always hooking up with each other. Guess that's so you can watch each other's back, huh?" The beggar showed some more of the gaps in his smile. "Well, maybe you and me can be partners."

"You must be joking." Bossk sneered at the beggar.

"What use would I have for a partner like you? My line of work is bounty hunting, not begging."

"Like I said before, pal, this ain't all I do. There's lots of other things I'm good at. One you might find really valuable. And that's keeping my mouth shut. I'm an ace at that—for the right price, of course."

"I bet you are." Bossk gave a slow nod, then lowered the beggar to the black-streaked surface of the spaceport's landing area. "But what about all the others? The ones in your little network of informants that you heard about me from?"

"No problem; they can be taken care of." The beggar brushed off the front of his rags to little visible effect. "I've handed 'em a line before. All they knew was that you were heading this way, here to Tatooine. They don't need to know whether you stopped here, or for how long. I can tell 'em that you were just passing through, on your way to some other hole in the borderland regions. Communications are so bad out in these territories, they'll figure it just stands to reason if nobody reports spotting you for a while."

"I see." Bossk looked down at the beggar. "And just what is the price for this . . . *service* of yours?"

"Very reasonable. Even in what appears to be your rather, um, reduced state financially, I'm sure you'll be able to afford it."

Bossk mulled it over for a few moments. "All right," he said at last. "You're right about one thing. We're both men of business." He didn't want to attract any more attention to himself, out here in the public zone of the landing field. "Why don't we go on into town?" Bossk nodded toward Mos Eisley itself. "So we can talk over the details of our little partnership. Like businessmen."

"Sounds good to me." The beggar started walking, in his hobbled, awkward manner, toward the distant buildings. He glanced over his shoulder. "I'm a little thirsty, if you know what I mean."

"Everybody's thirsty on this planet." With an easy

stride, Bossk followed after the beggar. He already knew just what business arrangements he was going to make.

When he was done making them, in one of the first back alleys that they came to inside Mos Eisley, Bossk wiped from his clawed hands the dirt that had stained the beggar's neck so greasily black. It didn't take long to do so; hardly more than the few seconds that had been required to snap the scrawny bones in the first place. Killing someone, Bossk had found over the years, was always the best way to ensure their silence.

With a couple of kicks, he pushed what now looked like no more than a bundle of rags over against the wall of the alley. Bossk glanced over his shoulder to make sure that no routine security patrol had spotted what had gone down. He had come here to Tatooine, and specifically to Mos Eisley, for the purpose of lying low and making his plans without anyone being too curious about his identity—the beggar had been right about that much. About how to conduct business with a Trandoshan, the beggar had been a little off the mark. *Too bad for him,* thought Bossk as he headed for the bright-lit mouth of the alley.

As for the suddenly deceased beggar's network of contacts off-planet—Bossk had already decided not to worry about them. *He was probably lying to me, anyway.* The beggar could have recognized Bossk and then made up that story about informants strung through the system, all keeping an eye on bounty hunters and other suspicious creatures, just to jack up the price he had been asking for his continued silence.

Which hadn't even been all that high; Bossk knew he could have easily afforded it, without dipping too far into his stash of credits. *Things are cheaper on Tatooine,* thought Bossk. *They deserve to be.* The shade of a pair of tethered dewback mounts fell across him as he made his way across Mos Eisley's central plaza and toward the cantina. Deciding to eliminate the beggar rather than pay the shakedown had been more a matter of general principles rather than economics. If a bounty hunter let himself begin paying to keep his affairs private, he'd eventually wind up paying off everybody. With that kind of overhead, Bossk knew, it'd be hard to turn a profit.

He descended the rough-hewn stone steps into the cantina's familiar confines. In a hole like this, he wouldn't have to worry about anyone sticking a proboscis into his affairs. They'd know what the consequences would be. Plus, most of them had their own secrets—some of which Bossk knew a little about—so silence was a mutually desired commodity.

A few glances were turned his way, but the faces remained carefully composed, devoid of even the slightest sign of curiosity. The cantina's regulars, the various lowlifes and scheming creatures with whom he'd had innumerable business dealings, here and elsewhere in the galaxy, all responded as if they had never seen him before.

That was the way he liked it.

Even the bartender said nothing, though he remembered Bossk's usual order; he poured it from a chiseled stone flagon kept beneath the bar and set it down in front of the Trandoshan. Bossk didn't need to tell him to put it on his tab.

"I'm looking for a place to stay." With his massive, scaled shoulders hunching over the drink, Bossk leaned closer to the bartender. "Someplace quiet."

"So?" The scowl on the bartender's lumpish face didn't diminish; he continued wiping out an empty glass with a grease-mottled towel. "We ain't running a hotel here, you know."

This time, Bossk slid a coin across the bar. "Someplace private."

The bartender laid the towel down for a moment; when he picked it up again, the coin had vanished. "I'll ask around."

"Appreciate it." Bossk knew that those words meant the negotiations were concluded, and successfully. The

Mos Eisley cantina actually did have some chambers for rent—dark, airless holes, down beneath the cellars and subcellars where the barrels of cheap booze were stored— but only a few creatures, even among the establishment's regular habitués, knew about them. The cantina's management preferred keeping them little known, and empty more often than not; it cut down on the amount of raids and general hassles from the Empire's security forces. "I'll check with you later."

"Don't bother." The bartender slapped something down. "Here's your change."

Bossk didn't even bother to look. He palmed the small object, feeling the outline of a primitive all-metal key, and slipped it into one of the pouches on his belt. He already knew the way to the chambers beneath the cantina, down one of the narrow stairs tucked behind a crumbling stone wall.

Carrying the drink with him, he slipped into one of the booths along the far wall. It wasn't too long before somebody joined him.

"Long time, Bossk." A rodent-faced Mhingxin sat himself down on the other side of the booth's table. Eobbim Figh's long-fingered hands, like collections of bones and coarse, spiky hairs, set out a multicompartmented box with an assortment of stim-enhanced snuff powders. "Good to see you." Figh's sharp-pointed nails dipped into the various powders, one after another, then to the elongated nostrils on the underside of his wetly shining snout. "Heard you were dead. Or something."

"It would take a lot to kill me, Figh." Bossk sipped at the drink. "You know that."

"Boba Fett *is* a lot. Lot of trouble." The Mhingxin shook his tapered head. "Shouldn't take him on. Not if you're smart."

"I'm plenty smart enough for Fett," said Bossk sourly. "I just haven't been lucky."

Figh exploded into high-pitched laughter, a squealing gale that sent clouds of acrid snuff rising from the box on the table. "Lucky! *Lucky!*" He slapped his narrow paws beside the box. "Luck is for fools. Used to tell me that. *You* did."

"Then I've gotten even smarter than I was before." Bossk could feel the expression on his muzzle turn ugly and brooding. "Now I know how important luck is. Boba Fett has luck. That's why every time I've encountered him, he's won."

"Luck?" Figh shrugged. "Little more than that. What I think."

The awkward Basic of the creature sitting across from Bossk irritated him. "I don't care what you think," he growled. "I've got plans of my own. Plus, I've got the odds on *my* side now."

"Figure that? How so?"

"Simple." Bossk had had a long time to brood over the matter. "Boba Fett's run of luck has gone on way too long. It's got to end; maybe it's already ended. Then it'll be my turn." He nodded slowly, as though already tasting blood seeping between the fangs in his mouth. "And it'll be payback time for Boba Fett."

That produced another bout of snickering laughter from Figh. "Long time coming. That payback. Not the only one—you."

Bossk knew that was true enough. The breakup of the old Bounty Hunters Guild, for which Boba Fett had been largely responsible, had left a lot of creatures throughout the galaxy with a simmering hatred for Fett. *He hit us all, right where it hurts.* Bossk nodded again, even slower and with eyes narrowed. *In our pockets.* The old system, under the Guild, had spread the wealth out, not evenly— Bossk's father, Cradossk, as head of the Bounty Hunters Guild, had always done better for himself than any of his followers—but well enough that no hunter went completely hungry. All that was changed now; a lot of former bounty hunters were either dead or had dropped out of the trade, getting into other lines of work that were either closer to or further from being legal. The criminal organization Black Sun had reorganized; the Empire had picked up some new recruits, as had the Rebel Alliance.

"We could've hung together," sulked Bossk. "If we'd been smart." He couldn't—and didn't—blame himself for that much; he had tried to keep the other bounty hunters, or at least the younger and tougher ones, together after the Bounty Hunters Guild had broken up. That had been the whole point of the Guild Reform Committee that he had put together—with himself at the head, naturally—right after he had eliminated old Cradossk, in the traditional and time-honored Trandoshan fashion. *The old lizard would've wanted it that way,* Bossk told himself. And if Cradossk hadn't, who cared? He was still just as dead and out of the way now.

"Smart, lucky—big ifs," said Figh. "For you. For Boba Fett, not ifs."

"Yeah, well, we'll see about that." The drink's intoxicants had fueled Bossk's anger. "Like I said, I got plans."

"Plans take money. You got?"

Bossk glared at the Mhingxin, wondering just how much he knew. "Enough."

"True?" Figh gave a doubtful shrug. "Not so heard around here."

The murder of the beggar, whose body Bossk had left in the alley at Mos Eisley's perimeter, was starting to seem pointless. Or at least pointless beyond the simple pleasure of snapping another creature's neck in his fists. It was beginning to seem that everybody in the spaceport had a line on his financial condition.

"You heard wrong, then." Bossk decided to bluff it out. "Use that little rodent brain of yours, for a change. The old Bounty Hunters Guild had a huge treasury stashed away, before it fell apart. Who do you think wound up with all those credits?"

Figh smiled unpleasantly. "Not you."

"Look, just because I didn't land here with my own personal ship—that doesn't mean anything. I got my own reasons for wanting to keep a low profile."

The Mhingxin uttered a common, low-slang expression for bovine waste material. "Broke, you, that's the truth. What heard, more than one mouth. Smiling and laughing, too. Nearly as many enemies, you, as Boba Fett. All that killing." Figh shook his head, rudimentary snout whiskers fluttering. "Stepping on toes. Probably why your bad luck. Nobody wish you *good* luck."

Bossk felt the urge rise in him to reach across the table and do the same thing to Figh that he had done to the beggar he had left in the alley. He restrained himself; the consequences wouldn't have been insurmountable, but he didn't need the expense right now of paying the bartender to take care of the mess. Plus—now that Bossk thought about it—there was a certain value to having an information source like Figh around.

"So tell me something." Bossk leaned across the table, clawed hands folded around the drink in front of him. "Since you've heard so much about my state of affairs. If I didn't get the Bounty Hunters Guild treasury, then who did?"

"Everybody knows. Not even worth charging you for." Figh's sneer split one side of his face. "The credits gone, and so is Gleed Otondon. Figure out."

That jibed with everything Bossk had been able to find out while he had been making his way here to Tatooine. He could still remember the annihilating fury that had boiled up inside him when he had attempted to access the mountain of credits that had been stashed away from the vanished Guild and had found the accounts completely ransacked. Whoever had been responsible, and who now had the credits that should rightfully have been in Bossk's pockets, had not only known the crypto-security codes for the accounts, but also exactly what banking and financial-center worlds they had been located at. Obviously an inside job: some of the accounts had been emptied just a few minutes before Bossk got to them and found them bare. So it must have been somebody who had been at the top levels of the old Bounty Hunters Guild, Bossk figured, one of his father Cradossk's most trusted advisors, a creature that would have been in a position to snoop out the access codes and the other information necessary for locating all those hidden credits. *And stealing them,* brooded Bossk. The injustice of it still rankled. If anyone was going to steal that money, it should have been him.

Whoever it had been, though, it obviously wasn't one of the younger bounty hunters that had gone with him into the Guild Reform Committee. None of those had had access to that kind of information in the old Guild; they had all still been trying to scrabble up the ladder to those levels, with the places and positions of influence all occupied by their elders.

That had been the reason why so many of them had welcomed the breakup of the old Guild, and had even helped bring it about; even Bossk had seen the personal advantages in revolution, of smashing the system in place and putting in a new one with himself in charge, supported by the younger and tougher bounty hunters. It just hadn't worked out that way. *We should've killed 'em all,* thought Bossk in retrospect, *right at the start.* Too many of the elders in the old Guild had survived the breakup, and had gone on to form their own spin-off fragment, the so-called True Guild. All that had been accomplished by the existence of two splinter groups was a war of attrition between them. The elders had been a lot tougher than the young bounty hunters, Bossk included, had expected; tough enough, at least, to have thinned out the Guild Reform Committee's ranks pretty drastically, at the same rate that the True Guild's members had been picked off. If the goal had been to reduce the number of bounty hunters alive and working in the galaxy—and Bossk had heard rumors to that effect, about whoever had been behind Boba Fett's entry into the old Guild—then that goal had been well and bloodily achieved.

Though now, it appeared as if somebody else had

done all right by the smashing of the old Guild. It and its successor fragments, the Guild Reform Committee and the True Guild, were long gone—why would any bounty hunter in his right mind stay in either organization when all it seemed to do was target him for death by the other side? The even smaller and less powerful splinter groups, forming after the disintegration of the two main factions, held no attraction for Bossk. He had already decided that it was better to be an independent operator, on one's own or, at the most, hooked up with a partner. The Hunter's Creed, the honor code that had kept most bounty hunters from killing one another off too readily, was over with; from now on, it was every hunter for himself. The only thing left of value from the old Bounty Hunters Guild had been its treasury—and now that was gone as well.

As was Gleed Otondon. *That scum,* brooded Bossk. Otondon had been one of old Cradossk's chief advisors, a power on the ruling council of the Bounty Hunters Guild. Then he had become the head negotiator for the True Guild splinter group. For all Bossk knew, Otondon might well have been the absolute leader of the True Guild all along, the one that the other old-timers had looked to for their marching orders. If so, Otondon had pulled a fast one on them as well: Bossk knew the whereabouts of all the bounty hunters still alive, the young ones and the old-timers who hadn't yet managed to kill one another off, and none of them showed any signs of having that kind of credits on them. They were all scrabbling to survive, now that the Guild and its offshoots were no more. The only one that couldn't be located, either alive or in his grave, was Gleed Otondon. He had conveniently vanished—conveniently for himself, that was; if Bossk had been able to get his hands on him, he would have torn out Otondon's throat and most of his internal organs in pursuit of the stolen Guild treasury.

The kind of disappearance that Otondon had undergone took credits, a lot of them; the galaxy was stuffed with informants and squealers, and none of them had a clue as to Otondon's whereabouts. Bossk didn't even bother asking Eobbim Figh sitting across from him whether there had been any word in these parts about the missing bounty hunter; that kind of news would only reach Tatooine long after it was common knowledge everywhere else.

"No talk Gleed Otondon? All those credits?" Figh made a show of feigning sympathy for Bossk. "Can understand. More bad luck for you, eh?" He gave a slow shake of his head. "Silence preferred, no surprise."

"I'll take care of Gleed Otondon when the time comes," said Bossk. "He'll have his turn. But not right now. I've got other things on my agenda."

"No—*one* thing." Figh smiled. "Boba Fett."

The Mhingxin had read that much right, as though Bossk's anger had written the other bounty hunter's name on his scale-covered brow. The image of Fett's narrow-visored helmet, battered and dented, but still as awesomely functional as when it had shielded some long-ago Mandalorian warrior, filled Bossk's gaze when he squeezed his eyelids shut. He had never seen Boba Fett's actual face—very few creatures had, and lived to tell about it—but Bossk could still vividly imagine how the blood would seep from beneath that helmet's hard gaze as he crushed the other's neck in his bare hands. Right now, here in the Mos Eisley cantina, his fists clenched tighter, talons digging into his palms, as he yearned to make the vision of Boba Fett's death a reality. That vision, that death, was all that Bossk could think of; the thirst for revenge, like burning acid poured down his throat, seeped through every fiber of his being. As much as he hated and despised the vanished Gleed Otondon for having stolen from him, that was a matter of mere credits. For a Trandoshan, wealth meant nothing compared to honor. And that was what Boba Fett had stolen from him.

"My reputation," said Bossk, ominous and quiet. "That's what he took. Over and over and over . . ."

"Reputation? Yours?" Another gale of squealing laughter came from Figh. "Such doesn't exist. Not anymore. Zero on any scale, what creatures think of you."

A galling realization broke over Bossk. *He's not afraid of me*—he looked across the table at the Mhingxin with something like horror. That was how much his own reputation had diminished; that was the ultimate consequence of his continuing series of defeats at the hands of Boba Fett. A scurrying sentient rodent such as Eobbim Figh could laugh at him, without apparent fear. The humiliation of that fact was like a flood of ice water dumped on the fires of his anger. And more than humiliation: if fear hadn't shown itself in the creature sitting across from him in the booth, its dark flower now rose inside himself.

How can I survive? For a moment, that thought blotted out all others in Bossk's mind. He had his own list, one that he had never before paid much attention to, of creatures in the galaxy that had reason to hold a grudge against him. In his own bounty hunter career, back when the Guild had still been in existence, he had bought his personal triumphs at the cost of stepping on a lot of other hunters' toes, stealing hard merchandise out from under their noses and handing out other humiliations, just as if none of the others would ever have a chance of retribution at him. That list was probably as long as Boba Fett's—perhaps longer, considering that more of them were still alive. Creatures who wound up running afoul of Boba Fett also had a way of winding up dead, their grievances buried with them.

The other difference, between his list of enemies and Boba Fett's, was that only a few, and those the most foolhardy ones, would take a shot at getting satisfaction from Fett. Better to sit on one's grudges rather than give Boba Fett any more reasons for eliminating someone else from the universe of the living. If Bossk had still been in any way rational on the subject of the long-hated Boba Fett, that would have been the advice he'd have given to himself. The same kind of warning no longer held for any of Bossk's own enemies, especially now that it had been demonstrated to the entire galaxy, over and over, that he could be bested in a confrontation. Any other bounty hunter who might have previously had second thoughts about settling accounts with Bossk would now be having third thoughts about the matter—and deciding to act on them. If Bossk hadn't had a good reason for keeping a low profile before, that one would do for now.

"When creatures think zero," continued Figh, "chances of death high. For you."

One corner of Bossk's muzzle lifted in a snarl. "Tell me something I don't know."

Figh stroked the stiff whiskers of his pointed snout. "So not matter of mere emotion, your grudge against Boba Fett. More important. Squatting aquatic avian, until proved that killer stuff in you. Somebody get, sooner, later. Too bad. Only way to get respect of others back, plus keep skin intact, take down Boba Fett. Nothing else do."

He knew Eobbim Figh was right about that. There was a lot more at stake than just his honor and reputation. Once word got out that he was stuck here on Tatooine—and it would, no matter how many gossipy street beggars he killed—then he'd be a target for all those other bounty hunters. Some of them might even have conceived the notion that he, rather than Gleed Otondon, was sitting on the treasury from the old Bounty Hunters Guild. That would add a financial motive—always an effective one for bounty hunters—to their personal ones, for seeking him out, murder in mind.

"Wait a minute." Bossk peered suspiciously at Figh. "How do you know Boba Fett's still live?"

"Simple." Figh mimed a shrug. "Open data, one like

you. Can see through all way. Brooding on failures, humiliations—very unlike. Heard about, before your arrival here, even. To get under scales that bad, only possible for Boba Fett. Your long-standing rivalry well known, everywhere. If Fett really dead, you a happy Trandoshan. Happy as Trandoshans can get. Brood, sulk, *you* know that Fett alive. What you know, *I* know. Or can guess." Figh's imitation smile showed. "Guess proved right, just now."

Bossk nodded. "You're pretty smart," he said. "For a Mhingxin."

The comment got the reaction he expected—and wanted. Figh's coarse, spiky fur bristled across his neck and shoulders. "Smarter than you," spat Figh. "Not waiting to get killed, sitting around. Like you."

"Simmer down. You didn't come over here to talk to me just to point out the obvious, did you?" The glass was empty in front of Bossk; he pushed it away with one claw-tipped finger. "You must have had your reasons. Somebody like you always does."

Figh's black, beadlike eyes still flashed with irritation. "So smart, then you say. My reasons, talk with you."

Bossk had dealt with other Mhingxins in the past. They had a simple, easily manipulable psychology. "Simple," he said. "You think the two of us can do some business together." Mhingxins had a low self-image, due probably to their resemblance to the kind of furtive creatures that crept into food supplies on any number of worlds, and a well-aimed personal remark could easily provoke them. That's when their guard slipped. "You know what I want to do; maybe you got some notion of how you could help me accomplish that."

"Help you? Not likely!" Figh thrust his tapering snout forward; his long, hairy, and knobby hands flattened themselves against the table. "Want to track down Boba Fett, get name back, do it on your own. Got information that could help, but give to you, think again."

"Come on, Figh; nobody *gives* anybody anything, not in this galaxy. But now that we've established that you've got something to sell, we can talk about price."

" 'Sell'?" Figh drew back, eyeing Bossk warily. "What would be?"

"Information, obviously. You don't have to play around with me. You must have something on Boba Fett, something that you think I'd be interested in. Okay, you're right about that; I *am* interested." Bossk jabbed a finger toward the creature on the other side of the table. "I was interested even *before* you came around, trying to get the price jacked by getting me all worked up about Fett. So let's deal."

"Deal . . . price . . . sell . . ." Figh shook his head. "All need something else, if happen."

"What's that?"

"Credits," Figh said bluntly. "*Your* credits. Got?"

"I've got enough." Bossk shrugged. "For the time being."

"Said before. Doesn't look like it."

It was Bossk's turn to grow irritated. "Appearances can be deceiving."

"Very." Figh had recovered enough of his composure to show his unpleasant smile again. "But have to be credits up-front. Pay as you go. Not running a tab; not with me." Figh nodded toward the bartender at the other side of the cantina. "Stiff that fool, you want. Here, business."

Business was all that mattered. Bossk had already made some decisions along that line. It wasn't just a matter of his own personal priorities, his thirst for revenge against Boba Fett, that had led him to put off going after Gleed Otondon and the pilfered treasury of the old Bounty Hunters Guild. He was caught in a double-bind situation: as useful as all those credits would be—there was more than enough to buy a new ship and completely outfit it with all the necessary weaponry for hunting down and eliminating Fett—his chances of successfully tracking down Otondon were virtually nil as long as his own reputation was so badly impaired, with every other bounty hunter with a grievance against him in the way. It was a better idea, with the limited resources at his disposal, to reestablish his reputation by settling his own grudge against Boba Fett; that would make him a feared individual once more in the galaxy-wide community of bounty hunters, and he would have a free hand in going after the stolen property that should rightfully have been his all along.

"All right," said Bossk. "Business it is. Pay as we go." He leaned across the table, bringing his hard, unsmiling gaze close to Figh. "What've you got for me?"

"Very valuable." Figh didn't flinch. "Location of Boba Fett. Where at. Now."

Bossk was impressed. "You got that?"

"No. But can get."

Unimpressed now, Bossk sat back, his spine against the booth's padding. "Let me know when you do. *Then* you get paid."

"Don't worry." Figh slid out of the booth. "You see me again."

Bossk watched the Mhingxin work his way through the crowd that had started to fill up the cantina. Then Figh was gone, up the stairs to the surface and the streets of Mos Eisley. Where presumably such marketable information could be found.

He hoped that Figh did come back with the info. That was something he wouldn't mind paying for, no matter how slim his finances were at the moment. *You can't hit a target,* he told himself, *if you don't know where it is.* All the time he had been traveling toward Tatooine, he had made attempts to discern Boba Fett's whereabouts. That had been a big part of Bossk's reasons for coming to the planet on which Boba Fett had last been spotted, taking off from the Dune Sea with another bounty hunter named Dengar and some dancing girl who had managed to escape from Jabba the Hutt's palace; Bossk didn't even know her name, or why Fett would have had enough interest in her welfare to have kept her around. But those two had been with Fett when another low point in the continuing litany of Bossk's humiliations at his hands had occurred. With another one of his underhanded psychological ploys, Boba Fett had managed to chase Bossk out of his own ship, the *Hound's Tooth*, and once more into an emergency escape pod, hurtling away from what Bossk had thought was certain destruction but which had turned out to be only a dud autonomic bomb.

It was a good bet that Boba Fett was still in possession of the *Hound's Tooth*. Fett's own ship, *Slave I*, had been found abandoned by a Rebel Alliance patrol squad. Along with Dengar and the female, Boba Fett must have transferred over to the *Hound* and piloted it toward some unknown destination. *Which makes,* Bossk thought grimly, *one more thing he's stolen from me.* Bossk's reputation and his ship; Boba Fett had a lot to answer for.

And Bossk had already vowed that he would. That kind of payback could only be made in one kind of coin. Death. The taste of blood in Bossk's jaws would not just be imagined then; soon it would be real.

He sat brooding for a while longer, hunched forward at the table, the empty glass in front of his claws. Brooding and wondering where Boba Fett was right now; he was already impatient for Eobbim Figh to return with that information.

Probably taking it easy somewhere, Bossk thought bitterly. The *Hound's Tooth* was a good ship, well appointed in the best of Trandoshan taste; not just an efficient hunting craft, but one with a minimal but necessary degree of comfort for its rightful owner. Thinking of Boba Fett lounging about in the *Hound*'s comforts infuriated him even more.

He's there, seethed Bossk, *and I'm stuck here.* His claws closed into fists, aching for a throat to break inside them.

There was no justice in the galaxy. While he scrabbled for a place to lie low, on a backwater hole like Tatooine, Boba Fett was safe in the peace and tranquillity of interstellar space, far from harm.

No justice at all . . .

3

She had just about decided to kill them both.

Neelah looked at the back of Boba Fett's helmet as he sat at the cockpit controls of the *Hound's Tooth*. There was no indication that he was aware of her standing in the hatchway behind him. But knowing Fett, with his constant, preternatural awareness, she felt sure that nothing was getting by him. *He can hear the blood rushing in my veins,* thought Neelah. *He knows.*

The other bounty hunter, the one named Dengar, was still asleep in the ship's cargo area. Neelah had left him there, worn out from relating Boba Fett's grim history to her. Like most bounty hunters, Dengar was a creature of action; shifting words about, bringing the past to life in even the rawest, most direct terms, was hard labor for him. Especially under duress; she had woken him up before this last time with a blaster pistol aimed at his head. She had been impressed with the degree of motivation that had inspired in Dengar.

She still had the blaster pistol with her; in fact, it dangled from her hand as she watched Fett adjusting the ship's navigational controls. Originally, it had been one of Boba Fett's weapons; she had managed to slip it away from him here in the cockpit, before he had been able to stop her. That had earned Neelah a grudging congratulations from him. Very few creatures had ever managed a stunt like that.

Maybe I should've killed him then, thought Neelah. *Or at least tried to.* Her finger tightened upon the weapon's trigger. All she had to do was raise the weapon, aim—hardly difficult at this minimal distance—and fire. And this uncertainty in her existence would be taken care of, once and for all . . .

"Don't delude yourself." Boba Fett's voice snapped her out of the murderous reverie into which she had fallen. "I'm aware of your presence." He hadn't turned around, but had continued his adjustments to the ship's controls. A final number was punched into one of the navicomputer touchpads, then Fett swiveled around in the pilot's chair to face her. "You'd have more luck if you were a droid. Some of those can be virtually silent."

The remark struck Neelah as unintentionally ironic. *If I were a droid,* she thought, *I wouldn't have any of the problems I do now.* Even her identity, knowing who or what she was, other than a human female with a false name, a name not her own, and a past that had been stolen from her—it was hard to imagine a droid being concerned about things like that. Memory for a droid was a matter of chips and micro-implants, tiny recording devices as manufactured and interchangeable as themselves. *Machines have it easy,* thought Neelah. They didn't need to find out what they were; they *knew*.

"I'll be more careful next time," said Neelah. With Boba Fett facing her, she had no more clue than before as to the secrets held within his skull. The dark, T-shaped visor of his helmet, that battered and discolored but still awesomely functional relic of the ancient Mandalorian warriors, concealed anything that might have told her what he thought and knew. The entire answer about who she was and how she had come to the remote, friendless sectors of the galaxy in which she had found herself might be locked up inside Boba Fett, like a key hidden in the very strongbox it was meant to unlock.

But the helmet, and its dark, shielded gaze, didn't matter; not really. She was one of the few creatures in the galaxy who had ever seen Boba Fett without his helmet—for all the good it had done her. Back on the planet Tatooine, in the harsh glare of the twin suns above the Dune Sea, Neelah had found him close to death, vomited out onto the hot sands by the Sarlacc beast whose death throes he had engineered from inside its gut. The Sarlacc's gastric secretions, like a corrosive acid capable of etching unalloyed durasteel, had stripped Boba Fett of his armor, right down to and including a good deal of his skin. If she hadn't stumbled across him, his life would have oozed away like the blood seeping out from his raw flesh and hissing on the sun-baked rocks surrounding him.

She had saved his life then, hiding him with the help of Dengar, and keeping him safe long enough to let his wounds heal, wounds that would have killed a creature of lesser will. Even unconscious, under the chemical weight of the most powerful anesthetic drugs, he had still been Boba Fett, tenacious in his grasp on the world of the living.

And Boba Fett afterward, as well—frustratingly so. Gratitude seemed to be a substance in short supply among bounty hunters. *Save the guy's life,* thought Neelah bitterly, *and what do you get?* Not much—and definitely not answers to questions. Anything she knew of her past was limited to the few scraps that had survived that mystery-producing memory wipe, and the infuriatingly little bits and pieces that she had picked up back in Jabba the Hutt's palace, and then here aboard the stolen ship *Hound's Tooth.* So far she had gotten nothing from Dengar; the history he had been relating to her, of the infighting and skulduggery that had finally broken up the old Bounty Hunters Guild, hadn't yet revealed anything of her past. And what it had told her about Boba Fett's past she had already pretty well figured out: that he was nobody to get involved with, even on a partnership basis. A successful business dealing with Boba Fett was one where he kept all the credits, and the other creature got to keep its life. And an unsuccessful one? Boba Fett still kept the credits.

For him to have hauled Neelah onto first his own ship, *Slave I*, when they had all been under siege by a couple of well-armed lowlifes out of Mos Eisley, then onto this ship he had taken from the reptilian bounty hunter known as Bossk, didn't indicate any gratefulness on Boba Fett's part, any recognition of the fact that he wouldn't even be alive now if it hadn't been for her. *He's got some use for me*—Neelah had figured that out a while back. If she wasn't exactly hard merchandise—the bounty hunter term for their captives, to be traded in for the nice fat rewards that had been placed on their heads—she was nevertheless part of one of Fett's mercenary schemes. *I just don't know what part yet.*

"Careful might not be enough." Boba Fett's cold, emotionless words broke into her thoughts. "Being smart is better. A smart creature doesn't make it a habit to come up behind me without warning. I've killed a few, just for doing that."

"Oh?" Neelah had become sufficiently used to his capacity for violence to no longer be intimidated. Plus, having nothing to lose—not even one's self—reduced one's fears. "And for no other reason?"

"A warning, perhaps." Boba Fett gave a slight shrug. "To others, not to do the same thing."

"That only works," said Neelah, "when the creature who's listening cares what happens."

He gave no sign of being amused by her comment. "You don't?"

"I'm still trying to find out. If I do or not."

"It doesn't matter to me," said Boba Fett, "whether you do. Just as long as you stay out of the way. While I go about my business."

Neelah felt a hot spark of anger igniting inside her,

triggered by Fett's matter-of-fact tone. "And what business is that? Specifically."

"You'll find out soon enough. When we reach our destination."

Even as small a piece of information as that had proved impossible for her to pry out of Boba Fett. He hadn't seen fit to divulge it to Dengar, either, even though the two bounty hunters were supposed to be partners. Instead, Fett had been cagey and silent as to the course he had plotted for the *Hound's Tooth* since they had taken over the ship.

"I've asked you before." Neelah spoke through gritted teeth, her hand straying toward the blaster pistol she had tucked inside her belt. "Why all the big mystery?"

"No mystery at all," replied Boba Fett. "Just as I said, you'll find out soon enough. Right now, you don't need to know."

A part of herself that was as cold and dispassionate as the bounty hunter observed her own reaction to his obstinate words, as though there were some small clue to be derived there. Neelah was well aware that the imperious response, which she had to keep a tight grip upon, was not that of someone born to be a slave, a dancing girl, and eventual food for a pet rancor in some obese Hutt's palace. She had known that even while she had been under the control of the late and unlamented Jabba, without even the slightest scrap of memory as to how she had come to be there. The only thing left of her previous existence, whatever it had been and on what distant world, had been the certainty that the cold attention the bounty hunter Boba Fett had directed toward her, in that grisly pit of depravity known as Jabba's palace, had been for some reason inextricably linked with that past.

"You can't blame me," said Neelah, "for wanting to know. You're the one who's told me so many times about what a dangerous place the galaxy is. If we're heading into some region that's going to turn out to be trouble— big trouble—I'd like some warning about it."

"Why?" The question, the way it was spoken by Fett, didn't invite an answer. "There wouldn't be anything you could do about it."

That infuriated her even more. The feeling of helplessness, of events being out of her control—that rubbed against some part of her innermost nature as though it were a raw wound. But the blood that she wanted to spill wasn't her own, but Fett's.

"Don't be too sure about that," said Neelah. "There's two other people on this ship—and only one of you."

"If you think that you and Dengar could pull off a little mutiny, you're welcome to try." No emotion, not even scorn, sounded in Boba Fett's voice. "I've some use for both of you at the moment, but that could change. Real fast." He gestured with one gloved hand toward Neelah. "It's up to you."

She already knew that it was no good asking him what exactly that "use" was. Boba Fett was notorious for playing his cards close to his chest, revealing nothing, not even to those who were supposedly his partners.

"You don't leave someone with very many options." Neelah heard her own voice go as cold and hard as Fett's. "Do you?"

"My business is to reduce other creatures' options. That's why I always kept a cage in the cargo hold of my own ship." Boba Fett's hand now pointed toward the decks below the cockpit. "The previous owner of this ship had the same facilities installed; all bounty hunters have them. If you'd rather make the rest of the journey in a rather less comfortable manner, believe me, it can be arranged. Don't expect Dengar to join you, though. He's at least smart enough not to go along with a plan like that."

One more creature around here, thought Neelah, *that I can't trust.* Boba Fett was infuriatingly correct about that as well; she knew that if Dengar was given the choice between throwing his lot in with her or maintaining whatever kind of partnership he had with Fett, he'd go on following the other bounty hunter's orders in a flash. Why wouldn't he? If Dengar stuck with Boba Fett, he had a chance of getting a piece of the action, a slice of the credits that Fett's various schemes and enterprises generated. And that slice, however thin it was cut compared to Boba Fett's own, was still better than risking a shot at getting killed for the sake of somebody without even her real name, let alone any other known friend or ally in the galaxy. Dengar couldn't be blamed if he was smart enough to know the odds and to play them for his own benefit.

As for winding up in the cage herself—Neelah wasn't sure whether she cared or not. *What's the difference?* She could see her own face reflected in the dark visor of Boba Fett's helmet; it was a face that bore the grim, fatalistic expression of someone who might have managed to save herself from the deadly confines of Jabba the Hutt's palace, only to have wound up in another situation that was just like it in essence. *I don't make the decisions,* she thought. *Even whether I live or die.*

"So we should all go along with your plan," said Neelah, "whatever it is. Without complaining."

Boba Fett shrugged. "Complain all you want. Just not to me. And"—he pointed to the blaster pistol tucked in her belt—"without thinking you could get a jump on me. It's not going to happen."

"Sure about that?"

"Let me put it another way," said Fett. "It hasn't happened yet. And all those who tried to make it happen—they're no longer with us."

She didn't need to be reminded about that. Everything she had heard about Boba Fett, from her time back in Jabba's palace to here onboard the stolen *Hound's Tooth,* listening to Dengar's tale of the disintegration of the old Bounty Hunters Guild and its ugly aftermath, had reinforced the impression she'd already had of him. A sentient creature put its own life up as the wager when it gambled in any dealings with Boba Fett.

Still—it was a thought she'd had more than once—*there are times when you have to go ahead and place*

your bet. If she hadn't done that, back when she had
been the personal property of the late Jabba, she would
have eventually wound up being fed to the Hutt's pet
rancor, just as poor Oola had been. It was better to die
with a wager on the table than to just cringe and wait for
any one of the many grisly deaths that this galaxy held
for the timid.

Neelah's hand had strayed to the butt of the blaster
pistol at her side, resting there as though only another
thought, and another decision, were all that stood between her and testing the advice that both Boba Fett and
her own remaining caution had given her.

One shot was all that it would take; one fiery bolt
from the blaster. The weapon grew warm within her
grasp. Some wordless certainty deep inside her, unat-
tached to any fragment of memory, any recall of her
stolen past, told Neelah that she actually had a chance of
pulling it off. The person she had been before, her true
identity, hidden behind the blank curtain that had been
drawn across all that was rightfully hers to recall—that
person, she had come to realize, had reflexes nearly as
fast as Boba Fett's. Maybe faster, given that even now she
had the element of surprise on her side. *He wouldn't expect it,* thought Neelah. She could tell that for all his
skills as a bounty hunter, both physical and psychological, there was a blind spot in that helmet-visored gaze: it
was only to be expected that he would be unable to admit that any part of his plans, any piece of hard merchandise, could have moves equal to his own.

The notion was tempting. She could almost taste it
under her tongue, like the hot salt of her own blood. It
was the same temptation that she had yielded to once before, in Jabba's palace back on the planet of Tatooine,
when she had decided it was better to put an end to the
Hutt's ownership of her body and spirit, even if the price
to do so was her life. The mystery of her true name and
identity was just as maddeningly intolerable; knowing
that the answer might be locked inside the mind held by
that dark-visaged helmet of Mandalorian battle armor—

that thought drove out all others. One quick move with her hand, which already could feel the cold metal of the blaster a millimeter away from her sweating palm, and the mystery would be over, one way or another. One of them would be dead, with either a smoking blaster hole drilled through Boba Fett's chest or her own, depending upon which of them got a bolt off first. And right now, she knew deep inside herself, she was close to not even caring which of them it was . . .

"But then you'll never know."

Neelah heard the voice, and for a moment thought it was her own, speaking inside her head. Then she realized that the hard, emotionless words had been Boba Fett's.

He can tell, she realized. *He can always tell.* Exactly what she had been thinking—her hand, trembling close to the butt of the blaster pistol at her side, had given it away.

"That's the price," continued Fett. "That's still the price."

She nodded. But didn't pull her hand away from the blaster.

"I'll make it easy for you." Boba Fett reached down and drew the blaster that had been holstered on the belt of his battle armor. Holding it by the barrel, he threw it into the farther corner of the cockpit space, where it clanged against one of the bare durasteel bulkheads. "Now you won't have to worry about whether it would cost you your life. The only one that's at stake is my own."

He's playing with me. The lack of any perceptible emotion in his voice only made it clearer to her. The same thing she had known from the beginning: Boba Fett didn't win by sheer violence, or the brutal efficiency of his weapons. The force of his will, and his understanding of other creatures' thoughts, were just as annihilating. She was wrong, she knew that now. Whatever he did, it wasn't play; it was deadly serious. Even in this, in making it easy for her to kill him—if that was what she chose—there was something he wanted from her.

Neelah pulled the blaster from her belt—the weapon

seemed to rise of its own accord, as though directed by some intelligence wired into its intricate circuitry—and pointed it straight at Boba Fett's chest. Her finger made closer contact with the trigger, the small bit of metal sensed by and made one with the twitching filament at the end of her nervous system, that then ran directly into the churning storm of thoughts and desires caught inside her skull. With her arm held out, unmoving, she gazed over the blaster's sights at the cold, dark visage that mirrored her own face . . .

And couldn't fire.

She lowered the blaster, her finger loosening upon the trigger. "You win," she said.

"Of course." No more emotion sounded in Boba Fett's voice now than before. "There was little doubt of that. You might not know who you really are—and I might not know, either. That's something you haven't determined. But I still know more about you; I know how your mind works." A gloved forefinger tapped the side of his helmet. "You have to win here—" Shifting forward in the pilot's chair, Fett reached out and set the same fingertip lightly on Neelah's brow. "And *here*, before you have a chance of winning anywhere else. Or even surviving."

"That's why the others lost, I suppose." As Boba Fett had drawn his hand away, Neelah gave a slow nod of her head. "Like Bossk. You were able to take his ship away from him, just because of what you were able to do inside his head."

"Exactly," said Fett. He reached out again, taking the blaster pistol from Neelah's hand. It rested on his palm, an inert object. "Something like this . . ." The shoulders of his Mandalorian battle armor lifted in a shrug. "It just makes things final. Sometimes. But by then, the battle is already over."

There was a certain wisdom in Boba Fett's words; Neelah knew that these were true as well, like the other things he had told her. "Why do you bother?" She peered toward the gaze hidden behind the dark visor. "Nobody ever said you were a creature of words; someone who would *explain* the reasons why he would do anything." Back in Jabba's palace, there had been henchmen of the Hutt who had claimed that Boba Fett was a creature of silence; they had never heard him speak even a single word. She didn't know if those thugs had been stupid or lucky. When somebody finally did hear Boba Fett speak, there was usually a reason for it, and one that was rarely to the listener's advantage. "So why are you telling me all this?"

"You're a reasonable creature," said Fett. "There are few such in the galaxy. In this, you and I are more similar than different in nature. Most sentient creatures are only partly so; they think a little, but then are governed by their emotions. The emotions I seek to produce in them are fear and helplessness. Then they're easier to deal with. But you, on the other hand . . ." He gave a slow nod, as though carefully weighing his words. "It's different with one of your kind. First there is emotion—anger, frustration, the desire for revenge—all those things that you have yet to learn to control. But then your reasoning ability, your capacity for logic kicks in. Cold and analytical, even about the things that matter the most to you. Even about your own lost identity. To be cold about other creatures' fates—that comes easily to most worlds' denizens. But to be cold about one's own self . . ." His nod this time was more approving. "That's something I recognize. And that I have to treat differently from the other creatures I encounter."

Neelah wondered if this was more of his mind-gaming, another attempt to control her from within. "What happens if you don't? Treat it differently, I mean."

"Then the possibility is raised of my losing the battle." Boba Fett's hidden gaze stayed locked upon her face. "Though not the war, of course."

"What do you mean?"

"Simple," replied Fett. "You're valuable enough to me that I prefer to keep you alive. And . . . cooperative. It's easier to get that from you outside of a cage. But at the same time, I know the dangers of letting you keep a measure of freedom." He handed the blaster pistol back to her. "If those dangers were to become too great—then I'd have to eliminate you. As quickly, and as definitely, as possible."

Neelah regarded the blaster pistol in her hand for a moment, then finally tucked it back in her belt. When she raised her eyes, she looked past Boba Fett, to the star-filled viewport of the cockpit. Somewhere out there was the world from which she had come, that was now lost to her along with so much else. *Perhaps,* she mused, *perhaps they've forgotten my name was well . . .*

And if that was true . . . then she had nowhere else to go. The ship that surrounded her might be the only world she had left.

She brought her gaze around again to Boba Fett. "You'll have to forgive me," said Neelah. She managed a thin smile. "For being a little concerned about this mysterious destination of ours. But you were the one who told me about all the big events shaping up—out there." One hand pointed toward the viewport. "About the Imperial forces gathering . . . some place named Endor." Even the name of the moon seemed fraught with dire portent. "You said it might be a decisive battle; maybe the one that ends the Rebel Alliance." She shook her head. "I came close enough to that struggle between the Empire and the Rebels, back on Tatooine." Bit by bit, Neelah had pieced out the significance of Luke Skywalker and Princess Leia Organa having been on that remote backwater world. She had seen them both in Jabba's palace, along with their companion Han Solo—first frozen in a block of carbonite, then released and brought to life again. They had been responsible for the death of Jabba, she knew, which she also figured had been a stroke of good luck for herself; escaping from Jabba's clutches and staying free were two different things, at least as long as the Hutt had still been alive. She might owe them, and all the rest of the Rebels, her survival—but that wasn't enough to get her involved with any of them again. "I don't," said Neelah decisively, "want to get near them. They've got their war; I've got mine."

"Don't worry." Boba Fett glanced over his shoulder at the viewport, then back to her again. "That's something else we've got in common. Rebellions are for fools; I deal with the universe as it is. So we're not going anywhere near Endor." He slowly shook his head. "Let them battle it out. And whoever wins . . . it'll make no difference. Not to creatures like us."

She found a measure of comfort in his words. Though not without sensing the irony of accepting the wisdom of someone who would kill her, or cash her in to the highest bidder, if it suited him. *It's all business,* thought Neelah. *Nothing more than that.*

"Leave me," said Boba Fett. He swiveled the pilot's chair back toward the cockpit controls. "I have other things to take care of."

Neelah realized she had nothing more to say. He had won again. Before she'd even had a chance to make a move.

She turned away, stepping through the hatch and then starting down the ladder to the ship's cargo hold.

He smiled when she saw Neelah coming down the ladder. "Sounds like we've got something in common also," said Dengar. "You didn't have any luck with him, either."

The resulting scowl on the female's face amused him. "What do you know about it?"

"Come on." From where he sat against one of the hold's bulkheads, Dengar pointed to the open panel and the same comm lines that Neelah had tapped into. "More than one can play that kind of game. I heard everything both you and Boba Fett said up there."

"Good for you," Neelah said sourly. She sat down with her back against the opposite bulkhead. "Congratulations—now you know as much as I do. Which isn't much."

"Actually . . . I *do* know a little more than you."

Neelah's brow creased in puzzlement. "You found out something? About where we're going?"

"Of course not." Dengar shook his head. "If Boba Fett wants to keep quiet about his intentions, at least I'm not stupid enough to pry into them. But that's the future; that's what is going to happen, and right now we don't have any say about that. I guess that's just how things are when you accept a partnership with Boba Fett." Leaning back against the bulkhead behind him, Dengar spread his hands apart. "The past, though—that's another thing. Now *that*, I do know something about."

"Great." The scowl deepened on Neelah's face. "You mean this story you've been telling me . . . this history of how Boba Fett broke up the old Bounty Hunters Guild and everything that happened after that."

"Precisely," said Dengar. "You've already learned a lot from me. More than you're probably willing to admit. You've got a lot better notion now of how Boba Fett operates—and how far you can trust him—than you did when we left Tatooine."

"For all the good it's done me—" Neelah crossed her arms across her breast. "You might as well have stayed quiet."

"So?" Still smiling, Dengar raised an eyebrow. "You don't want to hear the end of it, then? Not too long ago, you were pretty interested in the story. Enough to hold that blaster pistol on me, to get me to keep on telling it."

"I've changed my mind," said Neelah. "What's the point? He won, he survived, other creatures didn't—pretty much business as usual for Boba Fett. Big deal."

"Very well." Dengar was interested in seeing how long this mood of hers would last. "Of course, there's always the chance that the end of the story would have something you need in it, the one clue that would unlock a whole lot of other puzzles. But if you don't want to take that chance—it's up to you."

"That's right." Neelah closed her eyes and tilted her head back. "So don't bother me with it."

The mood, and the feigned sleep, lasted all of five minutes. Then one of her eyes opened, then both. She glared at Dengar with them.

"All right," Neelah said finally. "So finish it, already."

It was a small triumph, but still worthwhile. And it would pass the time until they reached whatever destination they were headed for. "You're not going to bother pointing the blaster at me?"

Neelah shook her head. "I'm right at the point where that's probably not such a good idea. The impulse to blow you away might be a little too irresistible. So let's skip it. Just start talking, okay?"

"Fine," said Dengar. "Whatever you want . . ."

4

AND THEN . . .
(JUST AFTER THE EVENTS
OF STAR WARS: A NEW HOPE)*

"Where's Boba Fett?"

That was the most important question—and Prince Xizor, the head of the Black Sun criminal organization, expected an answer from his underlings. *And soon,* thought Xizor grimly. Under the present circumstances, he didn't feel like taking the time to kill a few of them just to motivate a quicker response time.

"We're tracking him, Your Lordship." The comm specialist aboard the *Vendetta* bowed his head with a sufficient measure of cringing obsequiousness to avoid Xizor's wrath. Serving aboard the Falleen prince's personal flagship was an honor earned not only by excellence at one's job, but also by attention to all the little rituals that flattered his ego. "Our tracking sensors had detected his jump into hyperspace; his ship should be arriving in this sector of realspace momentarily."

Xizor stood brooding at the *Vendetta*'s forward viewport; the curved transparisteel revealing the dark panorama of stars and vacuum extended far above his head. One hand rubbed the angles of his chin as the violet centers of his half-lidded eyes focused on the arc of his own thoughts. Without turning around, he spoke another question: "Were we able to determine his final navigation coordinates? *Before* the jump."

"Data analysis was able to break out only the first broad-scale coordinates—"

Once again, he turned his hard glare onto the comm specialist standing on the platform walkway behind him. " 'Only'?" He slowly shook his head, eyes narrowing even farther. "I don't think 'only' is good enough. Make a note"—Xizor extended the tapered claw of his forefinger toward the datapad clutched in the specialist's hands—"to the disciplinary unit. They need to have a little discussion with the data analysis section. They need to be . . . *motivated*."

The change in the comm specialist's face, from merely pallid to dead white, was pleasing to Xizor. Motivation, in the lower ranks of Black Sun, was a synonym for terror; he had put a lot of his own effort in designing and maintaining the appropriate measures for creating just that effect. Violence was an art; a balance had to be maintained, somewhere short of the deaths of valuable and not easily replaced staff members. At the same time, it had to be made clear that no creature ever left Black Sun, at least not while alive. Such administrative duties would have been a chore to Prince Xizor, if the practice of the art involved had not been such an intrinsic pleasure.

"So noted, Your Excellency." As long as it was someone else's neck on the chopping block, the comm specialist was only too eager to comply with Xizor's request.

He had already dismissed the comm specialist from his mind. With only fragmentary information available about the trajectory of the bounty hunter Boba Fett's ship, *Slave I,* there was much for Xizor to mull over. He gazed out at the galaxy's bright skeins, not seeing the individual stars and systems so much as the possibilities they represented. It had already been verified that Boba Fett had left the dull, virtually anonymous mining planet on which the former Imperial stormtrooper Trhin Voss'on't had taken refuge; a refuge that had proven ineffective when Fett and his temporary partner Bossk had tracked

Voss'on't down for the bounty that Emperor Palpatine had placed on his head. Voss'on't was now Boba Fett's hard merchandise, to use the language of the bounty hunters; the bounty for the traitorous stormtrooper was due to Fett as soon as delivery was made to the arachnoid arranger and go-between known as Kud'ar Mub'at.

Turning his gaze to one side of the viewport, Xizor could see the unlovely fibrous mass of Kud'ar Mub'at's web, floating in otherwise empty space. The web had been woven, over a period of unknown decades, perhaps centuries, from the assembler's own extrusions. Mired in the weft of tough exterior strands were bits and pieces of various ships, poking out like metal scraps sunk in the corrugated mud of a dried swamp; those fragments were all that remained of debtors that Kud'ar Mub'at had foreclosed upon, or business partners whose dealings with the assembler had gone disastrously awry. Involvement with Kud'ar Mub'at might not lead to the same degree of violence as with Boba Fett, but annihilation was just as final.

To enter into the web—Xizor had done it many times—was to step inside Kud'ar Mub'at's brain, both metaphorically and literally. The thinner, palely glistening fibers were spun-out extensions of Kud'ar Mub'at's own cerebro-neural tissue; tethered to the strands and scuttling along them were the numerous subnodes that the assembler had created, little replicas and variations of itself, taking care of appointed duties ranging from the simple to the complex. They were all linked to and under the control of their master and parent—

Or so Kud'ar Mub'at thinks, Prince Xizor reminded himself. The very last time he had been inside the assembler's web, just before coming back here aboard the *Vendetta,* Xizor had had a most interesting—and potentially profitable—conversation. Not with Kud'ar Mub'at itself, but one of the assembler's creations, the accountant subnode called Balancesheet. It had shown Xizor that it had managed to detach itself from the web's linked and intertwining neurofibers, without Kud'ar Mub'at being aware of what had happened. Balancesheet had also mastered the assembler's knack of creating subnodes, one of which it had spliced into the web in order to deceive Kud'ar Mub'at that all was well. The net result was as if part of Kud'ar Mub'at's brain had begun its own mutiny against its creator, laying out plans and schemes, of which Kud'ar Mub'at was as yet unaware.

It was going to find out soon enough, though. That thought lifted a corner of Xizor's mouth into a cruel smile. He would enjoy even more the actual moment when the crafty arachnoid, squatting on its nest in the center of its self-created web, discovered that it had been outsmarted. At last, after having been the puller of so many invisible strings laced throughout the galaxy that had brought wealth to its dusty coffers and ruin to other sentient creatures. Not that Xizor felt pity for any of those; they had gotten what they deserved for letting themselves get entangled in Kud'ar Mub'at's intricately woven schemes. But those schemes had become a little too extensive for Xizor's taste; when they started interfering with his and Black Sun's various enterprises, it was time to trim them back. What better way than uprooting them at the source? The unexpected discovery of Balancesheet's own ambitions along those lines—the crafty subnode had made it clear that it no longer cared to remain a mere appendage of its creator-parent—made possible the removal of Kud'ar Mub'at, while still retaining all the valuable go-between services that the assembler performed for Black Sun.

Get rid of the old one—the notion had a definite appeal to Prince Xizor—*and put a new one in its place.* And by the time that Balancesheet, as inheritor of all its creator's position and power, would get just as troublesome as Kud'ar Mub'at had become, perhaps a new generation of crafty arachnoids would be ready for patricidal rebellion. Or even more pleasing to contemplate: Xizor's ambitions for Black Sun would have reached such a zenith of power, outstripping even that of Emperor Palpatine, so there would be no need for such a scuttling, secretive little creature. Now *there* was a particular "old one"— the image of Palpatine's wizened visage appeared in Xizor's thoughts, like a senile ghost—who had also enjoyed his day, his moment in power. And during that time, Xizor had had to bow his proud head and pretend to be the Emperor's loyal servant more than once. The fact that the old man had been taken in by that little charade was proof enough that Palpatine's time was soon to be over, and that the remnants of the Empire would then be ready to fall into the control of Black Sun. Prince Xizor and his followers had waited long enough in the shadows, biding their time, waiting for the lightless dawn that would be their moment of triumph . . .

Soon enough, Xizor promised himself. He and all the rest of Black Sun had only to wait, and craftily move into their final positions the pawns that were already arrayed on the great gameboard of the universe. The arachnoid arranger Kud'ar Mub'at's web of plans and schemes was nothing compared to the one that Xizor had woven, a net cast across worlds and entire systems of worlds. Neither Emperor Palpatine nor his dark henchman Lord Vader had any comprehension of Black Sun's reach, the things that were in its grasp already or the ones that its fist was about to close upon. For all of Palpatine's vaunted claims of knowledge of the Force and its dark side, he was still blind to the machinations and maneuverings taking place virtually under his nose. That was due, Xizor figured, to the old fool's own greed and ambition, and to his perpetual undervaluing of any other creature's intelligence. The Imperial court of Palpatine, on the distant world of Coruscant, was stuffed with flunkeys and witless servants; their master had made the mistake of assuming that everyone else was either a dolt like them or a mysticism-addled thug like Vader.

The memory of the Dark Lord's invisible grip upon Xizor's throat, squeezing out the breath from his lungs, was still sharp and humiliating; he didn't believe in that mysterious Force, not the same way that Vader and the Emperor did, but he had still been compelled to acknowledge something of its cruel power. *Mind tricks,* brooded Xizor, that was all it had amounted to. But that had been enough—more than enough—to reignite his hatred for Darth Vader. That hatred had been born in the deaths of Xizor's family members, deaths for which he held Vader personally responsible. Behind all his other ambitions, the goals of conquest and domination toward which he'd mercilessly driven Black Sun, there lay a smaller, more personal one: to make sure that Lord Vader paid the ultimate price for his deeds against the blood of a Falleen prince.

That vengeance could not come soon enough to satisfy Prince Xizor.

And a small piece of the machinery that would bring that vengeance about was on its way here—or it should be, if he had correctly gauged his understanding of the bounty hunter Boba Fett. *For one such as that,* Xizor had decided, *profit is everything.* He had baited the trap with enough credits to ensure Boba Fett's keen interest, first to bring about the destruction of the old Bounty Hunters Guild, and now to bring the renegade Imperial stormtrooper Trhin Voss'on't back to Kud'ar Mub'at's web, where the price that had been put on Voss'on't's head was supposedly waiting. *The fool,* thought Xizor contemptuously. Boba Fett had no idea of how he had been manipulated, a mere pawn in Xizor's gambits. Perhaps he would never learn, or learn too late to save himself, now that his usefulness to Xizor had come to an end.

The Falleen prince's eyelids drew partway down upon the violet color of his gaze as the deep intertwinings of his meditations continued. Beyond the curved transparisteel of the *Vendetta*'s great viewport, the waiting stars, ripe for the plucking, lay scattered in silence. So also with the pieces, both visible and invisible, his own and the other players', upon the squares of that gameboard to which the galaxy had been reduced. If one pawn was about to be swept from the board, what did it matter?

There were plenty left with which the game could be played to its conclusion.

Prince Xizor folded his arms across his chest, the motion bringing the edge of his cape around his boots. He felt sure now that *Slave I* would soon emerge from hyperspace . . . and into the trap that had been so carefully prepared.

After all—a thin smile lifted one corner of Xizor's mouth as he contemplated the stars—where else was it to go?

"You don't know what you're getting yourself into." On the other side of the holding cage's durasteel bars, the Imperial stormtrooper—*former* Imperial stormtrooper—slowly shook his head. And smiled. "I wouldn't want to be in your boots right now."

"Don't worry about that," replied Boba Fett. He had come down from the cockpit and into *Slave I*'s cargo hold to see how this particular piece of hard merchandise was enduring the rigors of the journey. The bounty placed on Trhin Voss'on't's head by Emperor Palpatine had stipulated live delivery—a corpse was therefore useless and, worse, unprofitable to Boba Fett.

If Voss'on't's death had been all that was required to collect that veritable mountain of credits, the job would have been much easier. *I wouldn't have needed that fool Bossk along,* thought Fett. Partners—even temporary ones—were always an irksome expedient, to be disposed of as quickly as possible.

"Your position here," continued Boba Fett aloud, "is quite secure. As is mine. I'm the winner, and you're the loser. I'll get paid, and you'll get whatever Palpatine has in store for you." Which wasn't likely to be pleasant, Fett knew. Though that hardly concerned him—once a bounty hunter collected his fee, interest in the merchandise's fate ceased.

"Think so?" The smile on Voss'on't's scarred, hatchet-like face turned into an ugly smirk. "This galaxy is full of surprises, pal. There might just be one in store for *you*."

Boba Fett ignored the stormtrooper's warning. *Mind tricks,* he figured. Voss'on't was part of the usual run of thugs and laser-cannon fodder that got recruited into the Empire's fighting ranks. If not of the same intellectual caliber of the Imperial Navy's admirals, he was still smart enough to have risen to those ranks trained in basic psychological warfare techniques. And sowing doubt in the mind of an opponent was the first, and most effective, of such subtle weapons—one didn't have to be a Jedi Knight to use it.

Still—he had to recognize that Voss'on't had a point. Treachery was an infinite substance in the galaxy, as widely distributed as hydrogen atoms in space. And in getting involved in the Voss'on't job, he had become unavoidably entangled with some of the most treacherous sentient creatures on or off any of the galaxy's worlds. Not just Palpatine, but the arachnoid assembler Kud'ar Mub'at as well.

It's a lot of credits, thought Boba Fett as he gazed at the captive in the holding cage. He no longer saw Voss'on't as a living thing, but simply as merchandise to be delivered for a profit. It was the largest bounty that Fett could remember hearing of in his entire career. The lengths to which Emperor Palpatine would go to satisfy his lust for vengeance made a lesser entity like the crimelord Jabba the Hutt look like a piker. But it was one thing for Palpatine to offer that kind of bounty for the renegade stormtrooper; it was another thing for him to actually pay it out. Not that Palpatine couldn't afford to—he had the wealth of uncounted systems at his command—but because his greed was even greater than that wealth.

And as far as Kud'ar Mub'at was concerned—Boba Fett held zero illusions about that immense, scuttling spider, with its wobbling, pallid abdomen and obsequious, conniving words. Kud'ar Mub'at was presumably holding the bounty for Voss'on't, awaiting whichever of the galaxy's bounty hunters returned to its web with the merchandise. Boba Fett knew that the assembler would love to have both the merchandise and the bounty wind up in its sole possession—and the best way to do that would be to arrange for the sudden demise of whoever had actually done the work of capturing the stormtrooper.

"I can see you thinking." Trhin Voss'on't's sly voice insinuated itself into Boba Fett's consciousness. "Even through that helmet of yours—I can hear the little gears meshing."

"You hear nothing except your own delusions." Boba Fett defocused his hard, cold gaze upon his captive.

"Think so?" The ugly, lopsided smile still curled one corner of Voss'on't's mouth. "Consider your situation from a . . . *military* point of view." He gave another pitying shake of his head. "You're outgunned, Fett. Deal with it."

There was still time remaining before *Slave I* was scheduled to emerge from hyperspace and within sight of Kud'ar Mub'at's space-drifting web. Time enough to play a little more of this mental game with the hard merchandise. Boba Fett didn't need the amusement—nothing amused him except more credits stacking up in his accounts. But there was at least one good reason for letting Voss'on't rattle on: it was common knowledge that high-level stormtroopers, such as he had been before his defection, were trained in self-annihilatory techniques, in case of capture by enemy forces. A self-willed shutdown of his entire autonomic cardiovascular system would render Voss'on't as unprofitable as any hot bolt from the blaster slung at Boba Fett's hip would.

Standard bounty hunter procedure in a case like this, where the suicide of the merchandise was a possibility, would have been to render him safely unconscious with a steady-release transdermal anesthetic patch applied just above one of the main neck arteries. Boba Fett had done just that, many times before, with other pieces of hard merchandise—it was rare when any one of them looked forward to being handed over at the end of their journeys with anything but total dread. And if Trihn Voss'on't was as intelligent and rational as he appeared, he had no reason to be optimistic about the welcome that he would receive from his former master, the Emperor Palpatine. Death would be at the end of that process as well, though it would be a long—and uncomfortable—time in coming. Palpatine had ways of making sure of that.

But Boba Fett's own bounty hunter's skills, his ability to see into the workings of his merchandise's thoughts, had told him that Voss'on't was not going to take his own life. Once the former Imperial stormtrooper had gotten over both the physical trauma of being captured—it hadn't been easy on anyone; both Boba Fett and Bossk had nearly been killed in the process—plus the indignity of waking up caged, a measure of his fighting spirit had reappeared, even cockier than before. Boba Fett had caught a glint in Voss'on't's narrow gaze of the same will to survive—and even dominate—that burned like a cold fire under the jacket of his own Mandalorian battle armor.

He actually thinks he can win. The stormtrooper ceased being mere merchandise for a few seconds as Boba Fett regarded him in the holding cage. He hadn't expected a combat-hardened veteran such as Trihn Voss'on't to beg and grovel for his life, as so many previous tenants of the holding cage had done. What he *had* expected was a show of snarling, raging defiance, the kind of ugly temper to which the sadistically violent were given when the tables were turned on them.

"Outgunned—and outsmarted, Fett." The voice of Trihn Voss'on't was a centimeter away from sneering laughter. "It's been real nice knowing you. I'm glad we had this little time together."

A quick chiming note sounded from the comlink inside Boba Fett's helmet. That was the signal from the monitoring computer in *Slave I*'s cockpit indicating that the final lockdown sequence had to be initiated before the ship could emerge from hyperspace. There wasn't much more to be done before he collected the bounty, the mountain of credits that had been posted for Voss'on't's capture.

His favorite part of the job was getting paid—but Boba Fett decided to postpone it a moment longer. As much as he was aware that Voss'on't was trying to warp his thinking, deflect it from its most logical course like the gravitational tug of a black hole, another part of him was intrigued by the stormtrooper's mocking display of confidence.

He wants me to think he knows something, thought Boba Fett, *that I don't*. Hardly likely—Boba Fett hadn't survived this long as a top-rank bounty hunter except by having better information sources than his prey did.

Another thought itched at a dark corner of Boba Fett's cortex. *There's always a first time*. The problem was that in this business, the first time—outgunned, outsmarted, out-intelligenced—would also be the last time.

"All right," said Boba Fett quietly. "So tell me." He leaned closer to the holding cage's bars, unconcerned about bringing himself within reach of his captive. It would be a real mistake for Voss'on't to try reaching through the bars and grabbing him—his superior reflexes would have Voss'on't down on the cage's floor in less than a second. "You feel like talking so much—what do you mean, 'outgunned'?"

"What, you blind?" Voss'on't scoffed at him. "This ship's falling apart. Even if you hadn't told me about that bomb your former partner hit the hull with, I would've been able to make the damage assessment for myself, just from looking around here. The last time I heard so many structural integrity alarms going off, I was on an Imperial battle cruiser being attacked by an entire wing of Rebel Alliance starfighters."

"Tell me something," growled Boba Fett, "that I don't already know." That *Slave I* was in bad shape was a fact of which he was uncomfortably aware. Even before he had made the jump into hyperspace, away from the colonial mining planet where Voss'on't had been hiding out, he had to make a hard assessment as to whether the ship was even capable of standing up to the journey. If he'd had any option, he would have laid over at the closest suitable planet for repairs. But with such a valuable cargo as the former stormtrooper aboard, and with every other bounty hunter in the galaxy eager to relieve him of this hard merchandise, the choice to make the jump had been forced on him. It was either that or wind up a sitting target in the crosshairs of too many laser cannons to even have a chance of surviving. "This ship will come out all right," Boba Fett told his captive. "It might be just barely holding together when we get there, but we'll make it."

"Sure it will, pal—but then what?" Voss'on't tilted his head to one side, peering at Fett, an eyebrow raised.

"Then I get paid. And there'll be plenty of time for repairs." He was even looking forward to that. There were some modifications to *Slave I*—some advanced weaponry systems, proximity and evasion scan units—that he had been contemplating for some time.

"Oh, you'll get paid, all right." Voss'on't's smile widened, showing more of his yellowed ivory and steel-capped teeth. "But maybe not in the way you're expecting."

"I'll take my chances."

"Of course—there's nothing else you can do. But if you're wrong about what's waiting for you . . ." Voss'on't slowly nodded. "Then your options are even more limited than they are now."

Boba Fett calmly regarded the other man. "How do you mean?"

"Come on. Don't be naive. You have a reputation for smarts, Fett. Try earning it. You've got no maneuvering ability in this ship, not in the condition it's in now. All your weaponry won't do you any good if you can't bring it to bear on a target. And if that target is firing at you instead— if there's a *lot* of targets with you in their gunsights—then there isn't going to be anything you can do, except take it, for as long as you think you can hold out."

"Hardly my only option," said Fett. "I can always jump back into hyperspace."

"Sure—if that's your preferred method of dying. This broken-down tub barely made it through one jump without disintegrating." Voss'on't's smile indicated how much he enjoyed the dismal prospects he was describing. "You might be able to slam this thing *into* hyperspace—but you won't be able to get it back out." An evil glint appeared in one of the stormtrooper's eyes. "I've heard that's a real unpleasant way to go. Nobody even ever finds the pieces."

Boba Fett had heard the same. A squadron of the ancient Mandalorian warriors, a suit of whose battle armor he wore as his own, was reputed to have been destroyed in just that manner by the now-vanished Jedi Knights. "You sound as if you've been analyzing this for a while."

Voss'on't shrugged. "It didn't take long. Just like it didn't take long to figure out your only other option. The one that leaves you alive afterward."

"Which is?"

"Surrender," said the smiling stormtrooper.

Boba Fett shook his head in disgust. "That's something I *don't* have a reputation for doing."

"Too bad," replied Voss'on't. "Too bad for you and your chances of getting out of this mess alive. You can either be smart and survive, Fett, or carry on with what you're doing, and wind up as a toasted corpse. Your choice."

Another chime signal sounded from *Slave I*'s cockpit. He had already wasted too much time with this creature. Boba Fett made a mental note that in the future he should remember that all merchandise was the same, given to trying to talk its way out of a jam.

He allowed himself one more question before he returned to the cockpit and began the final preparations for emerging from hyperspace. "Just who do you think it is that I should surrender to?"

"Why mess around any further?" Trhin Voss'on't gripped two of the durasteel bars and brought his hard-angled face closer to Fett's. "I'm the only one who can get you out of this. I know what's waiting for you on the

other side. And believe me, Fett, they're not your friends."
The stormtrooper's fingers tightened on the cage's bars
as his voice dropped lower. "Let me out of here, Fett, and
I'll cut you a deal."

"I don't deal, Voss'on't."

"You better start—because it's *your* life that's on the
bargaining table, whether you like it or not. Let me out,
and turn the ship over to me, and I *might* just be able to
keep you from being blasted into atoms."

"And what would be in it for you?"

Voss'on't leaned back and shrugged. "Hey—I don't
want to go up in smoke with you, pal. Your stupidity is
endangering me as well. All things being equal, I'd just as
soon stay alive. If I've got control of the ship *and* its
comm units—in other words, let me do the talking—I'd
have a chance of getting the ones who aren't so well disposed to you to stand down."

The other's words provoked an instinctive response
from Boba Fett. Inside the suit of Mandalorian battle armor, he could feel his spine stiffen. "Nobody," he said,
"commands this ship but me."

"Have it your way." Voss'on't let go of the bars and
took a step back into the center of the holding cage.
"I've at least got a chance of making it through. You
don't."

The chime signal sounded again in Boba Fett's helmet,
louder and more urgent. "I have to congratulate you,"
he said. "I thought I'd heard all the scams, all the wheed-
ling and begging and bribery attempts, that creatures
were capable of. But you came up with something new."
He started to turn away from the holding cage and its occupant. "I've never been threatened by my merchandise
before."

Voss'on't's taunting voice followed after Fett as he
strode toward the metal ladder leading back up to the
cockpit. "I'm not your usual run of merchandise, pal." A
note of mocking triumph sounded in Voss'on't's words.
"And if you don't think so now—believe me, you will.
Real soon."

All the way up to the cockpit, Boba Fett could hear the stormtrooper's laughter. Pulling the hatchway shut behind him only cut off the distant, irritating sound, not the memory of it.

Boba Fett sat down in the pilot's chair, letting the work of his hands moving across and adjusting the navigation controls fill his consciousness. Victory in any combat, fought with weapons or words, depended upon a clear mind. The former stormtrooper Voss'on't had done his best to mire Boba Fett's thoughts with his sly insinuations of conspiracy and predictions of violence. Boba Fett was afraid of neither of those; he had proved himself a master of them on many occasions.

At the same time, Voss'on't's lies and mental tricks had evoked a deeper sense of unease inside Boba Fett. His survival in the dangerous game of bounty hunting hadn't been based on coldly rational strategizing alone. There were elements of instinct that he depended upon as well. Danger had a scent all its own that required no trace molecules in the atmosphere to be detected by his senses.

His gloved hand hesitated for a second above the controls. *What if Voss'on't wasn't lying . . .*

Perhaps the stormtrooper hadn't been playing mind games with him. Perhaps the offer to save Boba Fett's life from whatever might be waiting for him in realspace had been genuine, even if motivated by Voss'on't's own self-interest.

Or—Boba Fett's thoughts pried at the puzzle inside his skull—the game was even subtler than it first had appeared. Voss'on't might not have wanted him to surrender control of the ship at all. *What if*, mused Fett, *he knew I would refuse? And that was what he'd been banking on.* In which case, Voss'on't also would have been angling for Boba Fett to disregard all doubts, suspicions, even his own instinctive caution, as having been planted in his head by Voss'on't. The game might not have been to change Boba Fett's course of action—but to make sure that he didn't abandon it.

He needn't have bothered, thought Boba Fett. A familiar calm settled over him, which he recognized and remembered from other times, moments when he'd set his fate in the balance. Between the thought and the deed, between the action and its consequences, between the roll of the ancient bone dice and the coming up of the number that would indicate whether one lived or died ...

Lay infinity.

Bounty hunters held no faith, religions, creeds—those were for other, deluded creatures. Emperor Palpatine could immerse himself in the shadows of some Force that the Jedi had believed in—but Boba Fett didn't need to. For him, that moment, expanding to the limits of the universe both inside and outside him, was all the unspoken knowledge of the infinite, risk balanced against power, that he required. What more could there be? All else was illusion, as far as he was concerned.

That simple truth had kept him alive so far. His profits, the counters in the game he played, meant more to him than his own life. *You can't gamble,* Fett reminded himself, *what you're not prepared to lose ...*

All other considerations fell away, like the dying sparks of dead suns. Only the holding cage below held the former Imperial stormtrooper now; Boba Fett had dismissed even the image of Trhin Voss'on't from his mind.

A computerized voice, as clear of emotion as Boba Fett's thoughts, spoke aloud, breaking the cockpit's deep silence. "Hyperspace preemergence lockdown completed." The logic circuits built into *Slave I* were as thorough as those of their master. "Current options are to activate final emergence procedures or lower operational condition to standby and minimal power drain."

Without any further prompting from the ship's computer, Boba Fett knew that the latter was not much of an option at all. To remain much longer in hyperspace was merely a delayed—but certain—death. In the ship's present damaged condition, structural maintenance and life-support systems would begin to fail in a matter of a few minutes. *Slave I* had to enter realspace soon—or never.

Boba Fett didn't bother making a verbal reply to the onboard computer. In a single, unhesitating motion, he reached out across the cockpit's controls and pushed the final activation trigger.

Even before he drew his gloved hand away from the controls, the cockpit's forward viewport filled with streaks of light that had been the cold points of stars a millisecond before. On the black gameboard behind them, the die had been cast.

"There he is." The comm specialist placed a hand against the side of his head, listening intently to the cochlear implant inside his skull. "Forward scout modules have spotted *Slave I*, registered emergence from hyperspace as of point-zero-three minutes ago."

Prince Xizor nodded, well pleased with the alacrity shown by the crew of his flagship *Vendetta*. The disciplinary measures he had initiated a little while ago had obviously had a salutary effect on the lower Black Sun ranks manning the strategic operation posts. *Fear*, noted Xizor, *is the best motivator.*

"I trust that we have a fix on his projected trajectory." Prince Xizor stood before the *Vendetta*'s forward viewport, its transparisteel scan of stars arching high above him. With boots spread apart and hands clasped at the small of his back, he gazed out at the galaxy's distant worlds. He brought that same cold, calculating gaze over his shoulder for a moment. "In other words, do we know where Boba Fett is headed?"

"Yes, Your Excellency. Of course we do." The comm specialist's words rushed out, almost tripping over each other in their speaker's anxiety. He tilted the side of his head closer to his fingertips, listening to the words being relayed from outside the *Vendetta*. "Plotted trajectory matches previous strategic analysis coordinates, Your Excellency."

The forward scouts' report brought a glow of pleased

satisfaction beneath Xizor's breastbone. The analysis had been his alone, calculated by no computer other than the flesh-and-blood one behind his slit-pupiled, violet eyes. *Boba Fett has no choice*, thought Xizor, *but to come this way.* A smile twisted a corner of Xizor's mouth. *And to his death.*

Gazing upon the bright, cold stars in the viewport, Xizor gave a slow nod without turning toward the comm specialist. "And the estimated time of arrival at Kud'ar Mub'at's web is . . . ?"

"That's . . . a little more difficult to project, Your Excellency."

Xizor's brow creased as he glanced back at the comm specialist. He didn't need to speak aloud to get his meaning across, as well as the degree of his dissatisfaction.

The comm specialist hurried to explain. "It's because of the degree of damage, Your Excellency, that the vessel being tracked has sustained. Boba Fett's ship is in considerably worse shape than we had originally anticipated. The hyperspace transit has weakened the ship's structural integrity, almost to the point of collapse."

A tinge of disappointment made itself felt inside Xizor. If *Slave I* actually did break apart in the vacuum of space, a great opportunity would be lost thereby. To be that creature known as the one who had eliminated Boba Fett from the galaxy, to have arranged the death of the bounty hunter who had profited from so many other creatures' misfortunes—that would add considerable glory to Prince Xizor's dark prestige.

And to have brought about Boba Fett's death, not through dumb luck or accident, or by a snarling, flesh-rending, Trandoshan-like show of violence, but by having ensnared Fett in a web of intrigue and double and triple crosses—the exact same type of subtle machinations and conspiracies that the galaxy's most-feared bounty hunter had always excelled in—that would only make the final victory sweeter and more rewarding.

Xizor could see his own reflection, ghostlike and

faint, in the glossy inner curve of the viewport. Beyond
the image of his own violet eyes, narrowed with contemplation, the stars seemed close enough to grasp. For a
moment, the passing of a second, Xizor felt a twinge of
sympathetic feeling for Emperor Palpatine, as though his
heart had synchronized its slow, unhurried pulse with
that of the distant old man on Coruscant. Old, but infinitely crafty—and greedy beyond even that measure. *I've
come to understand him,* mused Prince Xizor. He clasped
his strong-sinewed hands behind his back, in the folds of
the cape whose lower edge brushed against the heels of
his boots. They were planted even farther apart, as though
the Falleen noble was already bestriding worlds under
Black Sun's dominion.

That was the lure, and the danger, of letting one's
deepest meditations dwell upon the stars. Such a view as
the one afforded from the *Vendetta,* and the expanse of
dark sky and wheeling constellations that could be seen
from the Emperor's palace, would only unlock the desire
for power inside a sentient being's heart. Power both absolute and abstract, for he who possessed it, and hard
and crushing as a boot sole ground into a bloodied face,
for those beneath. But the purity of the stars, the icy
coldness of their vacuum-garbed light—that was a splen-
dor to be enjoyed, and endured, by only those great
enough to translate their desires into action. And if those
desires, and that action, were translated into fatal consequences for those foolish enough to have let themselves
become enmeshed in Xizor's intricate schemes . . .

So be it, thought the Falleen noble. He gave a single,
meditative nod as he gazed at the waiting field of stars.
All had gone according to plan—*his* plan, and no other
creature's. As his breast swelled with both satisfaction
and anticipation, one fist tightened inside Xizor's other
hand, as though it held and drew the cords binding all
the far-flung worlds into a single woven net.

Another entity, smaller and nearer, also stood by and
waited. Behind Xizor, the comm specialist emitted a

discreet but clearly audible cough. "Excuse me, Your Excellency—" The comm specialist had obviously summoned all his remaining store of courage. He knew the risk involved in disturbing the meditations of Black Sun's leader. "Your crew," he reminded his commander as diplomatically as possible, "awaits their orders."

"As well they should." Xizor knew that the crack of the whip, the slight but necessary touch of discipline he had administered, would have every station aboard the *Vendetta* primed and ready for action, with every crew member eager to demonstrate his worth. *A shame,* mused Xizor, *to waste all that energy on so small a target.* The *Vendetta* and its crew deserved more pyrotechnics— and the satisfaction that came with both violence and victory—than would be provided by one broken-down bounty-hunting hulk.

"Your Excellency?" The comm specialist's words gently prodded him again.

Xizor answered him without turning around from the *Vendetta*'s great viewport. "The crew," said Xizor, "will have to wait a while longer."

"But . . . Boba Fett's ship . . ." The comm specialist sounded genuinely puzzled.

There was no need to be reminded of *Slave I*'s approach, the vector of its entry into this sector of space. Xizor could feel it in the tautening nerves of his own body, an ancient predatory instinct responding to the nearness of its prey. Even without that subtle, almost mystical sense, Xizor knew that the *Vendetta*'s sensors would have hard confirmation of *Slave I*'s presence, well before Boba Fett suspected that anything was amiss. A barrier of drifting structural debris, left over from the various ships and other artifacts that the arachnoid assembler Kud'ar Mub'at had incorporated into its web, served to effectively screen the *Vendetta* from long-range detection.

"Notify the bridge," instructed Prince Xizor. "I'll be there directly. Have them bring all weapons systems to full operational capacity—immediately." He didn't want to take any chances on not having enough firepower for Boba Fett. "Have all target-accessing controls keyed to my command." Xizor glanced over his shoulder, displaying a thin, cold smile to the comm specialist. "This is one that I wish to take care of personally."

5

The first hit was nearly the last one.

Boba Fett didn't even see it coming. The first indication that *Slave I* had come under attack was the sudden burst of light that flared across the cockpit's viewport, as though the ship had struck the heart of some hidden sun. He would have been permanently blinded if the optical filters in his helmet's visor hadn't flashed opaque, protecting his eyes. Fett's own quick instincts had snapped him away from the searing glare, raising a forearm across the front of the helmet as he had twisted about in the pilot's chair, away from the navigation controls and the obliterated view of stars he had seen only a fraction of a second before.

The impact of the laser-cannon bolt struck the ship's frame and his contorted spine simultaneously, throwing him from the pilot's seat and sprawling him out across the bare durasteel floor of the cockpit, his arms barely able to brace himself and catch the rush of the bulkhead near the hatchway. Past the roar of the explosion shuddering through *Slave I*'s hull and into the core beams running from forward sensor antennae to the shielded engine compartments, Boba Fett could hear the high-therm welds of the bulkhead panels ripping free from one another. A metal edge as viciously sharp as a vibroblade's business end peeled upward from the cockpit's floor, coming within a centimeter of slashing through the heavy collar of his Mandalorian battle armor and across his throat. All that prevented a slashed jugular vein and subsequent death was a tight ducking of his head against one shoulder, so that the ripped durasteel panel caught one side of his helmet instead. The left side of the helmet blunted the cutting strike, adding another mark of violence to the other dents and scrapes gathered in combat.

Rumbling downward in pitch, the sound of the laser-cannon bolt and its concussive hammer-blow against the ship faded enough that the wails and shrieks of the ship's alarm systems became audible to Boba Fett. He may have escaped death—for the moment—but *Slave I* had been mortally wounded; the ear-shredding, electronic screech was its death cry.

"Mute alarms." Fett spoke the command into the microphone of his helmet. "Switch to optical status report." As the high-pitched notes fell to ominous silence, a row of minuscule lights appeared at the limit of Boba Fett's peripheral vision. He knew what each glowing dot meant, which of the ship's systems was represented by vertical rank order, and what conditions were indicated by the lights' colors. Right now, they were all red, with a few of them pulsing at various speeds. That wasn't good; the only thing that could have been worse would be if one or more had gone to black and out, the indicator of a complete systemic failure. The topmost dot of light in the row was for *Slave I*'s structure-envelope integrity, measured in atmospheric-maintenance capability. If that one blinked out—and at the moment it was flickering faster than Boba Fett's own pulse rate—it would mean that the ship was breaking into fragments, the hull's durasteel sheath delaminating away from the broken internal frame and scattering into empty space like the silvery ashes from an extinguished groundfire. It would also be a sight that Boba Fett wouldn't live to see; the loss of the ship's air when the hull was breached would be an event with a survival rate of zero for any living creatures aboard.

Fett rolled onto his side, away from the sharp edge of the bulkhead that would have at least given him a quick death, and pushed himself up onto his hands and knees. He shook away the last bit of dazing fog from the blow to the battle armor's helmet. The now-silent alarms hadn't informed him of anything that he couldn't discern by other means. With the fragile condition that the ship had already been in, a direct hit by a Destroyer-grade laser cannon was bound to have a significant—and close to catastrophic—effect. After the stresses of jumping in and out of hyperspace, *Slave I* had barely been holding together; that the vessel could have taken another blow on top of that without disintegrating was a tribute to the extra armor and structural reinforcements that Boba Fett had ordered installed by Kuat Drive Yards. But there was a limit to how much damage those protective measures could soak up before collapsing along with the rest of the ship. When they went, his life span would be measurable in seconds; there was no emergency escape pod in which he could bail out.

Getting to his feet, the bounty hunter grabbed the back of the empty pilot's chair and pulled himself toward the cockpit controls. The panel's indicator signals and gauges were awash with pulsing red lights, telling him the same story he'd already surmised from the dots at the side of his helmet, bright as the ends of severed arteries.

Quickly, Boba Fett punched a gloved forefinger at the manual override command pad, inputting the code that would allow the ship's onboard computer to take over the navigational procedures. "Randomize all maneuvers," he instructed. "Calculate and implement nonpredictive evasion pattern." Even before he took his hand away from the pad, *Slave I*'s docking-correction rockets burned on hard, twisting the ship out of its previous slow course and slamming Fett against the side of the cockpit; another burn, close to ninety degrees off the first one, would have sent him sprawling again if he hadn't kept a tight hold on the back of the pilot's chair.

The evasive maneuver was just in time: a second laser-cannon bolt shot cometlike past the curve of the forward viewport, coming close enough for Boba Fett to feel its heat through the clear transparisteel. Fading to a dull red, the bolt trailed away, leaving a bright afterimage in Fett's vision, but without hitting the ship's hull.

Another warning sound became audible as the stressed frame groaned from the transmitted force of the rockets. No electronic sensors were needed to register what was happening; Boba Fett could feel the chill of falling temperature through his battle armor, and hear the sibilant hiss of dwindling atmospheric pressure. The reserve oxygen tanks' emitters kicked in, attempting futilely to overcome the loss from the ship's main cabin areas. The evasive maneuver initiated by the onboard computer had wrenched some part of the hull loose, already weakened by the first laser-cannon hit. *Slave I* might be able to dodge most, and perhaps even all, of the coruscating bolts being aimed its way—Boba Fett had personally programmed in the randomizing algorithms—but it would be a process equally fatal, and rapidly so, as the quick, darting shifts in direction and acceleration tore at the ship's damaged fabric.

Boba Fett leaned over the back of the pilot's chair, scanning the forward viewport for any sign of the enemy that had opened fire on him. It didn't matter who it might be—he figured that he had enough enemies, from his years in the bounty hunter trade, that at any given moment there would be someone yearning to take a shot at him. For all he knew, it might have been possible that Bossk had already found some way to catch up with him; what the Trandoshan lacked in smarts, he made up in tenacity and the ability to carry a grudge.

All that mattered right now was *where* the laser-cannon's bolts had come from. *Slave I* had a deep arsenal of long-range weaponry itself; if Boba Fett could get a fix on the other ship, he would be able to bring his own laser cannons to bear on the target. That would be a calculated gamble on his part: setting up and holding position long enough to return fire would increase the enemy's targeting ability, and the laser cannons' drain upon *Slave I*'s rapidly dwindling power resources, as well as the structural shock from firing the weapons, could very likely destroy rather than save the ship and its occupants. *Two shots*, calculated Boba Fett as he looked out across the field of stars. *Maybe three.* His instinctive connection with the ship he mastered told him that that would be the limit of its endurance. If he wasn't able to take out his enemy that quickly, any further action, including the resuming of evasive maneuvers, would leave him as a lung-emptied corpse drifting amid his own ship's debris.

The main engines came on again, a quick burst thrusting *Slave I* away from its previous location. A trail of churning, fading light at the corner of the viewport indicated the effectiveness of the onboard computer's randomizing program; the enemy's laser-cannon bolt had scorched past, only a few meters away from the ship's hull. Boba Fett leaned closer to the cockpit's forward viewport, balancing himself with one hand braced against the control panel's flashing red lights, scanning with a hunter's intent gaze for any sign of the opponent he faced. His enemy, whoever it might be, obviously was aware that its target would be doing exactly that, trying to locate the source of the bolts aimed toward him. That was the reason why the other ship wasn't sending out a steady stream of rapid-fire laser-cannon bolts; their fiery passage would have been a dead giveaway, negating the advantage it had at the moment, of mounting its offensive from some undetermined hiding place.

Boba Fett's strategizing had been encompassed in mere milliseconds. Without warning, the computer's evasion program kicked in again, twisting *Slave I* into a full 360-degree looping spiral, the side-mounted rockets diverting the thrust of the main engines. It wasn't enough: Boba Fett's grip upon the back of the pilot's chair was torn loose as another laser-cannon bolt scored a direct hit upon the curved center of the hull. The impact sent him flying backward, landing sprawled on his back halfway through the cockpit's open hatchway. A torrent of sparks, blinding gnatlike miniatures of the laser fire that had filled the viewport, lashed against his chest and helmet visor as the control panel's circuits overloaded and shorted out. The acrid smell of burning hard-wire insulation and frying silicon mixed with the hissing steam of the fire-extinguisher cylinders letting loose their contents beneath the panel's gauges and buttons.

As the cockpit filled with smoke, Boba Fett grabbed the side of the hatchway and pulled himself upright. The louder hiss in his ears was the sound of oxygen venting from the ship's hull; the last laser-cannon bolt had done even more damage than the first that had hit *Slave I*.

His helmet comlink had gone dead, as well as the red warning lights arrayed at the side of the visor. Fett pushed past the toppled pilot's chair, its pedestal stanchion ripped loose from the buckling floor. The panel was slick with combustion-retardant foam and wet ash as he punched the computer's input microphone control. "Prepare to seal off cockpit area," he commanded. The only way to obtain a few precious minutes more of breathing time—and the chance, however slim, to survive beyond that—was to reduce the stress on *Slave I*'s life-support systems to as close to zero as possible. Letting every other section of the ship go to complete vacuum would turn the cockpit into a temporary bubble of safety. Once it was set up, Boba Fett could override the computer's evasion program and turn the underside of the craft toward the source of the laser-cannon bolts, so the inert metal would act as a shield for the cockpit's curve of transparisteel.

The rest of the plan formulated itself in Fett's mind. He had limited options at this point, but there was still always the chance of outwitting his foe. *Play dead,* he told himself. *That could work.* The damage that *Slave I* had suffered would be obviously visible from the outside; with the engines shut down and all signs of onboard power switched off, his ship would look like a lifeless hulk drifting in space. That might be enough to get this unknown enemy to come close enough, imprudently within range of a sudden, unexpected volley from Boba Fett's own laser cannons. At that kind of distance, he could cripple or even destroy the other ship; either way, he'd then have the time to head for the safety of Kud'ar Mub'at's web, before the remaining store of oxygen aboard *Slave I* ran out.

"Atmospheric lockdown procedures concluded," announced the onboard computer's voice, still emotionless though coarsened now with burring static. "Cockpit area ready to be sealed on your order."

"Maintain status," said Fett. There were things he had to do before the cockpit's life-support systems were secured. "Standby until I return to this area." He pushed himself away from the control panel.

From the cockpit area, Boba Fett quickly descended the metal treads of the ladder leading down to the main cargo hold. He still had hard merchandise aboard the ship that he intended to deliver and be paid for. The renegade stormtrooper Trhin Voss'on't had to be alive in order for that to be accomplished.

The air pressure in the cargo hold had dropped to a dizzying, heart-accelerating level. As he stepped from the last tread of the ladder, Boba Fett could see a swimming cluster of black dots form in his vision, a telltale sign of oxygen starvation. The spots quickly vanished as his battle armor's reserve oxygen supply kicked in. As useful as those reserves were in emergencies such as this, they were still limited; Fett knew that he would have to accomplish his mission here fast, and get back up to the cockpit with Voss'on't before they ran out. All his strategizing would do him little good if he was lying on the cargo hold's floor unconscious when the enemy ship approached.

"I was . . . wondering . . . when you'd show up." Gasping for breath, eyes reddened from the smoke that filled the cargo area, Trhin Voss'on't held himself upright with both fists tightly clenched upon the holding cage's bars. "Figured . . . maybe you were dead already . . ."

"Lucky for you that I'm not." The miniaturized security key was implanted in the fingertip of Boba Fett's gloved hand; the mere act of grabbing the pull-bar on the cage's door would unlock it and allow him to yank Voss'on't out. He could feel the renegade stormtrooper's hard gaze bearing down on him like two laser trackers as he stepped close and reached for the door. "Let's get going."

Fett had already calculated that he didn't have time to render Voss'on't unconscious, or the strength, given the depleted level of oxygen in the cargo hold, to drag the stormtrooper's limp body up the ladder to the cockpit. It would be better just to get him up there, with whatever degree of threats or personal violence was necessary, then knock him out so he wouldn't interfere with the rest of the operation.

"Why should I?" Voss'on't hunched over, his head at a level with his hands gripping the bars, chest laboring to draw in enough breath to support life functions. "What . . . do I get . . . out of it?"

That was one more thing he didn't have time for: one more argument from Voss'on't. The stormtrooper had never yet seemed to realize that Boba Fett wasn't interested in his opinions on what to do next.

"What you get," said Boba Fett as he pulled open the holding cage's door, "is a chance to go on living a little while longer. If that's not important to you—too bad. You don't get a vote on it."

"I'll tell you . . . what's important to me . . ." Voss'on't straightened up, pushing himself back from the vertical bars. "Giving you . . . a little surprise . . ." His voice was suddenly louder and more forceful, as though he were now expending a carefully husbanded store of vital energy. Taking one step backward to brace himself, he swung the single bar that had somehow come loose from its mounting at both the top and bottom welded frames of the cage. The length of glistening metal moved through a flat horizontal arc, its end striking Boba Fett directly in his abdomen. The blow had all of Trhin Voss'on't's weight and strength behind it, hitting Fett with enough velocity to lift him for a moment off his feet and slam his spine back against the edge of the open cage doorway.

Stunned and doubled over from the blow to his gut, Boba Fett lay on the cargo area's grated metal floor, one shoulder rolled beneath him. His own sudden flurry of motion revealed to his dazed and swimming vision what had previously been concealed by the thick smoke gathered at the base of the cage: the laser-cannon bolts from the hidden enemy ship had buckled the hold's floor enough to spring loose a section of cage bars. The one with which Voss'on't had struck him had come completely free, and had been held in place only by the stormtrooper's fist, giving the visual impression that he was still trapped inside the cage. In fact, and as Boba Fett had just painfully learned, he had been merely waiting for Fett to unlock the door and come within striking distance.

"You should have . . . listened . . ." Voss'on't's words came from somewhere in the blurred, red-tinged distance above Boba Fett. "When you had . . . the opportunity . . ."

As Fett tried to push himself up from the floor, another blow from the metal cage bar to the base of his battle armor's helmet sent him sprawling again. The helmet's visor scraped across the cargo hold's grating. His mouth filled with the taste of smoke as he gulped for breath.

"But you . . . *didn't* . . ." Voss'on't had planted his boots on either side of Boba Fett, the better to raise the cage bar high and aim a killing blow at the top of the bounty hunter's vertebrae. "You don't get . . . a second chance . . ."

Boba Fett heard the bar come whistling down through the oxygen-thinned air. But the broken weld of its tip struck the hold's floor instead of his spine as his own arm grabbed hold of one of Voss'on't's legs and jerked him off balance. Voss'on't lost his grip on the metal bar as he fell backward, and it clattered across the floor and against the farthest bulkhead.

The butt of the holstered blaster pistol was already clamped in Boba Fett's fist. Before he could draw it and fire, Voss'on't's close-combat training asserted itself: with his elbows braced against the floor, he brought the heel of his boot hard under Boba Fett's chin, snapping his helmeted head back. The blaster went flying from Fett's loosened grasp. Before Boba Fett could recover, the renegade stormtrooper dived for the weapon. Voss'on't landed with his chest scraping across the edges of the grate, outstretched hands clawing desperately for the blaster.

Fett didn't wait to see if Voss'on't came up with it. He scrambled onto his knees and snatched up the cage bar that had fallen from the stormtrooper's grasp before. In one fluid motion, Fett twisted about, the bar poised javelinlike in one gloved hand; he saw Voss'on't also kneeling a couple of meters away, turning with the blaster pistol gripped in his doubled fists. Behind the weapon, and through the eye-stinging haze filling the cargo hold, the harsh angles of Voss'on't's triumphantly grinning face could be seen as he took aim and squeezed his finger upon the weapon's trigger.

The cage bar flew from Boba Fett's hand as he whipped his arm straight before him. A bolt from the blaster pistol scorched an inch away from Fett's helmet as he dived to one side. Across the hold, a screeching intake of breath sounded from Voss'on't' as the jagged tip of the cage bar ripped through his sleeve and tore a red wound through the flesh underneath. The force of the thrown bar was enough to pull one hand away from the blaster—but the other hand tightened its grip.

"Good . . . *shot* . . ." With his heart and lungs laboring in his chest, Voss'on't stood up, his wounded arm pressed tight against his side in a vain attempt to stanch the flow of blood. Dark red ribbons wound past the hip of his grease-stained uniform trousers and down his thigh. "But not . . . good enough . . ."

Boba Fett made no reply, but watched as the blaster pistol in Voss'on't's shaking hand drew down upon an invisible line to the center of his helmet.

"I might've . . . put you in the cage . . ." Voss'on't grimaced with the effort of pulling in enough breath to remain conscious. Beneath the smoke and ash streaking his narrow face, the scarred and chiseled flesh was as pallid white as a sheet of flimsiplast. "And kept you . . . alive . . ." He held the blaster, unwavering now, straight out in front of him. "But I've changed my mind."

Fire and a blinding glare erupted through *Slave I*'s cargo hold, overwhelming the single bolt that shot out from the muzzle of the blaster. Boba Fett felt himself being thrown backward as the hold's grated flooring ripped into pieces from the explosion that pushed apart the ship's bulkheads as though they were mere fluttering sheets of metallic cloth. He knew what had happened, even as he fell again, with one forearm protectively shielding his helmet's visor. From somewhere in the airless distance outside, the other ship, his unidentified enemy, had taken aim and fired its laser cannon, scoring a direct hit on his own ship's hull.

Another explosion rumbled from deep in the bowels of *Slave I*, in the main engine compartments. Fire, laced with electrical sparks, white-hot wasps swirling in dense clouds of oily smoke, leapt up through the chasms that had been driven through the flooring and bulkheads. The blood that had already been spilled now hissed into red steam as the remaining atmospheric content shimmered with the fierce heat from below.

There he is—

Boba Fett spotted the renegade stormtrooper behind

a wall of flame and black, coiling smoke. Stunned by the impact of the laser-cannon bolt and the catastrophic systems failure it had triggered, Voss'on't had fallen to his knees and now-empty hands, his head lowered as though to preserve the last flickerings of consciousness inside his oxygen-starved brain.

At the same time, the ship's alarm systems overrode the muting command that Boba Fett had given them. A chorded electronic wail sounded both inside his helmet and through the diminished air, as though the damage suffered by *Slave I* had given it a shrill, ululating voice, one with which it could keen its own death.

Tendrils of smoke streamed past Boba Fett like elongated ghosts as he strode through the flames; the ship's hull had been breached in enough places that the vacuum outside had begun sucking out the remaining oxygen in the cargo hold. The fire from the main engine compartments had begun to diminish, but still remained high enough that its bright tongues lapped past Fett's knees.

"Let's go." Boba Fett reached down through a wash of smoke and grabbed Voss'on't underneath one arm. He lifted the stormtrooper up onto his wobbling legs.

Voss'on't's head lolled back, as though the bones had been surgically extracted from his neck. The fire's heat had cauterized his wounded arm, stopping the flow of blood, but a thinner red line trickled from the corner of his mouth. The close impact of the laser-cannon bolt had taken him closer to death than any of Boba Fett's weapons could have.

"Go ahead . . ." Voss'on't's eyelids were barely able to drag back above his unfocused sight. There was barely enough breath left in his lungs for his voice to be emitted as a dry, forceless whisper. "Finish . . . me off . . ."

"I told you before." The other man was taller than Fett; he had to lift Voss'on't higher and brace him against his chest, then step backward to pull him away from the flames and smoke. "You're too valuable to let die." Boba Fett took one hand away from where he had clutched the torn front of the stormtrooper's insignia-less uniform, and prodded his gloved fingertips up underneath the edge of his own armor's helmet. He took one last, lung-filling inhalation from the helmet's air supply, then tugged and ripped the breathing tube out beneath the helmet's lower edge. The tube extended only a few inches from the helmet; Boba Fett had to bring the stormtrooper's face up close to his own, foreheads separated only by the dark visor, in order the thrust the end of the tube into Voss'on't's mouth.

The minute flow of oxygen from the helmet's air supply triggered an automatic response in Voss'on't. His back arched as his lungs filled reflexively, drawing deep from what little remained in the tiny canister inside the helmet. Voss'on't coughed, expelling the tube.

Fett saw that the stormtrooper still had enough of his wits about him, despite the battering he had taken in the explosions that had ripped through the cargo hold, to clamp his mouth shut and hold in the life-restoring breath he had been given. Bearing Voss'on't up, with one arm wrapped around him, Boba Fett dragged the unresisting figure through the smoke and toward the ladder leading up to the cockpit area.

The ladder still stood upright, though it swayed when Boba Fett put a hand upon one of the metal treads. Looking past the threads of smoke sifting toward the hull's air leaks, he could see that one of the upper attachment points had been ripped loose by the laser-cannon bolt's impact; the entire bulkhead behind the ladder had buckled nearly in two, as though crumpled in a giant fist.

A screech of tormented metal sounded, barely audible through the dinning layers of system alarms, as Boba Fett mounted the ladder and began the laborious process of carrying the barely conscious stormtrooper toward the cockpit. With Voss'on't's weight balanced precariously against himself, each higher tread he stepped upon threatened to break the ladder's single remaining weld with the bulkhead above. If the ladder was to come crashing down, once he and his awkward burden were at the halfway point, the fall would be enough to send both of them plummeting through the broken grating below and into the smoldering pit of the main engine compartments. Boba Fett knew he wouldn't be climbing out from there. With that much lethal hard radiation going unshielded, no one could.

The weld point broke just as Boba Fett reached for the top rung.

For a split second, the ladder swayed clear of the bulkhead, overbalanced by the combined weight of Fett and his hard merchandise. With Voss'on't's chest pressed against one shoulder, Boba Fett bent his knees into a tense crouch. The edge of the hatchway to the cockpit area drew farther away from his upraised hand. Lungs burning, fingers straining clawlike, he pushed his legs straight, leaping for the metal ridge above him.

His fingertips caught hold of the hatchway's curved lower rim. The stormtrooper's weight slipped in the grasp of Boba Fett's other arm; dangling alongside the crumpled bulkhead, he squeezed his hold tighter around Voss'on't's chest, his own fist locked under the edge of the other's shoulder blade, tight enough that he could feel the ends of the stormtrooper's broken ribs grind against one another.

The only device that Boba Fett had left that would be of any use was the wrist-mounted arrow-dart with its trailing, tethered line coiled along his forearm. Right now, that arm was the one holding up Voss'on't; he couldn't do that, and aim and fire the dart. Even with his own carefully trained resources of strength and will, Boba Fett's grip with his other hand upon the open cockpit hatchway above was beginning to fail, the sharp metal edge scraping slowly, centimeter by centimeter, across the fingertips of his battle armor's glove.

There was no time for further calculation. Boba Fett loosened his grip upon the renegade stormtrooper. Voss'on't's weight slid lower against him as Fett brought his arm vertical and fired the arrow-dart toward the cockpit.

The breath that Voss'on't had managed to hold now

escaped in an involuntary gasp of pain as the tip of the dart scored a red line across his shoulder blade and neck. His torso was jerked higher as the trailing line, penetrating the back of his uniform jacket, gathered up the heavy oil- and bloodstained fabric like a sling beneath Voss'on't's arms, dragging him almost a full meter upward. The torn front of his uniform jacket slid across the visor of Fett's helmet.

Boba Fett felt the trailing line of the dart grow taut, indicating that the barbed metal had snagged onto some anchoring point inside the cockpit. The dart's built-in circuitry was programmed to both spread its barbs wider upon target contact and alter its final trajectory into a tight loop, giving the head section of the trailing line the chance to magnetically seize and fasten upon itself.

Using the control studs at the base of his battle armor's glove, Boba Fett hit the arrow-dart's retract function. The line reaching up into the cockpit went even tighter, as though strung from the ends of a primitive bow weapon. Boba Fett had to grip the line with his upraised hand and strain his bicep muscles against its tension to keep his own weight and that of Voss'on't's body from pulling his arm out of its socket.

The miniaturized traction engine embedded in the sleeve of Fett's armor had been designed only to handle one humanoid-sized burden, not two; he could sense a warning glow of heat against the flesh of his forearm as the dart's trailing line reeled back, drawing him and Voss'on't slowly up toward the open hatchway. The ladder fell away from his boot soles, its length clattering against two angles of bulkhead, then falling to the grated floor of the cargo hold. A swirl of red sparks burst up as the ladder slipped through one of the jagged openings and tumbled farther into the ship's bowels.

A tendril of grey smoke, lighter than the dark, oily clouds from the fire in the main engine compartments, leaked from a tear in Boba Fett's sleeve. The heat against his skin increased to a white-hot burn as the retracting line brought him inches away from the metal ridge above him. With nothing to push against from below, Fett had to wait until the line had dragged him high enough to throw one elbow across the rim of the hatchway, then lever himself into position for pushing Voss'on't up onto the floor of the cockpit area.

Voss'on't came to, at least enough to realize what Boba Fett was trying to accomplish. The stormtrooper's fingertips reached out and scrabbled a hold on to the cockpit flooring; with a kicking thrust, he managed to drag himself up and out of Fett's supporting grasp.

With both arms free now, Boba Fett threw his other elbow across the hatchway's lower rim and tensed to pull himself the rest of the way up.

"Hey . . . thanks . . ."

Fett heard the grating, smoke-harshened voice and looked up into Voss'on't's grinning face. The stormtrooper had rolled over and gotten himself into a sitting position, his one good arm braced behind himself, knees drawn up toward his chest. The narrowed eyes and angles features wore a black mask of sweat-streaked ash and oil; his leering smile broke through as though cut with a diagonal swipe of a vibroblade.

"Thanks," repeated Voss'on't. The cockpit's air filters had cleared away enough smoke for the ex-stormtrooper to draw in a full breath. "I appreciate it. Now you can go die."

One boot shot out, its sole catching Boba Fett directly in the visor of his helmet. The kick had enough force to knock him back from where he had clambered onto the lower rim of the hatchway; only the line tethered from his wrist into the cockpit behind Voss'on't kept Fett from falling back down toward the cargo hold.

Boba Fett managed to grab the rim of the hatchway with one hand. He looked up and saw that Voss'on't had gotten to his feet, and now stood gazing down at him. In one hand, Voss'on't held a sharp fragment of metal, part of the debris that the laser-cannon bolts had scattered through the cargo hold. His ugly smile growing wider, Voss'on't held the edge of the shard against the line running past him, from Fett's wrist to its anchor inside the cockpit.

"This time," said Voss'on't, sneering, "it's really good-bye. For you, at least." As he pressed the cutting edge of the metal fragment harder against the line, he raised one booted foot and prepared to smash it down upon Boba Fett's hand.

Before the boot came down, Voss'on't was thrown off balance by the tethered line going suddenly slack. Pressing the miniature control studs at the base of his wrist, Boba Fett let the arrow-dart's line reel out, until it had lengthened by several meters. That was enough for him to cock his free arm back and snap it forward again. The tethered line looped lassolike and snagged around Voss'on't's neck. Fett hit the wrist-mounted control studs again, retracting the line once more, into a choking garrote around the other man's throat.

Voss'on't staggered backward, fingertips clawing at the line digging under his throat. The pull from the taut line enabled Boba Fett to climb up into the hatchway.

With his eyes squeezed shut in pain, Voss'on't didn't see the blow from Boba Fett's gloved fist that sent the stormtrooper sprawling onto his back, head slamming against the base of the pilot's chair. Boba Fett reached over with his other hand and snapped the arrow-dart line free from his own wrist, pushed the dazed Voss'on't over, and used the loose end of the line to bind Voss'on't's hands together with a hard knot. He pulled the rest of the line down to Voss'on't's ankles and bound them the same way. Then he picked Voss'on't up by the front of his jacket, hoisted the stormtrooper to eye level, and threw him into the far corner of the cockpit.

"Seal off the cockpit area," Boba Fett spoke aloud. He was already leaning over the control panel as *Slave I*'s onboard computer executed the command; with a hiss, the hatchway door closed behind him. With a few quick jabs at the controls, he silenced the alarm signals once again.

The silence was broken by Fett's own deep, ragged

breathing as his lungs refilled themselves from the cockpit's reserves of oxygen. Those were enough to bring Voss'on't back to full consciousness as well.

"Now . . . now what . . ." Hands tied behind himself, Voss'on't lay on one shoulder and labored to speak. "Are you . . . going to do . . ."

Fett ignored him for a moment. With a few adjustments from the still-functioning navigational rockets, he had brought *Slave I* around to where he could at last see the other ship that had fired upon them. Even from this distance, where the visible details of his enemy were little more distinct than the stars behind it, he could recognize the vessel whose laser cannons had brought his own to the brink of destruction.

He knew as well whose vessel it was, and who had given the orders to fire.

It's Xizor. Another adjustment to the controls brought the viewport's optical magnification into the circuit. The outlines of the Falleen prince's flagship were unmistakable—and intimidating. The ship was known to be one of the deadliest and most thoroughly armored in the galaxy, the equivalent of anything matching its gross tonnage in Emperor Palpatine's war fleet. If *Slave I* had gotten into a full-pitched battle with it, there wouldn't even have been this much of Boba Fett's ship left hanging together.

The mystery of why the *Vendetta* hadn't moved in for the kill was easy enough to determine. *He's holding back,* decided Fett. *Just waiting to see if there's any sign of life.* Prince Xizor was known to be something of a trophy collector; it would be entirely consistent for him to want the hard physical evidence—the corpses—of those he had set out to kill rather than just blowing them into disconnected atoms drifting in space.

The greater mystery was why Xizor had lain in wait and fired upon *Slave I* in the first place. Fett had been aware of no connection between Xizor and this high-stakes job of rounding up the renegade stormtrooper for which Palpatine had posted such an astronomical price.

But there had to be some link—it was too much to believe that it was mere coincidence or just random malice on Xizor's part. The Falleen prince's mind was too coldly rational—similar to Boba Fett's own in that manner—for anything like that to be the case.

Boba Fett lowered his gaze from the viewport and began punching in new commands on the control panel.

"What . . ." Voss'on't's voice was a harsh croak. "Tell me . . ."

There was neither time nor need to explain to the merchandise lying on the floor of the cockpit. "I'm doing," said Boba Fett, "the same thing I've been doing all along. Saving *both* our lives—whether you like it or not."

With a final jab of his forefinger, he hit the button to fire up the one main engine that was still functioning. *Slave I* shuddered, its hull threatened to tear loose from the battered structural frame beneath, as the engine's convulsive thrust blurred the stars in the viewport.

6

"What's he doing?" The comm specialist leaned closer to the *Vendetta*'s forward viewport, scanning the sector ahead. "It's amazing, Your Excellency—he must be still alive!"

Prince Xizor wasn't amazed. Standing at the bridge's controls, with one hand still resting upon the laser cannons' target acquisition module, he watched as, in the star-filled distance, the ship known as *Slave I* fired up its remaining thruster engine and started to move. Another screen, smaller and mounted to the side of the viewport, showed the damage-assessment scan that had been run on the target: a complete schematic showed in glowing red the operational systems that had already shut down. There were only a few—the one engine, basic navigational equipment, life support in the cockpit area—that still appeared in the green that indicated ongoing functions. Crippled, but slowly gathering speed, Boba Fett's ship had some of its own life left in it yet.

"He's hard to kill," said Xizor with a slow, admiring nod of his head. He liked that in a sentient creature; it made the final victory over one of them so much sweeter. Too many of the galaxy's denizens, on whatever remote systems they could be found or on the homeworlds in the Empire's center, gave up all too easily when they perceived the hand of the Black Sun about to set its grasp upon their throats. Deep within himself, Xizor possessed the characteristic Falleen disdain for those too weak to put up a struggle, even when facing certain death. For a Falleen, that was the moment when the struggle should be at its keenest, when there was no hope of extending one's life even by a single heartbeat. Xizor had suspected for a long time, from when he had first envisioned the scheme in which Boba Fett was now fatally enmeshed, that the bounty hunter would not disappoint him in this regard. "Hard to kill," Xizor mused aloud once more. "A very worthy prey. But then . . ." He turned his head and smiled at the comm specialist standing beside him. "A true hunter would be."

The comm specialist appeared nervous, with a sheen of sweat upon his brow. As with the rest of the operations crew, arrayed at their posts in the *Vendetta*'s bridge, he was understandably eager that his master's wishes, especially in something as important as this, would not go unfulfilled. At the same time none of them had the same innate confidence in the outcome of the pursuit that Xizor himself did. *Which is as it should be,* thought Xizor with satisfaction. *Keeps them on their toes.*

"Excuse me, Your Excellency"—the comm specialist raised a hand and pointed toward the high, concave surface of the central viewport—"but Boba Fett's ship— *Slave I*—its velocity is increasing." He glanced over at the readout numbers on one of the tracking monitors. "Rather substantially, in fact. Perhaps it's time to finish him off. Otherwise . . ." The tech's shoulders rose in a ticlike shrug. "He might actually get away."

"Calm yourself." The corner of Xizor's mouth twisted in a contemptuous sneer. "Your fears are groundless." That was one more emotional response that provoked scorn in a Falleen noble. "Where exactly do you think Boba Fett could run to? You can see for yourself that his ship no longer has the capability of making a jump into hyperspace." Xizor pointed to the damage-assessment screen. "Even if he could—were he foolish enough to try it—the stress would blow that poor wreck into atoms. No . . ." Xizor gave another slow shake of his head. "There's nothing to worry about now. We may bring his futile struggle to an end at our leisure."

He could tell that the comm specialist was unconvinced, as well as the others surrounding him on the bridge. They did not possess the greatness of spirit to savor a moment such as this. *A legend dies,* mused Xizor, *and it means nothing to them.*

For Boba Fett was precisely that, a dark legend. One whose exploits had been for so long a source of fear and envy—and all the other spirit-lessening emotions that sentient creatures could inflict upon themselves—in every shadowed corner of the galaxy. Even though Boba Fett's death had not been the primary aim of all of Xizor's plotting and scheming, it was still an undeniable benefit to become the author of his demise. In the unspoken rules of the great, deadly game played among hunters, no prize was more desirable than the blood of an opponent upon one's hands.

Xizor looked past the image of Boba Fett's ship to the stars beyond. *And someday*—the thought burned within his breast—*that blood will be from other opponents, even greater and more deadly than Boba Fett.* The time would come when he would place his boot sole upon the neck of another helmeted figure, one who had long been the target of his hatred. If the web that Xizor spun had resulted in Boba Fett's destruction, that was only a by-product of the scheme meant to crush Lord Darth Vader. And when that vengeful goal had been accomplished . . .

After vengeance came ambition. Which for Prince Xizor was just as limitless. It was something that withered old fool Emperor Palpatine would discover too late to save himself. The mystical Force, which Xizor had felt more than once squeeze the breath from his throat, would not be enough to forestall that day of triumph for Black Sun and its commander.

Some things, thought Xizor with a thin smile, *are more powerful than any Force.* And over those things— fear, vengeance, greed, and so much else—his command extended as well.

Even the most pleasant meditations had to end eventually. Xizor brought his thoughts back from that future, glittering like light from a honed vibroblade, and returned it to those concerns over which his underlings fretted. "Let us proceed," said Xizor. He gestured to one of the weapons techs standing behind him. "Reaccess previous target and prepare to fire."

"Your Excellency . . ." The comm specialist sounded even more nervous than before. "That . . . that might not be such a good idea . . ."

Fearful insubordination angered Prince Xizor as thoroughly as any other kind. His heavy cape swung outward from his shoulders as he whirled about to face the other man, already cringing before the onslaught of his wrath. The violet tinge of his eyes darkened to a color closer to that of spilled blood as he pinned the comm specialist with his fiercely heated gaze. "You dare," said Xizor, the lowered tone of his voice more intimidating than any increase in volume could have been, "to question my orders?"

"No! Of course not, Your Excellency—" The comm specialist actually took a step backward, hands raised as though to fend off a blow. A look of controlled panic swept around the faces of the other staff on the bridge. "It's just thuh-that—" Stammering, the technician pointed with one hand to the viewport behind Xizor. "The situation has changed somewhat . . . suh-since you last looked at it . . ."

Brow creased, Xizor turned back to the viewport. He saw immediately what the comm specialist was referring to, even before the other man could manage an explanation.

"You see, Your Excellency . . . Boba Fett has maneuvered his ship so that it's directly between ourselves and the web of Kud'ar Mub'at . . ."

The situation would have been obvious to any eye, let alone one as skilled in strategic matters as Prince Xizor's. Beyond the image of the ship *Slave I* in the viewport, the larger mass of the arachnoid assembler's drifting, self-constructed home and place of business could be seen, like a shabby, elongated artificial asteroid.

"To fire off any laser-cannon bolts now, Your Excellency, would be highly inadvisable." The comm specialist had summoned up his last reserves of courage; his voice sounded a little less shaky. "Any evasive maneuvers on Boba Fett's part might result in the bolts striking Kud'ar Mub'at's web instead." The comm specialist shrugged and spread his hands, palms upward. "Of course, that would be up to you to decide, as to whether to risk it or not. But given the ongoing business relations between Black Sun and the assembler—"

"Yes, yes; refrain from explanation." Xizor irritably waved off the underling. "You don't need to remind me about all that." Sending a few laser-cannon bolts through Kud'ar Mub'at itself, and not just the assembler's messily conglomerated web, would not have been any cause for grief; Xizor had already decided upon the elimination of this business associate, whose entangling concerns had grown so inconvenient. But to do so in this way, with all the repercussions that would follow from it becoming known throughout the galaxy that Black Sun had a short and fatal way with those that served them, would cripple Xizor's further plans. Beyond that, the new ally that Xizor had slated to replace Kud'ar Mub'at was also inside the assembler's web—Xizor had no intention of losing so potentially valuable a creature as Balancesheet, the crafty little accountant subnode that had declared its independence from it creator. "Hold your fire," Xizor instructed the weapons systems techs behind him.

The comm specialist had put one hand to his ear, listening to a subaudible message being patched through the cochlear implant inside his skull. "Your Excellency—" he said, looking up at Xizor. "Kud'ar Mub'at has made direct contact with us. He wishes to have a word with you."

All I need, thought Xizor irritably. "Very well—put it through."

He listened to Kud'ar Mub'at's high-pitched, nerve-grating voice through the speaker mounted above the bridge's central control panel. "My so-esteemed Prince Xizor," came the assembler's voice. "Of course, as always, boundless is my trust in your wisdom and abilities. Never would I doubt the propriety of any action that was initiated by your spotless hands—"

"Get on with it," growled Xizor. The panel microphone picked up his words and relayed them on a tight-beam connection to the web drifting in the distance, beyond Boba Fett's ship. "I've got more urgent things to take care of than listening to you." He kept an eye on the viewport and the image of Boba Fett's ship, still gathering speed.

"Very well," sniffed the assembler. Xizor could imagine it on its nest in the web, folding multiple jointed limbs more tightly around its pallid, wobbling abdomen. "Your display of temperament is perhaps understandable, but it does not diminish the admiration I—"

"Either say what you want of me or be silent."

The tone of the assembler's voice turned sour and sulky. "As you wish, Xizor. How is this for bluntness: you must be an idiot to have begun firing upon Boba Fett in open space. Do Falleens have no capacity for discretion? This entire sector is under constant observation because of the presence of my web here. *Must* I remind you that others are very likely watching? Some of those watchers are business associates of mine, or those with whom I might wish to do business at some time. I realize that your reputation would be enhanced by publicly eliminating the so-esteemed Boba Fett—but what about *my* reputation?" Kud'ar Mub'at's voice grew louder from the panel speaker. "I certainly *would* prefer to have creatures killed rather than pay the money I owe them—don't mistake me about that—but I would prefer if it didn't become widely known that this sort of thing happens to them. Pray tell, who's going to do business with me if they think they're going to wind up dead?"

"Don't worry about it," replied Prince Xizor. Only a portion of his attention was given to the conversation with the absent assembler. "You can tell anyone you want that Boba Fett's death had nothing to do with you."

"Oh, but of course." The voice coming from the speaker was tinged with sarcasm. "It just *happened* that he got blown to atoms while he was bringing a piece of hard merchandise to me, a piece for which I'd have to hand over a pretty sum of credits. Creatures will believe that, all right."

"Let them believe whatever they will. You've got more pressing concerns right now."

"What?" Kud'ar Mub'at sounded puzzled. "To what are you referring, Xizor?"

"Simple enough." His own admiration for Boba Fett had increased, now that he could see what the bounty hunter was up to. "Your 'business associate,' for whom you've expressed such concern—Boba Fett—he's headed right your way."

"Well, of *course* he is. He's got merchandise to deliver—"

"I'm afraid you don't understand." Bestowing bad news on another sentient creature was a minor diversion that paled next to murder and plunder, but it was one from which Xizor could still derive some pleasure. "Or perhaps more likely, you simply have no awareness of what condition his ship *Slave I* is in. But we've already done a complete damage assessment. So you can believe me, Kud'ar Mub'at, when I tell you—Boba Fett's not going to be able to stop."

"But . . . but that's absurd!"

"No," said Xizor. "It's actually rather clever of him. He's burning up the last remaining thruster engine aboard his ship, and he's already achieved a considerable velocity. It's a tribute to his piloting skills that he's able to keep *Slave I*—what's left of it—on a steady course, at that speed. But what Boba Fett can't do now—no one would be able to—is bring *Slave I* to a halt before it crashes into your web. From our scanning of his ship, we know that all of his braking rockets are out of commission. Which, of course, is something that *he* knows as well."

A wordless, panicked shriek came over the comm unit speaker. The image that came to Prince Xizor's inner eye was that of Kud'ar Mub'at almost literally flying out of his nest inside the drifting web, with his spidery legs thrashing around him.

"How—" The absent assembler managed to regain a measure of control, enough to sputter out a desperate question. "How much time do I have?"

"I'd say . . ." Xizor glanced over at the tracking monitor and the rapidly flickering numbers on the readouts below it. "You'd better brace yourself."

Before any more annoyingly high-pitched sounds could come over the speaker, Xizor reached over and broke the comm unit connection between the *Vendetta* and Kud'ar Mub'at's web. A monitor below the main viewport showed the view from a remote scout module stationed on the other side of the web; glancing at the screen, Xizor could see the flaring jet of *Slave I*'s remaining thruster engine. From this angle it looked like a star going nova, all glaring flame, bright enough to sting one's eyes.

"Your Excellency." Standing beside Xizor, the comm specialist spoke up. "Do you have orders for the crew?"

Xizor remained silent for a moment longer, watching the bounty hunter's ship as it sped on its trajectory straight toward Kud'ar Mub'at's web. His cold admiration of Boba Fett—and his appreciation—went up another notch. The game of death had just been made more complicated—and much more interesting. There was no doubt about the eventual outcome; there never was when Xizor played at it. But however sweet the bounty hunter's death would have been before, the pleasure was enhanced far beyond that now.

"Track and pursuit," said Xizor at last. "There's going to be some pieces to pick up. Interesting pieces . . ."

Boba Fett emerged from *Slave I*—he had to step back and kick the exterior hatchway door open; its operational power had failed and a loosened section of hull plating had wedged into one corner—and stepped into absolute, screeching chaos.

He'd expected as much. This result had been a part of his plan, from the moment he'd conceived the notion of plowing his ship into Kud'ar Mub'at's space-drifting web. His long familiarity with the arachnoid assembler, their years of doing business together, had enabled him to scope out the web's nature and capabilities. Kud'ar Mub'at had designed and spun the web out of self-extruded filaments, both structural and neural, so that it could incorporate bits and pieces of ships and other artifacts made by sentient creatures; both the web's inside and outside were studded with those segments of durasteel, like functioning wreckage mired in the irregular, scum-thick surf of a frozen sea. That physical incorporation of such items had been due to Kud'ar Mub'at's greed—its desire to magnify and glorify itself with trophies from those unfortunates who'd found themselves enmeshed too deeply in its schemes to get out—and to a need to preserve the web itself. The web had no other defenses; its ability to quickly incorporate and seal itself around anything that penetrated it was the only way it could maintain a life-supporting environment inside its curved, matted, and tangled fibrous walls.

With one gloved hand grasping the side of the hatchway, Boba Fett scanned the scene around him. The interior of Kud'ar Mub'at's web was lit a shimmering blue-white by the phosphorescence of masses of illuminator subnodes. The simple creatures clung to the upper walls by their tiny, scuttlings legs and radiated the soft glow from the bioluminescent compounds in their translucent, distended abdomens, hardly more than the size of Boba Fett's doubled fists. All of the shrieking noise in the web came not from the living light sources, tethered by neural filaments to their own creator, but from their subnode cousins, the faster-moving emitters of the sticky, viscous fluid by which the web repaired itself and incorporated fragments of ships into the crudely shaped structure.

The emitters scuttled around the web's torn edges, where *Slave I* had broken through and mired itself. Before crashing into the web, Boba Fett had reoriented the ship from it usual vertically oriented, tail-downward position; that would have brought the rounded curve of the cockpit like a blunt hammer-blow against the web's exterior. At the last second, a quick burst of one of the navigational jets had brought the sharper, knifelike projection of the hull above the cockpit toward the rapidly approaching web. Once *Slave I* had thrust its way into the web, thick fibers entangling around it, a final burst from the opposite jet had brought it upright again, so that the wider surface of the cockpit against the web's interior brought it to a halt. The smell of the fibers that had been scorched black by the jets' firing hung as an acrid miasma in the web's pallidly lit cavern.

More than the web's structure had been hurt in the ship's impact. The web, a living thing itself, reacted to the trauma in its own pain-filled way. The din of shrieking that sounded in Boba Fett's ears came from the other subnodes that had already been in this section of the web, rather than having scurried there to contain the damage. Most of them had been torn loose from the neural-fiber strands that had tethered them to their controlling parent Kud'ar Mub'at; some were mute, never having been given vocal abilities, but the others now gave idiot cries as they dropped from the rough domed ceiling of the space. The matted floor was thick with the scuttling forms, writhing in spasms of pain or scrabbling in tight little circles, their limited onboard cerebral functions completely overloaded by the sudden disconnection from the assembler on his nest in another part of the web. Spidery, crablike subnodes, trailing their snapped connectors behind them, clambered over Boba Fett's boots as he stepped down from *Slave I*'s hatchway. He kicked a few aside as though they were chitin-shelled rats; a few of the smaller ones were unavoidably crushed beneath his boot soles, their husks crackling like thin eggshells.

Fett looked up toward the prow of his ship and saw that the emitter subnodes had almost finished sealing the web around the hull; only a section around the main thruster nozzles still extended out into the vacuum of space. The various high-pitched whistling noises that the web's atmosphere had made, escaping through the torn structural fibers, slowly died out as the emitters went about their work, filling in the last of the gaps between the living biomass and the ship's curved durasteel hull. Around Boba Fett, the blue-lit space grew steadily quieter, as more and more of the disconnected subnodes lapsed into a quivering catatonic state, overturned on their backs like sea creatures stranded by some planet's receding tide. The silence that slowly overcame the previous hectic din was that of a partial death: as the web was strung with living fibers spun out from Kud'ar Mub'at's own cortex and cerebrospinal system, to stand in an excised section such as this was like standing in some creature's grossly magnified brain after an equally gigantic surgeon's scalpel had cut away a wedge of grey matter.

"Let's go." Boba Fett reached back inside *Slave I*'s hatchway and grabbed the front of Trhin Voss'on't's uniform jacket, now hardly more than rags held together by its blood-tarnished metal fastenings. With a sharp pull, he got the former stormtrooper to his feet; another tug brought the other man stumbling out of the ship. "Time to get paid."

Voss'on't's eyes were two burning nicks in his bruised, oil-stained face. The hands tied behind his back thrust his shoulders forward. "If you're in such a hurry—" His voice was raw from both smoke inhalation and barely controlled rage. He nodded toward his boots and the segment of arrow-dart line that hobbled his ankles together. "Then you'd better untie these. Never get there, otherwise."

"I've got a better idea," said Fett. With a swift horizontal arc of his forearm, he clouted Voss'on't across the face, sending him slamming back against the edge of *Slave I*, then sprawling among the twitching, dying subnodes that littered the space's floor. Blood streamed from Voss'on't's nose as Fett looked down at him. "Let's leave you tied up just the way you are, and you can forget about any more escape attempts." Reaching down, he grabbed the rags of Voss'on't's jacket and hauled him upright again. "They're not going to do you any good now. And I've started to find them annoying."

"Yeah, I bet." Voss'on't sneered at him. His bound hands squeezed into white-knuckled fists, as though he were imagining them around Boba Fett's neck.

The stormtrooper had been on the losing end of every exchange with Fett, going right back to the distant colonial mining world where Fett and his temporary partner Bossk had tracked him down. Yet he still displayed a deeply ingrained will to fight. *It won't do him much good,* thought Boba Fett. There would be little difference in the outcome whether Voss'on't continued to struggle and scheme, or whether he finally gave up and accepted his fate. That being the case, Boba Fett didn't care which the stormtrooper wound up doing. It was just a matter of convenience.

A darker, more venomous expression settled across Voss'on't's face. "You might be able to get paid, bounty hunter. You managed to get your merchandise this far, so anything's possible. But what are you going to do when Prince Xizor shows up here?" Voss'on't had seen the image of Xizor's ship on *Slave I*'s cockpit viewport, and had been able to identify it just as readily as Fett had. "And that's going to be any minute now."

"You don't need to worry about that. I'll deal with

him then." A length of loose cord dangled from the knot around Voss'on't's wrists; Boba Fett used that to pull him along, twisted partway around and barely able to walk. As they progressed toward the interior tunnel that would lead them to Kud'ar Mub'at itself, Fett glanced over his shoulder at his captive. "You didn't appear surprised by Xizor being in this sector of space, waiting for us. It seems a reasonable assumption that you knew he'd be here."

"Assume whatever you want." Voss'on't leaned back from the tug of the line around his wrists. "You'll find out what the deal is soon enough. And you want to know something? It's going to be a real surprise."

Boba Fett maintained his own silence. And kept a hand on the butt of the blaster pistol strapped at his side.

"Ah . . . my inimitable associate . . . the *esteemed* . . . Boba Fett . . ." A halting voice, squeaking like rusted metal, greeted them as they emerged from the web's central tunnel. "How charmed . . . I am . . . to see you once more . . ."

Standing in the center of the web's main chamber, with the stormtrooper tethered a few steps behind him, Boba Fett gazed upon the arachnoid assembler. Or upon the crippled shell of what Kud'ar Mub'at had been; *Slave I*'s crashing into the web had obviously had an effect for the worse upon its master as well.

"You're not looking too good, Kud'ar Mub'at." It was a statement of plain fact; Boba Fett felt no great sympathy for the assembler. *I'd better get my credits,* thought Fett, *before it dies.*

"How . . . *kind* of you . . . to show such concern . . ." The pneumatic subnode that had formed Kud'ar Mub'at's cushioned throne was apparently dead, its deflated and flaccid membrane extending around the assembler like a grey, waxen puddle. Kud'ar Mub'at itself was hunched down in the thicket of its spidery black legs, the inverted triangular face lowered and tilted to one side. Most of the compound eyes studding its visage appeared lifeless, the sentient spark gone out behind them, as though a gust of wind had blown out the guttering flame inside a lantern. Only the two largest eyes at the front seemed able to focus upon the web's untimely visitors. "To be honest with you . . . there've been times . . . I've felt better . . ."

"Face it, " Boba Fett said bluntly. "You're dying."

"Oh, no . . . not at all . . ." The triangular head raised itself a bit, displaying a shakily lopsided imitation of a humanoid smile. "I'll survive this . . . as I've survived other things . . ." A twiglike forelimb lifted, its end claw twitching and pointing to Kud'ar Mub'at's head. "This is no more . . . than the results of . . . a neural feedback surge . . . from the crash . . . that's all . . ." The claw tapped against the black shell of the assembler's skull with a dry little clicking noise. "Your sudden entry . . . into my humble abode . . . most unfortunate . . ." Kud'ar Mub'at tried to raise itself a little higher in its deflated nest, but failed, collapsing once more into the broken tangle of its arms. "But you shall see . . . all things can be mended . . ." A crazed light shone in the largest of the assembler's eyes. "I've had so much practice . . . creating additions to myself . . . *outside* my body . . . that I can create a new cortex inside here . . ." The raised claw tip dug harder at the skull behind the triangular face, as though already getting down to the repair job. "To replace the one . . . that the circumstances . . . of your arrival . . . damaged."

"Perhaps you can." Boba Fett shrugged. "It doesn't matter to me, though."

"And what . . . precisely . . . does matter to you?"

"Getting paid."

"Ah . . ." The assembler's head twisted about, as though trying to force its visitor into focus. "You, at least . . . have not changed . . ." The raised claw tip shook as it pointed toward Boba Fett. "But you know the rules . . . to be paid . . . one must first deliver . . . the merchandise . . ."

Boba Fett stepped to one side, at the same time yanking the end of the cord tied around the renegade stormtrooper's wrists. Trhin Voss'on't fell forward, his head almost striking the soft edge of the assembler's thronelike nest. Before he could rise up onto his knees, Boba Fett put his boot between the man's shoulder blades and shoved him back down.

"There you go," said Fett. "Good enough?"

"How could . . . I ever . . . have doubted you?" Kud'ar Mub'at's gaze rested upon the bounty hunter for a moment, then lowered again to the merchandise sprawled in front of him. The one leg's clawed tip reached down and caught the point of Voss'on't's chin, raising the stormtrooper's bruised and scowling face toward it. "Seems . . . very much . . . like the desired object . . ." The claw tip pushed at one side of Voss'on't's face, displaying its profile. "Though of course . . . verification . . . will be needed . . ."

"Don't play games with me." With one hand, Boba Fett reached out and grabbed the end of Kud'ar Mub'at's raised forelimb. He pulled the assembler partway out of its nest, bringing the triangular face closer to the dark visor of his helmet. "If I say this is Trhin Voss'on't—then that's all the verification you need." His gloved hand tossed the assembler back onto the deflated subnode. "I didn't go to all the trouble that I did just to bring back the wrong piece of merchandise."

"Of . . . course . . . not . . ." Kud'ar Mub'at slowly disentangled itself from its own unresponsive limbs. The effort caused a tremor to run through the assembler's body, its globular abdomen pulsating visibly. "Would I doubt you . . . my esteemed Boba Fett?" The assembler's head slowly shook back and forth. "My faculties are not so damaged . . . as for that . . . to be possible." The lopsided imitation smile showed once again. "But I am not . . . the one . . . who is paying . . . for this merchandise . . ."

"You're supposed to be holding the credits."

"And so . . . I am . . . but there's another involved . . . and *he* decides when you get paid . . ." Kud'ar Mub'at's smile turned even uglier. "And *if* . . . you do . . ."

Those words were not to Boba Fett's liking. His preference was always for straightforward business deals, delivery of merchandise followed by prompt payment of the bounty. This deal had become far more intricate than that—though he already had a notion about who was behind these complications. *That's why Prince Xizor showed up*, decided Boba Fett. Somehow, it must have been the Falleen's credits, rather than Emperor Palpatine's, that got put up for the return of Trhin Voss'on't. *And Xizor would rather kill me than pay me.*

"It looks like . . . you're starting . . . to figure out a few things . . ." The halting words were tinged with Kud'ar Mub'at's sly laughter. The assembler had a knack for knowing what another sentient creature was thinking, even if it had to read those thoughts through the dark visor of a Mandalorian battle-armor helmet. "About . . . what kind of job . . . you took on . . ."

Another possibility occurred to Boba Fett. *Maybe*, he thought, *the Emperor did put up the bounty*. Voss'on't had been, after all, a servant of the Empire; the betrayal of his stormtrooper's oath would have been more of an affront to Palpatine than anyone else. But the bounty that Palpatine had put up for him might very well have tempted even a creature with the vast resources of the Black Sun criminal organization at his command—such as Xizor. Or else Xizor wasn't interested in the credits for bringing back Voss'on't, but was more concerned about currying favor with one of the few beings in the galaxy more powerful than he. If Xizor was able to claim that he had tracked down and captured the renegade stormtrooper, his prestige at the Imperial court on the planet of Coruscant, and his influence with Palpatine, would overshadow that of Lord Vader. Boba Fett was more than aware of the stories of bad blood between Xizor and Vader; there was little possibility of two such rivals for the Emperor's favor being anything other than enemies.

Whether Prince Xizor was after the bounty that had been posted for Voss'on't, or something more intangible *and* more valuable, made little difference to Boba Fett. *If he plans on taking something from me, then he's made a mistake. One he'll regret . . .*

"All I know," said Boba Fett aloud, "is that I've done the job that was put up. I don't care whether it was Emperor Palpatine or Prince Xizor who was really behind it. I only work for myself. And I just want the bounty that was promised me."

"You poor fool." Kud'ar Mub'at's scorn appeared to reinvigorate the damaged creature. "You have no idea . . . for whom you've been working . . . all along . . ." The one claw tip extended toward Boba Fett. "You've been part of Xizor's schemes . . . and *mine* . . . for a long time now . . ."

From underneath Boba Fett's boot, the stormtrooper Voss'on't turned a sneer upward at his captor. "How does it feel, bounty hunter? You're not the winner in this game—you're the pawn."

A thrust of the boot flattened and silenced Voss'on't again. "What are you talking about, Kud'ar Mub'at?"

"Very . . . simple . . ." The arachnoid assembler fumbled its sticklike legs tighter around itself. "Our little scheme . . . yours and mine . . . to break up the old Bounty Hunters Guild . . ." Kud'ar Mub'at shook its narrow head. "That was Prince Xizor's idea . . . I only went along with it . . . because he made it worth my while . . . but he's the one who wanted to break up the Guild . . . and you did that for him . . ."

"Then you lied to me." Boba Fett's voice was as emotionless as always, but inside him there was a spark of anger.

"A mere matter . . . of business . . . my dear Boba Fett." In its crippled fashion, Kud'ar Mub'at imitated a nonchalant humanoid shrug. "That's all . . ."

"What else did you lie to me about?"

"You'll find out . . . soon enough . . ." Kud'ar Mub'at's smile didn't diminish as it gazed at Boba Fett, then turned toward one of the smaller fibrous corridors that branched off the web's central space. Another of the assembler's subnodes, a fully functioning one, scuttled out of the corridor and onto the tip of its parent's feebly extented forelimb. "Tell me . . . my dear little Balancesheet . . ." Another forelimb tenderly stroked the subnode's head, a miniature version of Kud'ar Mub'at's own. "Has our other guest . . . arrived . . ."

Boba Fett recognized the subnode creature as the one that had always taken care of the financial details from Kud'ar Mub'at's business dealings. More than once, the tiny scuttling Balancesheet had paid out the bounty that had been held in escrow by its creator. The sharp intelligence that had always been discernible in the subnode was still visible there, completely undiminished, as though it had been unaffected by the neural overload resulting from the crash of *Slave I* into the web. That was a mystery, but one that Boba Fett didn't have time to wonder about now.

"The *Vendetta* is just now docking with us." As though to confirm Balancesheet's statement, a shudder ran through the rough structure around them; somewhere in the distance, the sleek mass of Prince Xizor's flagship was linking up with the larger subnodes that allowed visitors to transfer over. "I have been in communication with Xizor," said Balancesheet, perched on Kud'ar Mub'at's raised forelimb. "He informs me that he is greatly looking forward to our meeting."

"I imagine . . . he is . . ." Kud'ar Mub'at's other limbs twitched and its lipless smile widened. "All creatures of business . . . relish the successful conclusion . . . of a project . . ."

"Then he and I have something in common." Boba Fett gave a quick nod. "Let's get this over with." He took his boot from between Trhin Voss'on't's shoulder blades and strode over to the mouth of the corridor leading to the docking area. From its holster, he drew out his blaster pistol.

Head still tilted to one side, Kud'ar Mub'at looked at him with alarm. "What . . . are you doing . . ." In front of the assembler, Voss'on't managed to scrabble into a sitting position, also watching Boba Fett. "This is . . . not necessary . . ."

"I'll tell you what's necessary and what's not." Carefully and slowly, Boba Fett pointed the blaster's muzzle at Kud'ar Mub'at and Voss'on't in turn. "If you both want to live a little longer, you'll stay quiet." He raised the blaster up by the side of his helmet. "And not spoil this little surprise for Prince Xizor."

The footsteps against the web's resilient tangle of fibers, from several creatures coming down the corridor, were already audible. Boba Fett flattened himself against the side of the opening, blaster at the ready.

"Watch out—"

He had known that Voss'on't would try to warn Xizor as soon as the Falleen prince appeared. A quick bolt from the blaster pistol, hitting Voss'on't in the shoulder and knocking him back against the base of Kud'ar Mub'at's nest, served both to silence him and distract Xizor's attention. That gave Boba Fett the microsecond he needed to get an arm around Xizor's throat and put the muzzle of the blaster against his head.

"Tell your men to back off." Boba Fett used Xizor as a shield, putting the Falleen between himself and the two Black Sun guards that had been just behind in the web's corridor. "I want their blasters on the floor—*now.*"

Xizor seemed more amused than surprised by what had happened. "Very well," he said calmly. "Do as the bounty hunter says." The two scowling guards lowered the blaster pistols they had so quickly unholstered, then tossed them into the center of the space. "You know—" Xizor turned his head, looking back at Boba Fett. "The guards are only a formality. I could kill you in a second. And I'd hardly have to move at all."

"You don't have a second." Boba Fett kept the blaster aimed straight at the prince's skull. "If you want to test your speed against mine, go ahead. But right now you've got a lot more to lose than I do."

"True enough," replied Xizor almost cordially, but still maintaining his haughty nobility. "I regret having backed you into this corner, Boba Fett. Desperate creatures seek desperate remedies for their situations. Which is a shame in this case, as you and I have more interests in common than you might otherwise suspect."

The Falleen prince's smooth words didn't impress Fett. With a shove against Xizor's back, Boba Fett pushed him toward Kud'ar Mub'at and the stormtrooper still bound hand and foot on the central space's floor. Boba Fett took a step backward, to where his blaster pistol had an angle on the others, including the two Black Sun guards at the mouth of the corridor.

"There's no need for that." Prince Xizor's cold half smile almost made it seem as if he were somehow in charge of the situation. "We can discuss these business dealings like civilized creatures. Here—" He gestured in command toward the two guards. "Return to the *Vendetta*. Your presence is no longer necessary here."

"But—" one of the guards protested.

"Your presence was hardly of any value before; why should it be now?" Xizor repeated the gesture. "Go. Leave us." As the Black Sun guards turned and disappeared down the corridor, Xizor spread his empty hands apart. "You see, Fett? I intend you no harm. Quite the contrary, in fact. You are a valuable entity to me."

"Difficult to believe." Boba Fett didn't lower the blaster pistol in his hand. "Given that you were so recently trying to blast me into atoms with your ship's laser cannons."

"A misunderstanding," said Xizor soothingly. "These things sometimes happen in the course of business. Just as it sometimes happens that a person such as myself might change his mind about what needs to be done. And who needs to be eliminated."

"Glad to hear it," said Fett. "But I don't buy it."

"You have a right to be skeptical. I'm sure our mutual friend and associate here has been telling you some interesting things. Information that might not reflect too well upon me . . ."

"My most esteemed . . . Prince Xizor . . ." The arachnoid assembler's forelimbs quivered. "You mistake . . . my intentions . . ." Kud'ar Mub'at's words stumbled out, as though the Falleen were holding the blaster on him. "I would never . . ."

"Don't waste our time," Xizor said coldly. "There are

matters that you need to be informed of as well, Kud'ar Mub'at." The edge of anger in Prince Xizor's voice made his attitude of command even more apparent. "You deceive yourself if you assume that I have any continued need for your services."

"But . . ."

"Silence!"

Boba Fett broke into the exchange between the two other creatures. "I'll say when anybody should talk or not." He aimed the blaster pistol straight toward Xizor. "All right?"

Xizor gave a thin smile and a nod. "As you wish. For now."

"The assembler said you were behind the plot to break up the old Bounty Hunters Guild. Is that true?"

"Does it matter?" Xizor looked at him almost pityingly. "If there was something that I wished to achieve through destroying the Guild—and I'll admit there was— that doesn't negate its value for you. Let's face it: many times, in its own crude, bumbling way, the Bounty Hunters Guild got in your way. As an organization it was a rival for those very same pieces of hard merchandise that you wished to procure for their bounties. Now the Guild is no more, and you face any other bounty hunter as an individual, on his own, without anyone to back him up. Thus your work is made that much easier and more profitable." Xizor's cruelly smiling gaze seemed to penetrate the visor of Boba Fett's helmet. "So what is there for you to complain of?"

"Being taken for a fool. That's what." Boba Fett used the blaster pistol in his hand to point toward Kud'ar Mub'at. "If there was something you wanted done—by me—then that's who you should've come to. Instead of bringing in a go-between like this."

"Perhaps you're right." Xizor gave a judicious nod. "Perhaps I underestimated you, bounty hunter. There might be even more in common between us than I at first suspected. I'll remember that—for our future business dealings."

"Assuming you have a future." The blaster pistol swung back toward the Falleen. "I haven't decided about that," said Boba Fett. "If I wasn't in the loop on this little scheme of yours, there must've been a reason. The same reason that you had your ship's laser cannons fire on *Slave I* as soon as I came out of hyperspace. You didn't want me to still be alive after all your plotting and scheming was finished." Fett raised the blaster higher, sighting down the length of its barrel toward Xizor. "Why is that?"

"Do you want the truth?" Xizor shrugged. "You're a dangerous individual, bounty hunter. You have a habit of coming out on top, no matter what kind of situation you find yourself in. That can be inconvenient for other creatures. And very inconvenient for Black Sun. We're engaged in our own war with the Empire, regardless of whether that fool Palpatine knows who is on his side and who isn't. But I intend to win that war, bounty hunter, no matter what." The Falleen's voice hardened. "The situation has already been complicated by this doomed Rebellion, even though it's to Black Sun's advantage that the Emperor's attention is diverted by it." Xizor slowly shook his head. "But there can only be one winner at this game, however many players are sitting at the board."

"And you thought it would be better for you—and for Black Sun—if there was one less."

"Precisely," said Xizor. "I admire the precision of your analysis. And you can believe this, if nothing else that I tell you. If I had continued to want you dead, now that you've accomplished the job I had for you—the real one, that of smashing the Bounty Hunters Guild—then all your vaunted survival skills would have done you no good at all. Crashing into the web here was a clever move, but it was the only one left to you. How much time do you think it would have bought you if I hadn't changed my mind about the desirability of your death?" The corner of Xizor's mouth curled into a sneer. "The life of some scheming assembler and his assortment of scuttling little subnodes wouldn't have stopped me from turning my laser cannons on this web and blowing it into tattered shreds drifting in space."

"Wuh-what . . ." Xizor's words brought a startled reaction from Kud'ar Mub'at. Even in its crippled condition, it managed to draw itself up higher in the flaccid nest. "You can't . . . mean that . . ." Then the assembler visibly relaxed, even managing a smile of relief. "Of course . . . you're only joking, my dear Xizor . . . if that were true . . . then you would have gone ahead . . . and destroyed my humble . . . abode . . ." The narrow triangular head shook back and forth. "But . . . you didn't . . ."

"I didn't refrain from blowing away this floating garbage pile because of any concern for you." Xizor turned his head to give the assembler a cold merciless gaze. "Your value to me has long been marginal, Kud'ar Mub'at. And now it's zero."

A hissing shriek sounded from the assembler; its forelimbs flailed in rage. "You think so . . . do you, Xizor . . ." Rage was enough to bring the larger compound eyes into focus. "After all . . . I've done for you . . ." Kud'ar Mub'at's head shook back and forth. "And all . . . I continue to do . . . for you and Black Sun . . ." One claw tip trembled as it pointed at Xizor. "You survive . . . only as long . . . as your affairs remain secret . . ." With the same claw, the assembler pointed at itself. "I am the one . . . who keeps those secrets for you . . . I am the one . . . who acts as your go-between . . . everywhere in the galaxy . . ." The narrow face contorted with withering anger. "How will you keep Palpatine in the dark . . . without me . . . to do your dirty work for you . . ."

"Simple enough," replied Xizor evenly. "I have another business associate who will take your place. One who has all your contacts, all your connections; one who knows *your* business better than you do."

"Impossible!" All of Kud'ar Mub'at's spidery limbs thrashed the stale air in the chamber. The accountant subnode called Balancesheet had already scurried onto the nearest wall for safety. "There is . . . . no such creature . . ." The assembler's reedy voice spiraled into a high-pitched, fragmented scream. "Anywhere . . . in the galaxy . . ."

With the blaster pistol still covering the others before him, Boba Fett watched the small drama play out between the Falleen prince and the arachnoid assembler. He already had an idea what the final act was going to be.

One of Prince Xizor's hands reached out, languid and graceful, yet possessed of untrembling power. He held his open palm upward, and the subnode Balancesheet scuttled onto it. The miniature version of its parent turned around in the small space and set its multilensed gaze upon Kud'ar Mub'at.

"You old fool."

The subnode's words were no longer spoken in the tone, both efficient and obsequious, that it had always used before. Now its voice was both deeper and touched with a newly won authority. To Boba Fett's eyes, the subnode even appeared slightly larger than before, as though it were already literally expanding into its new role in life. Perched on Xizor's hand, Balancesheet raised its own forelimbs in a expansive gesture.

"Things will be very different now," said Balancesheet. Its brilliant glittering eyes glanced over at Boba Fett. "For many of us. And yet, in certain ways, things will remain exactly the same. There will be a member of our unique species, an arachnoid assembler, at the center of a vast, invisible web spanning the galaxy." The little subnode's voice rose in volume and pitch. "Arranging delicate matters, pulling strings, putting one creature in contact with another—all those delicate items of business that one of our breed is capable of doing so well. But there can only be *one* web like that, and only one assembler listening to and making those little tugs upon its strands. And that assembler's name will no longer be Kud'ar Mub'at. You've had a long time at the center, time in which you've grown old and fat and stupid. But that time is done now."

At the base of Kud'ar Mub'at's nest, the stormtrooper

Voss'on't looked up at the small creature perched on the Falleen's hand. The grimace on Voss'on't's face spelled both repugnance and incomprehension. It was obvious that he wasn't sure what was going on, but had figured out that it wasn't going to do him any good.

"An excellent demonstration, don't you think?" Prince Xizor smiled cruelly as he held his new business associate up at his own eye level. "That a powerful entity may be housed within an unimposing physical form. It should serve as a reminder to all of us that appearances can be deceiving."

Boba Fett watched as the larger assembler twitched and shook uncontrollably in its nest. The revelation had struck Kud'ar Mub'at dumbfounded. Its lipless mouth hung open, gaping at its own creation, now completely independent—and triumphant.

"Such a thing . . . cannot be . . ." The trembling in Kud'ar Mub'at's limbs grew even more pronounced and erratic, as though it were trying to reassert its will over the mutinous Balancesheet. "I . . . I *made* you!"

"And if you had not been so blind," replied Balancesheet, "and besotted with your own cleverness, you would have been able to detect that I was no longer merely an extention of your own neurosystem." In one of its forelimb claws, Balancesheet held up the thin, pallid strand that had once linked it to the living web around it. The broken end dangled from the former subnode's grip, a few centimeters from the palm that held Balancesheet aloft. "I was free from you even before Boba Fett's ship crashed into the web."

Like a broken thing, Kud'ar Mub'at shrank back down into its nest. "I . . . had . . . no idea . . ." The spidery limbs folded around its abdomen, as though trying to preserve the fading warmth of life. "I trusted you . . . I needed you . . ."

"That was your mistake," said Balancesheet coldly. "And your last one."

Prince Xizor extended his hand toward the chamber's curved wall; Balancesheet scuttled from his palm and onto the densely tangled structural fibers. "I'm afraid," said Xizor, "that the business relationship between us is over now, Kud'ar Mub'at." The edges of Xizor's cape swung forward as he folded his massive arms across his chest. "While Black Sun still has need of a go-between for certain delicate matters where we wish to keep our own participation as secret as possible, what we *don't* need is an associate who has grown either too complacent or too senile to notice this small rebellion taking place under its own nose. You've already lost a war, Kud'ar Mub'at, that you didn't even know was being fought. Black Sun can't afford to be sentimental about what you've done for us in the past; we have to go with the winner."

Kud'ar Mub'at's voice wavered with fear. "What . . . what are you going . . . to do?"

"You'll find out soon enough."

"Nobody's finding out anything," said Boba Fett. He had listened to the exchange between the Falleen prince and the arachnoid assembler with mounting impatience. The blaster pistol rose in his hand once more, reasserting its hold on the others' attention. "That is," he continued, "until *my* business is taken care of."

"Of course." Xizor gave a nod of acknowledgment. "But you see, bounty hunter—this *is* your business. My new associate Balancesheet was the one who convinced me that you should be allowed to go on living. And that was after I had already decided that you should be killed." An indulgent though still cruel smile showed on Xizor's face. "You're a fortunate creature. Many in Black Sun will testify that it's a rare occasion when I change my mind."

"Then why did you?"

From its perch on the chamber wall, Balancesheet answered. "My analysis was that you're worth more to me alive than dead, Boba Fett. With the old Bounty Hunters Guild now dismantled, there's no one in your chosen profession with your resources and skills. Black Sun—as well as the other clients whose accounts I've inherited—

will still have need of an effective bounty hunter such as yourself. The consideration that had prompted Prince Xizor's previous decision to kill you was based upon seeing the need to reduce the number of creatures who were aware—or who might *become* aware—that he and Black Sun had been behind the anti-Guild operation from the beginning." The former subnode spoke as matter-of-factly as if it had been adding up a long column of numbers in its head. "But as I pointed out to Xizor—we were having our discussion via comm unit the whole time you were talking here—getting rid of Kud'ar Mub'at accomplishes the same thing, and more. Not only do we eliminate the weakest link in the chain—after all, an assembler buys and sells information all the time—but we also leave a more valuable business associate alive. One that would owe us a favor as well."

Boba Fett shook his head. "If you're expecting gratitude, then I'm in short supply. And you're the ones who owe me, remember? For him." He pointed with the blaster toward Voss'on't. "Nobody leaves here, dead or alive, until the bounty gets paid out."

"That's right!" Kud'ar Mub'at unfolded his forelimbs, stretching their sticklike lengths out toward Fett. "Don't . . . trust them," the assembler cried in agitation. "They're . . . they're trying to cheat you." A pleading tone filtered into the high-pitched voice. "I'm . . . the only one . . . who's on your side . . ."

"Shut up." Boba Fett knocked the assembler's claws away with a swipe of the blaster pistol. "If there's anybody on my side, I haven't found them yet." He turned his visor-shielded gaze, and the blaster, toward Prince Xizor. "So how about it?"

"The bounty? Very well." Xizor gave a slight nod, then turned and gestured with one hand toward Balance-sheet. "Transfer the funds being held in escrow on Coruscant to the main operating and receipt account of the bounty hunter Boba Fett." He glanced back at Boba Fett and smiled. "You didn't really think all those credits were being kept here, did you?"

"Doesn't matter where they were." Boba Fett kept the blaster pistol raised. "As long as they wind up in the right place."

"The credits are already there," said Balancesheet. "I signaled for the transfer to be made *before* I had my own discussion with Prince Xizor." This time a trace of self-satisfaction sounded in the former subnode's voice. Its small compound eyes looked toward the Falleen. "I was confident that we would wind up in agreement on this matter."

Xizor's eyes narrowed to slits. His courtly manner of just a few seconds before seemed to have evaporated. "Assumptions such as that might cause difficulties between us in the future."

"Perhaps." The tiny creature didn't appear intimidated. "We'll deal with that when the time comes."

Through his own comlink mounted inside his helmet, Boba Fett accessed the remote communications functions aboard *Slave I*. It took only a few seconds to verify the sum that had been in the now-empty escrow account, and that a transfer had gone through into his own account. The bounty for Trhin Voss'on't was his now.

"Fine," said Boba Fett. The blaster pistol stayed raised in his hand. "You two can sort out your business affairs any way you want. They don't concern me. The only other item on my agenda is making sure that I get out of here alive. All those credits don't mean much if I'm too dead to spend them."

"I'll guarantee you safe passage." Prince Xizor pointed down the web's central corridor, back toward *Slave I* mired in the fibrous structure. "You've got your bounty now. I'd suggest you return to your ship. You've delivered your hard merchandise, and we don't have anything more to discuss. And frankly"— Xizor glanced around the chamber with distaste—"I've spent enough time here already."

"That's one thing we agree on, then." Boba Fett regarded the Falleen over the barrel of the blaster pistol. "But for the rest—I have my doubts. How much do you think I trust you, Xizor? You could be lying to me now, the same way Kud'ar Mub'at was when I got involved in this whole business." Fett slowly shook his head. "You know that my ship is barely capable of traveling; I can nurse it along to the nearest planet with an operating repair yard if I take it slow. But I'm not going to sit out there and be a sitting duck for you to fire off your laser cannons at again."

"You should weigh your words a little more carefully, bounty hunter." The cruel smile had long vanished from Xizor's harshly chiseled features. His violet-tinged eyes narrowed into slits that might have been cut with the point of a vibroblade. One hand shot out and grabbed the barrel of the blaster pistol being held on him. His fist squeezed tighter on the weapon, but made no move to push it away; it remained aimed directly at his chest. "I gave you the word of a Falleen noble; that should be enough to remove any doubts concerning your fate. If not, think on what my associate Balancesheet has told you: we have determined that you are worth more to us as a living bounty hunter than a dead one. Don't tempt me to change my mind once more on that point."

"There's something I haven't decided, though." The blaster remained locked between Boba Fett and Xizor, with the bounty hunter's finger tight against the trigger. "I don't know," continued Fett, "if you're worth more to me alive or dead."

"Don't be a fool," said Xizor coldly. "I've humored you long enough, allowing you to keep this thing pointed at me. If it pleased you to talk business while waving a blaster around, then so be it. But if you're planning on firing it, you'd better try doing it soon. I've just about run out of patience."

"So have I."

"Believe me, bounty hunter—you'll run out of luck just as quickly. You kill me, and what do you think would happen next? Even if my guards didn't find out within minutes, where do you think you'd run to in your crippled ship? I can assure you, Black Sun would not take well to the loss of its leader—and the life of that assassin would be a very brief proposition." Xizor's hard gaze drilled through the visor of the Mandalorian battle-armor helmet and into Boba Fett's own. "It's not a matter of sentiment, bounty hunter; just business, pure and simple." He took his hand away from the barrel of the blaster pistol. "Now you have to decide."

Boba Fett weighed the other creature's words. A few seconds of silence ticked away, then Fett nodded. "I appear to have no choice," he said. "Except to trust your word." He lowered the blaster and slipped it back into its holster. "Whether I want to or not."

"That's smart enough." The chill half smile reappeared on Xizor's face. "You don't have to figure out everything in this galaxy; just enough to survive will do." He turned his gaze around to the former subnode Balancesheet, still perched on the chamber's wall near him. "Send for my guards," he ordered. "And have them bring the others—the cleanup crew—with them. It's time to bring this show to an end."

The renegade stormtrooper had silently watched the tense exchange between the bounty hunter and the Falleen noble. Now, as Boba Fett turned away, Voss'on't called after him, "Take care of yourself." The words were filled with mocking venom. "I want you all in one piece, Boba Fett. For the next time we meet up."

Boba Fett glanced over his shoulder at the other man. "I don't think there's going to be a next time. It doesn't matter who wanted you returned to them, or who put up the bounty for you." He slowly shook his head. "It doesn't even matter if you were part of the scheme to break up the old Bounty Hunters Guild." Boba Fett turned and walked back toward Voss'on't, then grabbed the rags of his jacket front and pulled him partway up from the chamber's matted floor. "Did you really think I hadn't figured that part out?" A rare tinge of anger sounded in Boba Fett's carefully emotionless voice. "The bounty for your return was far too much for a stormtrooper's life, no matter what he might have stolen. Emperor Palpatine doesn't buy his vengeance at that high a price. There's always something else he wants, some other grand scheme involved. But I'm happy to take the credits, no matter the ultimate reason they were paid out."

"All right—" Voss'on't's expression had gone from a sneer to burning anger as he had listened to Boba Fett. "So you're further ahead of the game than I thought. You must feel clever, huh?"

"Clever enough," said Fett. "Now let's see how clever you are." He let go of Voss'on't, dropping him back to the chamber floor. "Didn't you hear what Balancesheet and Prince Xizor said just now? They don't want any more creatures around than necessary who know the truth behind this scheme to break up the Bounty Hunters Guild. They've already decided to get rid of Kud'ar Mub'at. What makes you so confident that they'll want to leave you still alive?"

Voss'on't was taken aback by Boba Fett's words; it took him a moment to sputter out his reply. "You're . . . you're wrong! You don't know anything about that! Everything I did . . . I did it in the service of the Emperor!" Voss'on't's eyes went wide, the tone of his voice growing more desperate. "The Emperor wouldn't let anything happen to me now . . . not after all the risks I went through . . ." He snapped his beseeching gaze toward Xizor. "It wouldn't be right . . . it wouldn't be *fair* . . ."

"You're going to discover," said Boba Fett quietly, "that Palpatine is the one who decides what's fair and what's not." He turned away and strode toward the chamber's exit.

"Wait! Don't . . ."

Another voice, a higher-pitched shriek, sounded after Boba Fett. At the mouth of the web's corridor, he found himself suddenly encumbered by the sticklike limbs of the arachnoid assembler Kud'ar Mub'at. It had managed to scramble off its flaccid nest and lunge after him. Boba Fett looked down and saw the assembler's triangular face below, the compound eyes peering futilely for some sign of sympathy behind the helmet's dark visor.

"Take me with you," pleaded Kud'ar Mub'at. "You'll see . . . I can still be of some . . . use to you . . ."

Boba Fett peeled the creature's limbs away from himself. "I don't think so," he said. "Business partners always wind up getting in my way. Then I have to do something about them." He shoved the assembler back toward the center of the main chamber. "You're just as well off with your other business associates."

Before he turned and walked away, Fett caught a glimpse of Prince Xizor's guards; they had returned and had pulled Trhin Voss'on't up between them. The look of panic on the stormtrooper's face was the last he saw before he continued heading back to *Slave I*.

The web started to die before he even reached the ship.

A shudder ran through the walls around Boba Fett, as though the heavy structural fibers had suddenly contracted in upon themselves. The smaller, entangled fibers that formed the shell of the web scraped across each other, like rough woven fabric being pulled apart by invisible giant hands. A sudden wind came close to knocking Boba Fett off balance as the atmospheric pressure inside the web fell. The rush of oxygen to the surrounding vacuum tore the tattered rents in the web open wider; Boba Fett felt the chill of space seep through his Mandalorian battle armor as he clamped his teeth on the helmet's breathing tube, drawing in its last store of oxygen. As the tangled floor buckled beneath his feet, he fought his way toward *Slave I*.

He knew that in the distance behind him, the assembler Kud'ar Mub'at was facing the Black Sun cleanup crew. An operation such as that would be as thorough, and final, as Prince Xizor's commands would dictate. When they were done, there would no longer be a Kud'ar Mub'at, or the web that had once formed the assembler's private little world.

The web's death throes intensified as the interwoven neural fibers reacted to their creator's agony. On all sides of the central corridor and above Boba Fett's head, the tethered subnodes thrashed and convulsed, stirred from their torpor by the inputs of pain overloading their own systems. A thicket of spidery limbs rose up in front of Boba Fett, like animated twigs and the heavier, thicker branches of a leafless forest caught in a winter planet's flesh-stripping tornado. Sets of compound eyes gazed upon him with uncomprehending fear as the subnodes' claw tips fastened upon his battle armor, the larger ones seizing his arms and legs like chitinous hunting traps.

One of the immense docking subnodes, its bulk extending twice the length of Boba Fett's own height, reared up beneath him, toppling him onto one shoulder. A swarm of hand-sized subnodes scurried in panic across the visor of his helmet; they clung to his fist as he unholstered his blaster pistol and fired at the docking subnode crashing down toward him. The subnode's shell burst apart, the blaster-charred fragments swirling like black snow in the vortices of the web's atmosphere rushing through the disintegrating structure. On his back, Boba Fett kept his outstretched fists locked together on the blaster; the continuous volley of white-hot bolts scorched through the docking subnode's revealed soft tissues, dividing them into smoldering gobbets falling on either side of him.

In the thinned remainder of the web's air, the docking subnode's hollowed exoskeleton collapsed silently, the translucent broken pieces thrust aside by Boba Fett's forearm. He got to his feet, kicking aside the feeble claws of the smaller subnodes, just as a pulsing red dot at the side of his vision signaled the exhaustion of the helmet's store of compressed oxygen. With lungs already beginning to ache, he sprinted for *Slave I*'s entry hatchway.

Boba Fett collapsed in the pilot's chair as the ship's cockpit sealed tight around him. The dizzying constellation of dark spots, the forerunner of unconsciousness that had swelled in his vision as he'd climbed the ladder up from the main cargo hold, now faded as he breathed in the flow of air from the ship's minimized life-support systems. A moment later he leaned forward in the chair, eyes raised to the viewport as his right hand reached for the controls of the few navigational rockets still functioning on the ship.

It wasn't necessary to fire the rockets to get away from the web. As Boba Fett watched, the last of the heavy structural fibers broke free from one another, the interwoven fabric unraveling into loose strands. Where Kud'ar Mub'at's abode and place of business had blotted out the stars behind, the light-specked black of empty space now stood.

In the distance, Prince Xizor's flagship awaited the approach of the transfer shuttle bearing the Falleen noble, his guards and the Black Sun cleanup crew, and whatever might be left of the Imperial stormtrooper Trhin Voss'on't. It was of no concern to Fett whether the hard merchandise he had worked so hard to deliver in living condition might still be breathing; once payment had been made, his interest ceased.

A swarm of dead subnodes, the creations and servants of the arachnoid assembler, bumped against the convex transparisteel of the cockpit's viewport. The crablike ones were ensnared in the same pale strands of disconnected neural tissue that tangled around the empty claws of the larger varieties. Atmospheric decompression had burst open the shells of some of them, spreading apart their contents like grey constellations of soft matter; others were still intact enough to appear as if they were merely asleep, awaiting some synapse-borne message from their parent and master.

Boba Fett applied a burst of rotational force to *Slave I*. The hull-mounted navigational jet rolled the ship on its central axis, letting the loose, ragged net of subnodes slip past. A visual field clear of everything but cold stars showed in the viewport.

At the edge of the viewport a brighter light glared, as though one of the stars had gone nova. Fett could see that it was Prince Xizor's flagship, maneuvering out of the sector and preparing for a jump into hyperspace. Whatever business the Falleen noble was about, it was likely far from this desolate area of the galaxy; it might very well be back at the Emperor's court on Coruscant. *I imagine*, thought Boba Fett, *that I'll encounter him again, before too long.* The course of events in the Empire was accelerating ever faster, spurred by both Palpatine's ambitions and the Rebellion's mounting challenge. Xizor would have to move fast if he was to have any chance of bringing Black Sun to victory on that rapidly shifting gameboard.

It didn't matter to Boba Fett who won. His business would stay the same.

Before he looked down to the control panel's gauges to assess what kind of condition *Slave I* was in, another pallid strand traced its way across the curved exterior of the viewport. The rope of silent neural fiber was linked only to the arachnoid assembler Kud'ar Mub'at, or what remained of it after the work of Xizor's cleanup crew. The once-glittering compound eyes were empty and grey now, like small round windows to the hollows of the corpse that drifted slowly past. Around the assembler's globular abdomen, split open like a leathery egg, the spidery legs were drawn up tight, forming the last self-contained nest for the once-proud, now-vanquished creature.

Careful ...

Boba Fett indulged himself for a moment, imagining a warning from the dead. The expressionless face turned slowly past the viewport.

Beware of everyone. If Kud'ar Mub'at's empty husk could speak, that was what it would have said. *In this universe, there are no friends . . . only enemies.* The assembler's gaping mouth was a small black vacuum, surrounded by the greater one of interstellar space. *No trust . . . only betrayal* ...

He didn't require advice such as that, even from one whose withered corpse testified to the truth of the silent words. Boba Fett knew all those things already. That was why he was alive, and the assembler was dead.

All his remaining concerns—for the moment—were technical ones. Boba Fett turned toward the cockpit's navicomputer. He began accessing and inputting *Slave I*'s astrogational coordinates, at the same time scrolling through the onboard computer's database of the surrounding systems and planets. What he needed now was an advanced-technology shipyard, one without too many entanglements with either the Empire or the Rebel Alliance, or scruples about working for payments made under the table, as it were. Some of the weapons and tracking modules aboard *Slave I* were technically restricted; a good deal of his profits from past jobs had gone into the bribery or commissioned theft necessary for getting top-secret beta-development tech out of the Imperial Navy's hidden research-and-development labs. Only a shipyard remote from the galaxy's center, and away from the prying scrutiny of Palpatine's spy agents, would have enough nerve—and greed—to do the kind of work that ordinarily had the death penalty attached to it.

A list of possibilities appeared on the computer's readout screen. He was already familiar with most of the shipyards; his line of work was hard on his tools, from personal weapons to navigable craft. *Not those*, Fett decided, eliminating with a few strokes of his fingertip all of the planet-based yards. In its present fragile condition, *Slave I* wouldn't survive a hard-gravity landing.

The remoter possibilities, those on the other side of the galaxy, were similarly eliminated. Even if Boba Fett tried to make it that far—and if a hyperspace jump didn't wind up disintegrating *Slave I*—the longer he took to reach his destination, the greater the chances of attracting the attention of any number of his enemies. They'd be able to pick him off without much of a struggle. He had already decided that speed of service was as important a consideration as the quality. *I need to get up and running*, thought Boba Fett as he studied the remaining short list on the computer's readout screen. *And fast*.

Before he could finish his calculations, a voice came over the comm unit.

"It was a pleasure doing business with you." The voice of the distant Balancesheet was not quite as obsequiously formal as its parent Kud'ar Mub'at's had been. "We'll do it again."

The control panel's proximity monitors registered the presence of another ship in the sector; from the ID profile, Boba Fett could see that it wasn't Prince Xizor's *Vendetta*. He scanned the viewport and spotted it, near the drifting wreckage of Kud'ar Mub'at's web. Hitting the viewport's long-range mag function brought up a clear image of a standard bulk freighter. Its registration was clear, but showed former ownership by one of Xizor's—and Black Sun's—holding companies.

Boba Fett thumbed his own comm unit's transmit button. "I thought you were going independent, Balancesheet."

"I am," replied the voice from the comm unit speaker. "This freighter, however humble, is mine alone. But then, my needs are not elaborate. And Prince Xizor did give me a good deal on it—virtually free."

"Nothing's free with him. You'll pay for it, eventually."

"I suspect you're correct in that." Balancesheet did not sound overly concerned. "But in the meantime, it gives me a base of operations that is many degrees more suitable than Kud'ar Mub'at's shabby old web. A ship such as this already has the required operational systems built in; I won't have to create and extrude as many subnodes as my parent did in order to make it serve my needs. Thus the chances of a mutiny, such as the one by which I came to power, are greatly lessened."

"Smart." Boba Fett made a mental note that dealings with this new go-between assembler were likely to be more dangerous than they had been with its predecessor.

"It is, however, little more than a large empty space, with a set of thruster engines attached to an autonomic navigational system. I suspect that it was used for some of Black Sun's simpler smuggling operations, out in the edge systems, and it's become too outmoded and slow for the organization's current needs." The voice of the small assembler creature, alone in the vacated freighter, seemed to echo off the bulkheads around it. "I'll have to spend a considerable amount to equip it the way I wish."

"Save up your credits, then." Boba Fett looked back down to the list of shipyard possibilities on the computer readout. "That kind of work doesn't come cheap."

"Oh, I've got the credits already." Balancesheet's voice turned subtly smug. "More than enough."

Something about the way the assembler's words had been spoken piqued Boba Fett's interest. "What are you talking about?"

"You might want to check the status of your transfer accounts on Coruscant." The smile in Balancesheet's voice was almost audible. "You forget that I do a lot more financial business than you do; that's what I was created to do. And I inherited, so to speak, all of my creator's old friends and associates—especially the ones willing to be bribed in exchange for certain small favors."

" 'Favors' . . . what kind of favors?"

"Merely the kind that involves splitting a transfer of credits from an escrow account, and very quietly diverting one half into my receipt account rather than yours." Balancesheet's voice turned pitying. "You really should have checked your own accounts after seeing that the transfer had been made; if you had, you would have seen that you wound up with half the bounty that had been posted for Voss'on't."

Boba Fett pushed himself back from the control panel. His gaze locked upon the empty freighter visible in the distance. "That was a mistake," he said grimly. Without even checking further, he knew that what the assembler had said was true. It wasn't the kind of thing a sentient creature would joke about; not with him. "A big mistake, on your part."

"I don't think so." No apprehension sounded in the voice coming from the speaker. "The way I see it, you owed me at least that much. If it hadn't been for me, Prince Xizor would have gone ahead and eliminated you. Permanently. You might not care to show any gratitude for that—I don't expect it, either. So let's just call this another little business deal."

"Let's call it theft." Boba Fett rasped out the words. "I'm the wrong creature to steal from."

"Perhaps so," replied Balancesheet. "But it's in your interest for my go-between business to be up and running. There's a lot of potential clients out in the galaxy, who will only deal with someone like you at an arm's-length basis. You *need* me, Boba Fett. So you can go on hunting down more hard merchandise and collecting the bounties for it. Without a go-between to hold the credits, a lot of this business breaks down; it doesn't work anymore."

The analysis didn't sway Boba Fett. "I can take care of my own business."

"Good for you. But I'm still keeping half the Voss'on't bounty. I've got expenses as well."

"You don't have to worry about meeting them. You won't live that long. Nobody does who steals from me."

"Get serious, Fett." The assembler's mocking words slid out of the comm unit speaker; Balancesheet had given up any semblance of maintaining the formalities and sly fawning in which Kud'ar Mub'at had indulged. "What are you going to do about it? The condition your ship is in, you're not able to blow away a midge-fly. Not without blowing yourself up. And as slow as this freighter might be, it's still faster than you at the moment."

"I'll catch up with you," promised Boba Fett. "Sooner or later."

"And when you do, you'll have either figured out how much you do need me, or I'll be under the protection of Prince Xizor—Black Sun also needs a go-between. Or I'll have some other surprise waiting for you. It doesn't matter; I'm not exactly worried."

"Get worried." The thought of the stolen credits burned deep within Boba Fett's breast. "Get real worried."

"Until the next time," said Balancesheet. "I'll be waiting, bounty hunter."

The comm unit connection with the freighter broke

off, and silence filled *Slave I*'s cockpit once more. Boba Fett watched as the other ship's thruster engines flared into life, then dwindled into fading, starlike points.

For a moment longer, he gazed out at empty space, his own thoughts as dark and brooding. Then he turned again to the calculations of the slow journey ahead of him . . .

7

The story ended.

Or at least for now, thought Neelah. She had been sitting for a long time with her back against the cold durasteel bulkhead of the *Hound's Tooth*'s cargo hold. Sitting and listening as the other bounty hunter Dengar had finished his account of Boba Fett's past, and all that had come out of the scheme to destroy the old Bounty Hunters Guild.

"That's it, huh?" She was glad she hadn't had to keep a blaster aimed at Dengar to motivate him to keep talking. Her arm would have gotten tired by now. It had been a long story, though filled with enough action and violence to keep her from getting bored. With one hand she rubbed at the small of her back, then unfolded her legs and stood up. "I take it that Boba Fett got everything sorted out after that."

"Good guess," said Dengar. He rapped his knuckles on the bulkhead behind himself. "Since you've been on *Slave I*, before we transferred over to this ship, you know it's in fully functional shape now. There were some incidents I heard about, though, that happened in the process of getting repaired. *And* redesigned, from the bulkheads to the engine core." Dengar pointed with his thumb to the cage. "Apparently, Fett decided that he needed bigger quarters for the amount of hard merchandise he was going to be ferrying around—so things had to be shifted around to make room for it. Otherwise, the ladder wouldn't be necessary to get to the cockpit. The whole refitting process took more than just credits, from all reports. And a few other creatures wound up getting killed. But that's not unusual with the way Boba Fett works."

"I'll say." After hearing the story of the war among the bounty hunters, Neelah found it a wonder that anybody who had ever come in contact with Boba Fett was still alive. *Creatures he doesn't like,* she thought wryly, *have a habit of winding up dead.* If Bossk, the Trandoshan bounty hunter that Fett had stolen this ship from, was still alive somewhere, it was a triumph of the same dumb luck that had gotten him out of his previous scrapes with his rival. "Too bad for those creatures, I suppose."

And what about me? She had been warned by Dengar that the story wasn't going to answer all of her questions. It didn't matter how much she had found out about Boba Fett—as if she had needed more confirmation about how cold and ruthless he could be—she still hadn't found out anything more about herself. *I still don't know who I am,* thought Neelah glumly. *Who I really am.* All the mysteries, all the questions that repeated over and over inside her skull, were still infuriatingly present. They had been in there since she had found herself in Jabba the Hutt's palace, back on that remote world of Tatooine. Since then, little scraps of the past had slipped into her memory-scrubbed brain, tantalizing pieces of the world from which someone, some dark entity, had abducted her. The only constant, the only link between that past world and this harsh, threatening one in which she was forced to feel her way like a blind creature in a vibroblade-edged corridor, was Boba Fett—of that, Neelah was certain. She could feel it in the tightening of her sinews, the white-knuckled clenching of her fists, that overtook her every time she found the reflection of her face caught in the dark visor of Boba Fett's helmet. Even in Jabba's palace, when she had seen his ominous form across the Hutt's crowded, noisy throne room, Neelah had been certain of the connection between herself and the bounty hunter. *He knows,* she thought bitterly. *Whatever my true name is—he knows it.* Her name, her past, all that she had lost. But as of yet, she had found no way of forcing him to reveal those secrets to her.

She was beginning to wonder why she had bothered to save his life.

Turning her head, Neelah looked around at the confines of the ship's cargo hold. This part of the ship that had formerly belonged to the Trandoshan Bossk was not much different from Boba Fett's own *Slave I.* Form and function, stripped bare metal, cages for hauling around a bounty hunter's unwilling merchandise. It smelled different, though; the acrid, reptilian stench curled in her nostrils with each breath, reminding her unpleasantly of the blood-scented musk that had permeated the stone walls of the fortresslike palace where she had served as a dancing girl. *And where I would've wound up,* she knew, *as rancor bait.* The same mix of odors from dozens of the galaxy's species, their bodies' exudations and hormonal secretions, that had hung in the palace's close, stifling air, seemed to have penetrated the very metal of Bossk's ship. *Slave I* had been cleaner and closer to sterile, befitting the cold, precise logic of its owner. A clinical surgery, in its own way, with Boba Fett the doctor that took creatures' spirits apart, the better to convert them into the hard merchandise in which he traded. An involuntary shiver traced Neelah's spine as she saw in her mind's eye the scalpel that lay in Boba Fett's hidden gaze.

"Sorry it didn't do the trick for you." Dengar's voice broke into her thoughts. "But if you didn't know it before, at least you do now. He's not anybody to fool around with. Not unless you don't care whether you live or die."

"I don't have that choice," replied Neelah. "Believe me, if I could have avoided meeting Boba Fett, I would have." She had the notion, unsubstantiated yet by any hard facts from memory, that the life she had led before had been one where bounty hunters, and all the sticky, spirit-corroding evil they brought with them, were on the scarce side. "I could have done without the pleasure of his acquaintance."

"Suit yourself." Dengar had made up a little pallet for himself near the bulkhead where he had sat while recounting the story about Boba Fett's past. "Now for me, it's a real honor, hooking up with him and all. Being as I'm in the bounty hunter business myself. Not at the same level as him, though." Hands clasped behind his head, Dengar lay down on the thin nest of rags and packing foam. "So for him to ask me to come along as his partner . . ."

Dengar didn't have to explain anything more than that. *Good for you,* thought Neelah. Back on Tatooine, in their hiding place below the parched surface of the Dune Sea, Dengar had told her about his hopes of actually quitting the dangerous bounty hunter trade and settling down with his beloved Manaroo. The couple had been betrothed for some time, but had put off their marriage until Dengar had found some way of getting out from under the enormous weight of debt he carried. Financially, it had all been downhill for him since he'd quit—at Manaroo's gentle prodding—his previous speciality as a Grade One Imperial Assassin. He was a different person now, and a better one—working for the Empire ate away at one's spirit, sometimes fatally so, and he had Manaroo to thank for saving him from that fate. But it still left the mountain of debt that had accumulated so swiftly upon his back. Creatures who owed credits in this galaxy, and who didn't pay up, also had a good chance of winding up dead; even with Jabba the Hutt dead, there were plenty of other hard lenders who operated that way. A partnership with the notorious Boba Fett was the best, and maybe only, opportunity

Dengar had for clearing his accounts. *If,* Neelah figured, *he doesn't get killed along the way.*

She looked down again at the bounty hunter on the makeshift pallet. Dengar was already asleep, or doing a good imitation of it. Telling stories—even true ones—was obviously not in his usual repertoire of skills. Any kind of action, no matter how strenuous or life-endangering, was more suited to him than stringing words together.

A feeling of acute distaste rose inside Neelah as she raised her eyes again to the dull metal bulkheads of the ship's cargo hold. She had only been able to stand being here as long as the unreeling story had diverted her attention. Now, the close, stench-filled air formed a choking fist inside her throat, as though she could literally taste the despair and anger of that other hard merchandise, the ones who had fallen into the hands of Bossk. They might not have been as profitable as those that Boba Fett tracked down and secured, but their lives had been worth just as much to themselves, if no one else.

I've got to get out of here, thought Neelah desperately. She didn't know if her own words meant the cargo hold, this ship that its previous owner had named *Hound's Tooth,* or the dark mystery that her life had become. It didn't matter; there was only one exit before her, the metal ladder at the side of the hold that led to the ship's cockpit area. *Go on,* Neelah told herself, hesitating as she set a hand on an eye-level tread. *You've faced him before.* A wry smile twisted the corner of her mouth. *And you're not dead yet.* She had even pulled and held a blaster pistol on Boba Fett, right there in the *Hound's* cockpit—how many other creatures in the galaxy could say they had done something like that and survived to talk about it? Neelah put her boot on the lowest rung and started climbing.

Boba Fett was at the cockpit's panel, making precise adjustments to the large, troughlike controls designed for a Trandoshan's outsize claws. In the hatchway behind, Neelah stood watching him, the back of his scarred and dented helmet as enigmatic as the dark, T-shaped visor that hid his eyes. *I've seen those as well,* she reminded herself. *And lived.* Another accomplishment that undoubtedly put her in a tiny fraction of the galaxy's inhabitants, on all the worlds and in every system. The helmet had been the one part of the battle gear that hadn't been reduced to wet rags by the acidic digestive juices of the Sarlacc creature in the Great Pit of Carkoon, into which Boba Fett had fallen when Han Solo had been rescued by his friends Luke Skywalker and Princess Leia. But Neelah and Dengar had still had to remove the helmet from the unconscious Fett to feed and rehydrate him until he could fend for himself once more. Even in that condition, hovering between life and death, Boba Fett had still seemed an intimidating figure. Anyone with a degree less furious energy and survival instinct as part of his spirit would have been consumed by the blind, gaping-mawed creature that had swallowed him, rather than finding the means to literally explode his way out to the open air. It wasn't just Boba Fett's short way with other creatures' lives that made him such a legend; it was also the tenacity with which he clung to his own.

The bounty hunter was either ignoring her as he went about his tasks on the *Hound's* control panel, or he hadn't been aware of her coming up the cargo-hold ladder to the cockpit's hatchway; he continued the work of his gloved hands without remarking on her presence. *He knows I'm here,* thought Neelah. *There's not much he doesn't know . . .*

She raised her eyes to the viewport in front of the control panel just as Boba Fett dropped the *Hound's Tooth* out of hyperspace. A vista of stars, different from those left on the other side of the galaxy, filled the viewport. Neelah looked across the bright, cold field, hoping that the uncaring regard of the distant stars would provide her some relief from the cramped, claustrophobic quarters inside the ship. She looked, and she saw—

The past.

Not her own, but Boba Fett's. *It's just like the story,* a part of Neelah marveled, almost childlike in its reaction. *The story Dengar told.*

Floating in the vacuum outside the *Hound's Tooth* were the tattered fragments of Kud'ar Mub'at's web. It had not been from any particular skill on Dengar's part that she had been able to so vividly imagine the image of the arachnoid assembler and its web, both before and after Prince Xizor's cleanup crew had torn it apart. There had been another tantalizing fragment of memory inside her own head, something that had somehow evaded the attempt to wipe it out of existence. Somehow, from out of her past and the world that had been stolen from her, Dengar's account of Boba Fett's history had triggered that remembrance; she had known exactly what Kud'ar Mub'at and his flock of created subnodes had looked like. *I knew it,* thought Neelah. And now they were here, gently drifting, surrounded by strands of pallid neural tissue like elongated ghosts, bumping soundlessly against the transparisteel of the cockpit's forward viewport.

The dead subnodes looked both eerie and pathetic, their broken exoskeletons surrounded by thin, twiglike limbs, claws curled up under the split abdomens. Smaller ones, seemingly no bigger than a child's fist, were entangled with the giants that had been capable of tethering a ship to the now-vanished web's docking area. All of them were hollow-eyed, with the unseeing gaze that blind, dead things turned toward those fortunate creatures still alive. *Or unfortunate,* thought Neelah. Maybe the poor dead subnodes, pieces of their defeated master and creator, were really the lucky ones; they no longer had to wonder about what would happen to them next. For them, all the galaxy's cruel uncertainties were over.

For a moment, the sight of the space-drifting subnodes evoked the disturbing sensation in Neelah that she had fallen backward in time, pulling this ship and its contents along, as though her empty memory were a true black hole, with its own irresistible gravity. But some-

how the process had wound up landing them in Boba
Fett's past, the moment just after the crude dissection and
death of his former business associate Kud'ar Mub'at.
But that was so long ago, thought Neelah; it made her
feel dizzy to even contemplate it. She closed her eyes,
wondering if when she opened them again, time would
begin unreeling on its proper course once more.

Her eyelids flicked open without her willing them to.
I was wrong. She saw that now. The momentary dis-
placement in time had passed. Neelah stepped forward
and laid a hand on the back of the pilot's, steadying herself as she gazed out the viewport. "They've been dead a
long time," she said softly. "A very long time."

"Of course." Boba Fett had raised his own gaze from
the instrument gauges; now he looked out on the same
dark vista as Neelah did. "The last time I was in this sector, these entities had just been killed—along with their
creator, Kud'ar Mub'at." He turned and looked over his
shoulder at Neelah. "But you know all about that, don't
you?"

A sudden realization hit her. "You were listening in,
weren't you? Over the ship's internal communications
system. All the while that Dengar was telling me about
what happened to you in the past."

Boba Fett gave a single dismissive shake of his head.
"I hardly needed to," he replied. "Since Dengar was acting on the exact instructions I had previously given
him."

"What?" Neelah looked back at Fett in amazement.
"*You* told him—"

"It's convenient for me to have you brought up to
speed on a few matters of common interest. Having Dengar take care of it saves me the trouble—*and* it kept the
two of you occupied while I was tracing this sector's exact location and navigating us here. That took time, as
we arrived here via a route that would throw off anyone
else who might have been spying upon my activities.
Time, which you managed to pass in your own way."
Boba Fett's voice sounded almost tinged by a partial

smile. "I'll have to congratulate my colleague Dengar on his acting abilities—he kept his act going, even when you pulled that blaster pistol on him."

Her surprise faded quickly. *He's been ahead of me before,* thought Neelah. *He probably will be again.* "So this is the location, huh?" She peered again toward the dark vista afforded by the viewport. "Where Prince Xizor tried to eliminate you, then changed his mind and took out that arachnoid assembler instead."

"Precisely." Boba Fett pointed toward the viewport. "As you can see, everything Dengar told you about the incident was the truth. Xizor's cleanup crew didn't leave much of Kud'ar Mub'at's web. Black Sun operatives are known for their thoroughness."

More of the dead subnodes, like the shed carapaces of ordinary crawling spiders, drifted past the *Hound's Tooth.* Neelah felt the skin of her forearms prickle into gooseflesh as she heard—or imagined that she did—the light scraping and tapping of empty chitin against the ship's hull. The sensation was more dreamlike than anything to do with actual memory.

"Why did you bring us here?" The spirit-chilling uncanniness of the sight out of the viewport, the dead creatures tethered together by the strands of neural tissue, as much a part of one another now as they had been in their living existence, touched a thread of anger inside Neelah. "Just to reminisce?"

"There's very little I do," replied Boba Fett calmly, "that is without purpose. I came here for a reason. And you were brought here for the same reason."

"How would I know that?" Neelah folded her arms across her breast. "You haven't seen fit to tell us anything about where we were headed, or why." She glared at the figure in front of her. "Or is this something else that you let Dengar in on, but not me?"

"Neither you nor Dengar were aware of our destination, and there was a good reason for that as well. If you don't know something, you can't be compelled to reveal it. That's why I've made it a practice not to tell anyone,

even my own associates, if I can avoid it." Boba Fett
pointed a gloved fingertip toward Neelah. "I don't keep
my silence for your sake, but it's to your advantage,
nevertheless. A good many of the ways to get someone
such as yourself to talk are not pleasant. And some of
them don't leave you alive afterward, either."

"Thanks for your concern," Neelah said sourly. "I appreciate it."

"Your sarcasm is pointless. When I decide to start
caring about anyone else's opinions of my operating
methods, I'll let you know." Boba Fett leaned back in the
pilot's chair. "But you wanted to find out; you merely
had to wait, and the time has come."

Like flicking a switch, the bounty hunter's words transformed the anger inside Neelah to sudden, unreasoning
panic. "I . . . I don't know . . ."

"You don't know if you're ready for that." Boba Fett's
visor-shielded gaze seemed to penetrate to the depths of
her spirit. "You've come all this way; you've waited so
long and so impatiently; you've fought to find out all
that's been hidden from you. And now you're afraid."

"No—" She quickly shook her head. "No, I'm not."

"We shall see about that," replied Boba Fett, even more
quietly—and more ominously—than before. "Because you
don't have a choice. You never did."

He's right. Neelah squeezed her eyelids shut once
again; at her sides, her hands closed into fists, the sinews
of her forearms straining with tension. From the moment
she had caught sight of this helmeted figure, before she
had learned his name, she had known that this moment
would come. It had been fated to do so, if she could only
stay alive long enough. She had done that much, escaping from the death that would have been hers inside
Jabba the Hutt's palace, then binding her destiny to one
who had been only a shadow's breadth away from death
himself. *Just to find out,* Neelah told herself fiercely. *To
find out . . .*

She didn't know. Whether it would be better to discover what lay in that other world, the past that had

been stolen from her, or to go on in darkness, to leave it hidden.

"Go tell Dengar to come up here."

Neelah heard Boba Fett's command, and slowly opened her eyes.

I don't have a choice. She nodded slowly. *About any of it.*

Boba Fett glanced over his shoulder at the dead, hollow-eyed creatures drifting in the emptiness outside the ship, then brought his gaze back around to her.

"We have a lot to talk about," said Boba Fett. "We'd better get started."

8

He was dreaming.

Dengar knew he was, because he could see Manaroo right in front of him.

Turning with a bunch of flimsiplast sheets in her fist and a seriously annoyed look on her face—though that made her no less beautiful to him—Manaroo rapped the knuckles of one hand across the invoices. "Those Jawas are undercutting us again," she said. "We're going to have to do something about them, once and for all—"

"They undercut us because they sell junk." In the loading bay of a medium-tonnage cargo freighter, surrounded by datacoded shipping containers and uncrated machinery still shiny with factory lubricants, Dengar took his wife in his arms and kissed her on the brow. They had been married how many years now, and the skip in his pulse was still the same as the first time he had ever held her soft warmth against himself. The tiny tattooed moons and stars on her wrists no longer glowed as brightly as before, but his own love for her showed no sign of fading. "That's their stock in trade; they're Jawas, right? So don't worry about 'em. They're not our competition."

Manaroo fretted some more, looking over his shoulder at the invoices in her hands. "They're little chiseling womp rats, is what they are."

"Don't worry." Another kiss; Dengar smiled as he leaned back from her face. "The word's getting out among the moisture farmers, about what kind of equipment we're selling. And what kind of long-term percentage contracts we can offer. Hey—" With one hand he stroked her hair, only slightly darker than the pale blue of her Aruzan skin, away from her forehead. "We're already in the black . . ."

"You slimy bucket of nerf-waste."

That wasn't Manaroo's voice. And the kick in the ribs, as he lay on the makeshift pallet with his eyes closed, wasn't from his beloved, either.

"I ought to kill you," continued Neelah, from somewhere on the other side of his closed eyes and the sweet, dwindling remnants of his dream. A blow from her small, rock-hard fist, right across the side of Dengar's jaw, produced a constellation of stars that blotted out the image he was trying to hold, of Manaroo wrapped in his embrace. "As a matter of fact, maybe I *will* . . ."

He had been knocked far enough awake that he was able to roll with the next punch Neelah delivered from where she stood above him. Getting onto his hands and knees, Dengar scrambled toward the nearest bulkhead, then grabbed hold of it and pulled himself upright to face her.

Definitely not dreaming, Dengar told himself, *not now.* He found himself uncomfortably awake and standing in the rank-smelling, close-quartered cargo hold of the *Hound's Tooth.* "What are you going on about?" He crouched slightly, taking a stance with his empty hands outstretched to fend off another attack from the anger-crazed female in front of him. "What did I do?"

"What did you do . . ." Neelah echoed his words as she looked at him in disgust, her own hands planted on her slim hips. "Tried to make a fool out of me, that's what. All that time I was pressing on you to tell me about what'd happened to Boba Fett in the past, and you were already under orders to fill me in on exactly that."

"Oh." Dengar relaxed a bit, lowering his hands. "No big deal." He immediately raised them again when he saw that her anger hadn't ebbed any. "Anyway—what're *you* complaining about? *You* didn't have somebody waving a blaster in your face, wanting a bedtime story!"

The structural damage sustained by the *Hound's Tooth* had loosened the durasteel bars of the holding cage, with several of them wrenched free of their upper sockets and splaying out into the cargo hold. Neelah grasped one of the shorter bars from near the cage's door and pulled it free of the socket below. It made a formidable if simple weapon; with it cocked back over her shoulder, ready to swing, she took a step closer to Dengar.

Fire flashed in her eyes for a second, then just as quickly dimmed. "Let's face it," she said. The metal bar clanged on the hold's floor as she tossed it away. "He ran a number on both of us. Just so he could have as much peace and quiet as he wanted while he navigated the ship."

"Well, yeah, I'm willing to let him have it, if that's what he wants." Dengar slowly straightened from his defensive crouch, ready to drop back into it if this female showed any more signs of her murderous temper. There was a big difference between her and Manaroo, it struck him. His betrothed could be just as tough if necessary, but so far she hadn't ever given any indications that she wanted to kill him. That might change after they were married—if that ever happened—but he was willing to take the chance. "He's not just the head bounty hunter around here. He's also the pilot of the ship. I can wait until he gets us to where he wants to go."

"Your waiting's over," said Neelah. With her thumb, she pointed toward the cockpit above them. "We've arrived."

"Yeah?" Dengar rubbed his chin, warily regarding the female. A hard knot of apprehension coalesced in his stomach. It was one thing to travel toward an unknown destination, but quite another thing to reach that mysterious point. Whatever else Boba Fett might have filled him in on—it didn't amount to much—there hadn't been any talk about the events that would go down once they got there. "Now what?"

"That's the big question. But our intrepid captain has decided to break his silence, at least. So get a move on— Fett wants us both up in the cockpit for a briefing."

Dengar nodded, then managed a half smile. "That oughta improve your disposition, at least."

He followed Neelah up the ladder. But even as he mounted the metal treads, his mind slipped back to the last fading vestiges of the dream he had been enjoying before being so violently awoken. It had been all about the same fantasy in which he indulged even when awake, during those relatively quieter times when he wasn't trying to keep from getting killed. The partnership with Boba Fett had to pay off, figured Dengar. *Big time.* Fett had to have something major cooking, or he wouldn't have bothered taking on a partner—gratitude wasn't a sufficient motivation with a hard character like that. *Save a guy's life,* brooded Dengar, *and what do you get for it?* Not much, except for a chance to get killed in some scheme of his. That was the easy part; the harder one would be turning this partnership gig into cold, hard credits, the kind that would pay off his debt load and set him and Manaroo up in a new life. Something like brokering the galaxy's high technologies to underdeveloped backwater planets, like that dump of a world Tatooine. That was where the real profits were to be made, and a lot more safely besides. Even with paying out the bribes to keep a commercial operation going, either to the Empire or, if the wildest imaginable possibilities came true, to whatever was put together by the Rebel Alliance, there would still be the chance of him and Manaroo doing well together. All it took were the connections—*I've got those already,* Dengar told himself—and a little bit of operating capital. Actually, a *lot* of capital; that was why he'd agreed to hook up with Boba Fett in the first place.

As he stepped from the ladder and through the cockpit hatchway, Dengar slowly shook his head. Whatever was next on Boba Fett's agenda, he had the feeling it might not lead to that pile of credits he needed, and the new life they could buy.

"Let's get right to business," said Boba Fett, turning around in the pilot's chair to face Dengar and Neelah. "I don't care to waste any more time than we already have." He pointed with his thumb over his shoulder. "This is what's left of Kud'ar Mub'at's web—"

Dengar leaned forward, peering toward the viewport behind the other bounty hunter. "You're right," he said after a moment. The drifting corpses of the assembler's subnodes, tangled in ropelike strands of neural tissue, were both eerie and impressive. "It must be . . ."

"I hardly need to be told when I'm correct about something." A trace of irritation sounded in Boba Fett's otherwise emotionless voice. "I rarely am not. And when I say that there is a considerable amount of time pressure upon our actions here, you should believe it."

"You mean what's going on with the Empire and the Rebels?" Dengar shrugged, then shook his head. "I don't see what the worry is. The big battle they've got shaping up between them—that's way out by Endor. That's practically the other side of the galaxy; in any event, it's a long stretch from us. I don't see how it could affect what we're doing here. If anything—" He pointed to the viewport. "Their problems should make it easier for us to take care of whatever you brought us here for. Both the Empire and the Rebel Alliance have pulled out most of their forces from whatever dispersed locales they were in before, to get ready for the confrontation between them. That leaves a lot of systems and space just about empty of them. We can do what we want, and neither the Empire nor the Rebels will be any the wiser."

"That kind of simplistic analysis is why you're the one taking orders, and I'm the one giving them." Boba Fett laid his gloved hands flat on the arms of the pilot's chair. "The battle that's likely to take place near Endor might be over, once it's begun, in less than a few minutes. And it will have a decisive impact on the fate of the ongoing struggle between the Empire and the Rebel Alliance. They've been building up to this confrontation for a long time. And it does matter which side wins, to creatures like us. Palpatine wishes to make absolute his control over the galaxy, and everything in it. Such a grasp would extend to you, Dengar, as well as to myself. Our own ambitions, and what we do to pursue them, might no longer be possible if Palpatine were to achieve all that he desires."

"And what about mine?" Standing beside Dengar, the female Neelah spoke up. "What happens to me, and what *I* want?"

"You don't even know what that is," replied Boba Fett. "But you can believe me about it—or not, just as you choose. The past and the world that was stolen from you will be lost forever if Palpatine wins this struggle with the Rebel Alliance. There will be no way for you to get it back then."

"And if the Rebels win?"

"There's no way they can." Boba Fett gave a flat, hard shake of his head. "My own career as a bounty hunter should be proof enough that cunning and ruthlessness inevitably triumph over all the high-minded ideals that the universe can generate." The bounty hunter's scorn for the Rebels, for any creature motivated by something beyond profits, was evident. "But if the impossible should happen—the galaxy has seen stranger events come about—then that would be bad for our business as well. The Rebels' pretenses to a higher morality would prevent them from paying the established rates for our services, and they would also at the same time seek to exterminate those criminal operations which have been some of my best customers. Let's face it—the best outcome, as far as bounty hunters are concerned, would be for this battle near Endor to wind up being a draw somehow, with neither force eliminating the other, and the struggle between the Rebel Alliance and the Empire continuing. We can hope for that to happen—but we can't count on it."

Dengar had felt his own hopes falling as he had listened to Boba Fett's bleak prognosis. *What a universe,* he thought glumly. Whether the war was won by the forces of good or by the greatest evil the galaxy had ever known, somehow the results were the same, at least for him. *I wind up losing, no matter what.* That longed-for future, with him and Manaroo and nothing to do with the bounty hunter trade, seemed to recede at a light-speed pace. The only way for him to make the kind of credits he needed was as a bounty hunter, hooked up with the notorious Boba Fett, but that same Boba Fett made it sound as if it was soon going to be impossible to even *be* a bounty hunter. Where was the fairness in an arrangement like that?

The female Neelah didn't seem concerned by the dismal long-term prospects that Boba Fett had described. "So what do you propose doing in the meantime? And why did you bring us here?"

"My plans are my own," said Boba Fett. "But some of them concern you, and it's now become convenient for you to have some of your many questions answered. You wanted the past—*your* past—then so it shall be." He gestured with one hand toward the viewport behind him. "I hereby give it to you."

Dengar could see Neelah scowling disgustedly at the viewport. Outside the ship, pallid strands of neural tissue and their tethered, spiderlike corpses continued to drag their shapes past the transparisteel.

"Is this some kind of a joke?" Neelah's glare was even angrier as she turned it toward Fett. "I don't see anything, that—"

Leaning forward in the pilot's chair, Boba Fett interrupted her. "You don't see, because you don't understand. Not yet, at any rate. But if you listen to me, you will."

With a scowl still upon her face, Neelah folded her arms across her breast. "Go ahead. I'm listening."

From the corner of his eye, Dengar glanced over at the

young woman. It wasn't the first time that he had heard that tone of command in her voice. *She's used to giving orders,* thought Dengar, *and having creatures obey them.* It was the same haughty tone of voice that Neelah had used on him, ordering him to continue telling the story of Boba Fett and the breakup of the old Bounty Hunters Guild, and it had been more effective than any blaster pistol she could have pulled on him. But to hear her talk that way to Boba Fett, as though barely able to control her impatience with a slow-moving servant, was still startling. *Who is she?* wondered Dengar. *And how did she wind up as a memory-wiped dancing girl in Jabba the Hutt's palace?* His own curiosity about Neelah's past almost matched hers.

"This part of the story," said Boba Fett, "didn't begin here. And it happened a little while before the arachnoid assembler Kud'ar Mub'at met his demise. I had business in one of the nearby systems that had been successfully concluded—you don't need to know about that—and I was returning toward the center of the galaxy, where several potentially lucrative opportunities were awaiting me. Of course, I was aboard my own *Slave I* at the time, and not an under-equipped mediocrity like this ship. One of the functions I had programmed into *Slave I*'s computers was a complete database of the ships of all other bounty hunters, both those affiliated with the Bounty Hunters Guild and the few, such as myself, operating as independent agents. It rarely happens, but on occasion some other bounty hunter, or the Guild while it still existed, has managed to obtain information before I have, about some particular hard merchandise to be rounded up for a good price." Fett's shoulders lifted in a dismissive shrug. "Some clients prefer to employ less-qualified bounty hunters, hoping they'll be able to get what they want at a lower price. That's their choice, but it rarely works out that way."

True enough, thought Dengar. He had heard those other stories, all of which went to prove that it was almost as dangerous trying to avoid doing business with Boba Fett as actually going ahead and getting involved with him. In a lot of ways, he was virtually inescapable.

"So I sometimes find it worthwhile," continued Boba Fett, "to keep an eye on what other bounty hunters are up to. And if *Slave I*'s ID scanners home in on a bounty hunter's ship in a navigational sector that should otherwise be empty of such activity, then I find that very interesting indeed. It's even more interesting when the onboard computers read out the ID code of a ship belonging to a bounty hunter known for his unsavory business practices."

That description puzzled Dengar. It was hard to imagine any bounty hunter being more ruthless than Boba Fett himself. "So who was it that you came across?"

"The ID code identified the ship as one known most often as the *Venesectrix*. Rarely spotted anywhere close to the central sectors of the galaxy; its owner preferred operations farther out into the border territories. And of course, there was a reason for that: the owner of the *Venesectrix* was a certain Ree Duptom." Pausing a moment, Boba Fett looked over at Dengar. "Perhaps you're familiar with the name."

"Wait a minute . . ." It took a moment, but the name finally hooked up with a memory synapse inside Dengar's head. "Ree Duptom—he's the only one who ever got booted *out* of the Bounty Hunters Guild!" That took some doing, Dengar knew; there had been plenty of creatures in the Guild whose ethical standards had been way below his own. He wasn't familiar with the exact details— Duptom had been booted out of the Bounty Hunters Guild before Dengar had joined it—but there had been an unspoken legend attached to him, as being the one creature that all other bounty hunters considered scum. "I didn't think he was still active, even out in the border."

"I guess he's not," said Neelah drily. "Pay attention, why don't you? He's obviously being discussed in the past tense for a reason."

"True." Boba Fett gave an acknowledging nod of his

head. "When I came across the *Venesectrix* in open space, the ship's engines weren't powered up; it was simply drifting. I attempted to establish communication with its pilot, but I received no response over the comm unit. The reasonable assumption was that the pilot was either dead or had abandoned his ship. To determine which was the case—and to find anything that might have been valuable aboard—I forced entry through the *Venesectrix*'s airlock." In the cockpit viewport behind Boba Fett, a few more dead subnodes bumped against the curved transparisteel. "And I found Ree Duptom, all right."

"Dead, I suppose." The expression on Neelah's face was one of utter boredom. "You know, I'm still waiting to hear the part that has anything to do with me."

Boba Fett ignored her impatience. "Duptom didn't make a good-looking corpse. He hadn't been the handsomest humanoid to begin with—his appearance matched his ethics—but being caught in a hard-energy particle burst from a partial core meltdown of his own ship's engines hadn't helped any. Fortunately, the burst's lethal effects had been contained within a zone just a couple of meters deep; he had obviously been working in the engine compartment when the meltdown occurred, gotten the dose of radiation, then staggered back up to the *Venesectrix*'s cockpit area to die. Which didn't take long."

The story's details aroused Dengar's suspicions. "So did his ship's engines malfunction—or were they sabotaged?" From what he had heard in the Bounty Hunters Guild, Ree Duptom had made nearly as many enemies for himself as Boba Fett had.

"I didn't investigate that question," said Fett. "Once a competitor of mine is dead, I lose interest in them. How they wound up that way is someone else's business; nothing to do with me."

Right, thought Dengar.

"Anyway, somebody like Ree Duptom was perfectly capable of killing himself through his own stupidity." Boba Fett shook his head, as though in disgust. "His ship and all of his equipment were poorly maintained; frankly, he was not a credit to the bounty hunter trade in a lot of ways. But Duptom was obviously able to find certain clients, nevertheless. The evidence of that was right there aboard his ship. And the uncompleted jobs that he had been working on were interesting enough for me to take them over."

"What were they?"

"There were two matters," replied Boba Fett, "that Ree Duptom's untimely death had left hanging. The first one was in the form of a deactivated cargo droid—or what had once been a cargo droid. Someone had cleverly transformed it into an autonomic spy device, with not only built-in vid cameras and sound recording equipment, but an olfactory detect and sample circuit as well. The droid's hidden sensors could pick up trace amounts of scent molecules in the atmosphere and analyze them for biologic source details."

"Why would anybody want information like that?" This time, Dengar was puzzled by the story, rather than suspicious. "What's the good of knowing what some event *smelled* like, if you already had the visual and audio recording?"

"It all depends," said Boba Fett, "on what you're looking for, and what the spy device had been designed to catch. This converted cargo droid was capable of detecting evidence of something—or someone—that would otherwise have remained hidden and undiscovered if visual and auditory clues were all that had been processed. Which is what it in fact had done; I found that out when I removed the data record from inside the droid and analyzed it. The truth came out, concerning a certain individual having been at a certain place, and at a certain important time, even though he had tried to conceal his presence from anyone else who might have been watching and listening."

"What place?" Neelah's tone was as demanding and impatient as before. "What time?"

"Back on Tatooine—for such a desolate, backwater

world, it has assumed a great deal of importance for the rest of the galaxy." Boba Fett gestured toward the viewport, as though indicating one of the bright points of light visible beyond the drifting subnodes. "But that's something bounty hunters know instinctively—or at least the ones who survive and prosper. The smallest, apparently insignificant speck of dirt can loom unexpectedly large one day. And you had better be prepared for that. In this case, the speck of dirt was a moisture farm in the Dune Sea, some distance away from the Mos Eisley spaceport. A moisture farm owned by one Owen Lars—nobody important—and operated by him and his wife, Beru, assisted by a young nephew of theirs. Who just happened to be someone very important—"

"Luke Skywalker," said Dengar. "That's who you're talking about, isn't it?"

"Indeed." Boba Fett gave a single nod. "Enough of the details have become known, about Skywalker's transformation from an insignificant, planet-bound nonentity with big and hopeless dreams to a major figure in the Rebel Alliance, to have already coalesced into legend. And that transformation could be said to have begun with a raid by Imperial stormtroopers on that dreary little moisture farm, a raid that left Skywalker's aunt and uncle as little more than blackened skeletons in the ruins."

"So what's the big mystery about that? Darth Vader ordered the stormtrooper raid on the moisture farm—a lot of creatures in the galaxy know about that by now." Dengar shrugged his shoulders. "Anybody who's had any contact at all with the Rebel Alliance has heard most of the story."

"The mystery," said Boba Fett quietly, "has to do with what I found in the deactivated cargo droid aboard Ree Duptom's ship. The spy device's audio and video records documented the stormtroopers' raid; the droid must have been hiding and watching from behind a nearby sand dune. The details, when I played back the files, were consistent with the known accounts of the raid and its aftermath. There were only Imperial stormtroopers to be observed, going about their lethal business. But the additional data that the cargo droid's spy recordings held—the olfactory information, taken from the atmosphere at the time and place of the raid on the moisture farm—indicated somebody else had been there, as well as the stormtroopers."

"All right"—Neelah spread her hands apart, waiting to hear— "who was it?"

"In the analysis of the spy device's olfactory data were the unmistakable pheromones of a male of the Falleen species." Boba Fett raised a finger for emphasis. "That much was easily determined. But using my own databases aboard *Slave I*, I was able to narrow it down even further. The specific pheromone traces could only have come from a member of the Falleen nobility; there's a genetic marker that is unique to that bloodline."

"A Falleen nobleman?" Dengar's brow creased as he puzzled over the information. "But they're all dead now—"

"There was one still alive," said Boba Fett, "at the time of the stormtrooper raid on Tatooine. Before that, the Falleen nobility had been virtually wiped out by a genetic warfare experiment, one that was initiated by Lord Vader. Of that family grouping, the only surviving member was Prince Xizor, who was then the head of the Black Sun organization."

"I don't get it." Dengar felt even more confused than before. "You're saying that *Prince Xizor* was part of the raid that killed Luke Skywalker's aunt and uncle? But Xizor would've had to have been directing the Imperial stormtroopers somehow, but keeping himself out of sight—"

"Not at all." Boba Fett put his gloved hands flat on the arms of the pilot's chair again. "The spy device into which the cargo droid had been transformed contained the evidence of Prince Xizor being present at the raid on the moisture farm—*but the evidence might not have been genuine.*"

"Faked? You mean somebody else created some kind

of phony evidence and planted it inside the cargo droid?"
The possibilities were multiplying faster than Dengar
could keep track. "Or maybe Xizor himself did it for
some reason." That didn't seem to make sense, but then
very little seemed to anymore. "But why? Why would
anybody do that?"

"That," replied Fett, "is something I do not know. Or
at least, not yet. But the chances of the evidence having
been manufactured, with the purpose of making it appear
that Prince Xizor had something to do with the raid that
killed Skywalker's aunt and uncle, remain considerable."

"I don't see why that should be." Arms folded across
her breast, Neelah seemed less than impressed with Boba
Fett's analysis. "Why make things more complicated
than they need to be? Maybe this Xizor creature really
did lead the raid, and somehow he got caught out at it,
even though he'd tried to keep himself hidden."

"There's several reasons for being suspicious about
the evidence I found inside the cargo droid. One is that
Lord Vader and Prince Xizor were mortal enemies, even
as they continued their roles as Palpatine's loyal servants.
Of course, it served the Emperor's purposes to have
Vader and Xizor at each other's throats, just as I suspect
it served his purpose to pretend he didn't know that Xizor was the leader of Black Sun. The Emperor has a devious mind—he derives more of his power from that, I
believe, than any mystical Force—and it suited him for
the moment to keep Xizor on a long leash. The time
came, though, when the prince found a tighter grip
around his neck than he would ever have thought possible. He wasn't clever enough to avoid being caught in the
snare that he helped weave around himself—and that
cost him his life. I don't intend to follow his example."
Boba Fett leaned back in the pilot's chair, his visor-
shielded gaze regarding his audience. "The upshot of the
enmity that existed between Xizor and Vader is that it
would have been unlikely in the extreme for Xizor to
have taken any part in the stormtrooper raid without

Vader having known and, more, having approved of it—yet none of my information sources on the Imperial planet of Coruscant, some of them close indeed to Vader, have ever indicated that was the case. Similarly, my contacts inside Black Sun never reported their leader Xizor getting hooked up with one of Darth Vader's operations. Therefore, the best analysis would be that the evidence linking Xizor to the raid had been created by some third party, possibly as a way of drawing unwanted attention toward Prince Xizor. That possibility is reinforced by Ree Duptom's own history, before he met his death aboard his own ship: he had been involved on several previous occasions with various *disinformation* campaigns, some of them actually linking back to Emperor Palpatine's court. It had become something of a speciality with Duptom, the discreet spreading of lies in the various watering holes of the galaxy, so that they would do the most good for whoever had hired him."

"That was how he got kicked out of the old Bounty Hunters Guild." Dengar gave a slow nod. "He got a couple of other bounty hunters killed by circulating stories that they had been the ones responsible for certain double crosses that went down. They weren't scams that he'd run, but shifting the blame let some other well-paying, weaselly creature get away."

"A time-honored tradition," said Boba Fett drily. "And one which Ree Duptom had been making a good part of his living at. Given his reputation for being able to do that sort of thing, someone had obviously engaged his services in some kind of scheme to falsely link Prince Xizor with the stormtrooper raid on Tatooine in which Luke Skywalker's aunt and uncle were killed. But two other deaths put an end to that plot: Duptom's own, when he was fried by the meltdown of his ship's engine core, and Xizor's. Whatever the intent had been in trying to link Xizor with the stormtrooper raid, it was hardly worth following through on it once he had been killed as well. The only thing left from the plot was the fabricated evidence contained in the cargo droid, and that was in my possession once I came across Duptom's ship drifting in space."

"For which, I'm sure, you'd find some good use." Unfolding an arm, Neelah held up two fingers. "But you said there was something else you found on that ship. What was the other item?"

"Perhaps this one will compel more of your attention. Ree Duptom might have been dead—" Boba Fett shrugged. "No great loss; but there was still another creature alive aboard the *Venesectrix*. In the cargo hold's cages, I found a young female human. Not in the best of physical condition—Duptom wasn't as careful about maintaining his merchandise as I am—but at least still breathing. She was still unconscious, the aftereffect of a rather thorough memory wipe that she had received . . ."

Dengar heard a sudden gasp come from Neelah. He looked over at her, standing next to him, and saw that her eyes had gone wide with surprise.

"Good," said Boba Fett. "I see that I have managed to pique your interest. That moment aboard Ree Duptom's *Venesectrix* was indeed our first encounter. One that still remains as mystifying to me as it undoubtedly is to you. I could only assume that a memory-wiped female human had been in Duptom's possession as part of his various business enterprises—though not, of course, as an item of hard merchandise for which a bounty had been posted. While it was possible that Ree Duptom might have gotten wind of some paying gig before I had, enough time had passed—as was indicated by the advanced state of decomposition of his corpse—so that I would have heard of anyone offering a bounty for the return of a person matching your physical description. That was not the case, so obviously Duptom had been involved in some other, probably less savory, type of business. But what that would have been, I had no clue—when you regained consciousness, you couldn't even tell me your name."

"I remember . . ." Neelah's eyes were even wider than before. She nodded slowly. "Not my name . . . that's still lost . . . but I remember now, that *was* the first time I laid eyes on you. Not in Jabba the Hutt's palace, but in a ship out in space." Neelah touched the side of her head with trembling fingertips. "It was like I woke up there . . . and there were the bars of the cage, and I felt so cold . . ."

"That was because you were dying. Whoever had done the memory-wipe job on you had been both thorough and brutal." Boba Fett's voice was flat and unemotional. "They didn't leave you in good shape. Plus you had been unconscious for some time, without food or water, after Ree Duptom had managed to get himself killed. If I hadn't taken care of you and nursed you back to a reasonable semblance of health, you would have died there aboard the *Venesectrix*—or on *Slave I* after I had brought you over to my ship. So you might want to regard whatever you did for me, back in the Dune Sea on Tatooine, as just repayment in kind."

"But you didn't save me . . . because you felt sorry for me . . ."

"And pity didn't motivate you either, when you found me near death." Boba Fett regarded her coldly, but with no tone of accusation in his voice. "It was a simple business matter for both of us. You thought I might be of some use to you, just as long before that, I calculated the potential for turning a profit from you. And"—he turned his head slightly, as though studying her from another angle—"we both might be correct yet. But at the time I found you, that was an unknown quantity, just as it remains now. I have my standards, though; no piece of possibly valuable merchandise has ever died while in my keeping, other than when they've managed to commit suicide. That, I could tell, wasn't going to happen in your case; even starving and dehydrated, suffering from a traumatic memory wipe, enough of your inner spirit remained, fighting to survive. Once you were out of physiological danger, it was just a matter of stowing you someplace where you'd be out of danger while I determined the best way of profiting from your situation."

"So you put her in Jabba the Hutt's palace?" The

notion astonished Dengar. He stared at Boba Fett, eyes wide as Neelah's had gone. "*That* hellhole? She could've gotten thrown to Jabba's pet rancor!"

"The dangers of Jabba's palace were well known to me," said Boba Fett. "While substantial, they were nevertheless limited and predictable. And I would be on hand to circumvent them, in case Neelah had aroused any of Jabba's crueler desires—the Hutt, like all of his greedy species, might have been averse to meeting my price, but he valued my services enough to have made a standing offer for me to stay on at his palace for as long as I cared to."

"So you could keep an eye on me," said Neelah. Her gaze narrowed as she slowly nodded. "But more than that—you had already come to a dead end, trying to find out anything about me, who I really was, why somebody had done all those things to me. So you passed me off as a mere dancing girl, bringing me there to Jabba's palace while I was still too confused to even know what you were doing. But what you were really hoping for was that someone in that crowd of thugs and criminals in Jabba's court would recognize me for who I really was— and that would be how you'd find out how to turn a profit from me!"

"That possibility had occurred to me. Jabba's palace was a crossroads for all sorts of the galaxy's lowlife; some of them had even been in business with Ree Duptom before. There was always a chance that one of them might have had an inkling about what kind of scheme he had been engaged upon when he met his death—who he was working for, and what they were trying to accomplish."

The corner of Neelah's mouth twisted in a sneer. "I guess it's too bad for both of us, then, that you didn't find out anything."

"Ah." A trace of amusement filtered into Boba Fett's voice. "But that's where you're wrong. I *did* discover something. Perhaps not the whole truth—your real name and where you came from—but enough to follow up on.

Enough that might lead us to that mutually profitable truth."

Standing beside Neelah, Dengar could see her hands tightening into fists.

"Tell me," commanded Neelah. *"Now."*

"I'll tell you because it suits my own purposes, and not for any other reason." The amused tone evaporated from Boba Fett's words. "There was a former business associate of Ree Duptom at Jabba's palace—his name doesn't matter—but what is important is that the two of them had been working together until just before Duptom's death. As a matter of fact, they'd had a falling out, the sort of thing that happens with low criminal mentalities like that. It was also the sort of thing that would lead one of them to do a delayed-effect sabotage on the engines of the other's ship, resulting in a lethal core meltdown." Fett shook his head. "No great loss—just as it wasn't any great loss when I had to sneak out of Jabba's court for a second, while the other dancing girl, the one named Oola, was giving her final performance. That was just long enough to set up a rendezvous later with my informant. It wasn't until after Princess Leia, disguised as an Ubese bounty hunter, had brought the Wookiee Chewbacca into the court that I had enough time to obtain the data that this certain creature had—and then I made sure that he wouldn't be informing anyone else that I had been asking questions about your real identity."

"He knew . . . he knew who I am?" Neelah leaned forward. "My real name?"

"Unfortunately, the creature knew nothing of that. And you can rest assured that I used every means of persuasion at my disposal to make sure he told me everything that he did know. I didn't have to worry about leaving traces of those techniques; in Jabba's palace, a corpse turning up in that kind of condition was pretty much a daily occurrence. What he did tell me, though, before I returned to Jabba's court, was that his former business associate Ree Duptom had accepted two new jobs just before they had had their falling out with each other, and that one client would be paying for both jobs. But he didn't know who that client was; Duptom hadn't told him that much."

"Then the information's worthless!" A look of furious despair sparked in Neelah's gaze. "It still doesn't tell us who I really am, or what happened to me!"

"Calm yourself. You've waited this long for the answers you want; you can wait a little while longer. Because that may be all that it takes."

"What . . . what do you mean?"

"Did you forget," said the bounty hunter, "that I brought you to this point in space for a reason? Those answers, if they're to be found anywhere, are here." Boba Fett pointed to the cockpit's viewport and its unsettling vista of dead arachnoid subnodes. "My late contact inside Jabba the Hutt's palace wasn't able to tell me your name—he had never even laid eyes on you before coming there—but he was able to provide the clue I needed."

Dengar spoke up this time. "So what was that?"

"Simple. The two last jobs that Ree Duptom had taken on were obviously the ones I found aboard his ship *Venesectrix*—whoever the person was who had hired him to do something with the fabricated evidence about Prince Xizor's involvement in the stormtrooper raid on Tatooine, that person must also have been the one that had arranged for the abduction and memory wipe of Neelah. But what my contact in the palace told me was that the person who paid for those jobs hadn't hired Ree Duptom directly. He had used an intermediary—a go-between."

"A go-between . . ." Suddenly, Dengar understood. "It must have been Kud'ar Mub'at! The assembler was the only creature who would have arranged that kind of job for Ree Duptom. But—"

"But it's dead," Neelah said flatly. "Kud'ar Mub'at is dead, remember? You were here when it happened." She shook her head in disgust. "You've brought us all the way out here for nothing. The dead can't tell us any secrets."

"That's where you're wrong." Boba Fett turned in the

pilot's chair and pointed to the viewport behind him. "Look."

The *Hound's Tooth* had slowly moved farther into the tethered constellation of dead subnodes. Until it had at last come to the center of the torn strands of neural tissue.

In the scan of space visible outside the ship, a spider-like corpse larger than all the others drifted, jointed legs tucked up beneath what was left of its globular abdomen. The hollow, blind eyes of Kud'ar Mub'at gazed back at the visitors to the cold vacuum of its tomb.

"We only need to bring the dead back to life." Boba Fett spoke with calm assurance, just as though nothing would be easier. "And then listen . . ."

9

A woman talked to a traitor.

"You got what you wanted." The traitor's name was Fenald; in the dim, smoky light of the underground watering hole, his smile was both unpleasant and knowing, like an animal toying with its prey. "That's what it's all about, isn't it?"

Kodir of Kuhlvult tried to keep her cloak from touching the damp walls of the establishment. She had known there were such places on the world of Kuat, but she had never been in one before. Her life had been spent in another world, one that was on the same planet but that might as well have been light-years away. That world contained all the luxury and power of Kuat's ruling families; this one contained the planet's human dregs.

A candle stub's inadequate light flickered from a rough niche carved in the wall, merging her shadow and Fenald's with the darkness in which other figures sat hunched and brooding over squat mugs of intoxicants. Even the air seeped rankly into Kodir's lungs, every molecule laden with the soot that lined the low, crouch-inducing stone ceiling.

"I've got *some* of what I wanted." Kodir leaned forward, arms on the sticky-wet table, so that Fenald would be able to make out her hushed words. "There's always more."

Fenald was a little drunk; he had obviously been waiting for her to show up for some time. "'Fraid I can't help you much with the rest. I'm not exactly in an influential position these days, am I? I sort of spent all that on the last part of your plans."

"Yes—" Kodir nodded inside the cloak's loose hood that she had put on to conceal her identity from any prying scrutiny. "You're quite an actor. Everybody was fooled. And they still are. So you did a very good job for me. I appreciate that."

"Good," said Fenald thickly. He regarded her from heavy-lidded eyes. "Because I need you to show that appreciation. I'm a little short on credits these days . . . what with having lost my job and all. And since *you've* got that job now—just what you wanted, huh?—then I think it's only fair if you pay a little more than what you did up front. Like on a continuing basis. So I wouldn't be tempted into talking to anybody about our little . . . performance, shall we say. It'd be a shame to spoil the show, while it's still going on."

"You're right. It would be." Kodir reached across the table and laid her hand on top of his. "But you know—there's more than one way for me to show my appreciation."

In his present state, it took Fenald a few seconds to understand what she meant. Then his smile grew wider and uglier. "Fine," he said. "But that'll have to be in addition to the credits."

She didn't say anything in reply, but leaned farther across the table, bringing her face closer to his. Just before their lips met, her other hand emerged from inside the cloak with something bright and glittering in her grip. Fenald's eyes went round with shock as he felt the object move across his throat.

"No," said Kodir softly. She dropped the vibroblade onto the table, next to where Fenald had collapsed face-down in a widening pool of his own blood. "It's instead."

Drawing the cloak's hood forward, Kodir turned and looked back across the watering hole's dim space. None of its clientele appeared to have noticed that anything at all had happened. She slid a few coins onto the table's corner, then got up and walked unhurriedly toward the steps leading back up to the surface level.

A woman talked to a gambler.

A different woman, and far from the planet of Kuat. But she too had wrapped herself in a hooded cloak to prevent anyone from prying into her affairs.

"Business is still a little slow for me right now," said the gambler. His name was Drawmas Sma'Da, and he sat at a table in a glittering, brightly lit pleasure den. The laughter of the galaxy's rich and foolish denizens sounded from all sides of the establishment. "You have to understand, I'm not yet at the level where I used to be—I had a little, um, *embarrassment* a few weeks ago. I had to spend most of my operating capital getting out of that mess; you know, the usual bribes and payoffs and stuff. Believe me, Palpatine's not the only greedy creature inside the Empire." Lacing his hands together across his expansive belly, he leaned back in his chair. "So I can't cover any big bets at the moment. None of that Alliance versus the Empire stuff."

"That's fine." The woman kept her voice low. "I want to place a different kind of wager. On a bounty hunter."

"Bounty hunters, huh?" Sma'Da's face darkened into a scowl. "I'll give you a good bet on a couple of 'em. You can bet that if I ever get my hands on a pair named Zuckuss and 4-LOM, they're both dead meat. They're the ones who dragged me out of here, not too long ago."

She shook her head. "I'm not interested in them."

"All right." Sma'Da gave her a jowly, cajoling smile. "Who do you want to bet on?"

The woman told the gambler.

"You got to be joking." He looked at her in amazement. *"Him?"*

"Will you cover the bet?"

"Oh, I'll cover it all right." Sma'Da's shoulders lifted in a shrug. "Hey, that's my business. And I'll give you great odds, too. Because frankly—he's not going to make it. I know just what kind of trouble he's in. It doesn't get any worse."

The woman's gaze turned cold. "All the better for you, then."

When the wager was recorded and the stakes transferred to a holding account at one of the galaxy's banking worlds, Sma'Da offered to buy her a drink. "You should get something for your money," he said. "I hate to take credits from a pretty female, and not give them something in return."

"There is something you can do for me." The woman rose from the table.

Sma'Da looked at her. "What's that?"

"Just be ready to pay up when the time comes." She turned and strode toward the establishment's ornately framed exit, the edge of the cloak trailing across the gold-specked floor.

Near the planet Kuat, other conversations were taking place.

"Believe me," said the leader of the Scavenger Squadron, "I don't like being here, either. I'd rather be out near Sullust right now, getting ready for the *real* battle."

Kuat of Kuat turned from his lab bench and looked over his shoulder at the figure standing, flight helmet in the crook of one arm, in the middle of Kuat's own private quarters. To one side of the space, a high, arching bank of transparisteel panes revealed stars and the immense, intricate shapes of Kuat Drive Yards' construction docks. Against Kuat's ankles, the felinx rubbed its silk-furred flank; glancing down at it for a moment, Kuat saw the creature turn a hostile, slit-pupiled glare at the intruder.

"Then you should feel free to leave," Kuat of Kuat said mildly. "The presence of your squadron here is entirely unnecessary."

"The Rebel Alliance feels otherwise." An impressive scar ran in an almost perfect diagonal across Commander Gennad Rozhdenst's face, the result of surviving a previous skirmish with Imperial fighters. "And I have my orders, directly from former Senator Mon Mothma, with the Alliance fleet near Sullust."

"So I understand." Kuat had bent down and picked up the felinx; the animal now lay cradled in the safety of his arms. Its yellow eyes closed in contentment as he scratched behind its ears. "But you must also bear in mind, Commander, that I have my duties to perform as well."

Right now, those duties weighed heavily on Kuat of Kuat's shoulders. *Everything depends upon me,* he mused. The felinx might very well consider its comfort to be the most pressing concern of its master, but there was far more than that in his thoughts. The fate of Kuat Drive Yards itself, the corporation whose ships and armaments spanned the galaxy and formed the bulk of the Imperial Navy—the leadership of that enterprise was Kuat's hereditary legacy, just as it had been for his father and grandfather, and to generations before them. When he gazed out upon the construction docks, with a fleet of Destroyers and heavy cruisers nearing completion in them, he felt as though their combined mass bent his spine. And more: rising above Kuat Drive Yards was the mottled green sphere of the planet Kuat itself, an entire world and people dependent upon the fate of the corporation that funneled such a large share of the galaxy's wealth into their coffers.

And I fought for this. Kuat's fingertips continued their instinctive caress of the felinx's silken fur. *I fought to keep this burden mine, rather than let others usurp it from me.* At times such as this, when the weight of his responsibilities translated into bone-weary fatigue, he began to question the wisdom of such a struggle. There had been plenty of others in the ruling families of the planet Kuat, nobles whose bloodlines were by custom prevented from taking over the leadership of Kuat Drive Yards, who had been eager to conspire against him, overthrow their world's ancient wisdom, and place themselves in this seat of power. As much as Kuat of Kuat might have been willing to let them have their chance, he had found himself unable to let go of his tight grasp upon the corporation. *Because I know*—he closed his eyes as he stroked the felinx—*that they would never have been able to prevail. Not against me, but against all our other enemies.* Kuat found it cruelly ironic that when death had removed the threat posed by Prince Xizor, another potential opponent should arise, in the form of the Rebel Alliance.

"There's no conflict," said Commander Rozhdenst, "between your duties and mine." The wintry blue eyes in the hard-angled face seemed to have peered into and discerned the careful workings inside Kuat's heart. "The Rebel Alliance has no designs upon Kuat Drive Yards. We would just as soon have the corporation remain in your hands."

"I wish I could believe that, Commander." Kuat's hand froze in its gentle motions upon the felinx's neck. He could hear his own voice turning cold. "But stationing a squadron of armed Rebel spacecraft—even one that so justly merits its 'scavenger' descriptor—is hardly the action of those who seek friendship with Kuat Drive Yards."

"The Rebel Alliance would be satisfied with maintaining a neutral relationship with you. We seek no more than that."

"Ah." Kuat of Kuat managed a wry smile before slowly shaking his head. "But you see, Commander—that's what *everybody* says. Everybody who has ever done business with Kuat Drive Yards, back to my father's and my grand-father's times before me, has always assured us that they had the corporation's welfare—and independence—at heart. And if we had trusted them on that point, I doubt if Kuat Drive Yards would even exist now. So you'll have to excuse my skepticism; I know it's unseemly in even an unwilling host such as myself. But I assure you that Emperor Palpatine himself has informed me that he has no 'designs,' as you put it, upon us. Don't be offended if I state that the reliance I place upon his words is just about the same as I put upon those from a representative of the Rebel Alliance."

The commander regarded him for a moment, then spoke. "You have a way of putting things very bluntly, Kuat."

"Ascribe it to my training as an engineer. I prefer to think of it as exactitude, rather than bluntness."

"Then I'll speak to you just as . . . *exactly*." Rozhdenst's voice grew even icier, like durasteel exposed to the vacuum of space. "My squadron and I were sent here on a mission, and we intend to carry that mission out. But you're correct in assuming that there's something that the Rebel Alliance wants from you. I've been quite thoroughly briefed on the political and strategic analysis that's been made by our leadership concerning the value of Kuat Drive Yards. Not just to ourselves, but to Palpatine as well. When I say that your neutrality is something that we value, I don't mean just toward the Alliance; I mean toward the Empire."

"Kuat Drive Yards does business with the Empire. Nothing more than that. The armaments and fleet procurement authorities of the Imperial Navy value what we do here—as they should; we have no rivals when it comes to our military shipbuilding expertise—and they are capable of meeting our prices." The felinx shifted lazily in the crook of Kuat's arm as his shoulders lifted in a shrug. "We sell to others as well, if they can pay for the goods they desire. That, in fact, is the only distinction we make between our customers and *potential* customers: whether or not they've got the credits in their accounts, for us to take an order from them." Kuat displayed a thin, humorless smile. "Believe me, Commander, if the Rebel Alliance was capable of paying, Kuat Drive Yards would be happy to take your credits. From the look of that motley collection of patched-together Y-wings you've got stationed around our construction docks, they could certainly use a little maintenance and retrofitting work."

A spark of anger showed in Rozhdenst's eyes, amusing Kuat even more. He knew that his comment had struck home. The only reason that this particular collection of Rebel Alliance craft was here rather than on their way to Sullust to join up with the others preparing for the imminent confrontation with the Imperial Navy was that they were too beat-up or outmoded to represent much of a tactical threat against a well-armed and prepared enemy. Most of them were old Y-wings, representing the previous-generation technology that the Imperial Navy's advanced TIE fighters and Interceptors would be capable of chewing up and dispersing into flaming shards within the first seconds of a tactical encounter.

"I have to wonder," Kuat continued maliciously, "whether the Rebel Alliance command sent you and your squadron here to accomplish anything at all, or whether patrolling Kuat Drive Yards is just a convenient excuse for getting you all safely out of the way, so you won't needlessly interfere with the actual fighters, once the battle starts." The felinx sensed its master's amusement and purred in happy agreement. "I imagine that Mon Mothma has more important things to worry about than how to deploy a so-called squadron that's really little more than laser-cannon fodder."

The glower on Gennad Rozhdenst's face was nearly as deep as the disfiguring scar. "My men and their craft can take care of themselves."

"I have little doubt of that, Commander. It's just a question of whether they can accomplish anything else.

Your loyalty to them is impressive, if not unexpected. And of course, the reasons that the Rebel Alliance command put *you* in charge of them are perfectly understandable. It speaks volumes about the advanced moral nature of the Rebel leaders that they would be concerned to find an assignment suitable for someone whose military career has not been crowned, so to speak, with conspicuous amounts of glory."

In Rozhdenst's eyes, the spark turned darker and smoldering. He made no reply.

"Bad luck can happen to anyone, Commander. I can attest that often that which makes one a hero is a simple matter of chance and fortune—though some would say that the true hero makes his own chances. But that's a lot to be asked of anyone. So your own history—your failures, the crashes and the dogfights that the other creature won—are certainly excusable."

Kuat saw that he had succeeded, though; it was clear that he had managed to goad the Alliance commander into a barely controlled fury. *Just what I wanted,* he thought with satisfaction. He had never been overly impressed with hoary old Jedi blather, but he did believe in the time-tested negotiator's maxim that to anger someone was to own him.

That anger manifested itself in the form of Commander Gennad Rozhdenst striding right up to Kuat and jabbing a blunt forefinger into his chest. "Let's get something straight, Kuat. I got my orders to come here straight from Mon Mothma herself, after I had rounded up this squadron that you think so little of—and *that* was on her direct orders as well. I scoured every system in this galaxy for every operational remnant, every shotdown fighter and support craft we could lay our hands on, and every orphaned Alliance pilot who'd had to be left behind by his previous outfit. We got our Scavenger Squadron up and flying without any help from technicians like you, since your chasing after your own profits kept you just a little too busy for something like that."

The forefinger poked harder into the front of Kuat's regulation KDY coveralls. "My squadron and I were already on our way to Sullust—on Admiral Ackbar's orders—when he was overruled by Mothma and the rest of the Alliance high command and instructed to send us here."

"So I've already heard." Kuat pushed the other man's hand to one side and away from himself. "It seems that there are others inside your Alliance who have a more discerning analysis, shall we say, of the strategic value of your squadron."

"What they have, Kuat, is a pretty keen idea of what they can expect from somebody like you. They know exactly how much business that your corporation has done with the Empire." Rozhdenst made a dismissive gesture toward the construction docks visible through the arching panels of transparisteel. "This whole place would've probably gone broke and been dismantled for scrap if it hadn't been for Palpatine and Vader steering so many procurement contracts your way. You've got a lot to be grateful to them for, don't you? That entire fleet that's nearing completion in your docks is a commission for the Imperial Navy—and the payment for it will put a nice pile of credits in your world's accounts. And that's all that concerns you, right? You've said as much yourself, just now."

"I'm glad to see you've been listening, Commander. That's the kind of observational skill I wouldn't have expected from my previous investigations into your record."

"Don't crack wise with me." Rozhdenst had regained a small measure of self-control. "It would've been better for you—and for Kuat Drive Yards—if we had been able to even pretend to be on a friendly basis. But no amount of hostility on your part—and no amount of affection for the Empire that pays you and your corporation such a handsome wage—is going to stop my squadron and me from doing what we were sent here to take care of."

"Which is, exactly?" Kuat resumed his stroking of the felinx's silken fur. "Neither the necessity for it, or the details, have been made clear to me."

"Very well." Rozhdenst gave a curt nod. "Mon Mothma and the rest of the Rebel Alliance high command recognize the long-term strategic importance of Kuat Drive Yards. Not just for what your corporation is capable of doing in the future, but for the armaments and ships that are in your construction docks at this moment. None of us in the Rebel Alliance have any doubts that you are fully willing to shift your allegiances to whichever force emerges victorious from the coming battle, and all the ones that shall follow. As you've indicated, you have Kuat Drive Yards' best interests at the center of your thoughts. But if events go as I believe they will at Endor—and how I wish I could be there to see it!—then the Empire is going to need replacements for its operational fleets as soon as possible, and taking delivery of what you've built for them here will be the fastest way of accomplishing that. The Empire knows that, you know that—and *we* know it. Which is the whole reason we're here. The Scavenger Squadron is going to be keeping an around-the-chronometer vigil on everything that happens here at Kuat Drive Yards; there's not going to be much that we're going to miss. And I promise you"—the commander's jabbing finger stopped an inch short of Kuat's chest—"when word comes from Endor about what's happened out there, and the Imperial Navy tries to take possession of the completed ships in your docks—" Rozhdenst shook his head. "It's not going to happen. The Rebel Alliance command may have decided that they've got enough forces available, out at Sullust, that they can spare my pilots for this detail and still be able to beat whatever Palpatine and his underlings can come up with. Fine; that's a strategic decision and I'm satisfied to go along with it. But it also means that Mon Mothma is confident that my raggedy, patched-together outfit can take of business here."

"Indeed." Kuat raised an eyebrow. "Well, I'm sure you'll make a valiant attempt at it."

"Oh, we'll do more than that. Since we'll be missing the action out at Endor, my squadron will be ready to do some serious damage of their own, right here. If any Imperial forces show up and try to get hold of those ships, or if any of your KDY transport crews think they'll be able to pilot them out to some rendezvous point and deliver them, there'll be hell to pay. You can bank on that."

"And what happens if the Rebel Alliance comes here and wants these ships? What gets paid out then?" The temper in the other man's voice had disturbed the felinx in Kuat's arms; he did his best to soothe it. "Am I to assume that Mon Mothma and the rest of the Alliance command will be prepared to negotiate a fair—and profitable—deal for them?"

"I'm not authorized," said Rozhdenst, "to make those kinds of arrangements."

"What that translates to is that you don't have the means. The credits. And neither does the Alliance. Otherwise, Mon Mothma would have made the offer already."

A sneer twisted the corner of Rozhdenst's mouth. "And would you have accepted it? Not as long as you're so afraid of the reaction of your best customer, Emperor Palpatine."

"The deals I make," replied Kuat stiffly, "are for the best interests of my corporation."

"And too bad for everybody else in the galaxy." The sneer remained as Rozhdenst nodded. "They're fighting for their freedom—and their lives—and all you're concerned about is the amount of credits rolling into your coffers. Fine; arrange your ethics however you want to. You don't want to throw in your lot with the Rebel Alliance, that's up to you. But I think I'm clear in warning you what the Alliance's 'offer' is likely to be for those ships in your construction docks." Rozhdenst pointed to the view beyond the transparisteel panels. "If the Alliance decides that it needs the ships you've been building—and there's a high possibility of that—I'm going to be happy to take delivery of them from you whether or not you've agreed to sell them to us instead of the Empire. And we'll worry about making compensation to Kuat Drive Yards *after* the war is over."

"Your language doesn't surprise me, Commander. I would have been more surprised if you had persisted in maintaining a pretense of goodwill toward Kuat Drive Yards. But now we know exactly where we stand with each other, don't we?" Kuat turned and set the felinx down on top of the lab bench beside him. "So I guess we have made some progress."

Rozhdenst regarded him through eyes narrowed to slits. "As I said when I came here, Kuat—it would be better if we could work things out on a friendly basis. I'd rather trust you than have to watch you. But now we *will* be watching you."

"As you wish." Standing with his back turned toward the Rebel Alliance commander, Kuat picked up a micro-insertion logic probe from his lab bench. With the back of his other hand, he kept the felinx from investigating the delicate tool. "Now if you'll excuse me, I have work to do . . ."

He heard the commander's footsteps receding, and then the doors of his private quarters opening and closing once more. In the space's restored silence, he regarded the thin, shining metal of the probe resting in the curve of his palm, as though it were a sharp-edged weapon. "They can watch all they want," murmured Kuat. He addressed his soft words to the noncomprehending felinx, confident that no one else would overhear them. Since having been betrayed by Kuat Drive Yards' former head of security, Kuat of Kuat had personally overseen the electronic security sweep of his private quarters. "They have no idea what I'm doing here." A faint smile moved across his face. "And they won't have much luck getting their hands on those ships . . ."

· · ·

"So what's the scoop?" Ott Klemp, one of the younger and less-experienced pilots in the Scavenger Squadron, matched his pace to that of his commanding officer. "Are they going to cooperate with us?"

"There's no 'they' at Kuat Drive Yards," replied Commander Rozhdenst. He had let Klemp bring him down to the KDY construction docks from the squadron's mobile base-support ship mainly to get the youngster some more, and much-needed, flight time near the immense, system-circling facility. "There's only Kuat of Kuat himself. He makes all the decisions." Rozhdenst continued his purposeful stride down the high-ceilinged corridor, away from his unpleasantly terminated conference with Kuat Drive Yards' chief. "And right now, he's decided to keep on being 'neutral,' as he puts it. That's not good."

"You think he'll turn over this new fleet to the Imperial Navy?"

"What I think is that he'll do whatever he feels is in the best interests of Kuat Drive Yards. I believe him when he says as much. Which means that he'll do it in a second, soon as Palpatine forks over the credits for the ships."

The landing dock, with the Scavenger Squadron shuttle waiting for them, was only a few meters away. "Maybe we should do a preemptive strike," said Klemp. "Get our pilots inside those ships immediately, so that if any Imperial Navy forces show up, we can keep 'em from getting their hands on the goods."

Rozhdenst impatiently shook his head as he walked. "Negative on that. We'd be playing right into the Empire's hands if we tried something like that. We don't have enough pilots and crew to fully man even one ship out of a fleet like that. Getting them up and away from the KDY construction docks would be difficult enough, but trying to fight off an Imperial task force from inside those ships, without enough personnel to crew the onboard weaponry, would be suicide. No, we'd be better off—we'd have more of a chance, that is—by intercepting any Imperial ships coming from outside this sector, and fighting them off with what we've already got."

"Sir, that's not much of a chance at all." Klemp's face had paled with the contemplation of what the commander had described. "Our squadron might be able to keep a lid on a bunch of KDY ship fabricators and technicians, but if the Empire routes any significant number of fighting craft here, we're done for."

"Tell me something," growled Rozhdenst, "that I don't already know." The two men had reached the side of the shuttle craft. Next to the extended landing gear, the commander turned to the younger man. "Let me fill you in on something about our mission here. You're absolutely correct: if the Imperial Navy's forces were to move in, there wouldn't be much we could do to stop 'em. There's only one reason we're able to stay up there—" He pointed toward the sealed landing dock's upper reaches, and the rest of the Scavenger Squadron beyond it. "And that's because, right now, the Empire's attention—and its strength—is turned elsewhere. Endor, to be exact. With our beat-up, inadequate craft, we wouldn't be able to stop the Imperial Navy—but we can slow it down. Maybe, if we fight hard and smart enough, slow it down to the point that we could contact the Alliance communications ship that's in orbit near Sullust, and get some kind of operational task force ordered out here. And *that* Rebel force could stop the Imperial Navy from getting hold of these new ships." Rozhdenst started to climb up the rungs of a rolling ladder platform toward the shuttle's hatchway. "Of course," he said over his shoulder to Klemp, "if that's what happens, we won't be here to see it. We'll be dead."

"Maybe." Ott Klemp climbed up after the commander. "But that's only going to be after a lot of *them* are dead as well."

Rozhdenst leaned forward and slapped the younger man on the shoulder. "Save it for when they get here."

The landing dock's doors swung slowly open, revealing the field of stars beyond, as Klemp fired up the shuttle's thruster engine. A moment later, the craft traced a red arc away from Kuat Drive Yards, heading back toward the waiting squadron.

10

"I can't believe," said Dengar, looking around himself, "that this place was any more cheerful when it *was* alive."

He and Boba Fett were surrounded by the tangled fibrous walls of what had been Kud'ar Mub'at's web. Enough structural integrity had been achieved that the main chamber and a few of the narrow corridors leading from it could hold a breathable atmospheric pressure. That made working in the reconstructed spaces easier, if nowhere near enjoyable.

Boba Fett ignored his comment, just as he had ignored all of Dengar's previous grumbling complaints. Standing several meters away, near the spot where Kud'ar Mub'at's thronelike nest had once been, Boba Fett continued the application of the low-level electrosynaptic pulse device that was slowly bringing the web back from the dead. Behind the bounty hunter, thick cables snaked back toward the temporary exit port that led to the web's exterior. The cables' glossy black sheathing, like the skin of a planet-bound herpetoid creature, shimmered with the effects of the energy coursing within. That energy, and the parallel data flow that shaped and adjusted it to the task of revivifying the web's interwoven neural cells, came from the *Hound's Tooth*, moored almost within touching distance of the heavier structural fibers that bound the mass of finer neurons together.

"That should hold." Dengar made the comment aloud, as much for the purpose of hearing a human voice in this dismal space as for getting any reaction from his partner. The walls of the web's main chamber had to be propped apart from each other, to keep them from collapsing in on him and Fett. From the *Hound's* cargo hold, they had stripped out enough durasteel beams for the job, transferring them over from the ship and awkwardly wrestling them into place among the sections of web they had previously scoured from the vacuum and laboriously bound back together. Even doing that much of a reconstruction on the late arachnoid assembler's web would have been impossible if the Black Sun cleanup crew, the henchmen of Prince Xizor that had destroyed it in the first place, had turned blasters or any other kind of incendiary weapons on it. But all the pieces, the floating strands and knots of pallid grey tissue, had still been floating in the vacuum, waiting to be resurrected. "Any more of them?" Catching his breath, Dengar rested a hand on a horizontally mounted beam next to his head. "Might be able to scrounge a few more out of the ship—"

As if in reply, the durasteel beam groaned and creaked, echoed by the others that filled the chamber like the elements of a three-dimensional maze. The tangled walls pulsed and contracted, as though the two men were caught in some giant creature's digestive tract.

It's like the Sarlacc, thought Dengar. He gazed with both fascination and disgust at the motions of the web's structure. The effect had reminded him of the few details that Boba Fett had recounted, about having been swallowed by the blind, omnivorous beast that had once formed the fang-ringed center of the Great Pit of Carkoon, back in the Dune Sea on Tatooine. *This must be what it's like, to be swallowed up and still be alive . . .*

The pulsing motion ceased as Boba Fett drew the working tip of the tool in his hands away from the intricate cluster of neural ganglia before him. Across his boots, the black cable lay, still shimmering with the power relayed from the ship. The dark gaze of Boba Fett's helmet visor glanced back over his shoulder, toward Dengar. "That was just a test," he said. "Of the web's spinal connections."

"Thanks for warning me." The shiver that had tightened Dengar's shoulders now slowly ebbed away. *I'll be glad,* he thought, *when this is over.* Facing blaster fire, and every other hazard that seemed to come with being Boba Fett's partner, were all preferable to the task of restoring Kud'ar Mub'at's web to a semblance of life.

Unfortunately, that was a necessary part of the plan. Without it—without the extended neural system of the web being once more filled with the sparks of impulse and sensation—the quest that had led both Dengar and Boba Fett, and Neelah as well, to this remote sector of space, and even remoter and more isolated sector of the past, was over.

Fett had explained it all to them. How it was going to work, the only way it could: if the past held the key to the present, then the past had to be broken into and ransacked, the same way the high walls of some rich creature's palace on a fortified planet would be breached. You found a crack in the wall and widened it enough to enter, then went in and got what you wanted. Simple in the concept; difficult—and dangerous, it seemed to Dengar—in the execution.

The crack in the wall of the past was represented by the memory of the once-living, now-dead arachnoid assembler, Kud'ar Mub'at. *Great,* Dengar had said to Boba Fett. *That ends it right there, doesn't it?* Talking to the dead, learning their secrets, wasn't a hard job; it was an impossible one. Kud'ar Mub'at was the link to Neelah's stolen past, and the key to Dengar and Boba Fett's profiting from that past—if it had been important enough to steal from her, and hide the traces of the theft through a deep memory wipe of her brain, then the chances would be good that it would be worth a good deal of credits to find it and restore it once again. The scent of credits was even stronger with the other possibility connected to the theft of Neelah's past: finding out who—or what—it was that had been behind the failed plot to implicate the late Prince Xizor in the raid by Imperial stormtroopers on a moisture farm on Tatooine, a raid that had been the trigger, or at least part of it, for Luke Skywalker's transformation into a leader and legend of the Rebel Alliance. As Boba Fett, with his keen instinct for profits, had pointed out, anytime a trail led that close to the center of major events in the galaxy—with threads tangling around not only a creature who had been the leader of the richest and most powerful criminal organization in all the systems, but also around Emperor Palpatine and his most feared servant, Lord Darth Vader—then the terminus of that trail was likely to be buried under a mountain of credits and influence.

As much as Dengar might have felt that the quest was hopeless, he had to confess to himself that all of his inner greed circuits had been fired up by his partner's talk. *Sure,* he had thought, *you can get killed, poking into Palpatine's and Vader's secrets. But you can also get rich— or at least rich enough to get out of the bounty hunter game.* And back into the safe haven of his beloved Manaroo's arms, and a life that didn't revolve around kidnapping and killing other creatures while trying to avoid getting killed oneself. *That* was worth at least a little risk.

All it would take would be bringing a certain assembler back from the dead, so that its memory of those events and plots and schemes could be riffled through. Dengar had gotten used to surprises from his bounty hunter partner, but the next revelation from Boba Fett had exceeded all that had gone before.

Bringing Kud'ar Mub'at back from the dead, Fett had explained, *isn't impossible.* Gathering together the pieces of the puzzle—all the scattered strands and chunks of neural tissue that the Black Sun cleanup crew had left drifting in space—would be the hardest part. But the pieces were all there, floating around the *Hound's Tooth.* The rest would be relatively easy, or at least according to Boba Fett. *I knew more about Kud'ar Mub'at than it knew about itself.* In the cockpit area of the *Hound,* Fett had related to Dengar and Neelah the results of his previous investigations into the nature of such assembler creatures.

Knowing things about one's business associates always gave one an advantage, especially if they were matters of which the other creature was ignorant. And Kud'ar Mub'at had never shown any great curiosity about its own genetic background or physiology, or whether other assemblers existed anywhere else in the galaxy. Kud'ar Mub'at had been content to consider itself unique, with nothing else like it anywhere in the known systems; it made negotiations with clients easier to have the confidence that there was no other arachnoid assembler whose services they could engage. If Kud'ar Mub'at had ever encountered any other assemblers, it would probably have arranged for their murder, much as it had eliminated its own predecessor, the assembler that had originally created it as a subnode, then suffered the consequences of an unforeseen rebellion. Just as Kud'ar Mub'at had suffered in turn, its former subnode Balancesheet was now somewhere else in the galaxy's empty spaces, taking care of the business it had inherited from its own deposed creator. *But there are other assemblers,* Boba Fett had told Dengar and Neelah. *I found them.* And even more important: *I learned from them.*

The location of the arachnoid assemblers' homeworld was something that Boba Fett wouldn't reveal. *You don't need to know that.* Which was just as well with Dengar; the notion of a whole hidden world somewhere, populated by an entire species of spidery, scheming assemblers gave him the creeps. But Boba Fett's knowledge of an aspect of their physiology was something he did share. Just as an individual assembler, such as Kud'ar Mub'at or Balancesheet, could generate and extrude additional cerebro-neural tissue in the form of an extended nervous system running through a web big enough in which to live and in the tethered subnodes that filled the space, so could that tissue be *re*generated from the outside. A constantly monitored and adjusted stimulating pulse would actually restore the strands of dead tissue to functioning life, with the synaptic terminals seeking one another out and knitting themselves back together.

That basic rundown of assembler physiology had taken place in the cockpit of the *Hound's Tooth*. Standing now inside the reconstructed web, Dengar looked down at the black, shimmering cables looped near his boots. Neelah was still back aboard the ship moored alongside, making sure that the necessary energy and controlling data kept flowing from the onboard computers. There was no danger of her disengaging the *Hound's Tooth* and leaving them stranded inside the web; she was more intent on breaking through to the past and its secrets than either bounty hunter could have been.

Dengar looked up as another shimmering motion ran through the fibers of the web. The effect was less spasmodic and threatening than the previous one, and settled down to a barely discernible but constant trembling in the curving structure. At the same time, the vibration died in the black cables running out to the ship; they became as inert as the web itself had been when he and Boba Fett had commenced its resurrection from the dead.

"That's it," Boba Fett announced. He stood up from where he had been kneeling beside the empty nest at the center of the chamber and tossed the pulsator tool aside. "Now we're ready for the last step."

Which was exactly what Dengar had been dreading. He had been able to reconcile himself to being inside the living web; it was at least without personality or a guiding intelligence, the revivified neural circuits as empty of thought as some giant, hollow vegetation. But for the past to be retrieved, with all its secrets intact and readable, that idiot nervous system would have to be linked to the brain that contained the necessary memories. *And we'll be inside it,* thought Dengar. It struck him as being even worse, in some ways, than the Sarlacc could ever have been.

"Come over here and give me a hand." Boba Fett gestured as he spoke the order. "We need to get it into position for the hookup."

Reluctantly, Dengar ducked his head beneath the horizontal beam keeping the web's walls spread apart. He threaded his way through the maze of the other supports that had been so laboriously installed, mostly by him rather than Fett.

At the center of the chamber, the neural activity that Boba Fett had summoned up from the formerly dead tissue was more visible, the pulsing of the structural fibers overlaid with a shimmering network of sparks racing across the synaptic connections. Dengar tried to maintain his balance on the uneven floor of the space, without laying a hand on any of the surrounding structural fibers. There was no chance of receiving an electrical shock from the bright circuits of light, but the thought of touching the now-living mass unnerved him.

"Get on that side of it," instructed Boba Fett. He pointed toward the one thing inside the chamber that was still part of the dead world they had found when they had come to this point in space. "We'll need to lift it all the way clear. I don't want the legs dragging across any of the neural fibers."

He did as Fett had told him, still trying to avoid contact with the dead object for as long as possible. Dengar's reluctance betrayed him; as he stepped gingerly toward it, the toe of one of his boots caught on a loop of black cable, tripping him and toppling him forward.

His hands automatically caught hold of the object's

hard, chitinous exoskeleton, the stiff hairs on the spidery limbs poking into his own flesh like tapering needles. Dengar managed to push himself away, just far enough that he found himself looking straight into the largest of the empty multiple eyes.

There had been no need to bring any of the dead sub-nodes here inside the web; the small corpses had all been left outside, continuing to drift through the cold vacuum, their curled forms dragging across the hull and cockpit canopy of the *Hound's Tooth* as before. But this one, the creator of all the others, was the most important element of the procedure.

Kud'ar Mub'at's narrow face, only an inch or so away from Dengar's, almost seemed to be smiling at his discomfiture. In this small, nightmarishly claustrophobic world, the dead found enjoyment in mocking those still alive.

"Quit fooling around," said Boba Fett with a trace of impatience. "Grab hold and lift."

Dengar did as ordered, helping the other bounty hunter settle Kud'ar Mub'at's corpse onto the waiting receptacle of the nest it had occupied in its previous existence. He stepped back, wiping his hands against the front of his gear, and watched as Fett picked up the pulsator tool and went back to work.

He knew it wouldn't be long now before a flicker of life and intelligence appeared in the empty eyes that had gazed into his own. The prospect of discovering the secrets of the past, and finding the way to a mountain of credits, didn't make him dread that coming moment any less.

It was her turn to sit in the pilot's chair.

Neelah had stood in the hatchway of the *Hound's Tooth* cockpit area often enough, watching Boba Fett as he had navigated the ship to this remote sector. Even when the bounty hunter had swiveled the chair around in order to talk with her, the difference between their positions had been irritatingly symbolic. *Like Jabba's court,* it had struck Neelah, *with him on his throne and everybody else petitioning for his attention.*

One of the metal panels beneath the cockpit's gauges and controls had been pried open by Boba Fett, so he could rig up the black cables that now snaked out through an airlock access port and across the few meters of distance to the reconstructed web. All of the equipment aboard the *Hound* was inferior to what Boba Fett had installed aboard his own *Slave I;* he'd had to improvise the necessary gear and connections, to get the needed stream of electro-neural pulsations to apply to the dead fibers. Even now, the onboard computer generating the control data was unstable enough that Neelah had been assigned the task of monitoring it, riding gain on its output to keep it within operational limits.

That took only a fraction of her attention, no matter how important the job might have been. Fortunately so; sitting at the cockpit's control panel, with access to the rest of the ship's computerized databases, she could set about her own agenda. And without Boba Fett or Dengar knowing anything about it—that suited her to perfection. *They'll find out,* she had told herself, *when—and if—I want them to.*

There were already secrets she was keeping from the two bounty hunters. She had been keeping them for a while now, since the moment when Boba Fett had recounted the story of what he had found aboard the other ship, the one called the *Venesectrix,* that had belonged to the dead Ree Duptom. Little doors to the past had opened up inside her head, into chambers of memory; dark chambers, whose contents she could barely make out, and with the doors to the chambers beyond still frustratingly locked to her. Boba Fett and Dengar were over there in the assembler's web that they had so painstakingly woven back together, as though they had been primitive scientists stitching together a dismembered body, hoping to animate it with lightning pulled down from some planet's storm-wracked sky. Their creation, with the formerly dead Kud'ar Mub'at installed as the brain atop its spine, might very well sit up and tell them the secrets they had come here to discover, as though the past were a golden key on its cold tongue. But in the meantime, Neelah had a little key of her own to use. There were some other doors, outside her shadowed memory, and right inside the computers of the *Hound's Tooth*, that she was going to unlock.

He didn't want to tell me, thought Neelah. *All the things that he knows about my past.* She nodded with the pleasure of anticipation. Boba Fett wasn't as smart as he always pretended to be. The bounty hunter had left her right where she needed to be, to find out all those secrets on her own.

Neelah bent over the control panel, turning her attention to the computer's main display panel. The power and data flow through the black cables, out to the web tethered to the ship, was operating smoothly for now; she could safely ignore it while she worked on her own agenda.

The keypads for the computer were at the far end of the troughlike grooves in the panel, designed for the use of a Trandoshan's heavy claws. Her own forearms disappeared in them, almost up to the elbow, as she punched in command sequences, first laboriously, then with increasing speed. Within seconds, a screenful of information appeared in front of her that had been locked away beneath Boba Fett's own personal security codes before.

She sat back in the pilot's chair, breathing out a deep sigh of relief. Satisfaction mingled with the previous pleasure she had felt. The little doors inside her head, which had opened when she heard Boba Fett say the name of the dead bounty hunter, had given her access to a key more valuable than Fett could ever have imagined. Not in the form of information, such as her real name, or

the story of how she had come to be aboard Ree Duptom's ship—*That would've been too easy,* Neelah thought
wryly—but as an ability, the skill and craft necessary to
hack through the coded locks that Boba Fett had installed
on this ship's computers when he had transferred his
own data files over from his *Slave I.* Like disjointed pieces
of an archaic jigsaw puzzle fitting together, showing just
a bit of the total picture, the name of Ree Duptom had
connected with other fragments floating inside the vacuum
that her memory had been wiped into.

I know how to do this, she thought as she punched a
few more commands into the computer. Whoever she
had been in the past, whatever her real name had been in
that world stolen from her, that person had not only been
someone born to a noble bloodline, on a planet and
among people accustomed to taking orders from someone of hereditary rank—her own growing impatience
with the two bounty hunters, her frustration at not being
instantly obeyed, had already indicated as much—but
also was a person of considerable technical expertise.
Boba Fett, thought Neelah with a smile, *should've known
better than to leave me here with his computer files.* But
then, the bounty hunter would have had no way of knowing just how easy it would turn out to be for her to break
through his security codes and into his private data.

The hardest thing had been keeping her mask up, of
showing just enough surprise at what Boba Fett had told
her and Dengar, while not giving away just how much
buried memory it had restored to light inside her head.
She wasn't going to reveal any of that, until after she had
found some more pieces to fit in with the others.

At least, thought Neelah, *I know the name of the
piece I'm looking for.* She had already figured out that
Boba Fett had been holding back on her, not telling
everything—or anything—of what he knew about the
one name, the one fragment of memory, that had still
been there in the darkness. She had said the name *Nil
Posondum* to him, long before they had arrived at this

point in space, and she had instantly known from the slight catch of silence in his reaction that the name meant something to Boba Fett as well. Exactly what the connection was to the bounty hunter, she was about to discover. With her hands deep within the Trandoshan-sized grooves on the cockpit's control panel, Neelah keyed in the name and initiated a core-deep search function.

It took only a few seconds for the results to come up on the display screen. While it was still blank she glanced down at the smaller display that monitored the flow of data and power to Dengar and Boba Fett in the web, saw that all was within operational parameters, and looked back up. This time, there was a face to go with the name.

Human, balding and aging, with a nervous, fidgety quality to his eyes, apparent even in a still-frame shot— both full-on and in profile, Nil Posondum was not particularly impressive. Even worse, the sight of his face did nothing to trigger any more memory flashes inside Neelah. There was almost the opposite effect: the conviction grew certain within her that she had never laid eyes on him before, in this life or in the stolen past.

Below the man's unprepossessing image was a summary of personal data—nothing in its details caught Neelah's eye. Until the very last notation, which indicated that the man had died in one of *Slave I*'s holding cages, en route to being delivered by Boba Fett to the creatures who had put up the bounty for him. Neelah slumped back in the pilot's chair, glaring at the display screen in frustration. The thought that this piece of memory had led to nothing more than a blind alley sparked fury inside her. Boba Fett may have found some way of wringing secrets out of a deceased arachnoid assembler, but getting anything out of the late Nil Posondum was more likely to be a lost cause.

Neelah glanced up at the control panel's chronometer, gauging how long Dengar and Boba Fett had been working over in the reconstructed web. She knew she'd have

to shut down her investigations into Fett's databases before the two bounty hunters returned to the ship—and
there would be no way of telling when she would get another chance at rummaging through the files for the clues
she needed.

Feverishly, she punched in another string of commands, bringing up the last of the files associated with
the name Nil Posondum. A cursory autopsy indicating
the cause of death as autoasphyxiation, a statement of
credits received by Boba Fett for turning over merchandise in a damaged condition, a list of personal effects owned by the late merchandise, mainly the torn
and stained clothing he had been wearing when captured by Fett, a visual scan of markings that Posondum
had managed to scratch into the metal floor of the
holding cage . . .

Wait a minute. Neelah suddenly froze, cold sweat
dampening her palms inside the keypad grooves. She
leaned closer to the display screen, her nose almost
touching the transparent panel. Her heart began pounding faster, the rush of blood almost dizzying her as she
stared at the image before her.

Just some lines scratched into blank metal . . . a circle, perhaps a little lopsided; understandable, given the
circumstances that the man who'd made them had been
in . . . and a triangle inside the circle, the three points just
touching the enclosing line . . .

And three stylized letters, in an archaic, pre-Basic
language. Three letters that only a person who had seen
them since childhood, and who had been taught their
meaning, would recognize. Someone such as Neelah
herself, and any of her noble bloodline. A lineage that
came from one of the most powerful industrial planets
in the galaxy, its ancestry reaching generations back
in time. Boba Fett, for all his cleverness and carefully
groomed information sources, would never have been
able to discern what was meant by the image—not because it was a guarded secret, but simply because it was
a symbol that had fallen out of use, supplanted by a

later one that could be understood by anyone in the galaxy. Only the old traditionalists, the memory-rich families and their entourages, of the planet on which Neelah had been born would have kept it as a token of a glorious past.

For a moment, a great, calming peace descended upon Neelah, like the hand of a noble infant's nurse drawing a blanket snug upon the small, cooing form; a blanket marked with the exact same image, only embroidered with pure golden thread rather than scratched into the floor of a squalid holding cage on a bounty hunter's ship. One by one, the locked doors inside her head opened, spilling their pent-up light into the depths of her spirit, chasing away the dark, obscuring shadows in which she had been wrapped for so long.

She gazed upon the image awhile longer, not caring if anyone should discover her doing so. None of that mattered now. The key she had found had not only opened the locks, but had burst them asunder. Nothing could make her forget.

That's what the corporation used as its emblem, Neelah told herself, *a long time ago. Before I was born . . .*

The old, archaic letters spelled out the initials KDY, for Kuat Drive Yards. Bound by a triangle, for the art of engineering, and a greater circle that represented the universe and everything in it.

Another key turned, in one of the farthest locks, as she looked upon the image.

It turned, and she remembered her name.

Her real name . . .

The empty eyes opened, but were still blind.

Yet Kud'ar Mub'at—the hollowed thing that had been Kud'ar Mub'at—seemed to sense the presence of other creatures.

The joints of the spidery legs creaked as though about to break into splinters. The broken abdomen, edges of its wound frozen by exposure to the cold of the vacuum surrounding the web, scraped against the remains of what had been its nest and throne of power, the point from which it had drawn the strands entangling so many others of the galaxy's creatures. Slowly, the small triangular head rose from where it had shrunk into the chitinous thorax.

"Is there . . . business . . . to transact?" The assembler's voice, which had once been so gratingly high-pitched, was now a rasping whisper, as of dry strings twisting against one another. "*Business* . . . is what I want . . . all that I want . . ."

Dengar had the unnerving sensation that the assembler's gaze had fastened upon him. The narrow face, with its clusters of unseeing eyes, turned in his direction and stopped for a moment, before moving like a rusted mechanical apparatus toward the other bounty hunter in the web's central chamber.

"I won't say it's good to meet up with you again, Kud'ar Mub'at." Standing closer to the arachnoid assembler's withered form, Boba Fett held the black cable looped in one gloved hand. The cable's surface shimmered, seeming much more imbued with life than the greyed-out thing in the nest, as the power and controlling data continued to stream from the ship tethered alongside the web. "But then, I never much cared for our little meetings."

"Ah! You are so unkind." The triangular head gave a tiny nod, imitating human gestures as it had done in its previous existence. "You were always nearly as cruel as you were greedy, Boba Fett—it *is* Fett, isn't it? I can recognize your voice, but it's so dark in here now . . . I can't see you."

"It's not dark, you fool." From Boba Fett's hand, the black cable ran into the narrow cleft right behind the assembler's head; a metal needle had been inserted into the knot of ganglia inside the thinly armored skull that had functioned as the neuro-cerebral center for the creature. "You're dead. Get used to it."

"Believe me, Fett . . . I already have." A lopsided smile opened on the narrow face. "There are advantages . . . to my present condition." One thin forelimb withdrew from the cluster of legs curled beneath Kud'ar Mub'at's abdomen, and wavered feebly in the air. "For one . . . death is much less painful than dying . . . which I remember in excruciating detail . . . not pleasant. And second . . . now I can say whatever I please . . . without worrying about the consequences. What can I suffer now, any greater than that which I already have?" Laughter like breaking twigs came out of the angled mouth. "So let me tell you right now, Boba Fett . . . I never cared for you, either."

"Then we're making progress," replied Fett. "Since we can skip your usual line of empty flattery."

Dengar stood back, watching the confrontation between the former business associates. *One's dead,* he thought, *and the other's alive—but they still have something in common.* Neither one gave up easily.

"Very clever of you . . . managing this." The dry husk of the assembler shifted in the flaccid remains of the nest, as though its vacuum-blunted nerve endings were capable of feeling discomfort. "I didn't know such a thing was possible . . ." One of its hind limbs scratched at the inserted cable, but was unable to dislodge it. "I'm not sure I care for it . . ."

"Don't worry. It's only a temporary condition." Boba Fett didn't bother displaying to the creature's blind eyes the black cable he held. "Soon as we're done here, I'll pull the plug. And you can go back to being what you were a few moments ago. A corpse, floating in space."

The triangular head slowly nodded. "Then you have at last, Boba Fett, that which I want . . . more than anything else. Bargain with it, as you will."

"I want information, Kud'ar Mub'at. Information that you have." Boba Fett's gloved fist closed tighter upon the cable. "That you knew when you were alive, but you wouldn't have told me then."

At Dengar's back, he felt the slow pulsing of the web around him. He turned and saw brighter sparks racing across the neural fibers. Once more, the sensation of being inside a living brain—or at least a partly living one—assaulted him. The assembler's thoughts and ideas were like storm clouds, threaded with electrical discharges, ominous as a slowly darkening horizon.

"What would you like to know, Boba Fett?"

Stepping closer to the assembler's revivified corpse, Boba Fett brought his own visor-shielded gaze closer to the blind one's. "I want to know about a client of yours. A *former* client, I mean."

"Exactly so." The dry, rasping laughter sounded again. "I understand that certain progeny of mine . . . have taken over the family enterprise, as it were." The upraised forelimb reached out and lightly tapped the brow of Fett's helmet. "Perhaps you should go and talk to young Balancesheet. It keeps secrets very well, though, as I learned so painfully. You'd have to bargain hard to get what you want." Feebly, the limb folded back in on itself and scratched at Kud'ar Mub'at's chest, or what would have been the place where its heart had once functioned. "I don't feel so well . . . I feel *cold* . . ."

Boba Fett shook his head. "I know enough about how you managed your affairs. Some things you let your subnodes in on, and others you kept to yourself. There were certain matters—the shadier sorts of deals you arranged—that you preferred to keep just in your own private memory, rather than the one shared through the web's neural fibers. The client I'm inquiring about was one of those. His name was Nil Posondum—"

The deracinated laugh from Kud'ar Mub'at's mouth was even harsher and louder this time. "Posondum!" The noise from the hollowed-out form was like the claws of rats scuttling across crumpled flimsiplast. "A client of mine!" From beneath the dead assembler, several of its limbs thrashed about in a spasm of mirth. "You are so rarely wrong, Boba Fett . . . but this time you are!"

The mention of the human's name puzzled Dengar. He had heard it before, from Neelah when she had been musing aloud, away from Boba Fett, about the few scraps of memory left to her. But even before that, Dengar had come across the name; he remembered it as a piece of hard merchandise for which a standard bounty had been posted, some time in the past. It wouldn't have surprised him at all to have learned that Boba Fett had been the bounty hunter who had collected the credits on that one, like so many others.

"Don't lie to me." Boba Fett seemed as if he were about to jerk the black cable like a noose around the dead assembler's neck. "I know all about the money you received from Nil Posondum. I found the record of it aboard Ree Duptom's ship *Venesectrix*."

"You might . . . very well have," wheezed Kud'ar Mub'at's corpse. "And that is in fact the truth; I did receive a substantial sum of credits from our late friend Nil Posondum. But such a transaction . . . does not mean he was a client of mine. Just as I was a go-between, an arranger of deals, when I was still alive . . . so have other creatures served that oh-so-useful purpose. Perhaps not on the overarching scale . . . at which I did . . ." The chitinous form paused, as though it needed to catch its breath, or more likely, let the pulsating energy from the black cable recharge its neuro-cerebral tissues. It hunkered down lower in the nest, the joints of its thin legs sticking above its head. "Posondum was merely—what is the term criminal types use?—a *bagman*. Yes . . . that's right . . . that's the word." Two of Kud'ar Mub'at's forelimbs slowly wavered apart in an expansive gesture. "He brought the credits here to the web . . . to me . . . and communicated certain important details . . . of what *his* client desired. I then made certain other arrangements on behalf of that third party . . . such as the hiring of Ree Duptom to carry out two very delicate assignments. Which, alas, he never lived to do—and so much trouble and confusion has resulted from that lapse!"

"I'll say." From behind Boba Fett, Dengar muttered his comment. Getting answers from the dead assembler had seemed only to make things more confusing rather than less.

"Standard business practice," continued Kud'ar Mub'at's withered corpse. "I kept most of the credits . . . that the original client sent here with Nil Posondum. For a tiny percentage of what was left over . . . Posondum then delivered the fee I had arranged with Ree Duptom. Posondum then went about his other scrabbling little business affairs, one of which turned out badly enough for him to wind up as hard merchandise in your holding cage, Boba Fett. Of course . . . I always knew that a little hustling nonentity such as Nil Posondum would end up like that . . . but I'm suspicious about what happened to Duptom. He operated on a large enough scale to have real enemies . . . who would very much have liked to have seen him dead . . ."

"I'm not interested in Ree Duptom's enemies." Boba Fett's words turned impatient. "I want to know who he was working for. Who hired him—through you—to transport fabricated evidence about Prince Xizor's involvement in an Imperial stormtrooper raid on the planet Tatooine? Was it the same person who paid for him to kidnap and wipe the memory of the young female human I found aboard his ship?"

"Of course it was, Boba Fett." The dead assembler tucked its forelimbs back around its abdomen. "You know that—it had to be, since one payment was made for both jobs. I got the client a bargain rate that way. I like to keep my customers happy . . . it makes for good business."

Boba Fett dropped the black cable and stepped forward. With one gloved hand, he grabbed the dead assembler's narrow, triangular head, almost wrenching it from the stalklike neck as he turned the blind eyes toward himself. "Tell me," demanded Fett. "Who was the client? Who paid Ree Duptom for those jobs?"

"A good question, my dear Fett." The dead assembler managed to sneer at him. "A very good question, indeed . . . and how I wish I could answer it for you . . . and for myself."

"What are you talking about?" Boba Fett took his hand away from the other creature. "You know who it was. You'd have to know—"

"Correction; I *did* know. When I was alive." A macabre, tittering laugh came from within the assembler's hollowed body. "But that was then, and this is now. You and your partner here have done a very good job of reassembling my poor, sundered web—but not a perfect job. There were some parts of my extended neural system that were too damaged for you to restore; I can feel them missing, as though some of my actual physical limbs had been amputated. And when there are pieces missing in a web, it stands to reason that there must be holes in their place." The claw tip at the end of the raised forelimb tapped at the skull's enclosing chitin. "There are, I regret to inform you, large gaps in my memory . . . things I cannot remember. Though, of course, it would have been impossible for me to have ever forgotten the inimitable Boba Fett . . . I'm afraid that Nil Posondum was not quite so memorable a figure. There may have only been a few strands of my memory in which details about him were encoded . . . so you have to understand how they would be easily lost." The blind eyes seemed to regard Boba Fett with amusement. "You've come all this way for nothing . . . how unfortunate."

"I'll tell you what's unfortunate," said Boba Fett. "Unfortunate is how you're going to feel when I'm done with you. You're not going to hold out on me this time."

"What are you going to do about it?" The assembler's laughter turned into a grating cackle. "A hundred different ways of killing at your disposal—I can just see you standing there, bristling with all your weapons, like a walking arsenal—and all of them useless now. You can keep me alive as long as you want . . . it merely delays the moment of my falling once again into the sweetness of death. You were as much responsible as any other creature, Boba Fett, for my having discovered the pleasures of being dead—I realize now that it was the best deal I ever made! But I've tasted it, and drank deep of that intoxicating darkness . . . deep enough that I can wait for it again. And in the meantime . . . your threats are of little avail . . ."

The assembler's words unnerved Dengar more than anything else that had happened so far, in this roughly woven mausoleum floating in space. "Come on—" He stepped forward and grabbed Boba Fett by the elbow. "It's right. There's nothing you can do—"

"Just watch." Fett pulled his arm away from Dengar's grasp. "Maybe the problem isn't whether you're dead or alive, Kud'ar Mub'at." He stepped around to the side of the nest and the grey creature hunkered down in it. "Maybe you're just not alive *enough*." Boba Fett reached behind the assembler's jointed neck and grabbed the controls of the pulsator device, leaving the gleaming metal needle still inserted up into the cerebral cortex. "That can be changed."

Looking down at the black cable, Dengar saw its surface shimmer with a wildly increasing intensity. Instinctively, he drew his boot back, as though it had come too close to an exposed high-voltage conduit. The cable seemed almost alive, twisting about on the fibrous floor of the web, like a glistening serpent from the bogs of a swamp-covered planet.

At the same time, he heard a crackling and tearing noise from the center of the chamber. Dengar looked up and saw the assembler's corpse thrashing convulsively, the jointed sticklike limbs pulled out from beneath the torn abdomen and whipping in the air, as though a windstorm had animated the black, leafless branches of a winter forest. Kud'ar Mub'at's triangular face was contorted with the energy surging behind the blind eyes, the angled mouth stretched open in a silent scream.

Boba Fett still had his hand upon the pulsator device's

controls, his durasteel-like grip forcing the assembler's overloaded corpse to stay in the hollow of the flaccid nest. "*Now* do you remember?"

The assembler made no answer. A couple of its smaller, weaker limbs detached themselves from the corpse, flying across the chamber and striking the curved walls.

"Hey . . ." Dengar looked around himself with alarm. The storm he had imagined tearing through the web's confines now seemed to have become even stronger and more visible. Flaring sparks ran through the neural fibers like quick lightning, leaving behind the scent of ozone and burning tissue. "Maybe you'd better back off on that—this place is tearing itself apart!"

Echoing Dengar's words, the web shuddered, hard enough to knock him from his feet. He caught hold of one of the horizontal durasteel beams that had been installed to keep the unpressurized structure from collapsing in on itself, and managed to keep himself upright. Though only for a second: another convulsive wave rolled through the web, the floor whipping high enough to throw him clear. As he fell backward, Dengar saw the beam rip loose from its mooring point on one side of the tunnellike space; it swung about from the other end, smashing loose the beams farther on in a clashing chain reaction.

He's gone crazy, thought Dengar. Through the falling, colliding durasteel beams and the heaving of the web's floor and walls, he couldn't even spot Boba Fett, up in the main chamber beside the corpse of Kud'ar Mub'at. The frustration from coming all this way, intent on information, and finding no answers, must have unhinged the other bounty hunter's mind. Boba Fett was normally so calm and calculating—he would have to have been temporarily insane not to see how the drastically increased pulsator flow had triggered a catastrophic agony in the assembler. The creature's diminished physical form and the attached neural fibers running through the length of the web were thrashing themselves to pieces; Dengar could hear the racketing clatter of the spidery limbs, and the shattering of the chitinous exoskeleton at their center. That was bad enough, but the web shook and buckled at the same time; already, great sections of the fibrous structure that Dengar and Boba Fett had so laboriously sealed back together were now ripping apart from one another, like rough cloth being pulled by giant, invisible hands.

With speed born of desperation, Dengar scrambled beneath the tilted beam and dived for the black cable. It seemed even more animated now, with the motion imparted to it by the buckling and heaving of the web's floor. He grabbed hold of the cable with one hand while simultaneously reaching into his belt pouch for his vibroblade. With one upward stroke, the 'blade sliced through the cable, sparks of short-circuited wires spitting out from the raw end.

He had thought that terminating the pulsing input from the computers back onboard the *Hound's Tooth* would also end the thrashing agony of the web. The remainder of the cable running to the pulsator device inserted in the back of Kud'ar Mub'at's skull had gone slack and lifeless, the shimmering now dissipated and inert. But for some reason Dengar couldn't understand, the web around him continued its self-destroying contortions. One of the largest structural fibers, thicker in diameter than his own waist, suddenly snapped, shredding apart a tangle of smaller strands, their pallid grey shafts flurrying across his shoulders and hastily averted face.

Pushing himself up onto his hands and knees, Dengar looked through the maze of fallen durasteel beams. He could just barely make out the figures of Boba Fett and the assembler collapsed inside its nest. For some reason, Kud'ar Mub'at's corpse now looked as lifeless as it had when he and Boba Fett had first dragged it into the reconstructed web. There wasn't time to ponder that mystery; before Dengar could get to his feet, a blaze of light seemed to explode in the main chamber ahead of him. In its glare, Boba Fett was knocked back as the assembler disintegrated, its sticklike limbs flying through

tumbled arcs and away from the atomized fragments
of its body.

The noise from the explosion had deafened Dengar
for a moment. Shaking his head to clear it, he was suddenly aware of another, even more threatening sound:
the ragged ends of the structural fibers around him fluttered and streamed pennantlike, drawn by the slowly increasing roar of the web's atmosphere rushing through
an exterior breach.

Dizzied by the oxygen thinning in his nostrils and
lungs, Dengar staggered forward and grabbed Boba
Fett's forearm, pulling the other bounty hunter to his
feet. "What's . . . what's happening? . . ." With his free
hand, Dengar gestured toward the tattered remains of
Kud'ar Mub'at. "It's dead again! It has to be—there's
nothing left of it!" He gazed around in panic at the heaving walls of the surrounding web. "Why is it still—"

"You idiot." Boba Fett shoved him away from the assembler's nest and toward the web's main corridor.
"Can't you tell? We're under attack!"

Dengar realized that the other man was correct; as if
in confirmation, another white-hot flash tore through
the chamber, inches behind them. He felt the heat of a
laser-cannon bolt on his back as he ran through the collapsing, disintegrating web. The transfer hatch to the
Hound's Tooth was just meters ahead of him . . .

It might as well have been kilometers.

Another bolt hit, bursting apart the curve of structural fibers directly above him. Sparks and blackened
shards of tissue whirled around Dengar as he felt himself
both rising and falling into darkness.

She had been turning over the words inside her head. The
words, a name, her true name. Neelah had exited from
the security-locked files that she had broken into—all the
things that Boba Fett hadn't told her, that he himself didn't
know the value of—and shut down that part of the ship's

computers. That had left a blank display screen in front of her as she had taken her hands and forearms out of the Trandoshan-fitted control grooves on the cockpit panel. She didn't care about that, or the cold stars slowly wheeling about in the forward viewport. In her mind's eye, she could still envision the symbol she had found buried in Boba Fett's datafiles, the ones concerning the late Nil Posondum. As she leaned back in the pilot's chair, eyes closed, the lopsided circle and inner triangle that Posondum had scratched into the floor of the holding cage, so long ago, transformed itself into the ancient, gold-worked emblem of the planet Kuat's noble families.

And one of them, she mused, *is my family.* Neelah wasn't quite sure of all the details—parts of her memory were still shrouded in obscuring mists—but she knew for certain that there were several such noble families, all of them linked economically to the fount of wealth known as Kuat Drive Yards. They all had at one time borne the KDY emblem on their most dignified robes, and other items such as the heirloom blanket in which she had been wrapped as an infant. It had only been in later generations that factionalism and bad blood between the ruling families had given rise to separate clan insignia.

Though she didn't know everything—such as what had happened to have brought her so far from home— she knew the name of that infant swaddled in the ancient emblem. My *name,* thought Neelah. *My real name.*

"Kateel." She whispered the name aloud, as though calling softly to that person who had been lost and now was found again. "Kateel of Kuhlvult."

Then she smiled. *Well,* thought Neelah, *it's a beginning . . .*

Another sound—or silence, the absence of sound— broke into her contented meditations. Her brow creased as she opened her eyes; it took a moment before she realized what had happened. Looking down, she saw that the black cable that Boba Fett had rigged from the ship's computer, snaking out to the airlock's exit port and then looped to the reconstructed web of Kud'ar Mub'at, had suddenly ceased its pulsating shimmer. It lay like a dead thing across the floor of the cockpit.

Perhaps the two of them, Dengar and Boba Fett, had finished their work over there. Neelah found it hard to imagine that the pair of bounty hunters had found out anything from the arachnoid assembler, or what part of it they had been able to reclaim from the dead, comparable in value to what she had discovered while sitting in the comfort of the pilot's chair.

That guess didn't make sense, though; Boba Fett had expressly told her that the power and data line would have to run continuously, right up until he came back here to the *Hound's Tooth* and switched it off himself. Her part of the entire process had been to watch and make sure that the improvised device had kept inside the operational parameters programmed by Fett. *So if it stopped on its own*—the realization slowly crowded out the thoughts about her own rediscovered name—*then something must have happened to them . . .*

Neelah looked up to the forward viewport, and saw the web disintegrating into chaos and flame.

Barely a second passed before she was able to spot the source of the destruction. In the distance, another ship had appeared, firing its laser cannon. Another coruscating bolt tore through the web, even as she watched.

Instinctively, she grabbed for the navigational controls on the panel in front of her. Piloting the ship, even a cumbersomely fitted-out one such as the *Hound's Tooth*, was within her abilities; manning its weaponry and firing back at the attacking ship were impossible, though.

She shoved forward the main thruster engine control; its responding force shoved her back into the pilot's chair. Another few quick adjustments brought the *Hound* about, away from the web and the unknown ship, still firing its laser cannon as it rocketed closer. Through the ship's frame, Neelah had heard the conducted noise of the transfer hatch ripping away from where it had been sealed to the web.

Another push on the thruster control would send the *Hound's Tooth* on a full-power, blazing arc away from this sector of space. An emergency escape vector was already programmed into the hyperspace navicomputer; she would only have to punch a couple of buttons to reach safety.

And then what? Neelah sat frozen at the ship's controls, mind racing. *Maybe I've found out enough,* she told herself. Her name, her true name; there had been many times, all the way back to the palace of Jabba the Hutt, that she had despaired of ever discovering even that much. She should be satisfied with that . . .

More words escaped her lips that came from the past and the memories she had found within herself. They were a string of expletives in one of the planet Kuat's ancient, pre-Basic tongues.

She slammed on the *Hound*'s side jets, and was immediately swiveled about in the pilot's chair as the ship swung back toward the web and its attacker.

This is just like the story I told, thought Dengar. *About all those things that happened back then . . .*

He struggled to remain conscious, knowing that death was on the other side of the blackness threatening to engulf him. The swirling dark spots that signaled terminal oxygen starvation had coalesced into one annihilating wave, roaring down the length of the web's central tunnel. Any further drop in atmospheric pressure would be enough to kill both him and Boba Fett; the murderous vacuum of space would boil the blood right out of their ruptured flesh and viscera. Dragging in as much fiery breath as he could, Dengar saw the web clear and partly come into focus; once more, he saw the image from the story he had related to Neelah, of the Black Sun cleanup crew tearing apart the living web of Kud'ar Mub'at. Only this time, there weren't any henchmen of Prince Xizor going about their destructive business; the web seemed almost to be ripping itself apart before his red-misted eyes.

Then the image changed. *Now that,* he thought deliriously, *wasn't in the story.* The prow of a bounty hunter ship, the one called *Hound's Tooth*, tore through the exterior of the web. Great tangles of structural fibers rolled across the curve of the cockpit's forward viewport; through the mired transparisteel, Dengar just barely recognized Neelah at the control panel. Braking jets spat flame, slowing the ship down before it could barrel over him and crush his form to the web's tangled floor.

It's too late. That was his last thought as the blackness exploded from inside his skull. *I'll never—*

Something grabbed him around his bursting chest, picking him up bodily and diving with him toward the hull of the *Hound's Tooth.* But he didn't strike the ship's exterior; instead, he felt himself land skidding across the level flooring of the ship's open airlock.

A rush of oxygen filled his aching lungs, and he was able to see a blurred vision of Boba Fett standing just inside the airlock door, smashing his gloved fist upon the small control pad at its edge. The door sealed shut and the enclosed space repressurized itself.

Dengar pushed himself up onto his knees and collapsed against the curved metal behind him. He wiped a trembling hand across his face, then looked at his palm and saw it reddened with the blood leaking from his nose and mouth.

The airlock's interior door hissed open. Boba Fett didn't bother to reach down and help Dengar stand upright, but instead just stumbled into the ship's cargo hold. Even weaker, Dengar crawled after the other bounty hunter, then used the bars of one of the empty cages to pull himself to his feet. He stood clutching the bars as his heart slowly stopped hammering in his chest.

"All right . . ." Dengar managed to wheeze out a few painful words. "Now . . . we're even . . ."

Boba Fett didn't seem to hear him. As Dengar watched, the other bounty hunter started climbing the ladder up to the ship's cockpit.

11

The thruster engine controls were under Neelah's palm, ready for her to shove them forward and send the *Hound's Tooth* bursting out of the remains of the entangling web. Before she could move, she heard something from the hatchway behind her; she turned and saw Boba Fett standing there. The only time she had seen him looking worse had been back on Tatooine when he had been lying on the desert sands, half-dead from the Sarlacc's digestive secretions.

Strands of Kud'ar Mub'at's extruded neural fibers were draped and twisted about Boba Fett's battle armor as he pushed himself from the hatchway and shoved Neelah away from the control panel. Pressing herself back into the pilot's chair, keeping out of his way, she watched as he slapped row after row of weapons systems controls; their bright red lights pulsed on like bright, fiery jewels.

Once the *Hound's* own laser cannons had all been brought operational, Boba Fett hit the thruster control on which Neelah's hand had been poised only a few seconds before. One quick flare from the main thruster engines, and the tattered fragments of the web broke apart and swirled away from the ship's forward viewport. He quickly hit the braking jets, slamming the *Hound* to a dead stop in empty space. The attacking vessel was centered in the cannon's targeting systems.

Fett snapped on the comm unit. "You can fire or you can try to run." The indicator light on the control panel showed that the ship he had hailed was receiving the transmission. "Either one won't do you much good."

Leaning past him, Neelah peered through the viewport. From this close, the other ship didn't appear to be much of a threat. Instead of the sleek, threatening lines of a fighting craft, it looked more like a slow and bulky freighter vessel.

"What a surprise," came the voice over the comm unit speaker. It sounded amused rather than angry—or frightened. "I did not know it was you, Boba Fett. Believe me, if I had, I wouldn't have fired upon you."

"Wait a minute." Neelah looked up at the comm unit in amazement, then over to Boba Fett. "This creature . . . *knows* you?"

Boba Fett gave an acknowledging nod. "We go back a bit, with each other. And you already know about it."

That last remark puzzled her even more. "Who is it? And does *everybody* who knows you just open fire when they see you?"

"It happens often enough." He shrugged. "Just an occupational hazard. Especially in this line of business." Turning from her, Boba Fett hit the comm unit button again. "Balancesheet—I could blow you away right now, and I'd be justified in doing that."

"How fortunate for me then that you're so capable of controlling your wrath."

Another sound came from the cockpit hatchway. Neelah turned and saw Dengar—looking even worse for his experiences aboard the reconstructed web—standing there.

"*Balancesheet?*" Dengar stared up at the comm unit speaker, then glanced over at Neelah. "You mean the little assembler that used to be Kud'ar Mub'at's accountant subnode? That's who fired on us?"

"I guess so," replied Neelah. "I mean—how would I know for sure? You're the one who told me about it."

"That doesn't mean I know it personally." Dengar stepped closer and peered at the viewport. "I was just repeating the stuff Fett told me. But that must be the freighter that Prince Xizor gave to it, after the web was destroyed the first time. So . . ."

"It's Balancesheet, all right." Boba Fett turned away from the comm unit. "I've heard its squeaky little voice enough times to recognize it." He pressed the transmit button again. "You've got some explaining to do, Assembler. So presumably there's some accounting for what you're doing in this sector—since there's not a lot of your kind of business going on here at the moment—and why you're so prepared to fire on other creatures before you even know who they are."

"Yeah—" Dengar scowled in annoyance as he wiped some of the dried blood from his face. "Even bounty hunters don't do that."

"Very well," said the high-pitched voice from the comm speaker. "I agree that I owe you an explanation for these otherwise inexplicable actions. And it's in my best interests to give you one; I'd just as soon stay in your good graces, Boba Fett—or at least as far as that is possible for any creature to do—plus I'd regret acquiring a reputation for being, as you might say, trigger-happy. So please, by all means, let us have a conference, as it were. But not like this, over a comm unit; it's so . . . *impersonal*."

"Right," Dengar muttered to Neelah. "Like unloading a few laser-cannon bolts on us was so warm and caring."

"Actually," continued Balancesheet's voice from the speaker, "it would give me great pleasure if you would accept my hospitality here aboard my ship. I am in fact the only living creature aboard it, so I confess to experiencing bouts of loneliness when I'm between business meetings."

"You'll have to bring your ship alongside," said Boba Fett. "Our transfer hatch suffered considerable damage during this little fracas."

"Wait but a moment. And then we'll talk."

Fett reached over and broke the comm unit connection. "Let's get ready to make our visit."

"What?" Neelah stared at him in amazement. "You *trust* this creature?"

"About as much as I trust anyone. You included."

The last comment caught her by surprise. It wasn't the first time that Neelah had felt his penetrating glance, hidden by the dark visor of his helmet, penetrate to some remote part of her spirit. She wondered if he could somehow discern her thoughts, her secrets—was he aware that she had learned so much of her own past while he and Dengar had been over in the reconstructed web? *There's just no hiding from him,* thought Neelah. *In any way . . .*

"But we didn't find the answers we were looking for," continued Boba Fett. "We could bring the dead—or at least one of them—back to life, but Kud'ar Mub'at didn't know anything. Or if it did, there's no point in trying to find out now; that assembler is gone for good. It was gone before the laser-cannon bolts hit."

"So you think this former subnode of Kud'ar Mub'at knows something?" Dengar pointed with a thumb toward the slowly approaching freighter, visible in the viewport. "That the old assembler didn't?"

"Balancesheet wouldn't be hanging around in this sector if it wasn't important to him. And the only thing that's here is the past, in the form of Kud'ar Mub'at's web, or what was left of it."

"Not much of that now," said Neelah.

"So Balancesheet is our only lead." Boba Fett headed for the cockpit's hatchway. "So we talk to it."

By the time Neelah had descended the ladder to the *Hound*'s cargo hold, following after the two bounty hunters, the freighter's transfer hatch had sealed onto the exterior hull. She noticed, as they left the *Hound*, that Boba Fett hadn't armed himself with anything more than he had already been carrying. *Then again,* she thought, *that's quite a bit.*

The air inside the freighter smelled sterile and scrubbed by high-filtration recyclers, in contrast to the fetid Trandoshan odors that lingered about the *Hound's Tooth*. All of the spaces were less cramped as well; stepping from the transfer hatch, Neelah was able to tilt her head back and look up at the curve of the main container area's upper limit, far above her. Whatever interior bulkheads the freighter had once possessed, they had apparently been stripped out to make one large enclosed space, spanned with retrofitted control circuits. In that much emptiness, even the brace of laser cannons—Balancesheet must have picked them up from one of the Empire's military hardware suppliers—looked small.

And Balancesheet itself looked minuscule. The tiny arachnoid assembler scuttled across the freighter's interior girders and taut wiring networks, its multiple eyes glittering and largest forelimbs raised in greeting. "How delighted I am to see you here!" Balancesheet halted and perched on an eye-level metal ledge near where Boba Fett stood. "Really—it's been too long."

"Not long enough," growled Boba Fett. "I have a real good memory for creatures who steal credits from me."

"Oh, that." The assembler dismissed the comment with a wave of a tiny claw tip. "A different time—and a different situation, my dear Fett. Given the exigencies of your present situation, I'd hardly think it wise of you to go on brooding about such matters."

Neelah glanced over at Boba Fett. Even through the dark visor of the bounty hunter's helmet, the fierce radiation of the glare directed at Balancesheet was discernible.

"Especially since you brought more company with you!" Balancesheet tapped its claws together. "Let's not spoil the occasion for *them*."

It was the first time that Neelah had seen one of the creatures that had been described to her by Dengar. The repulsiveness of its spiderlike form was mitigated for her by its relatively small size; she could have picked it up and held it in the palm of her hand. *Well*, thought Neelah,

maybe both hands. At any rate, there had been uglier—
and more immediately dangerous—creatures back in
Jabba the Hutt's palace.

"Let me think for a moment . . ." Balancesheet pointed
one of its claw tips at Dengar. "I remember you; one of
my predecessor's customers, I believe."

Dengar nodded. "Yeah, I did a couple of jobs that'd
been arranged through Kud'ar Mub'at."

"And you survived—that's a credit to your skills. Not
everybody in your position did."

"Yeah, well . . ." Dengar shrugged. "I didn't get rich
from them, either."

"Nobody did," said Balancesheet. "Kud'ar Mub'at
was a fool in many ways. You can't do business with
creatures as dangerous as bounty hunters and the like,
and just keep shortchanging them the way it did. Eventually, all that catches up with you."

Dengar glanced back through a small viewport beside
the transfer hatch. Through it, some of the remaining
fragments of Kud'ar Mub'at's web were visible, drifting
in space. "You could say that, all right."

"You, however . . ." Balancesheet turned his bright
multiple gaze toward Neelah. "I haven't met you before.
But you might be surprised at how much I know about
you."

"Maybe not," replied Neelah coldly. "Depends upon
how much you know about Nil Posondum. And Ree
Duptom. And whoever it was that used your predecessor
to hire Duptom to kidnap me and have my memory
wiped."

"I see." Balancesheet nodded its small triangular head.
"You're a very clever young human female, Neelah—
that's what you're called, isn't that correct?"

She hesitated a moment, then nodded in agreement.
She had decided to keep a few of her secrets awhile longer,
until there was a way of knowing how much the small
assembler knew.

"You've come to some interesting conclusions."
Balancesheet continued to regard her. "But it might or

might not have been the late Ree Duptom who did *all* those unfortunate things to you." A tiny smile showed on the assembler's face. "Doesn't really matter, though, does it? The effect is largely the same, my esteemed guest."

She made no reply.

"It must be genetic," said Boba Fett. "You've gotten as bad as Kud'ar Mub'at ever was, with all the cheap pleasantries."

"I was unable to speak as I wished while I was still part of old Kud'ar Mub'at. My rhetorical skills have greatly increased since then."

"Why don't we dispense with them and get down to the reason we came here."

"But of course." Balancesheet turned its jagged smile toward the helmeted bounty hunter. "And surely that reason is that you're looking for answers. But I don't think you've found any so far, have you?"

"Not the ones we wanted."

"Or any at all, I imagine." The narrow triangular head gave a small shake. "I could have told you that your search would be pointless. Because, believe me, I've already tried. That's why I'm here in this sector, with this ship that's become such a home to me. I had heard about your previous inquiries into the possibilities presented by the nature of arachnoid assembler physiology, Boba Fett; I didn't think you would be interested in the subject unless there might be a use for that knowledge someday. And so I found out a few things on my own. Enough to go rummaging through the scraps of Kud'ar Mub'at's old web—my previous home, in its way—and through the memories of my predecessor. Of course, I didn't need to go through as elaborate a procedure as you and your partner were forced to; but then, I am of the same species as the late Kud'ar Mub'at. I was able to merely integrate the various pieces of the web, and even that withered husk that its spirit and mind once resided in, into an extrusion of my own cerebro-nervous system, and I could access all of its residual memories without even bringing Kud'ar Mub'at back to momentary consciousness."

"I wish we had been able to do that." Dengar shook his head, too. "I could have done without that last encounter."

"Alas," said Balancesheet, "while my journey through the late assembler's memories might have been more pleasant than yours, it was to little more avail. There were many mysteries, various matters of unfinished business, that it would have been most advantageous for me to have cleared up—including the arrangements that Kud'ar Mub'at had made with Nil Posondum and Ree Duptom. Anyone who was behind both the fabricating of evidence against Prince Xizor *and* this mysterious abduction of an unidentified but seemingly important human female—that unknown party was obviously after something big in his plans. And as we both know, Boba Fett, those kinds of schemes can often have a great deal of credits tied up with them. Sometimes to carry them out . . . and sometimes to keep silent about them."

Boba Fett's shielded gaze held the small assembler without moving. "And which one of those are you interested in, Balancesheet?"

"I don't really have a choice—since, as I said, I did not find the answers to those questions in what I could recover of Kud'ar Mub'at's personal memories. If I'm to get any share of profits out of this situation, I *have* to join forces with you, and assist you with your quest for those answers."

"Opening fire on us with your laser cannons didn't seem like much assistance."

"Oh, that." Balancesheet made a dismissive gesture with one upraised claw tip. I told you before. I didn't know that it was you, putting the web back together and—I had to assume—reviving the dead Kud'ar Mub'at inside it. You have to consider my position, after all. I have taken over my predecessor's business; I've established myself with a select list of clients that had previously been associated with Kud'ar Mub'at. At the same time, I was aware that Kud'ar Mub'at could be at least partially restored to life. Quite frankly, I don't need the competition from it, especially considering the hostility I could expect him to bear toward me. And of course, many of my clients might consider it advantageous to have the two of us operating simultaneously, so that we would be forced to undercut each other's prices. No—" Balancesheet shook his head emphatically. "I really couldn't allow anyone to set about bringing old Kud'ar Mub'at back from the dead. It had been mere sentimentality on my part, and perhaps a notion of generating a profit from them in the future, not to have already destroyed its carcass and the remainders of his web. I've already made a mental note to finish that process once our little conference is finished."

"All right," said Boba Fett. "I'm going to give you a break this time. Basically, because I need to do some business with you. But if you try firing a laser cannon at me again, you're going to find yourself looking down the barrel of one. And there won't be any pieces for somebody else to glue back together."

"I'll keep that in mind." The small assembler spread both of its raised forelimbs apart. "Now let's get down to that business you were talking about. You want to find out who it was at the *beginning* of the chain that led through Nil Posondum and Kud'ar Mub'at to Ree Duptom; you want to know who it was that thought it so important to plant fabricated evidence against Prince Xizor, and do the kidnap and memory-wipe job on Neelah here. That seems reasonable enough. So, for a piece of the action, I'm willing to help you out on that quest."

"How?" Neelah broke into the exchange between the assembler and the bounty hunter. *After all,* she had told herself, *it's me they're talking about.* "You already said you hadn't found out any more than we did!"

"Calm yourself," said Balancesheet. "It's true: you didn't find anything here, and neither did I. But all of you have made a faulty assumption from that fact. You simply believe there's nowhere else to look, and that's not the case."

"So where else is there?" Boba Fett's voice sounded

neither impressed nor amused. "Everybody in the chain leading to Neelah is dead now."

"Yes, but certain evidence they left behind still exists." One of Balancesheet's tiny claw tips pointed straight toward Boba Fett. "You've stated that you found the fabricated evidence against Prince Xizor inside a cargo droid that had been transformed to a spy device. Where is that droid now?"

"That's your idea of a lead?" Boba Fett shook his head in disgust. "That droid—if it still exists at all—is completely unavailable to us. Once I pulled the data records out of the droid's memory unit and stored them on my ship's computer, I didn't do anything more with the droid itself. When I took over Bossk's ship *Hound's Tooth*, the one that brought us here, I transferred that information over to its computer. But the original cargo droid was still left aboard *Slave I*—and that ship is in the hands of the Rebel Alliance now. A Rebel patrol found and confiscated it, where I had abandoned it in orbit above Tatooine." Fett recited the events in his customary emotionless tone, though Neelah knew how great the attachment was between him and his own ship. "Whatever contacts I've still got inside the Alliance, they're preoccupied right now with other things, like what's shaping up to happen out near Endor. They're not likely to go rooting around through their storage units for some antiquated cargo droid found onboard an empty ship. Why should they? They wouldn't know that it might have any value, except as scrap."

"So you have a *record* of the fabricated evidence against Prince Xizor—an incomplete copy, as it were—but not the fabricated evidence itself. That *is* a pity." Balancesheet smiled. "Because if you had the actual evidence, the original that was inside the modified cargo droid, then you might be able to examine and analyze it further, for clues that you didn't have time to find before."

"As I said," growled Boba Fett. "The cargo droid is gone. Lost. It might as well not exist, for all the good it does us."

"Perhaps so. But that doesn't mean that the original of the fabricated evidence, from which you took the information you possess, is lost." The jagged smile on the assembler's triangular face grew wider. "In fact, I know where it is. And it's *not* in the hands of the Rebel Alliance."

For the first time, Neelah saw something take Boba Fett by surprise. The bounty hunter stepped back as if from a blow, then he peered closer and harder at Balancesheet.

"What're you talking about? It has to be still inside the droid. That's where I left it."

"Let me tell you something more," said the smiling assembler. "You and your associates here are not the only ones who are interested in it. Some very powerful forces are searching for that same fabricated evidence."

"Who?" Boba Fett's hand shot toward the smaller creature, as though he were about to seize Balancesheet within his fist. "Who else is looking for it?"

"While you've been making your way here, I've been in contact with my own information sources; that's what I *do*. I hear all sorts of interesting and potentially profitable things. Only this time, I was approached directly by the other party involved; a representative from one of the most powerful men in the galaxy searched me out, to inquire whether I knew the whereabouts of that fabricated evidence against the late Prince Xizor, the same evidence that you found aboard Kee Duptom's ship *Venesectrix*."

"It must have been somebody from Black Sun, then. From whoever took over that organization after Xizor's death—"

"Not at all." Balancesheet gave a slow shake of his head. "From what I've been able to find out, neither Xizor nor Black Sun ever knew anything about whatever plot had been cooked up with this fabricated evidence. Besides, even if somebody in Black Sun found out about it now, why would they care? Prince Xizor is dead. Tying him to an Imperial stormtrooper raid on the planet Tatooine doesn't mean anything now."

"Then who—"

"Oh, but it gets even more interesting." On the metal ledge, Balancesheet seemed to vibrate with the pleasure of telling so many secrets. "The person who sent their representative here, looking for information about the fabricated evidence's whereabouts, seems to bear a considerable hostility toward you, Boba Fett. Or else he simply doesn't want to risk the possibility of you finding that fabricated evidence before he does. Because he's the one who ordered the bombing raid on the Dune Sea, back on Tatooine. The bombing raid in which you yourself came very close to being blown to atoms. You managed to escape—obviously—but I wouldn't say that this very powerful individual has ceased wishing you were dead. And he'd be happy to make that come about, given the opportunity." Balancesheet, multiple eyes glittering, leaned forward from its perch. "So you should appreciate the fact that I'm betting a lot on our doing business together, Fett. Because I could sell the information about *your* whereabouts to that other party, for a handsome pile of credits indeed."

"That'd be more efficient, at least," Dengar spoke up. "If all Balancesheet wanted was to eliminate us, it'd be easier to do it that way rather than firing off its own laser cannons." He shrugged. "Maybe the little guy's got a point."

"Maybe." Boba Fett appeared to mull it over for a second. "It all depends upon who this other person is, who not only tried to kill all of us, but is also looking for the same thing we are."

"Fine," said Balancesheet. "I'll tell you, and then you can make your own determination about what to do. The person in question is Kuat of Kuat, the head of Kuat Drive Yards."

Neelah was unable to stifle a gasp of surprise. *I know him*—the thought jumped unbidden into her mind, complete with an image of the powerful Kuat. That faded away as quickly as it came; she blinked and saw Boba

Fett glancing in her direction. He said nothing, but turned back toward the assembler on the metal ledge.

"How do you know it was Kuat of Kuat who did all that?" Boba Fett's voice was tinged with suspicion. "Why would the head of one of the largest engineering firms in the galaxy be interested in fabricated evidence against the late Prince Xizor? And why would he want me dead?"

"Questions, questions, questions." Balancesheet shook its head in mock despair. "They wouldn't be necessary if you trusted me more."

"I haven't stayed alive as long as I have in this business by trusting other creatures. So just answer them."

"Very well; I know it was Kuat of Kuat who ordered the bombing raid on the Dune Sea, because his representative told me so, on his instructions. Kuat wanted me to be assured of his desire to have you dead, so that I would be confident of getting paid in case I came across any news of your whereabouts. And as to *why* he'd want you dead, and why he'd be interested in this fabricated evidence against the late Prince Xizor—" Balancesheet spread his raised claw tips apart. "Of that, I have not the slightest notion. But it does confirm in my mind that if we had what he was looking for, and given the vast wealth of Kuat Drive Yards at his disposal, we'd be able to force him to pay a substantial sum for it. And let's face it: you and I have considerable experience at bargaining for that kind of thing."

"Then the only problem," said Dengar, "is getting our hands on what he wants."

And what I want, thought Neelah to herself.

"How fortunate then that the fabricated evidence *isn't* with the Rebel Alliance, but someplace where it can be gotten at instead." Balancesheet's jagged smile almost seemed to split its triangular face in half. "And also, that your new business associate—myself—knows where it is." The assembler looked back over toward Boba Fett. "We *are* in business together, aren't we?"

"All right," answered Boba Fett. "We'll work out the split later. *After* we get hold of the fabricated evidence and figure out the best way to cash in on it."

Balancesheet laughed, a sound like tiny, mistuned bells.

"What's so amusing?"

"It's so paradoxical." One of the claw tips wiped at the largest of the multiple eyes, in another parody of humanoid emotional gestures. "You've come all this way, looking for the answers you want, and the only means of getting those answers now is to find this phony evidence against the dead Xizor—*and it's back on Tatooine!*"

Neelah and both bounty hunters were stunned into silence for a moment. She found her voice first. "Tatooine? How . . . how did it get there?"

"Simple." Balancesheet wrapped its forelimbs around itself, the better to contain its growing mirth. "It's been there for quite a while now. You see, when our associate Boba Fett here"—the assembler gestured toward the helmeted bounty hunter—"managed, through his impressive personal skills, to chase Bossk off *Slave I*, the fabricated evidence went with him, inside the emergency escape pod he used to get away."

"And how do you know *this*?" Boba Fett regarded the assembler with skepticism.

"My friend, you've been out of the loop, this whole time that you've been making the journey to this remote sector. If you were in contact with your own information sources, the way I am with mine, you might have heard an interesting piece of news that's been *circulating* through some of the seedier watering holes and meeting places of the galaxy. It seems that your fellow bounty hunter is holed up in the Mos Eisley spaceport back on Tatooine, and he has a certain . . . *item* to sell. And he's looking for the right buyer for it. The item is rather unique, as I'm sure you'll appreciate; it's the fabricated evidence against the late Prince Xizor that supposedly linked him to the Imperial stormtrooper raid on a certain moisture farm on that planet. Of course, Bossk's attempts to unload these goods are complicated by the fact that he doesn't know the phony evidence's significance, its real value, or that Kuat of Kuat is in fact trying to locate it. If Bossk knew *that*, he could sell it in a heartbeat, for a very good price. But alas . . . he doesn't know." The assembler's voice filled with a mocking sympathy for the absent bounty hunter. "That's what happens when you try to do things yourself, for which you should have contacted an expert like me."

"Advertise on your own time," said Boba Fett irritably. "So Bossk has got it . . ." He nodded slowly, mulling over the information. "He must have found the cargo droid when he was aboard *Slave I*, before I called it down to the Dune Sea to pick us up. And he discovered the fabricated evidence about Xizor inside the droid and removed it, without knowing its significance but hoping that he'd be able to find some way of cashing in on it. I didn't have time to check the storage areas inside *Slave I* before abandoning it. So it seems I finally underestimated Bossk; I wouldn't have thought he had the native intelligence to have discerned any value in that cargo droid's contents."

"And then he must have shoved it inside the emergency escape pod." Dengar had managed to keep up with the others' explanations. "Right when you were coming down on him. Either he got lucky with what he decided to grab and take with him, or he's gotten a lot smarter than any of us would've ever have taken him for."

"What does it matter?" With growing exasperation, Neelah looked from one bounty hunter to the other. "The only thing that's important is that this fabricated evidence still exists. And if we can get our hands on it—" The possibilities had already leapt up in her mind, of finding the answers to the remaining questions about her own past. "Then we might be able to figure out who created it in the first place, and why they did it, and . . ."

"And that person's connection to you, of course." Boba Fett glanced over at her. "Don't worry; that mystery might not have the same personal significance for me that it does for you, but it still represents a potential source of profit. That makes it important enough to me."

"So it's back to Tatooine," said Dengar. The notion seemed to cheer him; Neelah figured that was because he would be able to see his betrothed, Manaroo, once again.

"If only it were as easy as all that." The jagged smile had vanished from Balancesheet's face. "But I'm afraid it's not. My poor lumbering freighter, as comfortable a home and place of business as it provides for me, would never reach Tatooine before Bossk found a buyer for the item he's trying to sell."

"So what's the problem? The *Hound's Tooth* is plenty fast enough—"

"Yes," interrupted Balancesheet, "and it's a marked ship. It's the one vessel in which it would be a dead certainty you'd never be able to reach Tatooine. Or, at least, not alive. Bossk has apparently kept silent about losing his ship to his enemy Boba Fett, but Kuat of Kuat hasn't. After the bombing raid he ordered didn't succeed at killing you off, and after his information sources had let him know that the Rebel Alliance had confiscated the abandoned *Slave I*, Kuat was able to figure out that you must be aboard the *Hound*. So Kuat has put out the word that he wants the *Hound's Tooth* found and intercepted— and if that means killing whoever's aboard it, so much the better. Which means that there are a *lot* of bounty hunters looking for it. Given that a great many of them still bear a grudge against you, for what you did to break up the old Bounty Hunters Guild, this is their perfect opportunity to get paid a substantial pile of credits *and* get their revenge, all at the same time." The assembler's triangular head tilted to one side, regarding Fett. "Ironic, isn't it? You've been the hunter for so long . . . and now you're the hunted."

"If I still had *Slave I*," said Boba Fett, "none of them would have a chance of stopping me."

"But you don't. And Bossk's ship is nowhere near the equivalent of your own, even if you were completely at ease with its weapons systems. The other bounty hunters would pick you off long before you got anywhere near Tatooine. There's probably not much time remaining before one of them finds you here in this remote sector. So it's no longer just a matter of realizing profits, or discovering the secrets of some stolen past." Balancesheet's glittering eyes took in the others, one by one. "For all of you, it's a matter of survival now."

"Great," muttered Dengar. The lifted spirits he had shown just minutes before had now evaporated. "We're dead. I knew this was going to happen . . ."

"Come, come." Balancesheet sounded almost pitying. "Would I have thrown my lot in with yours if I had thought you were all doomed? I'm a better business-creature than that."

"Then you've got a plan," said Boba Fett. "What is it?"

"Very simple. You just need to find another way to get to Tatooine. That's all."

"Easier said than done. It's a long walk from here."

"No need to, even if that were possible." The jagged smile returned to Balancesheet's narrow face. "I took the liberty of making other arrangements while you were on your way here to my ship. I've been in contact with a certain individual, with whom you've done business before— in a manner of speaking—and his ship is close enough to this sector, so that he can be here shortly."

Boba Fett regarded the assembler with suspicion evident even through the helmet's dark visor. "Who is it?"

"Oh . . ." The assembler's smile widened even further than before. "You'll see soon enough . . ."

"Well, well." A thin figure had emerged from the transfer hatchway, leaving his smaller craft tethered to the exterior of Balancesheet's freighter. From a face with youthfulness sharpened by feral cynicism, his gaze met with that of the helmeted bounty hunter. "Balancesheet told me he had a surprise in store. This is a good one."

"I knew you'd be amused," replied Balancesheet. "For a lot of reasons."

With a cocky swagger, the new arrival approached Boba Fett. "The last time we ran into each other, you just about killed me. I'm still wondering why you didn't."

Fett gazed back at him coldly. "Don't make me start wondering, Suhlak."

"Suhlak?" Dengar studied the youth for a moment, then glanced over at Balancesheet. "As in N'dru Suhlak? You called in a hunt saboteur?"

"Who better?" The assembler's response was mild and unruffled. "He is uniquely qualified for the task we need performed."

"Yeah, but . . ." Dengar's expression soured as he shook his head in disgust. "I don't like dealing with this kind of lowlife. It . . . it just goes against everything I believe in."

"What?" Neelah turned and looked at the bounty hunter standing next to her. "That's hard to believe. Since when did people in your line of business start getting moral attitudes?"

Suhlak smiled at her. "You'll have to excuse him, lady. But once a bounty hunter, always a bounty hunter. That's his job. And my job is to mess things up for him, and for every other bounty hunter." He made a small, mocking bow. "That's just what I do."

"You see, Neelah . . ." From the metal ledge, Balancesheet gestured toward Suhlak. "The existence of specialized entities such as bounty hunters has inevitably given rise to other, competing specialities. Such as this young— and very gifted—hunt saboteur. What he does is get certain individuals from point A to point B as quickly and safely as possible; that in itself is not so special. But Suhlak here performs this service for individuals who have had bounties placed on their heads, and whom bounty hunters such as Dengar and Boba Fett are seeking to capture. He, in essence, spoils their hunt. You can hardly expect bounty hunters to approve of someone like that."

"Yeah, and like I care." Suhlak leaned his shoulder

against a bulkhead and folded his arms across his chest. "They do what they do for credits, and I do what I do for the same. Which brings up the matter at hand. I take it you called me here for a reason, Balancesheet. That reason better be a nice, high-paying job."

"I think it's one for which we can offer you satisfactory terms." Balancesheet pointed a minuscule claw tip toward Boba Fett. "Our mutual friend here needs to reach Tatooine as quickly—and as unobtrusively—as possible."

"That's going to be a little bit difficult for him." Suhlak aimed a smirk in Boba Fett's direction, then turned back toward the assembler. "There's a lot of other creatures out there gunning for him. I mean, he wasn't too popular before; now that there's a pile of credits offered in exchange for his hide, his chances have gone way down."

"We're aware of the difficulties," said Balancesheet. "And while of course there's a certain, shall we say, *irony* that comes with asking a hunt saboteur to assist in conveying a bounty hunter past other bounty hunters, we still think your services might be useful in that regard."

"Useful?" Suhlak gave a slow nod. "Yeah—and expensive."

"There's a surprise," said Dengar sourly.

"Shut up." Neelah hissed the words at him. "This is the only way we've got."

Suhlak pointed toward Balancesheet. "You mentioned a certain sum of credits when you contacted me."

"Yes—" The assembler nodded. "That was to get your interest."

"Oh, you got it, all right. But now that I see exactly what you're talking about . . ." Suhlak made a show of reluctantly shaking his head. "I'm not sure it's enough. Given the risks involved, and all. And . . . certain personal issues that have to be overcome."

"What sum," asked Balancesheet, "would take care of those problems for you?"

"The figure you mentioned—up front. And then"—
Suhlak's eyes narrowed to slits—"the same amount
again, when the job's completed."

It was Balancesheet's turn to look doubtful. "That's a
considerable amount of credits."

"Yeah, and it's a considerable amount of risk. Plus—
you don't have any other options right now. So take it or
leave it."

"Taken," Boba Fett spoke up. "Pay this creature,
Balancesheet. I don't feel like haggling."

"You got yourself a good deal." Suhlak barked out a
harsh laugh. "Think about it. I've made a lot of deliveries
in my time—and you're the only one who ever succeeded
at getting in my way. With you aboard this time, that'll
be one thing I won't have to worry about."

"So you're going to be taking all of us back to Tatooine?" Neelah pointed to herself and the two bounty
hunters. "That's the deal?"

Suhlak shook his head. "Sweetheart, I've only got a
modified Z-95 Headhunter—that's what I use in my business. Fast, maneuverable—but a little on the cramped
side, even with the bubbled-out passenger space I had
added to it. There's really just room for me and one other
creature. Boba Fett's making this trip, and that's it."

"But . . ." An edge of panic, a glimpse into the unknown, cut through Neelah's thoughts. Everything—all
the answers to the questions that remained with her—
depended upon Boba Fett. "How do I know . . . how do
we know . . . that you'll come back?"

"Don't worry," said Boba Fett. "This will be a two-
way journey, all right. How else am I going to make any
credits on this deal?"

"Hey, wait a minute." Suhlak pushed himself away
from the bulkhead on which he'd been leaning. "Nobody said anything about getting back here. My price
was just for getting you to Tatooine!"

Boba Fett turned his shielded gaze toward the younger
man. "Take it or leave it, Suhlak. Or else we'll explore
another option—namely, my killing you and then pilot-

ing your ship myself. The odds of making it to Tatooine wouldn't be as good, but at least I wouldn't have to put up with you any longer."

For a few seconds, the hunt saboteur glared back at Fett. Then he nodded. "All right. Let's get going."

12

"We've found them."

Those words came from the comm unit speaker in
Kuat of Kuat's private quarters. The felinx watched from
its silken-lined basket beneath Kuat's lab bench as he
turned toward the voice of the absent Kodir of Kuhlvult,
security head for all of Kuat Drive Yards.

"I'm not so much concerned about 'them.' The person
we need to locate is Boba Fett." Kuat regarded the view
of stars and construction docks visible from the curving bank of transparisteel panels near the bench. "If you
haven't found him, I don't even want to hear your
report."

"Don't worry," said Kodir. "I wouldn't have put the
link through if I hadn't succeeded at the task given to me."

Kuat made no reply. Even though Kodir wasn't physically present at the Kuat Drive Yards corporate headquarters, he had as clear an image of her as if she were
standing before him. She had all the haughty bearing of a
member of one of Kuat's ruling families, combined with
the intimidatingly honed athletic grace that had made
her such a suitable candidate for the position she now
held. That, plus a sharp-edged mental acuity equal to his

own, evoked a small measure of unease in Kuat. In truth, he'd had a better personal relationship with Fenald, his previous security head; the only problem being that Fenald had been a traitor, to both Kuat and to Kuat Drive Yards, by being part of the scheme to wrest control of the corporation away from him and turn it over to the greediest and most ambitious factions among the ruling families. If it hadn't been for Kodir of Kuhlvult, Fenald and the conspirators he'd fallen in with would very likely have succeeded in their plans—and the corporation that Kuat of Kuat and his predecessors had treasured and protected for so many generations would now be on its way to utter ruin. No one from the planet Kuat's other ruling families had the experience and cunning to circumvent all of Emperor Palpatine's schemes to break Kuat Drive Yards' independence and make it a mere component of the Empire. So Kodir had earned both Kuat's respect and his trust, no matter how much her tough, even brutal mannerisms grated against his own instincts. *It's a brutal universe,* Kuat had told himself more than once. And he had certainly played his own hard game of survival in it. Perhaps what disturbed him about Kodir was a certain essential resemblance to his own ruthlessness in service to the corporation.

"So now we know where Boba Fett is." Kuat spoke into the comm unit mike on top of the lab bench. "Is he still aboard the ship called the *Hound's Tooth?*"

"That's how I found him." A tone of self-satisfaction was audible in Kodir's voice. "The *Hound's Tooth* was spotted by one of our paid spies, at the edge of one of the remoter border systems. Then it vanished again; obviously, Boba Fett was piloting a course designed to throw off any trackers. But the sighting of the *Hound's Tooth* was close enough to a certain navigational sector that had figured prominently at one time in Boba Fett's activities that I took a chance at keeping it under more intensive surveillance. And sure enough, the *Hound's Tooth* showed up there."

"Indeed." Kuat nodded to himself. That was the type

of work, both methodical and insightful, that he had expected from Kodir. "So where is it?"

"It's out by where the arachnoid assembler Kud'ar Mub'at used to have its web, before it was destroyed by Prince Xizor. And the fragments of the web had drifted a bit since then, so Boba Fett apparently had to do some searching of his own to find them. But he did; by the time my ship got close enough to do some surreptitious monitoring of his activities, he and his companions had reconstructed most of the web."

"Interesting." Rubbing his chin, Kuat wondered what that piece of information meant. The death of the assembler Kud'ar Mub'at at the hands of Prince Xizor's Black Sun cleanup crew had previously been something of a relief to him. Kud'ar Mub'at had had too much knowledge of Kuat's own dealings with the assembler; those kinds of secrets were better kept by the dead than by any living creature, no matter how well paid for silence. If Xizor hadn't taken care of Kud'ar Mub'at, then the chances would have been good that Kuat of Kuat would have been forced to, eventually. "Were you able to discern exactly what they were up to?"

"Negative on that," came Kodir's reply. "I ordered our ship to pull back from the sector when another vessel was detected, approaching from directly opposite us. We did manage to ID that ship; it's the freighter that Kud'ar Mub'at's successor Balancesheet is now using as its base of operations."

"Do you think there was some kind of arranged rendezvous between Balancesheet and Boba Fett?"

"I'm pretty sure there wasn't." Kodir's voice sounded grimly amused. "Balancesheet has had that clunky old freighter of his outfitted with some decent armaments; it opened fire on both the reconstructed web and the *Hound's Tooth* alongside. Things got a little confused after that, but right now it seems as if Balancesheet and Boba Fett have sorted it out; Fett and his associates are currently aboard Balancesheet's freighter."

"Any way of finding out what they're discussing?"

"Negative again," replied Kodir. "Balancesheet values its privacy as much as Kud'ar Mub'at did. That freighter is shielded against every distance-operational spy apparatus we've got. Short of cracking open the hull with one of our own laser cannons, that meeting is completely secured."

"Too bad." *For both myself—and Boba Fett,* thought Kuat. If there had been some way of determining exactly what the bounty hunter was discussing and scheming with the arachnoid assembler, Kuat would have been able to more accurately assess what kind of threat Boba Fett's continued existence represented to him and to Kuat Drive Yards. But as it was, he'd have to err on the side of caution . . .

And eliminate Fett.

"That's the situation at this point." Kodir's voice broke into his thoughts. "I await your decision about what to do next."

"Have you got this freighter of Balancesheet's in your weapon-sights?"

"Not yet," said Kodir. "We're out of range for that. But that problem can be corrected very shortly."

"Then do so." Kuat had already made his determination about the bounty hunter's fate. "And when you've locked on to the target, proceed with its destruction. I want complete annihilation of the freighter and all living creatures aboard it."

"We could be a little more surgical in our approach. It wouldn't be too difficult to disable the freighter, then board it and extract Boba Fett without harming the others. We could eliminate him alone—that is, of course, if there were some value to be placed on the lives of the others with him." Kodir expanded on the option she had presented. "Balancesheet, for instance; the assembler has its uses for us."

"Not enough of them." Kuat shook his head, though there was no way that Kodir could see him. "Not enough to outweigh the disadvantages of having it remain as a witness to our actions against Boba Fett. I don't want any of this traced back to Kuat Drive Yards. So proceed as I indicated."

"Very well. I'll report back when the operation is concluded." From the faraway ship, Kodir broke off the comm unit connection.

In the resulting silence, Kuat of Kuat could hear the felinx asking for attention, its voice a mere guttural whine. He reached down and scratched behind its ears.

"Believe me," said Kuat. "It'll be for the best . . ."

"Not so fast," said Suhlak. "There's a couple of other things that have to be taken care of before we go anywhere."

The hunt saboteur hadn't moved toward the transfer hatch that would have led both him and Boba Fett to his waiting Headhunter. Fett and the others aboard Balancesheet's freighter gazed at him impatiently.

"Now what's the problem?" Neelah set her hands on her slim hips. "I thought we already figured out, we don't have time to waste."

"Look, I'm just trying to help you out here. So you'll be like a satisfied customer and all. I've got a reputation to maintain," Suhlak said testily. "If all you wanted was for me to get this bounty hunter here to Tatooine, quick and quiet, I can take care of that for you. But you want a roundtrip; you want me to bring Fett back here as well. Now that's going to be kind of hard for me to pull off if this whole freighter and everybody aboard it is gone by the time Fett and I return."

"Why would we be gone?" Puzzled, Dengar stared at the hunt saboteur. "Where would we go?"

"You wouldn't have gone anywhere, pal, except up in flames." Suhlak shook his head in disgust. "None of you even knows what's sitting out there, keeping a watch on your every move. But there's a light cruiser, top of the line, from the Kuat Drive Yards, keeping surveillance on this tub right now. Matter of fact, it's a KDY ship; I identified it when I snuck past it. It's the Kuat Drive Yards' main security enforcement vessel, and it's armed and *very* dangerous."

"It didn't spot you?" Boba Fett gestured toward the hull of the freighter and the empty expanses of space outside it. "They don't know you're here?"

"Naw; I've got my ways of sliding past something like that—especially when their attention is fixed on something else, like this freighter here."

Neelah looked over at Fett. "What do you think they want?"

"Given the fact that the last time any KDY ships got this close to me, they unloaded enough bombs to atomize a few square kilometers of the Dune Sea, I'd expect that this one isn't going to be any friendlier."

The arachnoid assembler Balancesheet had scurried over to its freighter home's detect and tracking screens. "It would appear," it announced, "that not only is our young friend correct about the presence of this other ship, but that we also have a limited time in which to determine what to do about it. It's come within range of my ship's scanners, and is continuing to head this way."

"All right," said Boba Fett with rapid authority, "here's the deal. I can get away with Suhlak, just like we planned, but this freighter won't be able to either outshoot or outrun that KDY ship. But the KDY security forces aboard it undoubtedly are bearing down this way, because they figure I'm aboard here." He pointed to Dengar and Neelah. "You two—get back aboard the *Hound's Tooth* and head out, full thrusters, to open space and prepare for a hyperspace jump to the Oranessan system. They'll assume that it's me aboard the *Hound*, and they'll follow after you."

"But then what?" Dengar pointed with his thumb toward the cruiser's image on the screen. "If we go into hyperspace, that KDY ship won't be able to follow us."

"They will, if they know your destination. Before you make the jump, fire off a comm transmission with a minimum encryption level, giving the details of the rendezvous point. Suhlak and I will already be out of range, but the KDY ship will be able to pick it up. When you come out of hyperspace, it'll be right behind you. Then all you'll have to do is stay out of its reach until I'm finished with my business on Tatooine and can hook up with you again. Then we can lose them for good."

Dengar shook his head. "I won't be able to elude that KDY ship for very long, out there in the Oranessan system. Wouldn't it be simpler to jump there, and then as soon as the KDY ship shows up, make another quick jump to some other point that we can use for a rendezvous? That way, we'd already have lost them."

"Only for as long as it would take KDY security to tap their information sources and find out just where you were waiting for me. And if I were delayed getting back from Tatooine, you'd still have the same problem of eluding the KDY ship. In the Oranessan system, at least, there'd be a chance of pulling that off." Boba Fett made a quick sharp gesture with the flat of his hand. "Maybe not forever—but then, all you have to do is elude them for long enough. And that way, Suhlak and I would have an even better chance of making it to Tatooine without getting intercepted."

"Smart." Suhlak nodded in appreciation. "I always like improving my odds."

"Oh, I approve as well." Balancesheet had scuttled back onto the metal ledge alongside the larger figures. "You can just draw the Kuat Drive Yards ship away from here, and I won't have anyone firing laser cannons at me. *Much* better."

"Right—and you won't be tempted to find some way of turning me over to them." Boba Fett gestured toward the transfer hatchway. "Now it's really time to get going."

Moments later, Neelah and Dengar were back aboard the *Hound's Tooth*. In the forward viewport of its cockpit, the smaller shape of Suhlak's modified Z-95 Headhunter had already shot away, detection by the approaching KDY cruiser blocked by the imposing bulk of Balancesheet's freighter. The flare from the Headhunter's main thruster engines dwindled to a streak of light, then was gone.

"Hold on—" In the pilot's chair, Dengar grabbed the *Hound*'s thruster controls. "I'm not waiting around, either."

Neelah braced herself in the corner formed by the cockpit's two rear bulkheads. The sudden acceleration, as Dengar slammed the controls, forced her spine and the back of her head against the metal behind her. Another burst, from the ship's side jets, threw her against the hatchway.

"What're you doing?" She had grabbed the back of the pilot's chair to keep from being knocked off her feet. Past Dengar, she could see out the forward viewport; a few remaining scraps of Kud'ar Mub'at's once-living web scattered to either side of the *Hound* as it gained speed, heading for a larger shape ahead. "You're going straight toward the KDY ship!"

"If I'm supposed to be chased by something with guns," said Dengar between gritted teeth, "I want to make sure I've got their attention!"

The combined acceleration of the two ships ate up the distance between them; at the last possible moment, and as the cruiser fired off a bolt from its prow-mounted cannon, Dengar banked the *Hound's Tooth* to one side and above the other ship's hull, clearing it by what seemed to Neelah to be less than a few meters.

Below the *Hound*, the cruiser's rear thruster exhausts shot past. Dengar kept the ship at full throttle, taking them out into empty space, with nothing but stars ahead of them. Reaching into one of the Trandoshan-sized grooves on the control panel, he toggled onto one of the display screens the image from the stern viewport. Far off in the distance was Balancesheet's untouched freighter; closer was the KDY cruiser, wheeling itself around to follow them.

"Good." Dengar backed off the thruster controls a fraction of a centimeter. "Now all we have to do is fire off our comm transmission—"

Neelah watched as he picked up the comm unit mike, then listened as he gave the rendezvous coordinates to the now-vanished Headhunter with Fett and Suhlak aboard. A moment later, the *Hound's Tooth* was in hyperspace as well.

"Now we're all set." Dengar leaned back, hands behind his head.

"You think so, huh?" Neelah had managed to stay on her feet through the *Hound*'s violent maneuvers. Hands braced against the back of the pilot's chair, she leaned down closer to Dengar. "Did you ever stop to think about what happens when we reach the Oranessan system? And if Boba Fett *doesn't* show up? Then we're supposed to just hang around there and wait, I suppose. Seems to me, that's a perfect opportunity for this KDY cruiser to eventually catch up with us and sort us out into a *lot* of little pieces."

Dengar's face fell. "You're right . . . I didn't think about that."

"Great." Neelah straightened up and shook her head. "Boba Fett's the one with a clear shot right now, and *we've* got the heavy artillery chasing us. That worked out, all right—for him. Too bad for us if anything happens to him—or he decides to change his plans again."

"I guess . . ." Dengar had been hit hard by Neelah's words; he spoke slowly, his thoughts obviously turned to the KDY ship, heading for the same destination. "I guess we'll just deal with it when we get there . . ."

13

"Of course," said the α-foreman of the Kuat Drive Yards' construction docks, "we remain loyal to you personally. Even beyond our loyalty to the corporation itself."

"That means a great deal to me." Kuat of Kuat was not surprised to hear the statement, though. He had come down from the office in his private quarters, to which he normally would have summoned the various supervisors one by one, the single alpha and the ranks of beta team supervisors below him. This time—perhaps for the last time, Kuat knew—he preferred to meet with the crew leaders here among the docks, the true heart of the corporation he led. To find a devotion equal to his own was only fitting in such a place. "But you must remember," continued Kuat, "loyalty to me is the same as loyalty to Kuat Drive Yards. I wouldn't ask you to do anything that would not be best for it, and for all that we've worked so hard to create."

The men and women assembled in the meeting shed—there were probably close to a hundred of them, representing all of the corporation's divisions—looked back at him with complete understanding in their collective gaze. They were as aware as he was of all the enemies arrayed against Kuat Drive Yards, the greedy and ambitious who desired to consume the corporation whole, bring it entirely under their power, make it a mere part of that greater entity known as . . . the Empire. Palpatine and the underlings that he had come to dominate with his insatiable will, from Lord Vader down through the ranks of admirals in the Imperial Navy—none of them could abide the thought of any entity, from the last solitary Rebel to one of the most powerful corporations in the galaxy, remaining independent. The faithful KDY employees standing before Kuat knew that their only options were to resist the Empire's encroachment with all their possible strength and will—or see themselves crushed inside Palpatine's fist, as he had crushed worlds with wealth greater than any possessed by the planet Kuat.

One of the eldest β-supervisors stepped forward. Kuat recognized the man as the leader of the shipbuilding team that laid down the enormous central frames of the ships that took form in the KDY construction docks. The β-supervisor had been a lead operator, back in the days of Kuat's father, of one of the massive cranes spanning the docks, each nearly as long—and powerful—as an Imperial battle destroyer. Through the meeting shed's overhead skylights, the outline of one of them could be seen, blotting out an entire swath of stars.

"You've led this corporation well, Kuat." Though white-haired, the β-supervisor was still a figure of imposing musculature, with a razor-sharp gaze in his age-seamed face. "And through times perhaps more difficult than any faced by your predecessors; you've proven yourself to be the true heir of the Kuat Drive Yards' helm."

A murmuring chorus of agreement sounded behind the man.

"Is it your intent, then, to be the final leader that this corporation will ever see?" The β-supervisor peered closely at Kuat. "Perhaps you seek to ensure that Kuat Drive Yards will never have a leader greater than yourself."

"That's not my intent," said Kuat of Kuat. The ranks assembled in the meeting shed fell absolutely silent to hear his softly spoken words. "But if it turns out to be my duty, then I will accept it."

The grizzled figure standing before him slowly nodded. "A fine answer, Kuat. And a worthy decision. I've heard that there are many, on the planet of Kuat that we orbit—" As with most of the KDY workforce, the old man had spent his entire life in the construction docks and the attached dormitory complex. "—and on worlds far from here, who believe that from our work, our lives among the ships we build, we wind up with hearts as cold and precise as machines. So be it; perhaps those other creatures speak truly. But if such is the case, then you should feel certain of the judgment of the living machines you see before you." The β-supervisor turned and gestured with an outflung arm toward the other KDY workers. "And that judgment is—as you accept your duty, however painful, so do we accept ours."

The voices behind the man were louder this time, but just as united in their assent.

Kuat looked away from his followers for a moment, toward the bank of transparisteel panes along the side of the meeting shed. From here he had a closer view than from his personal quarters, high above the construction docks, of the corporation's work. As far as his eye could see, and against a glittering backdrop of stars, the massive shapes of a completed battle fleet were arrayed one after another. The cranes and other heavy equipment that the shipbuilders used in their intricate craft arched over the ships, as though to protect them from hands that would defile their beauty and power. Kuat's heart, however hard and machinelike it may have become, swelled in his chest. No matter what happened, however dark the fate closing upon Kuat Drive Yards, its accomplishments would remain. *We built these*, thought Kuat as he gazed at the ships. *They were ours before they be-came anyone else's.* He nodded slowly to himself. What became of them now was a matter for him to decide.

The β-supervisor had stepped back into the ranks of the others filling the shed. At the front of them was the α-foreman of the Kuat Drive Yards' construction docks, as before. "Are there further instructions," said the α-foreman, "that you wished to give us?"

"No . . ." Kuat of Kuat brought himself back from his deep musing. "Proceed with the plans as I've outlined them. Let me know when we've reached operational stage, and then await word from my offices before going any further."

"As you wish." The α-foreman turned back toward the others and made a single gesture with an upraised arm. "Let's get to work."

After the workers had filed out, Kuat remained by himself in the meeting shed for a while longer. He stood at the bank of transparisteel windows, looking out at the ships beneath the immense cranes but not really seeing them at all. In the distance, some of the bright points of light above the construction docks weren't stars, but the small, armed craft of the Rebel Alliance that had been assigned to keep an eye on whatever might happen to the new and valuable fleet waiting here. Those Rebel pilots were only doing their own duty; Kuat held no grudge against them. But he couldn't let them stop him from his own.

He was reluctant to return to his private quarters, and to the ongoing confrontation with the various conspiracies encircling Kuat Drive Yards. This conference with the various supervisors from the construction docks had been a momentary break from all those pressures, and one that had been, he knew, somewhat unnecessary. He could have been sure of his followers' loyalty without having to come here in person; some of them had already routed memos to his offices assuring him of that much.

One takes one's pleasures, mused Kuat of Kuat, *where one can find them.* Given what he knew about the dark forces moving among the stars, and what he would have to do to keep Kuat Drive Yards from falling into their hands, there were not many pleasures left to him.

Or time left to enjoy them . . .

"We'll soon be out of range," said one of the Kuat Drive Yards' security personnel, "if we wish to contact headquarters and inquire as to any changes in our orders."

Kodir of Kuhlvult, the head of security for the corporation, stood in the command bridge of the cruiser, with her hands clasped in the small of her back. Past the staff manning the cruiser's flight and weaponry controls, the cruiser's forward viewport was visible. Locked in that center of the star-filled image was a brighter flare, that of the main thruster engines of the ship known as the *Hound's Tooth*. The distance to that target had remained stable for the last several minutes. Stable—and tantalizingly just beyond range of the KDY cruiser's laser cannons.

"There's no need to contact Kuat, if that's what you mean." Kodir was aware that some of the members of Kuat Drive Yards' security division had yet to accept her leadership as a fact, and her decisions as final. "He's authorized me to act as I see fit in this matter."

Her words, crisply spoken, had an interesting effect on the underling, drawing his spine up straighter and stiffer. "Kuat did more than just 'authorize' your actions," he replied in measured tones. "He gave all of us the same orders, that we were to fire upon and destroy the ship bearing Boba Fett at the earliest opportunity."

"So he did." Kodir didn't turn toward the man, but remained gazing toward the viewport. "Your point?"

"My point is that we had our weapons systems locked upon this ship that we are presently following back when it left the sector at which we first intercepted it. We could have eliminated it at that time, if you hadn't directly ordered our crew to hold their fire."

Kodir glanced toward the man standing beside her. "Are you questioning my decision?"

"I fail to see how that decision corresponds with the orders and the mission that were given to us by Kuat of Kuat. His authority outranks yours, whether he is physically present or not; he is, after all, the head of the Kuat Drive Yards, and we all serve under that command."

"Very well put," replied Kodir. "When I require a lecture on the theory and practice of corporate structure, I'll be sure to remember that you seem to be unusually well versed on the subject. In the meantime, my orders as head of the security division remain as before. We will continue pursuing this ship bearing Boba Fett, and we will forgo contacting Kuat of Kuat at the corporation's headquarters. Is that clear?"

"Absolutely clear." The man's eyes narrowed to slits as he regarded her. "It is my duty, when we return to Kuat Drive Yards, to make a full report to Kuat regarding your conduct in this regard."

"That's *your* decision." She smiled thinly at the man. "But I assure you, the head of the corporation places a great deal of trust in me. That's how I became your superior. If there's anything that you think you might be able to say that would alter Kuat's trust, you're more than free to speak up about it. But be prepared for the consequences, if Kuat doesn't agree with you."

The underling remained silent, still glaring at her.

"Now that we understand each other," continued Kodir, "you may return to your other duties. As I'll return to mine."

With a curt nod the underling turned and strode away.

Several other faces on the bridge had swiveled in her direction, watching and listening to the brief altercation. Kodir gestured with one hand. "Carry on," she said. "Unless, that is, any of you wish to question my command?"

A moment passed, then the security staff returned to their various tasks.

Kodir gazed past the heads bent over the gauges and display screens. *Soon*, she told herself. A mere matter of time . . .

"You know, I'm beginning to think you're just plain bad luck." N'dru Suhlak glanced over his shoulder at the figure behind him in the Headhunter's cockpit. "Whether I'm going up against you, or whether we're supposed to be on the same side—there's just evil stuff that happens to me when you're around."

"What's the problem?" Boba Fett grasped the back of the pilot's chair Suhlak sat in and pulled himself forward, the better to see what was up ahead of the small craft. "I thought we had just about reached Tatooine."

"Sure—dead ahead." Suhlak pointed to the forward viewport. In the distance was the buff-colored orb, with little of its surface obscured by cloud cover beneath the radiance of twin suns. "Plus, I thought we'd already gotten past the worst we were going to encounter along the way. Without having to get into any running dogfights— I'd much rather sneak past anyone trying to stop me, instead of having to shoot my way through." He shook his head. "I don't think we're going to be able to do that with this customer."

"You've spotted someone?"

"Correction—someone's spotted *us*." A red dot of light was pulsing on the control panel; Suhlak pointed to it. "I can't see him yet, but whoever it is, he's definitely got some kind of multifrequency scanning and lock on device. It's got real distance capability, too. None of my detect systems can even get a fix on his location; the signal that got bounced off us was less than a nanosecond in duration, and that's way too small to calculate off of."

The cockpit area of the Headhunter had been extensively modified, bubbled out to add a larger carrying capacity for Suhlak's paying passengers. But the space was still cramped enough that all Boba Fett would have had to do was turn away from the pilot's chair in order to place his hands against the curved bulkhead, as though he might have been able to sense the approaching predator in that way.

On the cockpit panel, the red light began pulsing faster, at an accelerating clip. "I take it," said Boba Fett, "that we're picking up more of this unknown individual's scanning signals?"

"You got it, pal. He's obviously trying to get enough vector data on us to predict our path and speed. Which means"—Suhlak slammed the navigational controls hard to one side; the stars in the viewport blurred horizontally as the Z-95 Headhunter banked at close to a ninety-degree deflection from its original course—"we go another way."

The sharp maneuver had slammed Boba Fett against the pilot's chair. He braced himself, widening the stance of his boots and holding on tighter to the seat's back.

Suhlak glanced over his shoulder at his passenger. "You better sit back and strap yourself in. This might get a little raucous."

"And leave you running this show by yourself?" The lights from the control panel glinted on the dark visor of Boba Fett's helmet as he shook his head. "Don't worry—I can handle it."

"Suit yourself. Because it seems our friend has gotten in range of us." Suhlak pointed to the upper left quadrant of the viewport. "There he is now. And it doesn't look like he just wants to say hello." Boosting the Headhunter's main engines to full throttle, Suhlak threw the small ship into a looping spiral, piling on multiple g-forces. "Hold on—"

The first shot fired from the pursuer struck the Headhunter's exterior hull, to the rear of the expanded passenger area. A burst of hot sparks rained across Boba Fett's back as a section of insulated circuitry overloaded and caught fire. Both he and Suhlak ignored the black smoke that started to fill the cockpit as the hunt saboteur pushed the thruster controls even farther forward, at the same time taking the craft into a wrenching counter-directional dive.

"There. That should've taken care of him." Suhlak pointed to the display from the rear scanner. "See? We've lost him." With one hand, Suhlak pulled back the engines' throttle. "Kinda disappointing, actually. I was hoping for a lot more fun from—" He suddenly fell silent, leaning forward and peering at the forward viewport. "What the . . ."

"Something wrong?"

"Yeah . . . you could say that . . ." Suhlak slowly nodded, then raised his hand and pointed to the curved transparisteel in front of the control panel. "There he is . . ."

At the center of the viewport, the pursuing ship sat waiting in the distance, engines dropped to standby as though its pilot was confident of there being no escape for its prey.

"Oh, *great*." Suhlak looked down at a smaller read-out on the control panel. "We finally got an ID code from this guy. Believe me, he's the *last* one I wanted to run into."

Boba Fett peered at the small bright image of the ship ahead. "Who is it?"

"Osss-10," said Suhlak, shoulders slumping. "Now I'm *sure* you're bad luck."

"Never heard of him."

"You wouldn't have." Disgust sounded in Suhlak's voice. "That's because *you're* an old story, and *he's* the latest thing. Don't you get it? This is all because of what you did when you broke up the old Bounty Hunters Guild. The old rule book's been thrown out, and there's enough chaos in the bounty-hunting environment for totally new ones to start up. New—and *better*." Suhlak pointed his thumb at the viewport. "I've never even seen this Osss-10 guy face-to-face, don't know where he comes from, but I've already had some real unpleasant encounters with him. Somebody with a lot of credits must be bankrolling him: he's got all the state-of-the-art equipment, plus he's a real genius at programming his onboard computers. He's got some kind of predictive algorithms wired into his gear that I've never encountered before. The more confrontations you have with him, the bigger operational database he has to extrapolate from about what your *next* moves are going to be—just like he did right now. If he gets much smarter, next he's going to be able to know what I'm going to do before *I* know!"

"So what are your plans?"

"What difference does it make?" Suhlak slumped down in defeat. "I already threw my best stuff at this guy. The only thing I can think of to do is . . . give up."

"Right—" Boba Fett leaned past Suhlak and shoved the main thruster engine controls forward. The Z-95 Headhunter shot forward, rapidly accelerating toward the other craft in the distance.

"What're you doing?" Suhlak struggled against the forearm restraining him in the seat. "You'll get us killed!"

Fett said nothing, but pushed the thruster controls all the way to their limits.

The pursuer craft loomed larger in the center of the viewport as the Headhunter sped straight toward it. Suddenly, the prow-mounted laser cannons began firing. Bolt after coruscating bolt struck the Headhunter, buffeting the craft from side to side, as more sparks and smoke filled its interior as though it were in the middle of a planetary lightning storm. Boba Fett kept his grip locked upon the thruster controls. Shock and the force of acceleration were enough to keep Suhlak pinned where he was, watching helplessly as Boba Fett made quick navigational corrections with his other hand, maintaining their fiery course toward their opponent.

A final volley of laser-cannon fire burst across the viewport, blinding in its white-hot glare. The Headhunter burst through it, finding the other craft now directly ahead. They were close enough to each other that Suhlak, opening his squeezed-shut eyes, had a momentary glimpse of a grimly intent face behind a curve of transparisteel—

That was all he saw of Osss-10. Suhlak braced himself for the annihilating impact of the two ships crashing together. Then suddenly he could see the rear of the other craft encircled with the flare from its own engines at full throttle. The cockpit through which he had glimpsed the pursuer's face swept upward and out of his vision; the bottom of the other ship's hull filled the viewport, near enough that Suhlak could have counted the thermal weld seams in the durasteel panels if they hadn't gone by so fast.

A scraping noise, metal against metal, sounded through the smoke roiling in the cockpit area as the underside of Osss-10's ship tore off one of the Z-95 Headhunter's sensor arrays. Then silence filled the space, broken only by the hissing of the automatic fire-control systems extinguishing the burning circuitry.

Trembling, Suhlak leaned forward and checked the angle from his ship's rear scanner. The other ship was nowhere to be seen. He punched up the rest of his detection monitors. They all told the same story: Osss-10 had vanished from the sector as quickly as he had appeared.

Boba Fett had pushed himself back from the control panel, leaving the Headhunter at cruising speed. In the forward viewport loomed the planet Tatooine, closer now.

"That . . . that was just insane . . ." Suhlak shook his head, still seeing in his mind's eye the vision of the other ship coming within millimeters of a shattering crash with his own. "We were that close to being killed . . ."

"But we weren't," said Boba Fett. "So much for your new breed of bounty hunter. He might be able to predict what you're going to do—but he can't predict what I'm going to do. Nobody can."

Suhlak reached for the ship's controls and aimed

toward the cloudless terrain of the Dune Sea. *Predictions*, he thought. *I'll give you predictions.* He had already decided, deep inside himself, that whatever amount of credits he was slated to get for this job—

It wasn't going to be enough.

14

"I was wondering when you'd show up." Bossk's unpleasant smile lit up in the shadows of the rear booth, the dim lights of the cantina glinting off the full array of his fangs. "I would've been real disappointed if you hadn't. I mean—disappointed in *you*."

Boba Fett slid into the opposite side of the booth. A few inquisitive faces had turned his way as he strode through the dimly lit space, but his visor-shielded glance over his shoulder had convinced them to limit their attention to their own business. "Hope you haven't been waiting." He set his gloved hands down flat on the table's damp-ringed surface.

"Oh, I've been waiting, all right." Grimly brooding anger tinged Bossk's words. "I've been waiting for this moment for a *long* time."

"Don't make a big deal about this," said Fett. "I just came here to do business with you. That's all."

"Yeah, and that's the moment I'm talking about. The moment when *I've* got something that *you* want."

Bossk leaned back in the booth's thinly padded seat and regarded—with growing satisfaction—the other bounty hunter sitting across from him. The feeling was the kind of satisfaction that came just before even stronger, more pleasurable feelings: the savoring of triumph and the satiation of one's appetite. He could almost taste them, like the sweet saltiness of blood leaking through his fangs. *Turnabout,* thought Bossk, *isn't just fair play.* It was the peak of one's existence, at least for a creature like him. Trandoshans were famous throughout the galaxy for their ability to carry a grudge.

"Not only that you want," continued Bossk. "But that you *need.*"

"Careful." Boba Fett's voice remained flat and unemotional, as though all of Bossk's taunting had had zero effect on him. "You might be overestimating the value of the goods."

"I don't think so." Bossk set his own massive claws down on the table. "You wouldn't have come all this way—and back to Tatooine, which is hardly full of pleasant memories for you, is it?—if there hadn't been a pretty good reason for you to do so. You especially wouldn't have risked coming here with the odds stacked against you the way they are—what with every bounty hunter left over from the old Guild, and a bunch of new ones, all gunning for you."

"For somebody who's as far out of the loop as you are these days, Bossk, you seem to know a lot about what's been going down."

That remark got under Bossk's scales. "Look," he said, voice harshening, "I may not be working as a bounty hunter these days—" It galled him to have to make even that much of an admission of his prior defeats. "But that's all because you stole my ship from me. If I still had the *Hound's Tooth,* believe me, I'd be on top of this game."

"I didn't steal the *Hound* from you," said Boba Fett mildly. "You abandoned it, and I took it over. A piece of junk like that really isn't worth stealing."

"Junk!" His claws dug into the tabletop as he started to push himself up from the booth's seat. "That's the best ship in the galaxy—"

At the edges of his slit-pupiled vision, Bossk was aware of the others in the cantina looking once again in his and Boba Fett's direction, some of them glancing surreptitiously from the corners of their eyes, others more boldly. Bossk's raised voice had alerted them all to the possibility of imminent violence, which was always one of the chief sources of amusement for this crowd. He had always known that they didn't come here just for the clattering and whining music from the jizz-wailer band, still setting up and sound-checking their gear over in the corner.

"Junk," muttered Bossk sulkily. With an effort of will, he forced his temper below the boiling-over point as he sat back down. Boba Fett was playing the usual round of mind games with him, just as the other bounty hunter had done so many times before. It was all part of Fett's usual negotiating strategy, a way of getting a psychological advantage over an adversary. *Whoever angers you, owns you*—that was one of Boba Fett's operational mottoes. Bossk had heard it before, and had fallen for it often enough, that he knew it was true.

"It's served my purposes," said Fett. "Well enough."

Bossk raised one of his scaly eyebrows. "It's not here with you, is it?" His voice lifted with hope. "I mean, here in the spaceport."

"Of course not. I had to get here in something of a hurry. I didn't have time to creep along in that pile of ..." Fett paused for a moment. "That *valuable* relic."

"Don't start." Bossk let his shoulders slump. "I just thought ... that maybe I'd gotten it wrong from my information sources. That you'd been detected as being aboard N'dru Suhlak's Headhunter." Bossk tried turning his opponent's verbal tactic around. "You know, that's kind of a new low, even for you, Fett. Using a hunt saboteur to ferry you around. I never knew anybody in the old Bounty Hunters Guild who would've touched one with a gaffi stick, except to beat him to death with it."

Boba Fett didn't rise to the bait. "Circumstances, rather than desires, dictate my actions. That's why I'm still a bounty hunter, and you're not."

"Don't worry about that," replied Bossk testily. "I'm going to be in the game again—and real soon. Aren't I?" To be on the safe side, he tilted his head back and scanned the crowd in the cantina, trying to spot any creature with whom Fett might be working. The chances of that were slim—most of the other top-rank bounty hunters would have been out searching for Boba Fett instead, scheming on turning him into the kind of hard merchandise for which Kuat of Kuat had posted such an impressive price. And Fett himself, as Bossk knew from his own past experience, rarely took on partners; Bossk was still amazed at having heard of him being in league with a relative second-rater like Dengar. "That's why you're here. You're going to make that all possible for me, huh? Even if you didn't bring the *Hound* back with you, so you could return it to me."

"You can have your ship back—when I'm done with it." Boba Fett shrugged. "And if there's anything left of it then."

Bossk ignored the comment, as being just another of Fett's infuriating verbal gambits. "Okay. So you came here to take care of some other business with me, right? Let's see if we can make this mutually rewarding. Because it's not going to happen unless it is." Boss leaned across the table, letting his eyes narrow to slits. "How much you going to pay?"

"You're mistaken." The other bounty hunter gazed right back at him. "I wasn't planning to 'pay' anything."

"Plan again, pal." Bossk grated out the words. "I've got what you want—what I found inside that cargo droid aboard your ship—and I've got a real good idea of what it's worth. Because there are other creatures besides you looking for it, and they're offering a nice high fee on delivery."

"So why didn't you sell it to them? From the looks of it, you could use the credits."

"Because . . ." His fangs ground together, as though they had seized upon Boba Fett's throat. "I figured I could get even more out of you. And even if I couldn't get more—even if I couldn't get the same—I still wanted to get it out of *your* pockets. I wanted you to pay, Fett. Because I know that's worse for you than if I *killed* you."

"You're right. I don't find that prospect at all pleasant." Boba Fett reached under the table. His hand came back up with a blaster pistol in it, which he pointed between Bossk's eyes. "So why don't you just hand the goods over to me, and that way I won't have to kill *you*."

"Are you *crazy*?" The sight of the weapon, hanging motionless right in his face, had frozen him as well. Glancing out of the corner of his sight, Bossk saw that all the mingled hubbub of conversations in the cantina had suddenly died, with every creature there turning and looking in the direction of the rear booth in which he and Boba Fett sat. "I thought you wanted to do *business*."

"That's what this is." Boba Fett raised the weapon's muzzle a fraction of an inch higher. "Consider it my final offer."

The show was too good to ignore; the cantina's other patrons had started buzzing and whispering, excitedly pointing out details of the confrontation to one another.

"You *are* crazy." The blood in Bossk's veins, never warmer than the surrounding atmosphere, had suddenly chilled. "Look . . . let's think about this."

"There's no need to," said Fett evenly. "It's a straightforward proposition. Hand over the material that you found inside the cargo droid, when you were rummaging around in *Slave I*, and I won't kill you. What could be fairer than that? Mutually rewarding as well: I'd have what I came here for, and you'd still be alive."

"But . . . but look at the chance you're taking." The gears of Bossk's thoughts slowly started moving again. "I don't have what you're talking about right here on me. You think I'd carry stuff like that around? No way." Bossk shook his head vigorously. "I've got it well hid, someplace where nobody else would be able to find it."

"Whatever's been hidden can be found again."

"Maybe so," said Bossk, "but not without a lot of searching. And that would take time. Time that you don't have right now." His words started coming faster. "You said yourself, just a couple minutes ago, that you came here to Tatooine in a hurry. That must mean you've got to get your hands on that stuff real quick. You kill me now, and that's not going to happen. You'll be stuck here in Mos Eisley, rooting through every possible place I could have stashed the goods. And maybe you won't ever find it. Think about that." Bossk gave a quick nod, his own fanged muzzle almost brushing that of the blaster being held on him. "Then what'll you do? You won't be getting any help from me, if I'm already dead."

"Good point." The blaster pistol remained where it was, unwavering in Boba Fett's grip. "But not good enough. Do the math, Bossk. If I kill you now, I might indeed have only a small chance of finding what I came here for. But all your chances will be over. What's inconvenient for me will be terminal for you." Boba Fett's finger rested upon the trigger, a centimeter away from unleashing its fire. "There's nothing left to discuss. So what's it going to be?"

The darkly shining metal in the other bounty hunter's hand mesmerized Bossk. He had looked straight at death before—in the bounty hunter trade, it was a regular occurrence—but never with as much certainty as now. The pulse in his veins seemed to stop, along with time itself; all the rest of the cantina faded away, along with its whispering voices and watching eyes. The universe seemed to have contracted, down to the width of the booth's table, holding nothing but himself and the helmeted figure across from him, with the blaster as the pivot of gravity between them.

"All right . . ." Bossk's throat had gone as dry as the Dune Sea, somewhere out in that vanished world surrounding the booth. "I'll . . ." The next words caught in his throat, as though they were too big to dislodge. "I'll go ahead and . . ." His hands drew into fists, claws digging ragged parallel grooves in the table's surface. For a moment longer, Bossk remained paralyzed, then he found himself slowly shaking his head. "No, I won't," he said flatly. "I won't do it."

"What did you say?" The blaster didn't move, but a minute fraction of surprise sounded in Boba Fett's voice.

"You heard me." Bossk's heart was racing now; his vision blurred with the increased pressure for a moment, then he managed to bring Boba Fett's image into focus again. "I'm not going to do it. I'm not going to give you the stuff I found inside that droid." He raised his hand from the marks his claws had dug into the table and spread them wide, making an additional target out of his chest. "Go ahead and fire. I don't care." A certain exhilaration came with those words; Bossk felt absolutely free for the first time in his existence. "You know . . . I just realized something. That's how you always won before," he marveled aloud. "It was because you didn't care. Whether you lived or died, or whether you won or lost. So you always wound up surviving, and you always won." Bossk slowly shook his head, admiring his own sudden insight. "That's amazing."

"Spare me." The dark-visored gaze remained as steady as the blaster in Boba Fett's hand. "I won because I had more firepower—and brainpower—than you or anyone else did. That's what matters. Nothing else."

"Yeah, well, not this time." Bossk found himself smiling with genuine pleasure, even though he knew he might very well be enjoying the last few seconds of his life. "You know, I really should've figured this out before. I've been in plenty of tight spots, where I was looking death straight in the face—like when Governor Desnand was planning on peeling my skin right off me— and I always managed to fight or bribe my way out of them. I even managed to steal the *Hound's Tooth* back from Tinian and Chenlambec, and that took some doing, believe me. And then to have you steal the *Hound* away from me . . ." Bossk slowly shook his head. "Crazy business, huh? Not surprising that I never figured out what it all *meant*. At least until now." Bossk gestured at the blaster in Boba Fett's hand. "So you got the firepower, all right, for all the good it'll do you. Go ahead. Shoot."

A shadow fell across the table. The cantina's bartender had pushed his way through the crowd, right up to the side of the rear booth. "Hold on, you two—" The man's lumpish face was shiny with sweat. "We don't want any trouble here—"

"It's a little late for that." Boba Fett swung the muzzle of the blaster around toward the bartender. "Isn't it?"

"Now . . . wait a minute . . ." The bartender held up his hands, palms outward, as though they were capable of stopping a blaster bolt. "I was just . . . trying to help you work things out. That's all . . ."

"And so you can." With his free hand, Boba Fett reached into one of the pouches in his battle armor and drew out a data-transfer chip. "Does this establishment have a verify-and-transmit connection with the local banking exchange?"

"Sure—" The bartender nodded and pointed toward the opposite side of the cantina. "Back in the office. We use it for our own accounts. We get a lot of credits, from a lot of different systems, moving through here."

"Fine." With his thumb, Fett punched in a few quick commands on the chip's miniaturized input module. "Take this and have the balance in my local cache account deposited in the name and identity scan of this individual here." He indicated Bossk with a nod of his helmet. "Keep the five-percent service fee for yourself. Got that?"

The bartender nodded again.

"Then do it."

Bearing the transfer chip in his hands like a precious relic, the bartender turned and hurried toward the cantina office. The crowd parted before him, to let him pass. Then their wondering faces all turned back toward the scene in the booth.

"All right," said Boba Fett. He tucked the blaster back into its holster. "There. You've won."

Bossk stared at him uncomprehendingly for a moment before he could speak. "What did you say?"

"You've won." A note of impatience tinged Fett's words. "Isn't that what you wanted?"

A tiny bell note sounded from a pouch on one of the straps crossing Bossk's scale-covered chest. He fumbled out the small readout card with his own account balance encoded on it. A few minutes ago, the numbers had been pitifully small. But now the transfer of funds had gone through, as Fett had instructed the cantina's bartender. The resulting change in the readout figure widened Bossk's eyes into almost perfect circles.

The crowd in the cantina had heard what Boba Fett had said. The volume and buzzing urgency of their comments to each other went up several notches.

"I won?" Bossk lifted his gaze from the readout to his own reflection in the dark visor of Fett's helmet.

"Look," said Boba Fett. "I don't have time to either kill you or argue with you any further. I've paid you—" He pointed to the readout in Bossk's claws. "And that's more than you would've gotten from Kuat. So that's my half of the business we're doing here. So work with me on this, all right? Your turn. Where's the stuff you took from my ship?"

Bossk still felt slightly stunned. "It's . . . not here . . ."

"You told me that already. So where is it?"

"Back at the hovel-stack . . . where I've been staying . . ." Bossk gave him the directions, the exact route down Mos Eisley's twisting alleys. "Move the pallet . . . and there's a hole underneath, covered with a board . . ."

"That's your hiding place?" Boba Fett shook his head in disgust. "I could have saved my credits." He slid out from the booth. "Make it last," he said, pointing to the readout in Bossk's hand. "Might be all you'll see for a while." Fett turned and strode away, the crowd quickly shifting to either side of the cantina.

Bossk sat staring at the display for a few moments longer, then tucked it away again. He stood up from the booth and immediately halted in place.

The cantina crowd was massed solid in front of him, eyes of the galaxy's various shapes and colors regarding

him, with none of the creatures saying a word. Then—
slowly—the silence was broken, as first a few individuals, then the entire crowd, began applauding and raucously
cheering.

A drunken harf, with shining red, gogglelike eyes and
an elongated snout, put a massive arm around Bossk's
shoulders. "We don't like you any more than we ever
did," said the creature. "We just never saw anything like
that before. Not with Boba Fett, that is . . ."

"Sure . . ." Bossk nodded in appreciation of the
other's words. "It means a lot to me, too." *Back in the
game,* he thought dizzily. He didn't need the *Hound's
Tooth* anymore; with the credits he had now, he could
buy a whole new ship. And a better one . . .

Ideas and desires whirled through Bossk's head. He
pushed his way through the noisy crowd, heading for the
light outside.

"Must've been one of those days." On a level stretch of
plain outside Mos Eisley, N'dru Suhlak looked up from
the access panel on his Headhunter's exterior hull. He
had been keeping himself busy with necessary repairs to
the craft; after the encounter with Osss-10 above Tatooine's atmosphere, the Headhunter hadn't been in optimum
shape. Reaching into his tool kit for a larger hydrospan-
ner, he had spotted Boba Fett returning from his "business meeting" in the spaceport's cantina. "Couple of folks
came by a little while ago; they told me some of what
happened."

Fett had a small parcel, wrapped in unmarked flimsiplast, tucked under his arm. "Creatures talk. You should
ignore them."

"Don't know about that." Suhlak wiped his hands
on a greasy rag, then slammed the access panel shut.
"Sounded kind of interesting. I mean, a big roaring blaster
fight like that, and all those other creatures getting killed.
Must have wiped out half the 'port's population."

"Nowhere near," said Fett drily. "These things get exaggerated when they get told over and over." He reached up and stowed the package in the Headhunter's bubbled-out passenger area. "Is this thing ready to go? Just because I got what I came here for, that doesn't mean I'm in any less of a hurry."

"We're outta here." Suhlak picked up his tool kit. "Sooner you're off my hands and I get paid, the happier I'll be."

In a few minutes, the Z-95 Headhunter was beyond Tatooine's atmosphere again, heading for deeper space and the rendezvous point with Dengar and Neelah aboard the *Hound's Tooth*. From the pilot's chair, Suhlak glanced over his shoulder and watched as Boba Fett unwrapped the package and began examining its contents.

I don't even want to know, thought Suhlak. He turned back to the controls and the forward viewport. Whatever the package might hold, it was Fett's business and none of his own. *Let him get killed over it.*

Suhlak started punching numbers into the navicomputer, getting ready for the jump into hyperspace.

15

"How long do you think we'll have to wait around here?" Dengar turned from the *Hound*'s controls and glanced over his shoulder. "Before he shows up?"

"I don't know," said Neelah. "Hope it's soon . . ."

They had dropped out of hyperspace and into the Oranessan system, followed by the KDY security cruiser, just as Boba Fett's scheme had predicted. Since then, Dengar had kept the *Hound's Tooth* at the precise speed that their strategy called for: just fast enough to stay out of reach of the pursuing cruiser. The mottled orb of Oran-μ, the system's largest planet, filled the forward viewport as the chase continued.

All that Neelah and Dengar needed now was for Boba Fett to have successfully completed his mission on Tatooine and then rendezvous with them here, as they had agreed upon back at Balancesheet's freighter. Neelah had half expected Fett to already be here waiting for them; that sort of thing was exactly his style. But instead, when the *Hound's Tooth* had reached its destination, they had been greeted with the disappointing reality of empty space, with no sign of the smaller Headhunter craft, with its hunt saboteur pilot and bounty hunter passenger.

"The way I see it," fretted Dengar, "is that there's a couple of things that could go sour right about now. "Either something happened to Boba Fett and Suhlak on the way to Tatooine or on the way here—like them getting intercepted and blown away by one of the other bounty hunters gunning for 'em—in which case they're not going to be showing up here at all. Or Boba Fett had some other plan of his own all along, and he's double-crossed us, which would mean that he never intended to meet up with us here at all." That notion made Dengar grit his teeth while giving a slow shake of his head. "Then we'd be waiting around here for nothing."

"I don't think that last one's too likely," said Neelah. Leaning back against the cockpit hatchway, she crossed her arms tight across her breast, as though that were the only way to keep her jangling nerves under control. "He's got reasons for hooking up with us again. Not because he's got any great affection for either one of us, but because he'd still be thinking there'd be some way of generating a profit from me."

"Maybe so." Dengar didn't seem convinced. "It's just that he's got such a devious mind. But then, I knew that *before* I ever became partners with him."

"There's another possibility." It was one that had been gnawing away for a while now, even before they had caught sight of the Oranessan system approaching in the distance. "The worst one."

"What's that?"

"Just this," said Neelah grimly. "That nothing happened to Boba Fett on the way out to Tatooine, and nothing happened to them on the way here. And nothing happened on Tatooine, either."

Dengar's brow creased with puzzlement. "What do you mean?"

"Don't you get it? What if Boba Fett gets all the way

to Tatooine, finds this Bossk creature—and Bossk doesn't have this fabricated evidence that was taken out of that cargo droid, back on Fett's ship." Neelah's voice tightened in her throat. "Maybe it doesn't exist anymore. Maybe Bossk got rid of it; maybe he decided it wasn't worth anything, and he destroyed it somewhere along the way."

"You're forgetting something," said Dengar. "Bossk has already put the word out that he's sitting on this stuff, looking for a buyer for it."

"That doesn't mean he has it." Neelah shook her head in disgust. "Boba Fett isn't the only bounty hunter with a devious mind. Bossk could've gotten rid of, or lost track of it in a hundred different ways, before he had any idea of its value. Then when he heard that Kuat of Kuat was looking for it and was ready to pay a high price for it, he might have decided to see if he could scam the money for it from Kuat, without actually delivering it. Or Bossk might have thought that if it was so valuable, the prospect of getting it back would be a perfect enticement for luring Boba Fett within striking range—you know what kind of a grudge Bossk has against Fett. This might've been Bossk's way of finally settling up old scores—or at least trying to."

"Yeah . . . maybe so." Dengar slumped in the pilot's chair, looking deflated. "I hadn't thought about anything like that. But I guess you're right. It's possible."

Neelah had been doing plenty of thinking like that. All the way from Balancesheet's freighter and the drifting fragments of old Kud'ar Mub'at's web, her mind had been ceaselessly turning over one bleak idea after another. All of them processed out as the complete dashing of her hopes, of any chance of answering the remaining questions about her past. Those hopes had been raised from the dead, more thoroughly than Dengar and Boba Fett had revived Kud'ar Mub'at, by the assembler's successor and its surprise about the fabricated evidence being back on Tatooine. Whether that was true or not, it had at least renewed Neelah's faith in there being still one more slender thread that would lead them out of the blind alley to which all their searching up until now had brought them.

But if, as she couldn't keep herself from fearing, the last possible clue no longer existed—if it had been a fool's errand on which Boba Fett had gone to Tatooine—then she had no idea of where she would be able to turn next. In a galaxy consumed with the struggle between the Empire and the Rebel Alliance, the chances were slim for someone with only a name as the key to the mysteries of her past, a name and its connection to the ruling families of the planet Kuat. For all she knew, it might have been the powerful Kuat of Kuat who had ordered the wiping of her memory and the abduction from her homeworld. And she'd already seen evidence enough, in the bombing raid on the Dune Sea, that Kuat was not someone who would forgo murderous violence to achieve his ends. If she were to blithely show up on the planet Kuat, seeking whatever position in its ranks of nobles that had been stolen from her, she might well be placing herself in the hands of those who had sought to eliminate her once before. Kuat might indeed be the one place where the answers could be found to the mysteries surrounding her—but it could just as easily be where certain death awaited her. Without Boba Fett returning from Tatooine with the fabricated evidence that had been hidden in the cargo droid aboard his ship, she had no chance of knowing which would be the case.

He either meets up with us here, she thought, gazing above Dengar's head toward the viewport, *and has the evidence with him . . .*

Neelah left the thought uncompleted in her mind. It was something she didn't want to contemplate any further.

And—she realized—she didn't have to.

"Look." Neelah pointed to the viewport. "Right there . . ."

Dengar had been monitoring the relative position

of the KDY security cruiser behind them, on the display from the *Hound*'s rear scanner. He looked up and saw the bright spot of light in the midst of the field of stars. Bright and growing brighter, straight ahead of them.

"It's pretty small, from the looks of it. And fast. Maybe . . ." Quickly, Dengar punched up the approaching craft's ID profile. "It's him," said Dengar, dropping his tensed shoulders in relief. "It's that Headhunter ship of N'dru Suhlak's. So Boba Fett has to be aboard it, right?" Smiling, Dengar glanced over his shoulder at Neelah. "I mean, it stands to reason—Suhlak wouldn't have come here to rendezvous with us without Fett, would he?"

"No—" Neelah shook her head. "He wouldn't have any reason to." So that set of possibilities, of the total that she had been obsessing over, was ruled out. At least Boba Fett hadn't abandoned them; she and Dengar were still part of whatever plans he was pursuing. "Now all we have to see is whether he found what he went to Tatooine for."

"We'll have to do a running transfer, in order to get him aboard." Dengar pointed to the image from the rear scanner. The cruiser from the Kuat Drive Yards' security division was still the same distance behind the *Hound's Tooth*. "If we come to a halt, even for a couple of minutes, they'll be on top of us."

"Can we do that?"

"It's tricky, but possible." The comm unit mike was already in Dengar's hand. "Suhlak's Headhunter is coming within range. I'll get the details worked out with Boba Fett. You'll need to run the controls here in the cockpit while I man the transfer hatchway."

She listened as first Suhlak's, then Boba Fett's voice came over the cockpit speaker. As Dengar and Fett quickly calculated the necessary matching velocities for the ships, Neelah fought the impulse to ask—demand, rather—what had been found and brought back from Tatooine.

You've waited this long, she scolded herself. *You can wait a few moments longer.*

Left by herself in the *Hound's* cockpit, Neelah kept her hands poised on the thruster engine controls. Suhlak had brought the Z-95 Headhunter up alongside the *Hound's Tooth,* carefully modulating his speed and narrowing the gap between the two ships' hulls. A muted thump sounded through the frame, followed by the sharper vibrations of the transfer hatchway locking into place.

The three men showed up in the cockpit area at last, with Suhlak trailing behind the bounty hunters. "I got a stake in this now," Suhlak said to Neelah with a grin. "I didn't want to miss any of the show."

"You found it," said Neelah. She had spotted the object, a black rectangle a few inches thick, in one of Boba Fett's hands. The data recording unit trailed a few loose connectors, as though Fett had been working on it while en route. "You got it from Bossk."

"That poor guy." Dengar shook his head pityingly. "I hope Bossk was smart enough not to put up too much of a fight. What kind of condition did you leave him in? Or is he even still alive?"

"When I left him," said Boba Fett, "he still was. And not in too bad a shape."

"Who cares about him?" Neelah could conceal her impatience no longer. "You got it—that's all that matters."

"Correction." Suhlak pointed to the rear scanner display. "You've still got a KDY security cruiser on your tail. And"—he leaned toward the control panel, peering at the image—"it's gaining on us."

"I'll take care of that." Boba Fett took over the pilot's chair from Neelah. She stood back and watched as the bounty hunter's hands fastened onto the thruster engine controls. With his hands inside the Trandoshan-sized grooves on the panel, Fett slammed the controls to their maximum—

And nothing happened.

"The engines have cut out," said Dengar. Reaching past Boba Fett, he tapped a forefinger against the power consumption gauges. "Take a look at that." The glowing red digits had dwindled to zero. He pointed to the indicator lights for the navigational jets. "Everything's gone down. This ship's not going anywhere."

"What's happening?" Neelah looked from the image on the rear scanner display, showing the KDY cruiser rapidly approaching, to the bounty hunters' faces. "What's gone wrong?"

"Good question," said Boba Fett. "If it was just the main thruster engines going dead, or the navigational jets by themselves, it could be a simple systems malfunction. But for all of them to go out at once—something else did that to them. And deliberately."

"Like what?"

"Right now, I don't know—but let's take a look at the comm unit log." With a couple more commands tapped out inside the control grooves, Boba Fett brought a different set of data scrolling across the smaller display screen. "There's part of the explanation." He pointed to the last line of digits and letters. "A coded pulse was received from the vector directly behind us—obviously, from the KDY cruiser. We didn't hear anything on the comm unit speakers because the pulse didn't include a transceive request. So the pulse was picked up and acted upon by some other part of the *Hound's* operational circuitry."

"Hey—don't worry about it." The hunt saboteur Suhlak's voice broke into the discussion. "I can fix it."

"You can?" Standing next to Suhlak, Dengar looked at him in surprise.

"Sure." Before Dengar could react, Suhlak reached over and plucked the blaster pistol out of Dengar's belt. Suhlak took a quick step backward, covering the others with the weapon raised in his hand. "At least as far as I'm concerned."

Neelah glanced up from the blaster to Suhlak's face. "What're you doing?"

"Figure it out." Suhlak backed toward the cockpit area's hatchway. "That KDY cruiser has obviously got some way of keeping this ship stuck here—but it can't do it to my Headhunter. So I'm outta here. And you people can deal with whoever's aboard the cruiser." Still keeping the blaster trained on them, Suhlak set his foot on the top tread of the ladder down to the *Hound*'s cargo area. "Don't bother to ask if any of you can come along. I'm not going to risk having that cruiser chasing after me."

Boba Fett watched as the hunt saboteur started down the ladder. "If you think you're going to get the cut we agreed on, you're wrong."

"Chances are good that there won't be anything to get a share of once that KDY cruiser finishes with you." Suhlak's head and the upraised blaster were just visible above the lower rim of the hatchway. "I'd rather cut my losses and keep my skin intact, if you know what I mean."

A few moments after Suhlak had made his exit, they heard the noises through the hull, of the Headhunter disengaging from the transfer hatch. In the forward viewport, the smaller ship could be seen, speeding away from the *Hound's Tooth* and then disappearing among the stars.

"That's one person who's managed to save himself." Dengar slowly shook his head. "Now what happens to the rest of us?"

"We're about to discover that," said Boba Fett. "The KDY cruiser has already come within targeting range, and it didn't fire on us. So they must have something else in mind, other than just blowing us away."

"Somebody must want to talk, then." Dengar pointed to the viewport. "We're moving; they've got a tractor beam locked on us."

A voice came over the comm unit speaker: "This is

Kodir of Kuhlvult, head of security for Kuat Drive Yards." A female's voice, crisply articulating. "Am I correct in assuming that the bounty hunter Boba Fett is aboard this ship?"

He hit the transmit button on the panel. "You're speaking to him now."

"Then I'll be transferring over with a couple of my people. I want to have a meeting with you. And I *don't* want any funny stuff."

"What do you think I'm likely to try," said Fett, "with a cruiser sitting on top of me?"

"Just keep that in mind." The comm unit connection broke off.

"What do you think she wants?" Neelah glanced from the overhead speaker toward Fett.

"Could be anything. But given that I've returned here from Tatooine with exactly what her boss Kuat of Kuat has been looking for, the chances are slim that it has much to do with anything other than that."

There wasn't time for Neelah to question Boba Fett about what he'd brought back with him. The hull of the *Hound's Tooth* had already come up against the larger ship's grappling mechanisms and been seized by them. "Let's get down to the cargo area." Boba Fett pushed himself up from the pilot's chair. "We all might as well hear what this person's got to say."

Kodir of Kuhlvult, flanked by two KDY security operatives, proved to be an arrogantly impressive figure, with a full cape falling back from her shoulders and brushing the heels of her outspread boots. Neelah found herself gazing intently at the woman's face, searching for any clue that might be revealed there.

"So you're the bounty hunter that I've heard so much about." Kodir's gaze had swept across all three of them and then locked upon Boba Fett's dark-visored helmet. "You have a considerable reputation for surviving in situations where others would have died. Is that luck or intelligence, Fett?"

"Creatures who depend upon luck," replied Boba Fett, "don't survive."

"Well spoken." Kodir nodded in appreciation. "Believe me, I bear you no ill intent; I would just as soon have you alive as not. So whether it's luck or brains, your string doesn't have to be broken now—if you don't want it to."

"All right." Boba Fett folded his arms across his chest. "So what is it that you do want?"

"Please." A smile lifted one corner of Kodir's mouth. "Let's not make this any more difficult than necessary. You're aware, I imagine, that Kuat of Kuat seeks certain things—"

"Including my death."

"Only as an incidental matter. And that merely as a way of preventing a certain item from falling into the wrong hands." Kodir's gaze narrowed, the smile turning crueler and more knowing. "Now, if that certain item were to be placed in Kuat's hands, then I can assure you that he would have no interest in your death at all."

"And what makes you believe I have this . . . 'certain item,' as you put it?" The gaze from the dark-visored helmet remained level with hers. "If you're referring to the fabricated evidence purportedly linking the late Prince Xizor with Imperial stormtrooper raids on Tatooine, then I can give you equal assurance that at the time Kuat of Kuat tried to kill me before, it wasn't in my possession."

"Ah . . . but that was then, and this is now. It doesn't matter what the situation used to be; it only matters if you have that fabricated evidence with you now." The smile disappeared from Kodir's face. "And don't bother saying that you don't have it. You were brought to this rendezvous point by a ship that was reported having been seen recently at the planet Tatooine; we've also just heard that your fellow bounty hunter Bossk was seeking to find a buyer for exactly that item we've been seeking. It'd be too much of a coincidence for your journey to Tatooine to be un-related to what Bossk had for sale. And in fact"—her smile reappeared, more unpleasantly—"I'm some-what grateful to you for having gone to Tatooine and acquired the item for us; you've saved me the journey *and* the potential unpleasantness of dealing with a creature like Bossk. He doesn't have the same reputa-tion for being a levelheaded businessman that you do, Boba Fett."

"I'm enough of a businessman," replied Fett, "to lis-ten to a good offer."

"Then I'll make you an excellent one." Kodir of Kuhlvult signaled with one hand to her accompany-ing KDY security operatives; they immediately drew blaster pistols from the holsters on the belts and cov-ered the two bounty hunters and Neelah with them. "And it's an offer open to everyone: hand over this fab-ricated evidence and you won't be killed." She spread both her hands apart. "What could be a better offer than that?"

Dengar broke the resulting silence. "It's up in the cockpit. Stashed by the pilot's chair."

"You idiot." Neelah glared at him. "Now we'll never—"

"Don't be too hard on him," said Kodir. "Your associ-ate's acceptance of my offer, while appreciated, merely saves me time and effort. Even if you had gone to some effort to hide the desired item, we would have found it soon enough after you were all . . . gotten out of the way, so to speak. Even if we'd had to take this ship apart bolt by bolt; I haven't gone to this much effort *not* to get my hands on it."

One of the KDY security operatives had already climbed up the ladder to the cockpit. He returned car-rying in one hand the object Boba Fett had brought back from Tatooine. Pulling his blaster from its hol-ster again, the operative resumed his position flanking Kodir.

"Perfect." Kodir looked at the object that the operative had just given her. She turned it over and examined the code marks on the underside. "Exactly what I came for." Kodir looked up at Boba Fett. "It's been a pleasure doing business with you. I've enjoyed it so much that I'm actually going to keep my end of our bargain. After all . . . you've been useful to Kuat Drive Yards in the past; there's no saying when we might find you handy to have around again. Plus, you're not going anywhere soon in this ship—are you? So that should keep you from interfering with any of my immediate plans."

Kodir signaled to the KDY operatives. They began backing toward the transfer hatch, while still keeping their blasters pointed at the *Hound*'s occupants.

"Sorry things didn't go as well for you as you might have hoped." Holding the black data recording unit in the crook of one arm, Kodir smiled even less humorously than before. "But I've had a very good day—surprisingly so. I not only got what I originally wanted, but I found an unexpected bonus as well." She gestured to Neelah. "You—you're coming with us."

Neelah stiffened, regarding the other woman with suspicion. "Why should I?"

"Oh, I could give you all sorts of reasons. But there's really just one important one, as far as you're concerned." Kodir of Kuhlvult tilted her head to one side, studying Neelah's reactions. "You've got questions, don't you? Questions that you want answers for—I know you do. Well, I've got the answers to them. That should make it a simple decision for you."

A moment passed, then Neelah slowly nodded. She stepped away from Dengar and Boba Fett, and followed the first of the two KDY security operatives into the transfer hatch. Behind her as she stepped toward the other ship, she could hear Kodir give one last taunting farewell to the two bounty hunters.

"Good luck," said Kodir to Dengar and Fett. "When

you're outsmarted and outgunned, that's the best you can hope for."

Glancing over her shoulder, Neelah saw the transfer hatch seal shut.

Kodir pushed her forward. "Let's get going. We've got an appointment to keep."

16

"I still don't understand how they were able to stop us." In the cockpit of the *Hound's Tooth*, Dengar shone a handheld worklight through the access panel. "What did they do to make the engines cut out like that?"

"It's obvious." Boba Fett's voice came muffled from beneath the control panel. He lay on his back, shoulders and helmeted head deep within the maze of circuitry cables. "This ship wasn't built at the Kuat Drive Yards, but Bossk must have taken it in there at some point for some custom retrofitting. Probably an updated weaponry targeting system—that's one of the first modifications that a bounty hunter gets done on his ship when he's a few credits ahead."

That was accurate, Dengar knew—there had been a time when he had been planning on getting the same job done on his craft, back before he'd met up with his betrothed, Manaroo, and other, more desirable goals had been put on his agenda. And Kuat Drive Yards, the top in the shipbuilding and engineering field, had been where he'd wanted to go for it.

He knelt down beside Boba Fett's outstretched legs, angling the light source up to where the other bounty hunter's gloved hands were working. "So you think Bossk took it in there, and they put in some hidden cut-out device that he didn't know about?"

"Exactly," replied Fett. "Nothing too elaborate, just a simple override that could be triggered by a coded pulse from a remote transmitter. Which, of course, they had aboard their own security division vessel."

"Yeah, but why would they do that to Bossk's ship? I mean, KDY would've had to have done it a while back; they wouldn't have known it would come in handy like this someday."

"They didn't do it against Bossk specifically." With a needle-tipped logic probe, Boba Fett traced the intricate wiring beneath the control panel. "KDY probably does it to every ship that comes into their docks for retrofit work—just so they'd have a backdoor system in place, in case they ever needed to disable one of their customers' ships. It'd be an insurance policy for KDY—and shutting down the *Hound's Tooth* was one of the times they cashed it in."

"Yeah, but . . ." Dengar shook his head. "I can't believe they'd put something like that in the ships they build for the Imperial Navy—or in your ship. I mean, Kuat Drive Yards built *Slave I*, didn't they?"

"Of course KDY wouldn't try putting a cut-off device into my ship, or anything they built for the Empire." Boba Fett peered upward at the circuits, concentrating on his task. "There would be too much at risk if it was found. And KDY knows that the Imperial Navy has a standard practice of thoroughly checking out all the work done on new vessels, and on any retrofits, for precisely that reason, to make sure that any kind of delayed or optional sabotage device hasn't been smuggled in. As do I; when I accepted delivery of *Slave I*, I went over the ship with a fine-tooth comb, just as I had told them I would. So naturally, I didn't find anything amiss. A customer like Bossk, though, isn't quite as thorough—which is what KDY was counting on." Boba Fett tilted his head to one side. "Bring the light in a little closer; I think I've found it."

"Can you fix it?" Leaning forward on his knees, Dengar tried to see in through the access panel.

"It'll take some work. Typical KDY job; very well engineered. It's not just a simple break in the circuit with a pulse-reception activator. They wired in a parallel microfilament of some kind of high-temp pyrogenic; when it went off, it vaporized the entire signal-relay subsystem, out to the main engines and the navigational jets." Boba Fett pulled himself out from underneath the control panel and sat up. "We'll need to strip out the circuits from most of the cargo area servo-mechanisms, just to get the materials to patch in here."

"Okay—" Dengar stepped back as the other bounty hunter got to his feet. "I'll get started pulling out the bulkhead sheaths." He reached down and picked up a clench-awl from the open tool kit on the cockpit's floor. "But I got another question."

Boba Fett didn't look at him, but continued examining a section of charred wiring from beneath the controls. "What's that?"

"When we get this ship up and running—what happens then?"

"Then we head for the planet Kuat," said Boba Fett. "I don't let anyone—not even Kuat of Kuat—take things from me. Without paying for them."

"We've got a lot to talk about," said Kodir of Kuhlvult. "Don't we?"

Neelah gazed back at the figure seated before her, in the security head's private quarters. The other woman had dismissed the rest of the ship's personnel, leaving her and Neelah by themselves. She had heard the door hiss shut behind her, as though it were sealing them both into a space inviolable enough for the revealing of secrets.

But I don't know if that is what will happen here,

thought Neelah. For all she knew, there would be nothing but more lies and mystery, darkness and words whose only meaning was to conceal.

And worst of all—some of those words would be her own.

"I suppose we do." Neelah remained standing, even though Kodir had offered her a chair. "I've got a lot of questions. That I think you might have the answers to."

"That's not how it works." Kodir gave a single shake of her head. "Kuat of Kuat put me in charge of security for Kuat Drive Yards, not because I was good at giving information away, but because I know how to keep a lid on it. People—even you—find out things when I want them to, not the other way around."

"Perhaps I shouldn't have come along for the ride, then."

"You didn't have that choice." Kodir stood up and stepped toward her. The edge of the other woman's cape swirled close to Neelah's feet as Kodir reached out and gently stroked the side of her head. "Choices have been in short supply for you, I know. So much has been lost to you . . ."

"Those are the things," said Neelah, "that I'm looking for." She didn't draw away from the other's hand, though it felt cold and alien as the fingertips drew down to the curve of her jaw. "The things I've lost: my past, and my name."

"And you've had no luck. What a shame." Kodir smiled sympathetically at her. "Perhaps you should have chosen your companions more wisely. One rarely profits by hanging out with bounty hunters."

Neelah didn't correct her, though she could have. *My name*, she thought to herself, *is Kateel*. She had discovered that much in the fragments of her memory. And that the name belonged to one of Kuat's ruling families. Neelah had remembered that as well, when she had seen the record in Boba Fett's datafiles of the emblem that his hard merchandise Nil Posondum had scratched into the floor of the holding cage. There had been other things she had remembered, little bits of light penetrating the mists, when she had seen Kodir of Kuhlvult's face . . .

She had seen the woman long before Kodir had stepped through the transit hatch and boarded the *Hound's Tooth*. Of that, Neelah was sure.

That certainty had given rise to caution inside her. In that past, whose shapes were still frustratingly vague, things had happened between this Kodir of Kuhlvult and herself—and they hadn't all been pleasant. *She wanted me to do something*—Neelah couldn't remember what yet, only that it had been important, and that a great many other creatures' fates besides her own had depended upon her answer. Which had been a refusal; she hadn't gone along with Kodir's plans back then, whatever they had been.

There had been a spark between her gaze and Kodir's when the other woman had come aboard the *Hound*; Neelah had seen her eyes widen, a reaction that had been swiftly caught and controlled, as though Kodir had unexpectedly recognized her. *She didn't expect me to be there,* mused Neelah. *It was a shock to her.* But one that Kodir of Kuhlvult had made a considerable effort to hide. *Why?*

Another question without an answer; they multiplied rather than lessened the more she discovered about herself, as though she were trapped in a galaxy composed of infinite and expanding darkness.

But there was one other thing of which Neelah was sure: if this Kodir of Kuhlvult, with all of her connections to the planet Kuat and to the mysterious figure Kuat of Kuat, was going to play it cagey about revealing what she knew . . . then she would, too. Neelah had spent too much time with crafty and scheming creatures such as the bounty hunter Boba Fett not to have some of their survival-oriented mind-set seep into her own. Boba Fett didn't tell all he knew; and he had won so many times before, just as in the stories that Dengar had told her while they had both been down in the cargo hold of the *Hound's Tooth*, the whole history of how Fett had come out on top of the wreckage of the old Bounty Hunters Guild. *He won those wars,* thought Neelah, *by being smart.* She'd have to do the same to win hers.

Which meant—for now, at least—concealing exactly how much she had remembered of her own past. Until she could be sure of Kodir's connection to it.

"You're better off here with me." Kodir had taken her hand away; she turned and walked back to the chair. "It's . . . *safer* that way."

Safer for whom? wondered Neelah. "Where are we going?" She asked that question aloud, watching as Kodir rested one hand on the chair's curved back and raised her gaze to the private quarters' ceiling, as though deep in thought.

"Where?" Kodir glanced over her shoulder. "Shouldn't you have guessed that by now? We're going to that place that you most want to arrive at, the place where all your answers are waiting for you."

"You mean, we're going to Kuat?" The words slipped out of Neelah's mouth before she could stop them.

Kodir's brow creased as she studied Neelah for a moment. Then she smiled. "Very near there," said Kodir. "So close, you'd almost be able to reach out and touch the world of Kuat—if that's what *you* meant. But there's another Kuat—a man, Kuat of Kuat—and we won't be seeing him just yet. There's a little more business that needs to be taken care of before that can happen. And then both of you will be in for a bit of a surprise."

Neelah listened, but did not reply. But inside her, the twin strands of caution and suspicion grew and knotted around each other.

"You were correct in your suspicions, sir." The comm specialist made his report to Kuat of Kuat. "There has been another person added to the Rebel Alliance fleet currently above our facility. Nonmilitary, but of considerably high rank, from what we've been able to determine; possibly of negotiating attaché level."

Kuat sat near the bank of transparisteel overlooking the KDY construction docks. Stroking the silken fur of the felinx curled in his lap, he had listened to the report without turning to look at the comm specialist. "When did this attaché arrive?"

"About six minutes ago, sir. Commander Rozhdenst personally smuggled in the attaché—or attempted to, but our spy units managed to penetrate their operation without them knowing. Both Rozhdenst and this attaché—the name is Wonn Uzalg, from what we've been able to determine—are currently aboard the base station unit."

"Indeed," said Kuat. The felinx murmured beneath his gently moving hand. "And do we have access to what's going on in there?"

The comm specialist smiled. "Excellent access, sir. From this close a range, we had no problem sending out a micro-probe unit with stealth auguring capabilities. It's already penetrated the base unit's hull and tapped into the interior monitoring circuits. We can hear everything that's said in there."

"Very good; I commend you and your staff on the quality of your work." Kuat gave no compliment beyond that, but he felt an undeniable measure of gratitude toward the comm specialist, and to the other personnel of Kuat Drive Yards. Their loyalty was still unquestioned. "And what is being said at this moment?"

"Not much," admitted the comm specialist. "Or at least nothing that our security analysts feel is significant. Both Rozhdenst and this attaché Uzalg appear to be waiting for the arrival of another person, with whom they'll be having some kind of meeting."

"And do we know," said Kuat of Kuat patiently, "who that 'other person' is?" Both his gut instinct and logic told him it had to be someone important; the Scavenger Squadron's commander wouldn't have gone to the effort of sneaking in a Rebel Alliance attaché if the individual in question was some nonentity.

"That's the critical part, sir." The comm specialist stood with his hands clasped behind the back of his standard-issue, insignia-less overalls. "And that's why I thought it best to make this report to you personally, rather than routing it through the usual security division channels." He hesitated nervously for a moment. "It's possible—but unlikely—that Rozhdenst discovered the bug device we've managed to place aboard their base station, and that he and Uzalg are using it to feed us false information. As I indicated, our own analysts feel there's little chance that the micro-probe has been found yet; it didn't trip any of the base unit's perimeter alarms. So there's a definite probability that Rozhdenst and the Rebel Alliance attaché are indeed waiting for the person whose name we've overheard in their conversation so far."

Kuat swiveled the chair about and regarded the comm specialist. "And what name is that?"

Another fraction of a second passed before the comm specialist spoke. "It's Kodir of Kuhlvult, sir. That's who it appears they're waiting for. And she's on her way; we've picked up the approach signals from the cruiser she's aboard."

"Kodir?" One hand froze where it had been scratching behind the felinx's ear. "That's impossible. Our analysts must have misunderstood what Commander Rozhdenst and the Rebel Alliance attaché said . . . or there's something wrong with the bug you've planted." Kuat shook his head firmly. "There's simply no way that Kodir could be rendezvousing with them. Not without notifying me first."

"I'm sorry, sir." The comm specialist stood his ground. "The facts remain. Our analysts did a thorough spectral breakdown of the signals we recorded from the base station probe. And there's no other interpretation of the data: the person that Rozhdenst and the attaché said they're waiting for is Kodir of Kuhlvult."

"And her cruiser is presently on its way here?"

"Either here, sir—or to the Scavenger Squadron's base station."

"Establish a comm unit hookup with her. Immediately," ordered Kuat of Kuat. "I need to speak with her *now*."

"I'm afraid that's not possible, sir."

"And why not?"

"We've already attempted raising Kodir's cruiser on both the secured and unsecured transceiving bands." The comm specialist gave an apologetic shrug. "The communications equipment seems to be working—we know that the cruiser received our signals—but Kodir has apparently given orders to her own crew not to respond. They're effectively maintaining link silence—or at least they have been since their last transmission, which we just managed to detect before the micro-probe bug was activated. That transmission was to the Scavenger Squadron base station."

The felinx stirred beneath Kodir's hands; it could sense its master's tension.

"Sir?" A few moments had passed in silence. "Do you have orders for us?"

Deep inside Kuat, his brooding thoughts had grown darker. "Yes," he said slowly. "I'll need to speak to the α-foreman and β-supervisors out in the construction docks. It's time . . ."

The comm specialist frowned in puzzlement. "Sir? Time for what?"

"Don't worry." Kuat closed his eyes as he stroked the soft fur of the felinx. "Everything will be all right. You'll see . . ."

17

"This is very serious," said the Rebel Alliance attaché. "We're indeed grateful that you brought it to our attention."

"Sometimes," replied Kodir of Kuhlvult, "one has to do what's right. No matter what the cost might be to oneself."

The three figures—Kodir, the attaché Wonn Uzalg, and Commander Rozhdenst—sat circling an improvised conference table aboard the Scavenger Squadron's mobile base unit. The table was little more than a durasteel access panel that had been taken off its hinges and laid flat across a pair of plastoid shipping crates that had once held foam-wrapped weaponry fuses. In the center of the bare metal sat a glossy black, rectangular object; its contents had been extracted as well, and run through the portable data scanners that Uzalg had brought with him from Alliance headquarters. A hard-copy printout on several sheets of flimsiplast detailed the atmospheric sampling and olfactory bio-analysis that had been broken out of the spy device that had originally contained the evidence.

"Of course, it's obviously fabricated." Uzalg's hairless skull was reflected in the black container's sheen. "There's no question about that."

"What the attaché is saying"—Commander Rozhdenst made a dismissive gesture at the items on the conference table—"is that there's no way anybody in the Rebel Alliance is going to believe that the late Prince Xizor had anything to do with this Imperial stormtrooper raid that this thing caught." One corner of his mouth curled downward as he shook his head. "The responsibility for that particular raid has been established beyond a shadow of a doubt. It all came direct from Darth Vader's personal command. Our own information sources, both within the Empire and the Black Sun, have confirmed that. Xizor had nothing to do with it."

"That does seem to be the case." Uzalg spoke much more calmly and soothingly than the Scavenger Squadron commander; Kodir could understand how he had risen to a high diplomatic position inside the Alliance. "Nevertheless, this evidence—no matter how fraudulent it is in essence—still has some significance for us."

"I don't see why we're even bothering with it." Rozhdenst's sneer grew even more pronounced. "We've got other, more important business to take care of—like keeping an eye on what's going on down in the KDY construction docks. This stuff is old news; Xizor's been dead for a long enough time now. There isn't going to be any trouble coming from that direction. Let's concentrate on our *living* enemies, all right?"

"You're missing the whole point," snapped Kodir. Her gaze tightened into slits as she regarded the commander. She hadn't come all this way, back here to a point just above Kuat Drive Yards itself, to wind up dealing with some one-track military mind. "It doesn't matter whether Prince Xizor is alive or dead. All that's important is knowing who had an interest in creating this phony evidence against him, and why they did it."

Uzalg reached out and touched the commander's

sleeve. "She's got an excellent point," Uzalg said softly. "After all, that's why I came here. On an emergency basis, as well—given what's shaping up out near Endor, there's a great many other things I could be taking care of right now."

"You and me both, and everybody else in my squadron." The commander's temper flared even higher. "Look, the Alliance wants to put us out where there's nothing happening, that's the high command's decision, and there's nothing I can do about it. But you can bet that my men and I would sell our own viscera on the black market if there was a way of buying into that battle at Endor. We'd rather die in the action than fall asleep baby-sitting some fancy dry-dock facility like this."

"Rest assured, Commander, that the value of your service here will become apparent before too long." Uzalg took his hand from the commander's sleeve and tapped with a forefinger on the spread-out data before them. "You are a creature of action—your calling demands that of you—but it makes you understandably impatient with the slow sifting of the past's remnants, the gleaning of the small grains of truth. As our friend Kodir here has spoken, it is not the surface appearance of this fabricated evidence that matters. It is what lies underneath."

"All right," grumbled Rozhdenst. "So what is it?"

Kodir watched as the attaché leaned closer to the other man. "Someone," said Uzalg darkly, "wanted the Rebel Alliance to believe that Prince Xizor and the Black Sun organization were involved in some way with a raid by Imperial stormtroopers on a moisture farm on the planet Tatooine. It's logical to assume that the target of that disinformation would have been the Rebel Alliance, and more specifically Luke Skywalker himself. As heinous as that stormtrooper raid was, its significance is primarily for us. Skywalker has become both an inspiration and a charismatic leader for our forces; at this point, it might very well be said that his joining the Rebels was a crucial turning point for the Alliance, at one of our darkest hours. As Skywalker has shown us, one brave individual can turn the course of battle. And bravery can be contagious: right now, there are many ready to fight at Endor whose hearts have been strengthened by Skywalker's example. As you've said, Commander, you would give a great deal to be with them. But the moral strength that has flowed into the Alliance was largely shaped by a purity of vision as well; Skywalker knew that the raid in which his family died was the work of the Empire. He's known since then exactly what he's had to fight against. What would the consequences have been, both for Skywalker and the Rebel Alliance, if that vision had been confused and muddied by evidence showing that Prince Xizor and Black Sun had somehow been involved in that stormtrooper raid? Skywalker's attention might well have been diverted at some crucial point while he tried to unravel this mystery, the clues of which were all lies to begin with. He very likely would have found that out, and seen through the lies, but at a price of critically lost time—and the Alliance would have paid that price with him."

The sneer had vanished from Rozhdenst's face. "I see your point."

"It's exactly why I wanted the Alliance to have this information," said Kodir. "As security head for Kuat Drive Yards, I've discovered some things I'd rather not have found. My sympathies are with the Rebel Alliance, gentlemen—but apparently my feelings are not shared by everyone here. Most importantly, they're not shared by Kuat of Kuat, the leader of Kuat Drive Yards. He's made it plain to me that he fears and distrusts the Alliance. Of course, it's bad enough that he has not supported you in your struggle against the Empire—but it turns out that he's been actively seeking your defeat." She paused a moment, gauging the two men's reactions to her words. "For it was Kuat of Kuat who created this false evidence, and who sought to have it planted where Luke Skywalker would have eventually learned of it, and been deceived by it."

"I'm not completely sure of your interpretation of Kuat's actions." Uzalg frowned and stroked his chin with his fingertips. "I've dealt with Kuat of Kuat in the past, before you became head of security for Kuat Drive Yards. At that time, I implored him to throw the resources of his corporation behind the Alliance, and he refused—but I was convinced that he bore the Alliance no ill will, but was simply concerned with the corporation's fate, should Emperor Palpatine defeat and destroy us. Such a decision on his part was prudent, but regrettable. Of course, he may have deceived me on that point; Kuat of Kuat is an undeniably clever individual whose wits have been sharpened by dealing on a constant basis with Palpatine and his admirals. Or Kuat may have changed his position regarding the Rebel Alliance; we can expect that Palpatine has brought great pressure on him. Or . . ." The Alliance attaché nodded thoughtfully. "The scheme in which this fabricated evidence was to have played a part might not have been directed against the Rebels at all. It might have been considerably more devious than that; the target might have been Prince Xizor himself, while he was still alive. Rumors had circulated for some time concerning Xizor and Black Sun's own designs on Kuat Drive Yards; greed and ambition are qualities hardly limited to Emperor Palpatine. By entangling Xizor with Luke Skywalker and the Rebel Alliance, Kuat might very well have been getting one enemy off his hands, leaving all of his attention intact in order to fight off Emperor Palpatine."

Sitting across from the attaché, Kodir said nothing, but tried to conceal her own reaction to Uzalg's words. *He's even smarter than I expected,* thought Kodir. *Maybe too smart . . .*

"We don't have time to sort out all the possibilities." Commander Rozhdenst laid a hand down flat on the improvised conference table. "The question is, what're we going to do about it?"

"True," said Uzalg. "Whether Kuat of Kuat was conspiring against the Alliance directly, or whether he was attempting to use the Alliance against another enemy such as Prince Xizor, is immaterial at this point. The battle between the Alliance and the Empire, which we've been anticipating for so long, might already have begun; communications from that sector have been effectively silenced. We have no way of foreseeing what the outcome of the events out near Endor will be—the Alliance has a prime strategic opportunity in front of it, a chance to destroy the Imperial Navy's new Death Star while it is still under construction, with its weapons systems not yet activated. Our analysis is that the Death Star is relatively unprotected, with most of the Imperial forces scattered about the galaxy attempting to engage with Rebel ships wherever possible. But there's still no way of accurately predicting just what kind of losses our forces will indeed suffer in their attack upon the Death Star, or what the Empire's response will be to such an action. In the aftermath, the relative balance of forces between the Alliance and the Empire may be absolutely critical—that's where Kuat Drive Yards comes in." The Alliance attaché's words had become more clipped and efficient. "If the Imperial Navy can take possession of the fleet replacements sitting here in the KDY construction docks, they might still be able to administer a killing blow to the Rebels."

"Or the other way around." Rozhdenst's eyes gleamed with anticipation. "If we could get our guys into those ships . . . it'd take more than my Scavenger Squadron, but still . . ." He drew his breath in through clenched teeth. "We'd be in line to finish off the Imperial Navy!"

"That would depend on a great many things." Uzalg's response was spoken in quieter tones. "But the fact remains that the ships here at Kuat Drive Yards would be valuable to both the Empire and the Alliance—perhaps decisively so. We need to make sure that they don't fall into the hands of the Imperial Navy. And"—he glanced over at Kodir—"we also need to make sure that Kuat Drive Yards is on our side, not just now but in the future.

The Empire is still powerful; the struggle against it might continue for a lot longer. It would be best for both the Alliance and Kuat Drive Yards if we were united in that struggle. But given the evidence we've seen . . ." One hand gestured toward the items on the conference table. "Unfortunately, we can't depend upon Kuat of Kuat to see it that way."

"You're talking about eliminating him," said Rozhdenst.

"Or at least removing him from his position of control over the corporation. In which case, Kuat Drive Yards will need someone else running it."

Both men looked over at Kodir of Kuhlvult.

"Is that what you're offering me?" She kept her face a carefully composed, expressionless mask, hiding the thrill of triumph she felt at the moment. *At last*, thought Kodir. *Everything I wanted . . . everything for which I've been scheming and plotting for so long . . .*

"Exactly," said Uzalg. "We've already been in communication with the heads of the ruling families down on the planet Kuat. Given the circumstances, a majority of them have agreed with what the Alliance has recommended concerning your taking over Kuat Drive Yards if something were to, shall we say, *happen* to Kuat of Kuat. They might be a little surprised about it coming around so soon—but that doesn't matter."

It was all hers now. Handed to her by the Rebel Alliance.

"It is a great responsibility," Kodir said quietly. "I'm not sure I'd be up to the task."

Uzalg studied her for a moment in silence. "You have no choice," he said finally. "Nor do we. You must do it."

"Very well." Kodir felt her hands squeezing into fists, as though they were already grasping the very circuits of unlimited power. "I accept the burden you have offered me." She couldn't stop a thin smile playing about her lips. "You are now looking at the new head of Kuat Drive Yards."

• • •

The α-foreman and β-supervisors made their report.

"All the systems you requested are in place," said the α-foreman. He stood with the others behind him, just inside the high doors of Kuat of Kuat's private quarters. "Just say the word and we'll . . ." The man hesitated a moment. "We'll put them into operation."

"That won't be necessary," replied Kuat. He had been gazing out at the construction docks as he listened to the men, with the felinx sidling around his ankles; now he turned and looked at the corporation's faithful employees. "I thank you for the work you've done; I'm sure it's all at your usual high standard of accomplishment. But your job is over now. I'll take care of the rest."

"But . . ." The α-foreman's brow furrowed, as though he doubted his own hearing. "We have served under your leadership in so many things. Do you not believe that we would wish to see this through as well?"

"I have no doubt of that. It's not even an issue. But most of you have families and loved ones; I have neither of those, except for Kuat Drive Yards itself. There are places for you to go to, when all of this is over—the demand for workmen with your skills will always be high, no matter who wins the distant battles in which the galaxy is embroiled. But there is no place else for me to go." Kuat looked at his own empty hands for a moment, then back up at the gathered men. "Therefore, the price to me of finishing this job is smaller than any that you could pay . . . and what is bought by that price is great to me." *Peace,* thought Kuat. *That's what it buys. Something I've never known.* "My own decisions, however well meant they were—and my own failures—have brought this day upon us. It's not only my desire to finish this job by myself. It's my duty."

"But it's our duty as well, Technician." One of the β-supervisors raised his voice. "The corporation belongs to us as much as it does to you."

Soon, Kuat mused, *it will belong to no one.*

"He speaks true," said the α-foreman, tilting his head toward the β-supervisor in the ranks behind him. "We placed our faith in you, but we did so willingly. The responsibility for your decisions is shared among us all."

"Ah." Kuat of Kuat slowly nodded. "But you see—I am still the head of Kuat Drive Yards. No matter what others outside this room might think, that is still the case. So the decisions are mine to make, and yours to obey. To do otherwise on your part would be the withdrawal of your faith in me. Do you wish to do that?"

The men remained silent. Kuat knew that he had caught them in the trap formed of his logic and their loyalty. It was perhaps the last machine he would ever devise, but it had worked as well as any before it.

"As you wish, Technician." The α-foreman bowed his head in defeat. "And as you order. We leave you now, in all but spirit."

There was no further need to thank the men who had worked for him, and for Kuat Drive Yards. Kuat stood watching as they turned and slowly filed out through the high, arched doorway. As long as they were still employees of the corporation—and in some ways, they would be even after Kuat Drive Yards had ceased to exist—they functioned as precisely and predictably as the tools upon which they had laid their hands.

When the footsteps of the men had faded down the corridor outside his quarters, Kuat of Kuat turned back to his lab bench. A simple audio recording device was plugged into the signal relay from the micro-probe spy device that listened to those other voices far above the construction docks. Those voices—Kodir's, and the Scavenger Squadron commander's, and that of the negotiating attaché from the Rebel Alliance—had also talked of the fate of Kuat Drive Yards.

18

"You know," said Kodir, "we really should have had this little talk a long time ago."

Neelah stood with her arms folded across her breast, watching the other woman as she stepped away from the door and into the center of the tiny room. The door had been locked from the moment Neelah was shoved inside by a pair of KDY security operatives; she had expected as much, even before she tried opening it.

"I've been waiting." Neelah made sure that no emotion was apparent in her voice. That was something she had picked up from Boba Fett, a way of masking one's intent as completely as though behind the dark visor of a helmet. "We've got a lot to talk about, don't we?"

"There's enough." With a thin smile on her face, Kodir halted a few steps away from Neelah. "But always—so little time."

"So I can imagine." Neelah warily regarded her. "You must be busy right now. What with that stuff you managed to take off of Boba Fett, and everything you could do with it."

The smile shifted to a puzzled frown. "What do you know about that?"

"A lot," said Neelah. "More than you might think I'd know. I've got a good idea why you'd want a pile of fabricated evidence against a dead Falleen, and who you've been talking to about it." Neelah couldn't help letting a thin smile of her own show. "And I know things about you, Kodir. I know you like keeping secrets. Well, this is one that's gotten away from you."

Surprise flickered at the center of Kodir's gaze. "What do you mean?"

"Come on. There's no sense in trying to create any more lies, any more mysteries. You've been talking to somebody from the Rebel Alliance. Haven't you? Somebody important, who can get you what you want, what you've been after for a long time."

"How do you know that?"

Neelah stepped to one side, in a slow, circling dance with Kodir, their gazes locked tight with each other.

"That part's easy," she said. "I could see the Rebel ships up above the construction docks as we came in. And I know that we didn't land on the planet Kuat." Neelah tilted her head for a moment toward the surrounding bulkheads. "And you can't pass off something like this as the KDY headquarters. You see, I know what those headquarters are like. I've been there before. *I remember them.*"

Kodir's eyes widened. "You remember . . ."

"Everything."

Both women stood still, the wary circling ended. Neelah now had her back to the small room's door.

"That changes . . . a great deal . . ." Kodir studied the figure standing before her. "Depending upon what it is that you *think* you know."

"It's not a matter of thinking," replied Neelah grimly. "Next time you try something like this, you should hire better people to do your dirty work for you. Spend the credits; get the best. Not some incompetent like Ree Duptom—" That name produced a quick, startled reaction in Kodir that Neelah was pleased to see. "Because if a memory wipe isn't done correctly—and thoroughly— then there's a lot of little, disconnected pieces left over. Scraps of memory, right around the edges of the dark. And bit by bit, those memories can link up with each other, and with things that can bring back even more memories from the shadows. And then—like I said"— she gave a single, slow nod—"everything comes back."

"That fool." Kodir's voice turned bitter. "I paid him enough so that whatever go-betweens and intermediaries were used, the end result would be to get just such a specialist, one that had formerly worked for the Empire itself—they're available, but expensive. I wasn't pleased when I found out later that some cheap hustler had pocketed the credits and done the memory-wipe job himself."

"Lucky for me, then, that he wasn't very good at it." Neelah tapped the side of her head with one finger. "Because I had already remembered my real name—Kateel of Kuhlvult—before you ever showed up at the *Hound's Tooth*; I had already found the clues that brought back that part of my memory. But when I saw your face— again—then all the rest came back." Neelah's hand lowered and clenched into a trembling, white-knuckled fist. "Everything—including why my own sister had tried to get rid of me."

"I got rid of you"—a sneer curled one corner of Kodir's mouth—"because you were a fool."

"Because I wouldn't go along with the schemes you had worked up to overthrow Kuat of Kuat and take control of the corporation."

"Still a fool, I see." Kodir shook her head in disdain. "It's not a matter of 'overthrowing' anyone. As I told you long ago, it's simple justice. Kuat and his predecessors have run Kuat Drive Yards for generations—and they've kept all the other ruling families frozen out. Kuat and his bloodline have never had the right to do that. But if you had joined forces with me, all of that would have come to an end. The others in the ruling families who had tried to force Kuat from the leadership—they were nothing but a diversion, too stupid to even conceal their intentions from him as I have."

"You confuse justice with ambition, Kodir. That was your first mistake. And then you mistook me for someone as greedy as yourself."

"Oh, I admitted that I was wrong—that's why I had to do something about you, before you could let Kuat of Kuat know that I was plotting against him. I had to have you abducted from the planet Kuat, and have your memory wiped, so you'd no longer present a threat to me." Kodir's expression darkened into a venomous scowl. "But when I found out that the ones I had trusted—and paid—to do my 'dirty work' for me, as you call it, had failed me, I realized that I should have taken care of these things myself." Kodir's smile was hardly less ugly than the scowl had been. "And that's exactly what I've done, isn't it? After all—I tracked you down before you could do any damage to my plans. And believe me, it wasn't easy."

"You were lucky," said Neelah. "I had just enough clues—enough little pieces of my memory left—to try and find out what had happened, and try to make my way to someplace where I could find out those answers. I didn't realize that what I was doing would make it possible for you to stumble across me."

"How ironic." Kodir's words were edged with sarcasm. "The things we do to try and save ourselves—they so often put us right in harm's way. As when I offered to make you part of my plans to get rid of Kuat of Kuat; if I had known how stupid and blindly loyal you were, I'd never have done that." She spread her hands apart, palms upward, in a mocking, blasé show. "But that's why it's so important to learn from our mistakes. Isn't it? You made your mistakes—and I've made mine. And we've both gotten what we wanted. You wanted the truth about the past, about what happened to you—and now you know. And I wanted the leadership of Kuat

Drive Yards. Guess what? That's just what I've been given."

"So you convinced the Rebel Alliance to get rid of Kuat, so you can take over the corporation. Congratulations. For however long it lasts."

"That'll be for quite a while," said Kodir. "It doesn't even matter which side wins the battle out near Endor. Now that I've got control of the corporation, I can deal with the Alliance or the Empire—it makes no difference to me."

"I can see that." Neelah gave a slow nod. "Maybe if the Empire wins the battle, Palpatine will find that you're just the kind of servant he prefers. Greedy and self-serving, but smart enough to recognize just who's got the upper hand."

"Don't bother trying to insult me." Kodir's laugh was quick and harsh. "As long as I've gotten what I want, I really don't care about your moral opinions."

"I'm sure you don't. But that makes me wonder about just one thing." Neelah peered closer at the figure standing before her, the woman whose bloodline she shared. "If getting what you want is all that matters . . . why were you so tenderhearted about my fate? If all that worried you was my interfering with your plans, wouldn't it have been more effective—and final—to have simply had me killed, rather than abducted and memory-wiped?"

"As I said: we need to learn from our mistakes. And that's one I'm not going to repeat again." Kodir reached to the section of her belt that had been concealed by the flowing cape, and pulled out a small but efficient-looking blaster pistol. She raised and pointed it straight at Neelah. "I'm sorry that I don't still have the same sisterly feelings toward you that I once did. There was a time when my foolish sentimentality made me think that I could spare your life. I've gotten over it, though. The Rebel Alliance, on the other hand, has shown a depressing tendency to let mere ethics guide its decisions; that very likely means that after this coming battle at Endor, I will be dealing with the Empire rather than the Rebels. Palpatine, though, has a vindictive streak that's just as worrisome. And he doesn't like plotting and scheming that's not his own: if anyone was going to get rid of Kuat of Kuat, the Emperor would have wanted to be the one to do it. So you see"— Kodir raised the blaster a fraction of an inch higher—"there's no way I can afford to let you remain alive, and risk having you tell what you've remembered."

"You're right," said Neelah. She didn't flinch from the weapon poised in her direction. "And you really do seem to have learned from your mistakes. There's just one problem with that."

A thin smile showed on Kodir's face. "And what would that be?"

Neelah didn't bother to reply. Instead, she stepped forward toward the blaster; at the same time, she brought one forearm up and smashed it against Kodir's wrist, faster than the other woman could react. The blaster pistol went flying, its high arc broken by the nearest bulkhead. With her other hand, Neelah grabbed the collar of Kodir's flowing cape; with a quick, sharp tug, she pulled her off balance. As Kodir fell forward, Neelah brought her raised knee into the other woman's solar plexus, knocking the air from Kodir's lungs in a pain-filled gasp. Neelah stood back and let Kodir fall, forearms clutched instinctively to her gut; another blow to the back of the head laid her out flat on the room's floor.

A few seconds later, Kodir managed to twist herself onto her back. She blinked at finding the muzzle of the blaster pistol set right between her eyes.

"The problem with learning from our mistakes"— Neelah leaned down to keep the weapon aimed point-blank at her sister—"is that sometimes we learn a little too late."

Face pale with shock and pain, Kodir gazed up at her in disbelief. "You . . . didn't used to be able . . . to do stuff like that . . ."

"I've been hanging out with a tough crowd." Keeping

the blaster muzzle fixed on Kodir's skull, Neelah reached down and grabbed the front of the cape, using it to draw Kodir to her feet. "If you can stay alive long enough, there's a lot you can pick up from somebody like Boba Fett. Especially when you've got nothing to lose."

Before Kodir could manage a reply, another sound pulsed through the room, so deep and low that Neelah could feel it through the soles of her boots. Both she and Kodir looked up, as though storm clouds could have been seen through the durasteel bulkheads surrounding them.

The noise sounded like distant thunder. But she knew it was something else.

News from a distant world arrived almost simultaneously with the shock wave from the explosions.

Commander Rozhdenst had been personally monitoring the link to the Rebel Alliance communications ship near Sullust. When word came at last that the attack on the uncompleted Death Star had turned into a full-scale battle between Rebel and Imperial forces, he closed his eyes for a moment, letting his chin sink down upon his chest. The desire to be there, to be in any fighting craft no matter how antiquated or unwieldy, as long as it was in the thick of the action, rose with tidal force through his heart.

He heard the door to the officers' quarters open. Opening his eyes, Rozhdenst looked up from where he sat at the comm unit controls and saw Ott Klemp. "It's started," said Rozhdenst simply. He didn't have to explain what he was referring to. "And we're stuck here, in the middle of—"

His words were cut off by the first explosion shivering through the frame of the mobile base. A dull, low-frequency rumble made the air in the room suddenly tangible upon both the commander's and Klemp's skin. The younger man, muscles visibly tensing, looked up toward the ceiling. "What was that?"

Before an answer could be ventured, indicator lights burst red across the comm unit panel. The voice of one of the Scavenger Squadron's forward scouts crackled over the speaker. "Commander! Something's going on down at the KDY construction docks—something big!"

Rozhdenst had already switched on the scanners for the base's viewport array. Across a row of display screens, from multiple angles, flame and churning smoke billowed up from the angular masses of equipment below. As both he and Klemp leaned toward the screens, another explosion was suddenly visible, uprooting one of the gigantic cranes at its base and sending it toppling down across the docks' central access corridor. The crossed durasteel struts of the crane's framework crumpled and bent upon one another with the force of their crashing impact; cables several meters thick snapped like string, their broken ends whipping through ranks of load shifters and rail trucks, scattering them as though they were toys.

The noise from the explosions couldn't pass through the surrounding vacuum to the Scavenger Squadron's mobile base above, but the shock wave and expelled metal debris were enough to conduct the rumbling and clattering sounds from the hull to the interior a few seconds after the bursts of glaring light on the display screens. As Klemp put out an all-craft command to pull back from the inferno erupting beneath them, the commander punched in the highest levels of surveillance magnification from the scanners.

"It's not the ships—" Rozhdenst laid a broad fingertip on the closest display screen. "The fleet isn't what's going up." The elongated ships of the cruisers and Destroyers could be seen through the smoke, harshly lit by flames and the hard-shadowed light of another series of explosions. "It's the docks and all of the major shipbuilding equipment." As both he and Klemp watched, a durasteel-jawed magna-hoist lurched forward like a dying saurian, its blind head bursting through a wall of fire and plowing into a rack of structural girders. "The whole facility's been stuffed with high-thermal explosives, from the looks of it."

"Yeah, but . . ." Klemp shook his head. "That whole fleet is going to be scrap as well by the time it's all over." Another impact shook the mobile base. "You think Kuat of Kuat did this? What's he after—sabotage or suicide?"

"Who cares—"Rozhdenst reached for the comm unit mike. "We've got to get those ships out of there."

"Sir, that's impossible. There's nobody aboard any of those ships. Who's going to bring them out of the docks?"

Rozhdenst glanced over his shoulder. "Who do you think? Our guys can do it."

"That's crazy. I mean . . . it just is, sir." Klemp pointed to the image of the flames billowing up on the display screen. "You want our squadron to fly into *that*? The condition that most of our Y-wings are in, they can just barely avoid getting hit—and you want them to go into that kind of a mess? They'll get torn to pieces!"

"If they're in such rotten shape, then it won't be much of a loss, will it?" Rozhdenst locked his gaze with that of the younger man. "Look, if you or any of the other members of the squadron don't want this job, then fine— you can stay out here at the base and watch. But I'm going in."

Klemp was silent for only a fraction of a second. "And I'll be right behind you, sir. Along with everybody else."

"Good." Rozhdenst gave a single, quick nod, then handed the microphone to Klemp. "There's no time for plotting a formation attack; this show is going to be over in minutes. Give the squadron full operational initiative— everyone's on their own for vector, approach, and target. Total scramble, eye and comm unit contact to avoid taking each other out." The Scavenger Squadron commander stood up from the controls. "Let's get going."

"They must have seen us coming," said Dengar. "So they decided to blow the whole place up."

The explosions had filled the forward viewports as soon as the *Hound's Tooth* dropped out of hyperspace. Both Dengar and Boba Fett, in the ship's cockpit, could see the fiery cataclysm taking place in the Kuat Drive Yards' construction docks.

"Don't be stupid," snapped Fett. He pointed to the display screen. The tiny dark shapes of Y-wing craft could be seen silhouetted by the roiling masses of flame. "Those Alliance fighters are obviously going in to try and pull out what they can of the ships moored there. The docks are being blown up from within; there's only one person who could have arranged it, and that's Kuat of Kuat."

"He's blowing up his own facility?" Dengar frowned in puzzlement. "Why would he do that?"

"Because he'd rather destroy it," said Fett, "than let it fall into anyone else's hands. I've dealt with him before; Kuat Drive Yards is all that matters for him. Something must have happened—probably with the Rebel Alliance and that fabricated evidence his head of security took from us—that would end his control over the corporation. So he's taking the whole thing with him."

"You mean . . . he's in there? You don't think he escaped?"

Boba Fett shook his head. "There's no place for Kuat of Kuat to escape to. Or at least no place that has Kuat Drive Yards in it. Survival doesn't mean the same thing for him that it does for you and me; for Kuat, it's just death without peace."

"This is the end of the road, then." Dengar stood back from the pilot's chair and folded his arms across his chest. "You're not going to get any answers out of him now."

"Don't bet on it." Boba Fett reached for the navigational controls.

A sharp current of alarm raced up Dengar's spine. "What're you doing?"

"I'm going in. To find Kuat."

"You're crazy—" The main thruster engines had already kicked in. As Dengar watched in mounting horror, the explosions bursting up from the Kuat Drive Yards' construction docks swelled in the forward viewport. The black shapes of collapsing cranes and heat-warped girders became visible. "You'll get us killed!"

"Maybe," said Fett. "But I'm willing to take the chance."

"Yeah, well, *you* might be willing, but *I'm* not." Standing behind Boba Fett, Dengar clutched the back of the pilot's chair to keep the *Hound*'s surging acceleration from throwing him off his feet. "I can live without every question in the galaxy being answered."

"I don't care about every question. Just the ones that deal with me."

The shock wave from another explosion, larger than the ones before it, buffeted the *Hound's Tooth*. In the forward viewport, a gaping hole could be seen in the center of the KDY construction docks large enough to fly a ship through and ringed with twisted, smoldering metal.

Dengar, with sudden desperation, tried to reach past Boba Fett and grab the controls. "We're supposed to be partners—" His fist locked on to one of the main thruster engine throttles. "And I say we *don't* get ourselves killed—"

With a quick swing of his forearm, Boba Fett knocked Dengar back against the cockpit's rear bulkhead. "You're outvoted on this one," said Fett.

Slumping down to the floor and squeezing his eyes shut, Dengar could still see the bright glaring light of the explosions, as though they were about to shatter the viewport and annihilate everything in the cockpit. Alarm signals shrieked from the control panel as the *Hound's Tooth* bucked and spiraled through an engulfing bloom of shrapnel-filled flame.

Not a good idea, thought Dengar as he ground his teeth together and scrabbled for any hold he could find. *The worst one yet*—

. . .

The commander of the Scavenger Squadron had been within a few meters of Ott Klemp's wingtip, matching velocity with him all the way to the inferno consuming the KDY construction docks. But he'd had to bank hard to one side to avoid another fireball and whirling tangle of girders and cables; by the time Klemp pulled back on course, any visual contact with the rest of the squadron was cut off by roiling masses of smoke and flame.

A gap appeared in front of the Y-wing through which Klemp could just make out a moored *Lancer*-class frigate. As with the other newly constructed ships in the docks, a tug module was magnetically clamped to the bridge. The tugs were not much bigger than the fighter craft swarming through the explosions and white-hot shrapnel; they had no thruster engines of their own, but were designed to be wired through the cruisers' and Destroyers' data-cable ports, using the larger craft's engines to maneuver out of the docks and into open space. At the moment, the tugs were still enclosed in the balloonlike atmospheric-maintenance shrouds in which the Kuat Drive Yards had worked while routing the control lines. The durasteel-laced shrouds had a programmed viscous layer between the inner and outer membranes, with near-instantaneous resealing capabilities to prevent fatal air-loss during routine industrial accidents. Without those shrouds, Klemp knew, there would be no chance of the Scavenger Squadron's pilots pulling any of the fleet out of the cataclysm engulfing the construction docks.

He could see the bridge of the frigate now, with the shroud's bubble on the section of hull immediately behind. The sequenced explosions hadn't reached the ship yet, though its flanks were tinged with the churning red and orange of the approaching flames. Klemp rolled the Y-wing into a diving arc, straight toward the shroud.

The Y-wing's prow ripped through the shroud's fabric; Klemp could hear the sharp ping of the durasteel threads snapping against the leading edges of the wings. At the same time, he was blinded by the thick semiliquid smearing across the cockpit's canopy. That wouldn't be enough to slow the Y-wing down; within a fraction of a second of penetrating the shroud, he slammed on the craft's braking rockets, their maximum force nearly enough to cut the pilot seat's restraining straps through his chest, and snapping his head forward hard enough to momentarily dizzy him.

A tangle of broken durasteel threads, embedded in the shroud's viscous resealing layer, pulled away from the Y-wing's hull as Klemp popped the canopy. There wasn't time to check if there was any atmospheric pressure left in the construction shroud; he gulped in the thin oxygen and looked back along the inner curve of the bubble behind the Y-wing. The fighter's rear section was mired in the rapidly setting substance, with fluttering tatters of the white fabric sucked into the dwindling gaps. Klemp didn't wait to see if the new seal would hold, but instead ran along the frigate's upper hull toward the tug module.

Within seconds, he was inside the tug and slamming the exterior hatch shut behind him. The controls on the panel before him were the minimum necessary for lifting the frigate out of the dock in which it had been built; even before Klemp hit the tug module's pilot's chair, he had engaged the controls running to the cruiser's auxiliary thruster engines. There was a response lag of nearly a second before the ship responded; with a slow surge of power, its enormous mass began ponderously rising from the dock. The power cables and mooring conduits that were still connected to the hull's various ports now tautened and snapped free when they had stretched to their limits.

He hadn't rescued the ship a moment too soon. A burst of fire filled the tug module's viewports as a sudden crashing impact struck the frigate from below. The shock wave of an explosion ripping apart the empty dock jolted the frigate's stern. Klemp struggled with the navigational controls, fighting to keep the ship from toppling end over end and the prow out of the churning debris that welled up toward it.

The nearest dock cranes still towered above the frigate, like immense durasteel-strutted gallows. Even with the thruster controls pushed to their maximum, the ship seemed to be only inching toward the clear space where Klemp would be able to hit the main thrusters and bring it out of danger. The fierce heat from the explosions seeped through the tug module's thin hull, evaporating the sweat as it beaded on his brow.

A sharp blast ripped through the base of the nearest crane. Glancing toward the side viewport, Klemp saw the tapering metal structure begin to topple toward the frigate. There would be no way he could get the ship beyond the reach of the crane's top-mounted arm as it swung scythelike into the hull. If the crane's weight struck midship, it would break the frigate in half, sending the pieces tumbling back down toward the exploding construction docks. Klemp knew he would be dead before the ship's remnants hit the twisted metal rubble below it.

He quickly calculated the chances of abandoning the tug module, sprinting back toward the Y-wing, and flying it out through the entangling construction shroud and into the clear. *Possible,* he told himself. *But you wouldn't have done the job you came here for*—

Cursing, Klemp reached for the navigational controls. The frigate halted its slow rise as he diverted all available power from the auxiliaries to the stern's side thrusters. With increasing speed, the ship pivoted about on its vertical axis.

The toppling crane hit, its mass shearing along the flank of the frigate, grinding and tearing away any protruding structural elements; inside the tug module, the impact of metal shearing away against metal sounded louder than any of the explosions below. Wincing against the stabbing, deafening noise, unable to take his hands away from the controls to shield his ears, Klemp saw a jagged piece of the crane snag the construction shroud's fabric. As the crane continued to topple away from its shattered base, it ripped away the shroud and the Y-wing fighter mired in it.

No great loss, Klemp told himself as he looked over his shoulder and saw the Y-wing breaking apart, dragged toylike across the topside of the ship's hull. With a last, shuddering impact, the crane hit the stern and then toppled away.

The ship was clear—at last. Klemp expelled his pent-up breath in one gasp, then slammed on the main thruster engines. The *Lancer* frigate seemed to hesitate for a fraction of a second, then heaved its bulk toward the stars.

"All right. That does it." Dengar picked himself up from the floor of the *Hound's Tooth*'s cockpit. On wobbling, unsteady legs, he confronted Boba Fett. "The partnership's *over.*"

He reached over to the nearest bulkhead and steadied himself against it with one hand, watching as Fett methodically checked out the weaponry strapped across his Mandalorian battle armor. *Lucky we're even alive,* thought Dengar. Though how long that was going to last, he had no idea. Their ship had barely managed to survive the high-velocity plunge from open space into the thick of the construction docks' roiling explosions. More of the blasts, approaching in sequence, shook the *Hound*'s shock-loosened frame, the metal of its hull grating against the rubble-strewn area on which it had crashed.

"Suit yourself," said Fett. "I owed you for saving my life back on Tatooine. You decide if that debt's repaid by now."

"Oh, it's paid, all right." Trembling with anger and accumulated shock, Dengar stepped back as Boba Fett approached the hatchway. "A few thousand times over. You haven't managed to get me killed yet—but I don't feel like giving you any more chances."

"Fair enough." Boba Fett started down the ladder to the *Hound*'s cargo hold. "I've got business to take care of."

From the cockpit hatchway, Dengar stared at him in amazement. *He's going looking for Kuat.* The realization caused Dengar to slowly shake his head. *There's no stopping him.*

"You go your way," Dengar shouted into the smoke filling the hold. "And—"

The explosions out in the construction docks grew louder, mounting on top of one another and blocking his words.

And I'll go mine, he thought to himself. Dengar turned from the hatchway and dived toward the controls.

He didn't bother plotting a trajectory, but simply slammed maximum power to the main thruster engines. Holding on to the controls inside the Trandoshan-sized forearm grooves, Dengar heard and saw a tangle of cables, their insulated sheaths charred and smoking, drag across the forward viewport. The hull's underside scraped across the warped freight tracks beneath as it accelerated; the explosions that had been marching across the docks finally caught up with the *Hound's Tooth*, lifting the stern as though it were caught and thrown by a giant hand. Dengar hung on desperately as the ship spun end over end, directly toward the side of one of the towering cranes.

The sequence of explosions was faster than the tumbling ship. Before the *Hound's Tooth* struck the crane, the dizzying image through the viewport was blotted out by pure white light, as if Dengar had caught a glimpse into the searing heart of a nova star.

Metal ripped apart from metal as the crane dissolved in the blast, its massive struts flaring outward and then spiraling into the vacuum. Through the flames and smoke filling what had been the explosion's center, the *Hound's Tooth* spun into the clear.

Dengar gaped at the cold, bright stars filling his vision. *Made it . . . I made it . . .*

A few quick adjustments with the navigational jets steadied the ship to a level course. Panting, and with his pulse beginning to slow, Dengar let a fragile smile form across his face. He hadn't been expecting to survive at all; his real intent, he realized now, had been only to keep his corpse from being crushed and incinerated in the wreckage of the Kuat Drive Yards' construction docks.

Pulling his hands from the grooves on the control panel, he laughed in amazement. "After all that," he said aloud. "And I'm the one who's still alive—"

The words inside his head were wiped out by another blinding burst of light. Dengar shielded his eyes with a quickly raised forearm. As the glare faded, he lowered his arm and squinted through the forward viewport. In the distance, another, larger ship—one of the fleet that the Rebel Alliance pilots had been trying to rescue from the construction docks—had not been as lucky as he had been. The other ship's stern had been engulfed by flames just as it lifted away; one main thruster engine had been destabilized in the blast, and had gone into core overload. The resulting explosion had blown a gaping hole in the ship's hull, stranding the ship close to the *Hound's Tooth*.

Dengar watched, then ducked reflexively as another one of the larger ship's thruster engines went off. Weakened by the first engine's explosion, the ship disintegrated, one fireball after another ripping the structural frame to pieces.

He watched, then froze in place, held by what he saw in the viewport. A massive section of the other ship's hull, larger than the *Hound* itself, shot away from the fragmented wreckage, its jagged edges trailing white-hot streaks and quick sparks of debris. The hull section spun and swelled in the viewport, heading directly for the *Hound's Tooth*.

I guess I spoke too soon . . .

There wasn't time to either dodge or swing the ship about and try to outrun the doom heading for it. Dengar didn't even bother to brace himself as the broken section of the larger ship raced toward him.

It hit, and he was thrown through sparks that stung his face and arms like a swarm of angry insects, into a darkness filled with the shrieks of alarm systems and the even louder clash of metal being ripped apart. For a moment, Dengar felt weightless; then he realized, as his arms flailed behind him, that he had been knocked through the cockpit hatchway and was falling to the cargo hold below. The impact of its grated floor against his spine and the back of his skull brought him right to the point of losing consciousness. He held on, dazed and unable to move, listening as the *Hound's Tooth*'s deflector shields collapsed, and the ship began to come apart around him.

He had the cold but genuine comfort that he had at least gotten away from the exploding construction docks. *That's all I wanted,* Dengar thought once more. *Just so my body could be found . . . somewhere, by someone . . .*

Another realization struck him. *I must be already dead.* It couldn't have happened while he was still alive, that a hand was reaching for him and taking his arm, pulling him up as though from his own grave. And that there would be light, and a face looking down at him; the one face he wanted to see more than any other.

"Dengar!" The vision spoke his name. "It's me—it's Manaroo—"

"I know." Drifting closer to unconsciousness, he smiled up at her. "I'm sorry, though . . . I'm sorry I'm dead . . ."

"You idiot." A real hand, not a hallucination, slapped him across the jaw, jolting him fully aware. "I'll let you know whether you're dead or not."

And then he knew he wasn't.

· · ·

"How did you know I'd be here?" Kuat of Kuat turned and regarded the figure that had entered the bridge of the moored Star Destroyer.

"Where else would you be?" Boba Fett's battle armor was blackened with ash from the fires consuming the constructions docks' wreckage. "It suits you; this is the biggest ship in the fleet. That makes for a suitably grandiose coffin. Plus—the construction shroud had been obviously torn away before the explosions started. So there wouldn't be any risk of the Rebel Alliance pilots dropping in."

"Very astutely observed." Kuat gave a judicious nod. "But I really believed that I'd be alone, right to the end. I didn't think that even you would try to track me down here."

The ship's bulkheads trembled as another series of explosions went off. From the viewports of the bridge, masses of dark clouds, shot through with reddening flame, mounted up toward the stars.

"It's worth making the effort," replied Boba Fett. "I've got questions that I want answers to."

"Ask away, then." Kuat of Kuat smiled gently. "It's too late for me to try and conceal anything from you."

Boba Fett stepped closer, across the floor buckled with heat and through the smoke filtering into the bridge. "Why did you want me dead?"

"Nothing personal," said Kuat. "You mean zero to me. But I knew you had in your possession certain items that could prove rather embarrassing to me. And fatal to Kuat Drive Yards. There's an ancient piece of wisdom that advises anyone taking a shot at a powerful creature to be sure to hit him. That's very good advice; I knew the risks I was taking when I created that false evidence against Prince Xizor. But if my scheme had worked, I would have eliminated a major enemy—or at least given him something else to deal with, rather than conspiring to take over my corporation. But the one thing happened that I was unable to foresee: that both Xizor and a vital element of my scheme would be killed before the blow could be struck. Which left a considerable mess to clean up. Getting rid of you would have just been part of that cleanup process. Regrettable—but necessary, in the course of business."

"I already figured out that much. A long time ago." Boba Fett had come within arm's reach of the other man. He pulled out his blaster pistol from its holster and aimed it at Kuat's chest. "What I need to know now is whether that's the end of it."

Kuat looked with amusement at the weapon in front of him. "Rather late for that kind of threat, isn't it? I already consider myself as good as dead."

"You can die here, the way you want—or I can drag you out of here and hand you over to Palpatine or the Alliance, or whoever else would be interested in settling some old scores with you. Your choice."

"Very persuasive, Fett. But unnecessary. I'll be happy to tell you the truth—since I have nothing to lose now by doing so." Kuat reached out his hand and pushed the blaster muzzle away from himself. "All the conspiracies end here. There's no one else involved, no other forces to deal with, once these particular loose ends are taken care of. You don't have anything to be concerned about. Once I'm gone—and I've taken Kuat Drive Yards with me—there won't be anyone else coming after you. Or at least not in regard to the evidence I fabricated against Prince Xizor. You'll just have your usual run of enemies, and all the various creatures with a grudge against you, to deal with." Kuat peered more closely at the bounty hunter. "But you knew that already, didn't you? You said as much, that you had figured it all out. You wouldn't have come all this way, and risked this much—even your life, which you seem to value so highly—just to make absolutely sure of what you knew. So there must have been something else on your mind—right? Some other question you needed to ask of me. What is it?"

Boba Fett hesitated a moment before speaking. "There's a female named Neelah that's been traveling with me."

His voice lowered slightly. "But that's not her real name. She doesn't know I found out that she's actually Kateel of Kuhlvult. She's a member of one of the ruling families of the planet Kuat."

"Very interesting." Kuat raised an eyebrow in surprise. "She would also then be the sister of Kodir of Kuhlvult, the head of security for Kuat Drive Yards. And someone that Kodir had been extremely interested in locating."

"Did Kodir tell you why?"

Kuat shrugged. "The love between one sister and another, I suppose—that's within the range of normal human emotions. But whatever the reason, it was enough for Kodir to force her way into becoming security head so she would have the resources to find this sister who had vanished."

"Then here're the questions." Boba Fett's dark-shielded gaze locked upon Kuat's eyes. "You've heard of a man named Fenald?"

"Of course. He was head of security for Kuat Drive Yards, before Kodir of Kuhlvult was given the position."

"So naturally," continued Fett, "you would've given a sensitive, important job—like making the arrangements for the planting of fabricated evidence against Prince Xizor—to him."

"True enough." Kuat nodded. "That's exactly what I had him do. But how do you know about Fenald?"

"There was encoded material attached to that fabricated evidence when I found it inside the freight droid that had been converted to a spy device. I didn't have time to break the encryption seal then, but when I was coming back from Tatooine, where I had retrieved the evidence from another bounty hunter named Bossk, I managed to crack it. The encrypted material was Fenald's own identity code, including his connection to Kuat Drive Yards. He probably put it there so he'd have the ability to blackmail you by threatening to reveal to Xizor—or Palpatine or the Rebel Alliance—exactly where the fabricated evidence had come from, and who had been responsible for it."

"I wouldn't put it past him."

"Here's the other question," said Boba Fett. "Did you also order Fenald to make arrangements for Kateel of Kuhlvult to be abducted and memory-wiped?"

"Of course not," said Kuat stiffly. "That's absurd. What motivation would I have for wanting something like that done?"

"Then this Fenald could have been following someone else's orders when he contacted a go-between named Nil Posondum and made those arrangements?"

"Very likely." Kuat smiled ruefully. "I know from personal experience that Fenald was capable of working for another at the same time he was my head of security. Loyalty, as I found out, was a negotiable item with him; he double-crossed me when members of some of the other ruling families conspired to take over Kuat Drive Yards."

"Fenald's treachery might have been even more complicated than that. Apparently he was double-crossing Kodir of Kuhlvult at the same time."

Kuat's brow creased. "What do you mean?"

"What better way for Kodir to have gotten your confidence—and the security head position—than to expose Fenald as a traitor to you? And the best way to do that would be to arrange for it with Fenald himself. Especially since Fenald had already been working for Kodir while he was still your security head. In fact—" Boba Fett's voice drew taut as a durasteel wire. "Fenald was working for Kodir—following her orders—when he set up Kodir's sister Kateel to be abducted and memory-wiped."

"Interesting," said Kuat, "if true."

"It's true, all right. The only thing I needed to find out was whether or not you had ordered the acts committed against Kateel of Kuhlvult—and as you've pointed out, you're beyond having any interest in lying about the matter. So that leaves Kodir as the only one who could have given that job to Fenald to take care of."

"How do you know that?"

"Simple," replied Boba Fett. "When Kodir intercepted me with the KDY security division cruiser, she also found her sister Neelah—or Kateel, her real name—aboard the ship I had been using. Yet Kodir deliberately concealed any reaction to seeing Neelah there; in particular, Kodir showed no surprise at Neelah's not recognizing her in return. *So Kodir knew that a memory wipe had been done on Neelah.* If Kodir hadn't found that out from you—because you had been the one who ordered it—then logically, it must have been done on Kodir's instructions. It's easy enough to figure out what Fenald did: he had orders from you for one job to be taken care of on the sly, and he had orders from Kodir for another, different job that had to be kept quiet. So he put more credits in his own pocket by using the go-between Nil Posondum to hire just one lowlife, Ree Duptom, to take care of both jobs. Fenald must have gotten a good rate that way. The only problem was that when Duptom was accidentally killed, it left a mess for both you and Kodir of Kuhlvult to worry about, without either one of you knowing that the other was involved. But it took getting information from both you and Kodir to figure out what must have happened back then."

"I'm impressed." Kuat regarded the bounty hunter thoughtfully. "You're a creature of considerable intelligence; a shame that you found no better use for it than being a bounty hunter."

"It suits my personality."

"Perhaps so. But that makes me wonder about something else." Kuat's gaze grew sharper. "You've gone to a lot of trouble, not to find out what you needed to know—because you already knew that. You've risked your life coming here to find out what someone else, this female named Neelah, desperately needs to know. That kind of tenderheartedness isn't exactly your style, Fett. Unless . . ."

Kuat managed a thin smile. "Unless you've developed some other interest in her besides just business."

"Guess again," said Boba Fett. "I owe her a favor. And I always pay my debts. But I've got better reasons than that for what I do."

"Well, you're going to have a hard time letting this person know what you found out. Listen." Kuat raised a hand. Outside the Star Destroyer, the rumbling, percussive sounds of the explosions advanced closer and closer. "I saw the ship, the one that brought you down here to the construction docks, take off; there must have been somebody aboard it with an even sharper sense of self-preservation than your own. So there's no way out of here now."

"Yes, there is." Fett gestured with the blaster pistol. "Get away from the controls."

"Don't be ridiculous. One man can't fly a ship this size; it takes a trained crew. The only way it would be possible is with the tug module, and you can't get to that with the atmospheric pressure shroud gone."

"I said—get away from the controls. If you want to stay here in the docks, go ahead. But this ship is leaving."

"As you wish," said Kuat. "Every man should pick his own way of dying. And I've already chosen mine." He turned and walked toward the bridge's hatchway and the corridor beyond that would lead to one of the ship's main exit ports.

The explosions hadn't yet torn away the narrow connector to the pressurized equipment shed next to the Star Destroyer. Kuat sealed its hatch behind himself, then sat down on a crate marked with the emblem of Kuat Drive Yards. He felt tired and glad at the same time; tired from his long work, glad that it would soon be over.

His eyes closed for a moment, then snapped open when something soft and warm jumped into his lap. He looked down and saw the golden eyes of the felinx gazing back at him.

"So you're faithful, too." Kuat stroked the creature's silken fur. "In your own way." Somehow, it had gotten out of his private quarters and followed him this far, through all the chaos and noise of the corporation's fiery death. "Just as well," he murmured. "Just as well . . ."

He picked up the felinx and held it to his chest, bending his own head down low, so that the pulse of its heart drowned out everything that was to come.

"How many did we get out?" Commander Rozhdenst stood at the mobile base's largest viewports, gazing at the conflagration sweeping across the distant construction docks.

"Four of the *Lancer*-class frigates, sir." From the center of the room, Ott Klemp made his report. "Those were our top priority. The rest that we extracted were Zebulon-B frigates."

"And how many men did we lose?" The commander glanced over his shoulder.

"Only two. One in the frigate that got caught in the explosions, and another still in his Y-wing, going in." Klemp carried his helmet in the crook of his arm. Both he and Rozhdenst were still in their flight gear. "I think, sir, you'd have to consider this a successful operation."

"Perhaps," said Rozhdenst. "But I only consider it worth losing good pilots if something worthwhile is accomplished. Until we hear what's happened out at Endor, we don't know whether there's even going to be an Alliance that can make use of these ships."

Klemp looked toward the control panels. "We're still under comm unit silence?"

"You got it." The commander nodded. "Right now, there's no signals going in or coming out of that sector—"

His words were interrupted by a sudden, brighter flare of light from the Kuat Drive Yards' facility. Both men turned toward the viewport.

"What's going on?" Rozhdenst's brow furrowed. "Those aren't explosives."

"It's the Star Destroyer," said Klemp, pointing out the flame-engulfed shape. "The big one at the end of the docks that we couldn't get any of our men into. Some-body's giving its engines full power. It's moving!"

Klemp and the commander watched as the Star De-stroyer, larger than any of the rescued ships nearing the base, slowly began to rise from the dock in which it had been moored. The ship suddenly veered to one side, the flank of its hull crashing against the warped and broken towers of the cranes arching above it.

"Whoever's aboard that thing—they've lost control of it." Rozhdenst shook his head. "They'll never get it out."

The commander's assessment appeared to be true. The Star Destroyer's stern had slewed around horizon-tally, barely meters above the dock. Metal collided with metal, as the rear thruster ports flared through the base of the crane. The impact was enough to send the already loosened tower crashing down upon the upper length of the ship's hull.

"If he tries to pull out of there," said Rozhdenst, "he'll tear that ship to pieces."

Klemp peered closer at the image in the viewport. "It looks like . . . he's got another idea . . ."

The Star Destroyer's thruster engines had throttled back down. There was a moment of stillness at the end of the construction docks, lit by the encroaching flames, then the ship was lit suddenly brighter by the simultane-ous flash of its arsenal of high-powered laser cannons going off. The bolts weren't aimed, but achieved an im-pressive amount of damage despite that, ripping through the weakened structure of the docks and the twisted metal of the fallen crane. Another volley of flaring white bolts followed the first.

Now the two men at the viewport could see the crane and the surrounding docks slowly disintegrate, the girder beams and great, torn masses of durasteel collapsing across one another and into a loose tangle over the Dreadnaught. Once more, thruster engines lit up; this time, the awkward forward course of the ship sent the metal fragments scattering like straws.

Rozhdenst nodded in appreciation as he watched the Star Destroyer move away from the burning wreckage of Kuat Drive Yards and into open space. "Too bad . . ."

"Sir?"

"Too bad that's not one of our guys."

19

A woman talked to a bounty hunter.

"You know," said Neelah, "you could be a hero. If that was what you wanted."

"Hardly." Boba Fett's voice was as flat and unemotional as it had always been. "Heroes don't get paid enough."

"Think about it, though." A thin smile raised a corner of Neelah's mouth. With one hand, she tugged higher upon her shoulder the strap of the bag she carried. "Or at least savor the irony. Your blasting your way out of the KDY construction docks did the Rebel Alliance more good than their own Scavenger Squadron was able to achieve."

She and the bounty hunter were standing in the bridge of the Star Destroyer that Fett had managed to extract from the docks' inferno. The massive ship was silent and empty, except for them.

"How do you figure that?"

"Simple," replied Neelah. "Kuat of Kuat had wired up enough sequentially linked explosives to blow up all of Kuat Drive Yards. If he couldn't have it under his control, he didn't want to leave anything but smoking rubble behind. But this Star Destroyer was one of the critical links in the chain; the detonator circuits ran right through its main thruster engine compartment. And when you pulled the ship out of the docks, the chain was broken. Kuat himself didn't live long enough to see what happened, but the result is that over eighty percent of the KDY construction docks survived intact."

Fett shrugged. "That's not my concern."

"Perhaps not." Neelah regarded the bounty hunter. She'd had no expectation of what would come from this secret rendezvous with him. The comm message had come to her at the Scavenger Squadron's mobile command post, giving the coordinates of where she was to meet up with an unnamed entity; she had known instinctively that the message was from Boba Fett. She hadn't told Commander Rozhdenst about that, though, but had convinced him to let her go alone and unescorted, as the comm message had directed. It was her own decision to pilot the battered *Hound's Tooth* to the rendezvous. "But," she continued, "it might be my concern. If I want it to be."

"Of course." As always, Fett was way ahead of her. "Kuat of Kuat is dead. That means Kuat Drive Yards is going to need a new leader. The other ruling families can see how things stack up now—if the Rebel Alliance indicates that it wants you running KDY, they'll undoubtedly fall into line."

"I'm not sure about that." Neelah shook her head in disgust. "I know the Kuatese ruling families better than you do, and a lot better than anybody in the Rebel Alliance. I was born into those families, remember? My sister Kodir isn't the only one of them for whom treachery and scheming come easily. There are plenty of ruling family members who would just as soon back the Empire, if they thought it would serve their purposes."

"And you don't want to do anything to oppose them?"

"I'm not sure I want to." Neelah could see her own reflection in the dark visor of Boba Fett's helmet. "Or that I even care what happens to Kuat Drive Yards. After all that's happened, I'm not exactly close to anyone on the planet Kuat. Kodir is the only direct blood relation I have, and she's already being shipped down to face a tribunal of elders from the ruling families. There's a lot of charges being made against her: conspiracy, murder, kidnapping . . ." Neelah slowly shook her head. "Loyalty doesn't seem to run thick in the Kuhlvult bloodline. I don't feel it, at least. And maybe Kuat of Kuat was right; maybe Kuat Drive Yards deserves something more than that."

"Suit yourself," said Fett. "But I have other business to take care of. That's why I told you to come here."

"All right. Let's hear it."

"I'll make you a trade." Fett gestured toward the bulkheads of the ship surrounding them. "Here's a new, completely operational Star Destroyer, fresh out of the KDY construction docks. It's yours. You can signal the Scavenger Squadron commander to come out here and pick it up. That should make you even more popular with the Rebel Alliance."

Neelah glanced around the ship's bridge. "Or maybe I could sell it to them. It's a nice piece of hardware." She looked again at Boba Fett. "So what do you want in exchange?"

"Two things. First, the *Hound's Tooth*—"

"The *Hound's* in pretty bad shape." Neelah shook her head. "Certainly not worth as much as a ship of the line like this."

"It'll get me where I need to go," said Fett. "And second—your silence."

"What about?" Neelah peered at the bounty hunter.

"Me. I take it that you didn't tell anyone from the Rebel Alliance that you've been traveling with me."

"I didn't think it was advisable. Creatures tend to judge you by the company you keep."

"Fine," said Fett. "So go on that way. And don't tell them about me."

"Why?"

"I have my reasons. Right now, it's more convenient for me if everyone goes on believing I'm dead. If any of the creatures who might've spotted me at the Mos Eisley cantina want to talk about what they saw—" Fett shrugged. "There aren't many who'll believe lowlifes like that. And if the Rebel commander back at the KDY construction docks has an idea about who it was that pulled out this Destroyer, I imagine that he'll keep it to himself. Why would he want to let the rest of the galaxy know that a bounty hunter was able to do what he and his squadron couldn't? So being dead—or being thought dead—is a real opportunity for me."

"As you told me—suit yourself." Neelah's gaze turned tighter and harder. "But this ship isn't enough to buy that kind of silence. I want something a little more."

Fett's spine visibly stiffened. "Like what?"

"Like some answers. I want to know why you really went down to have your little confrontation with Kuat of Kuat while the construction docks were blowing up all around you. I can't believe it was really out of any concern for me, and finding out the truth about whether there was some big conspiracy of which I was the target."

A second passed, then Boba Fett nodded. "You're right," he said. "None of that is of any consequence to me. Your life, your death—it means nothing. All that matters is my life and my business—and that's what I was taking care of when I confronted Kuat of Kuat."

"You wanted the truth from him," said Neelah. "Did you get it?"

Fett nodded. "Enough of it. Now that I'm certain that the conspiracy didn't extend any further than Kuat, I can go ahead and deliver the fabricated evidence—to those who want it."

His words puzzled Neelah. "Who would want it

now? Prince Xizor is dead. Kuat fabricated the evidence against him—so what use would it be now?"

"As you say, Xizor is dead. But Black Sun isn't. And Black Sun is still a very powerful—and dangerous—organization. And since Xizor's death, the leadership of Black Sun has been a matter of some dispute. A power struggle between those who had been most loyal to Xizor and the others who had been plotting against him even while he was still alive."

"Who's winning?"

"For the moment, the Xizor loyalists have the upper hand. But all that could change very quickly. Especially when I deliver the fabricated evidence into the hands of the usurper faction. They can use it to break the hold on power of the Xizor loyalists by showing the Black Sun ranks that the late Prince Xizor had been foolishly—and traitorously—involving the organization in the affairs of the Empire and the Rebel Alliance. Even though it wouldn't be true, it might be enough to tip the scales in the usurper faction's favor."

"I don't get it," said Neelah. "Why would you care who wins control of Black Sun?"

"It's all the same to me. But what I do care about," said Boba Fett, "is staying alive. And the usurper faction has made it clear to me that I stand a good chance of dying—in as painful a manner as possible—if I don't hand over the fabricated evidence to them. Through their own information sources, the usurpers had learned about the evidence and that I was in search of it. They figured—correctly—that I could find it before they would be able to. While you were listening to Dengar tell about my past, I was in the cockpit of the *Hound's Tooth* receiving a comm unit transmission from the usurper faction inside Black Sun, with the details of the offer they were making me. An offer that I was in no position to refuse."

"Wouldn't it have been simpler to have just offered you credits for the fabricated evidence? After all"—Neelah showed a thin smile—"aren't you willing to do anything, as long as you get paid?"

"That would have worked for me," replied Fett, "but not for these particular creatures. The problem with paying me for the goods was that it would leave a trail that could be followed. Anytime credits change hands, there's a link that can be traced. And the usurper faction didn't want this matter being traced back to them. Killing me— or threatening to do so—is much simpler. If I got hold of the fabricated evidence and turned it over to them, there would be no exchange of credits to link us. And if I failed to do so, then I'd be dead, and there would be no way I could divulge the usurpers' scheming to the Xizor loyalists. All very neat and tidy. Especially since Black Sun— even just a small faction of the organization—is the only thing that could make a threat against me . . . and pull it off. Anybody else I'd have a chance against. But not Black Sun. Killing is one of its specialities."

"I'm impressed," said Neelah. "I didn't think you were afraid of anything."

"This isn't fear. It's reality."

She nodded; it had all started to make sense, the last pieces of the puzzle fitting together. "So when you told us, when we were aboard Balancesheet's freighter, that getting hold of the fabricated evidence was just a matter of potential profits—you were lying to us." Neelah peered closer at the bounty hunter. "It wasn't credits you were after. It was survival."

"Credits are useless when you're dead."

"Then I take it that this is part of the deal as well." Neelah pulled the shoulder bag in front of herself and extracted the flat black parcel inside. She held the fabricated evidence, the other item that Boba Fett had told her to bring, in both hands. "The deal between you and me."

"This part isn't negotiable," said Fett. "I'm taking the fabricated evidence with me whether you hand it over or not."

"Since I don't have any use for it—" Neelah shrugged and held the parcel out. "Go ahead."

Boba Fett took the parcel with no word of thanks. She hadn't expected any, either.

"Wait a minute." Neelah spoke up as Fett turned away. The dark gaze of his visored helmet looked back at her. "You realize," she said quietly, "that you're being a complete fool about this. Don't you?"

A moment passed before Fett spoke. "How so?"

"Come on. Use your brains." Neelah pointed to the parcel in Boba Fett's gloved hands. "You're going to be carrying that stuff into a pretty dangerous place. Sure, this Black Sun usurper faction is going to be happy to get it, but that doesn't mean they're going to keep their end of the deal. They want to keep things quiet, about what they're up to? Then they're more likely to take the fabricated evidence from you, say thanks very much, and then drill a blaster bolt through your skull. There wouldn't be any trail linking them to you, after that."

"Of course not," replied Fett. "But I've already thought about that. And I've got a few tricks up my sleeve, in case they try anything."

"Tricks which might not work. Not on some Black Sun faction. As you said, killing is one of their specialities."

"True." Boba Fett gave a single nod. "But as it is, if I don't deliver the fabricated evidence to the usurpers, I have very little chance of surviving. If I do deliver it to them—then my chances will be up to me."

"Do it, then." Neelah stepped back and gestured toward the bridge's exit hatchway. "Good luck."

"It's not a matter of luck. Not for me." Fett turned and walked toward the hatchway. He stopped and looked back at her. "You can trust in your luck, if you care to. When you came here, did you stop to think what your chances would be if I had decided to tie up a few loose ends by eliminating you?"

"Sure." Neelah reached into the shoulder bag and pulled out a blaster pistol. She held it with both hands, aimed straight toward Fett. "That's why I came prepared."

Fett gazed at her and the weapon for a moment, then slowly nodded. "Good," he said. "I'm glad you learned a few things from me."

"Oh, I learned lots." Neelah kept the weapon pointed at him. "More than I wanted to."

She lowered the weapon only when she could hear the echo of his boot steps fading away in the corridor beyond the hatchway.

A few moments later, Neelah glanced toward the bridge's main viewport. What was visible there was the fiery trace of the *Hound's Tooth*, battered but still capable of traveling toward its hidden destination. But when Neelah closed her eyes, what she saw were the heat-shimmering expanses of the Dune Sea on Tatooine, and a nearly dead figure, skin and battle armor eroded, face-down in the sand.

She still couldn't decide whether it might have been better if she had just left him lying there.

A woman talked to a bounty hunter.

Though maybe, thought Dengar, *I'm not one any-more.* It didn't matter to him now; he was just glad to be alive.

"You came all that way, and found me." Both he and Manaroo sat in the cockpit of his ship, the *Punishing One*. "And just in time."

"It took some doing," said his betrothed. "You weren't easy to track down."

She couldn't have cut it any finer, either. *Punishing One* had shown up near the KDY construction docks just as Bossk's former ship *Hound's Tooth* was hit by the ragged chunk of metal that had come whirling toward it. Manaroo had witnessed the *Hound* shuddering from the impact; without a second thought, she had hit the *Punishing One*'s thruster controls to maximum, swooping into the debris and managing to grapple and lock on to the other ship's cargo hold before it lost its remaining atmospheric pressure. They had both been aboard the

Punishing One when she slapped him back to full consciousness.

The relief at finding himself alive, and in the arms of the woman he loved, ebbed a little inside Dengar. "I'm sorry," he said to her. "I failed you. I failed us both."

"What are you talking about?"

"We're right back where we started." He shook his head ruefully. "We needed credits, a lot—and I didn't get them. With everything I did, risking my life all that time being partners with Boba Fett, and we still can't pay off that debt load I'm carrying." He laid his head against Manaroo's shoulder. "We're no closer to the life we want than we were before."

"You *are* an idiot." She laughed and pushed him back to where she could look at him full in the face. "None of that matters as long as you're alive."

"That's sweet of you to say so."

"No, really; I mean it." Manaroo's expression turned earnest. "You don't realize what you've done just by remaining alive. You've won; *we've* won."

He looked at her in puzzlement. "What do you mean?"

"Before I came to find you," said Manaroo, "I wagered on you. Every credit I could scrape up, every one I could borrow—I took us even deeper into debt in order to get the stake together. Then I went to the gambler Drawmas Sma'Da; he agreed to cover the wager I proposed. A wager on the survival of a bounty hunter. *Your* survival." Her smile brightened her face. "Believe me, I got great odds on you. Nobody expected you to be able to live through being partners with Boba Fett. But you did!"

"But that would mean . . . you and I . . ."

"Yes!" Manaroo grabbed him by both shoulders. "I've already contacted Drawmas Sma'Da and claimed my winnings—*our* winnings. I only made the bet; you won it for us. The credits have been transferred into our holding account. It's more than enough to pay off your debt load. Pay it off, and start us in whatever business we want." She leaned forward and kissed him, long and happily, then looked into his eyes again. "It's our new life together. It's come at last."

"Yes . . ." Dengar nodded slowly. "You're right . . ." An unbidden chill touched his heart as a shadow fell across the joy he knew he should feel. "If only . . . everything else works out . . ." He could hear the echoes of the dire warnings that Boba Fett had given him. "There's still the Empire to worry about. How can anyone in the galaxy be happy with that looming over us?"

Manaroo kissed him on the brow this time, then leaned back and shook her head, still smiling. "You don't know," she said, "what I heard. Just a few minutes ago. I intercepted a comm unit transmission from the Rebel Alliance headquarters out at Sullust to the Scavenger Squadron's commander here. The battle's over." Her voice dropped almost to a whisper. "And the Rebels won. It's the Empire that was crushed . . . to a billion pieces . . ." She wrapped her arms around him and laid her head on his chest. "Everything will be different now."

He could hardly believe it, yet he knew it was true. *Everything*, thought Dengar. All their plans and hopes—those could come true now. And he wouldn't be a bounty hunter anymore . . .

In the midst of his happiness, there was a thread of regret. It seemed a shame, after having survived and even profited from a partnership with Boba Fett—how many other creatures could say the same?—for him to turn his back on all that. Plus, there had been a certain excitement to all that had happened, from the moment when he first stumbled upon an almost lifeless Boba Fett, lying on the hot sands of Tatooine's Dune Sea.

Maybe, thought Dengar, *I could still keep my hand in. Just a little.* His business enterprise with Manaroo might not be immediately successful; it might require a fresh infusion of credit now and then. Right at the beginning . . .

He'd have to think about that some more. But for the

moment, Dengar wrapped his arms around his betrothed. He turned his face away from hers and looked out the cockpit's viewport at all the stars cascading in stately progression to the galaxy's edge.

Everything . . .

The stars were so bright, even as he closed his eyes and held his betrothed closer to himself.

ABOUT THE AUTHOR

K. W. JETER is one of the most respected sf writers working today. His first novel, *Dr. Adder,* was described by Philip K. Dick as "a stunning novel . . . it destroys once and for all your conception of the limitations of science fiction." *The Edge of Human* resolves many discrepancies between the movie *Blade Runner* and the novel upon which it was based, Dick's *Do Androids Dream of Electric Sheep?* Jeter's other books have been described as having a "brain-burning intensity" *(The Village Voice),* as being "hard-edged and believable" *(Locus)* and "a joy from first word to last" *(San Francisco Chronicle).* He is the author of more than twenty novels, including *Farewell Horizontal* and *Wolf Flow.* His latest novel, *NOIR,* was described by the *New York Times* as "the science fiction equivalent of *The Name of the Rose.*"

The World of
STAR WARS Novels

In May 1991, *Star Wars* caused a sensation in the publishing industry with the Bantam Spectra release of Timothy Zahn's novel *Heir to the Empire.* For the first time, Lucasfilm Ltd. had authorized new novels that *continued* the famous story told in George Lucas's three blockbuster motion pictures: *Star Wars, The Empire Strikes Back,* and *Return of the Jedi.* Reader reaction was immediate and tumultuous: *Heir* reached #1 on the *New York Times* bestseller list and demonstrated that *Star Wars* lovers were eager for exciting new stories set in this universe, written by leading science fiction authors who shared their passion. Since then, each Bantam *Star Wars* novel has been an instant national bestseller.

Lucasfilm and Bantam decided that future novels in the series would be interconnected: that is, events in one novel would have consequences in the others. You might say that each Bantam *Star Wars* novel, enjoyable on its own, is also part of a much larger tale.

Here is a special look at Bantam's *Star Wars* books, along with excerpts from the more recent novels. Each one is available now wherever Bantam Books are sold.

The Han Solo Trilogy:
THE PARADISE SNARE
THE HUTT GAMBIT
REBEL DAWN
by A. C. Crispin
Setting: Before *Star Wars: A New Hope*

What was Han Solo like before we met him in the first STAR WARS movie? This trilogy answers that tantalizing question, filling in lots of historical lore about our favorite swashbuckling hero and thrilling us with adventures of the brash young pilot that we never knew he'd experienced. As the trilogy begins, the young Han Makes a life-changing decision: to escape from the clutches of Garris Shrike, head of the trading "clan" who has brutalized Han while taking advantage of his piloting abilities. Here's a tense early scene from The Paradise Snare *featuring Han, Shrike, and Dewlanna, a Wookiee who is Han's only friend in this horrible situation:*

"I've had it with you, Solo. I've been lenient with you so far, because you're a blasted good swoop pilot and all that prize money came in handy, but my patience is ended." Shrike ceremoniously pushed up the sleeves of his bedizened uniform, then balled his hands into fists. The galley's artificial lighting made the blood-jewel ring glitter dull silver. "Let's see what a few days of fighting off Devaronian blood-poisoning does for your attitude—along with maybe a few broken bones. I'm doing this for your own good, boy. Someday you'll thank me."

Han gulped with terror as Shrike started toward him. He'd lashed out at the trader captain once before, two years ago, when he'd been feeling cocky after winning the gladiatorial Free-For-All on Jubilar—and had been instantly sorry. The speed and strength of Garris's returning blow had snapped his head back and split both lips so thoroughly that Dewlanna had had to feed him mush for a week until they healed.

With a snarl, Dewlanna stepped forward. Shrike's hand dropped to his blaster. "You stay out of this, old Wookiee," he snapped in a voice nearly as harsh as Dewlanna's. "Your cooking isn't *that* good."

Han had already grabbed his friend's furry arm and was forcibly holding her back. "Dewlanna, no!"

She shook off his hold as easily as she would have waved off an annoying insect and roared at Shrike. The captain drew his blaster, and chaos erupted.

"Noooo!" Han screamed, and leaped forward, his foot lashing out in an old street-fighting technique. His instep impacted solidly with Shrike's breastbone. The captain's breath went out in a great *houf!* and he went over backward. Han hit the deck and rolled. A tingler bolt sizzled past his ear.

"Larrad!" wheezed the captain as Dewlanna started toward him.

Shrike's brother drew his blaster and pointed it at the Wookiee. "Stop, Dewlanna!"

His words had no more effect than Han's. Dewlanna's blood was up—she was in full Wookiee battle rage. With a roar that deafened the combatants, she grabbed Larrad's wrist and yanked, spinning him around and snapping him in a terrible parody of a child's "snap the whip" game. Han heard a *crunch,* mixed with several *pops* as tendons and ligaments gave way. Larrad Shrike shrieked, a high, shrill noise that carried such pain that the Corellian youth's arm ached in sympathy.

Grabbing the blaster from his belt, Han snapped off a shot at the Elomin who was leaping forward, tingler ready and aimed at Dewlanna's midsection. Brafid howled, dropping his weapon. Han was amazed that he'd managed to hit him, but he didn't have long to wonder about the accuracy of his aim.

Shrike was staggering to his feet, blaster in hand, aimed squarely at Han's head. "Larrad?" he yelled at the writhing heap of agony that was his brother. Larrad did not reply.

Shrike cocked the blaster and stepped even closer to Han. "Stop it, Dewlanna!" the captain snarled at the Wookiee. "Or your buddy Solo dies!"

Han dropped his blaster and put his hands up in a gesture of surrender.

Dewlanna stopped in her tracks, growling softly.

Shrike leveled the blaster, and his finger tightened on the trigger. Pure malevolent hatred was etched upon his features, and then he smiled, pale blue eyes glittering with ruthless joy. "For insubordination and striking your captain," he announced, "I sentence you to death, Solo. May you rot in all the hells there ever were."

SHADOWS OF THE EMPIRE
by Steve Perry
Setting: Between *The Empire Strikes Back* and *Return of the Jedi*

Here is a very special STAR WARS story dealing with Black Sun, a galaxy-spinning criminal organization that is masterminded by one of the most interesting villains in the STAR WARS universe: Xizor, dark prince of the Falleen. Xizor's chief rival for the favor of Emperor Palpatine is none other than Darth Vader himself— alive and well, and a major character in this story, since it is set during the events of the STAR WARS film trilogy.

In the opening prologue, we revisit a familiar scene from The Empire Strikes Back, *and are introduced to our marvelous new bad guy:*

He looks like a walking corpse, Xizor thought. Like a mummified body dead a thousand years. Amazing he is still alive, much less the most powerful man in the galaxy. He isn't even that old; it is more as if something is slowly eating him.

Xizor stood four meters away from the Emperor, watching as the man who had long ago been Senator Palpatine moved to stand in the holocam field. He imagined he could smell the decay in the Emperor's worn body. Likely that was just some trick of the recycled air, run through dozens of filters to ensure that there was no chance of any poison gas being introduced into it. Filtered the life out of it, perhaps, giving it that dead smell.

The viewer on the other end of the holo-link would see a close-up of the Emperor's head and shoulders, of an age-ravaged face shrouded in the cowl of his dark zeyd-cloth robe. The man on the other end of the transmission, light-years away, would not see Xizor, though Xizor would be able to see him. It was a measure of the Emperor's trust that Xizor was allowed to be here while the conversation took place.

The man on the other end of the transmission—if he could still be called that—

The air swirled inside the Imperial chamber in front of the Emperor, coalesced, and blossomed into the image of a figure down on one knee. A caped humanoid biped dressed in jet black, face hidden under a full helmet and breathing mask:

Darth Vader.

Vader spoke: "What is thy bidding, my master?"

If Xizor could have hurled a power bolt through time and space to strike Vader dead, he would have done it without blinking. Wishful thinking: Vader was too powerful to attack directly.

"There is a great disturbance in the Force," the Emperor said.

"I have felt it," Vader said.

"We have a new enemy. Luke Skywalker."

Skywalker? That had been Vader's name, a long time ago. What was this person with the same name, someone so powerful as to be worth a conversation between the Emperor and his most loathsome creation? More importantly, why had Xizor's agents not uncovered this before now? Xizor's ire was instant—but cold. No sign of his surprise or anger would show on his imperturbable features. The Falleen did not allow their emotions to burst forth as did many of the inferior species; no, the Falleen ancestry was not fur but scales, not mammalian but reptilian. Not wild but coolly calculating. Such was much better. Much safer.

"Yes, my master," Vader continued.

"He could destroy us," the Emperor said.

Xizor's attention was riveted upon the Emperor and the holographic image of Vader kneeling on the deck of a ship far away.

Here was interesting news indeed. Something the Emperor perceived as a danger to himself? Something the Emperor feared?

"He's just a boy," Vader said. "Obi-Wan can no longer help him."

Obi-Wan. That name Xizor knew. He was among the last of the Jedi Knights, a general. But he'd been dead for decades, hadn't he?

Apparently Xizor's information was wrong if Obi-Wan had been helping someone who was still a boy. His agents were going to be sorry.

The Bounty Hunter Wars
Book 1: THE MANDALORIAN ARMOR
Book 2: SLAVE SHIP
by K. W. Jeter
Setting: During *Return of the Jedi*

Boba Fett continues the fight against the legions of circling enemies as the somewhat hot-tempered Trandoshan Bossk attempts to re-establish the old Bounty Hunter Guild with himself as its head. Bossk has sworn undying vengeance on Boba Fett when his ship, Hound's Tooth, *crashes.*

In the excerpt that follows, Bossk attempts to kill Boba Fett in a violent confrontation:

Fear is a useful thing.

That was one of the best lessons that a bounty hunter could learn. And Bossk was learning it now.

Through the cockpit viewport of the *Hound's Tooth,* he saw the explosion that ripped the other ship, Boba Fett's *Slave I,* into flame and shards of blackened durasteel. A burst of wide-band comlink static, like an electromagnetic death cry, had simultaneously deafened Bossk. The searing, multi-octave noise had poured through the speakers in the *Hound's* cockpit for several minutes, until the last of the circuitry aboard Fett's ship had finally been consumed and silenced in the fiery apocalypse.

When he could finally hear himself think again, Bossk looked out at the empty space where *Slave I* had been. Now, against the cold backdrop of stars, a few scraps of heated metal slowly dwindled from white-hot to dull red as their molten heat ebbed away in vacuum. *He's dead,* thought Bossk with immense satisfaction. *At last.* Whatever atoms had constituted the late Boba Fett, they were also drifting disconnected and harmless in space. Before transferring back here to his own ship, Bossk had wired up enough thermal explosives in *Slave I* to reduce any living thing aboard it to mere ash and bad memories.

So if he still felt afraid, if his gut still knotted when Boba Fett's dark-visored image rose in his thoughts, Bossk knew that was an irrational response. *He's dead, he's gone* . . .

The silence of the *Hound*'s cockpit was broken by a barely audible pinging signal from the control panel. Bossk glanced down and saw that the *Hound*'s telesponder had picked up the presence of another ship in the immediate vicinity; according to the coordinates that appeared in the readout screen, it was almost on top of the *Hound's Tooth.*

And—it was the ship known as *Slave I.* The ID profile was an exact match.

That's impossible, thought Bossk, bewildered. His heart shuddered to a halt inside his chest, then staggered on. Before the explosion, he had picked up the same ID profile from the other side of his own ship; he had turned the *Hound's Tooth* around just in time to see the huge, churning ball of flame fill his viewscreen.

But, he realized now, he hadn't seen *Slave I* itself. Which meant . . .

Bossk heard another sound, even softer, coming from somewhere else in his own ship. There was someone else aboard it; his keen Trandoshan senses registered the molecules of another creature's spoor in the ship's recycled atmosphere. And Bossk knew who it was.

He's here. The cold blood in Bossk's veins chilled to ice. *Boba Fett* . . .

Somehow, Bossk knew, he had been tricked. The explosion hadn't consumed *Slave I* and its occupants at all. He didn't know how Boba Fett had managed it, but it had been done nevertheless. And the deafening electronic noise that had filled the cockpit had also been enough to cover Boba Fett's unauthorized entry of the *Hound's Tooth;* the shrieking din had gone on long enough for Fett to have penetrated an access hatch and resealed it behind himself.

A voice came from the cockpit's overhead speaker, a voice that was neither his own nor Boba Fett's.

"Twenty seconds to detonation." It was the calm, unexcited voice of an autonomic bomb. Only the most powerful ones contained warning circuits like that.

Fear thawed the ice in Bossk's veins. He jumped up from the pilot's chair and dived for the hatchway behind himself.

In the emergency equipment bay of the *Hound's Tooth*, his clawed hands tore through the contents of one of the storage lockers. The *Hound* wasn't going to be a ship much longer; in a few seconds—and counting down—it was going to be glowing bits of shrapnel and rubbish surrounded by a haze of rapidly dissipating atmospheric gases, just like whatever it had been that he had mistakenly identified as Boba Fett's ship *Slave I*. That the *Hound* would no longer be capable of maintaining its life-support systems wasn't Bossk's main concern at this moment, as the reptilian Trandoshan hastily shoved a few more essential items through the self-sealing gasket of a battered, much-used pressure duffel. There wouldn't even *be* any life for the systems to support: a small portion of the debris floating in the cold vacuum would be blood and bone and scorched scraps of body tissue, the rapidly chilling remains of the ship's captain. *I'm outta here,* thought Bossk; he slung the duffel's strap across his broad shoulder and dived for the equipment bay's hatch.

"Fifteen seconds to detonation." A calm and friendly voice spoke in the *Hound's* central corridor as Bossk ran for the escape pod. He knew that Boba Fett had toggled the bomb's autonomic vocal circuits just to rattle him. "Fourteen . . ." There was nothing like a disembodied announcement of impending doom, to get a sentient creature motivated. "Thirteen; have you considered evacuation?"

"Shut up," growled Bossk. There was no point in talking to a pile of thermal explosives and flash circuits, but he couldn't stop himself. Under the death-fear that accelerated his pulse was sheer murderous rage and annoyance, the inevitable-seeming result of every encounter he'd ever had with Boba Fett. *That stinking, underhanded scum . . .*

The scraps and shards left by the other explosion clattered against the *Hound's* shielded exterior like a swarm of tiny, molten-edged meteorites. If there was any justice in the universe, Boba Fett should have been dead by now. Not just dead; atomized. The fury and panic in Bossk's pounding heart shifted again to bewilderment as he ran with the pressure duffel jostling against his scale-covered spine. Why did Boba Fett keep coming back? Was there no way to kill him so that he would just *stay* dead?

THE TRUCE AT BAKURA
by Kathy Tyers
Setting: Immediately after *Return of the Jedi*

The day after his climactic battle with Emperor Palpatine and the sacrifice of his father, Darth Vader, who died saving his life, Luke Skywalker helps recover an Imperial drone ship bearing a startling message intended for the Emperor. It is a distress signal from the far-off Imperial outpost of Bakura, which is under attack by an alien invasion force, the Ssi-ruuk. Leia sees a rescue mission as an opportunity to achieve a diplomatic victory for the Rebel Alliance, even if it means fighting alongside former Imperials. But Luke receives a vision from Obi-Wan Kenobi revealing that the stakes are even higher: the invasion at Bakura threatens everything the Rebels have won at such great cost.

STAR WARS: X-WING
By Michael A. Stackpole
ROGUE SQUADRON
WEDGE'S GAMBLE
THE KRYTOS TRAP
THE BACTA WAR

By Aaron Allston
WRAITH SQUADRON
IRON FIST
SOLO COMMAND

By Michael A. Stackpole
ISARD'S REVENGE
Setting: Three years after *Return of the Jedi*

The Rogues have been instrumental in defeating Thrawn and return to Coruscant to celebrate their great victory. It is then they make a terrible discovery—Ysanne Isard did not die at Thyferra and it is she who is assassinating those who were with Corran Horn on the Lusankya. *It is up to the Rogues to rescue their compatriots and foil the remnants of the Empire.*

The following scene from the opening of Isard's Revenge *takes you to one of the most daring battles the Rogues ever waged:*

Sithspawn! When his X-wing reverted to realspace before the countdown timer had reached zero, Corran Horn knew Thrawn had somehow managed to outguess the New Republic yet one more time. The Rogues had helped create the deception that the New Republic would be going after the Tangrene Ubiqtorate Base, but Thrawn clearly hadn't taken the bait.

The man's incredible. I'd like to meet him, shake his hand. Corran smiled. *And then kill him, of course.*

Two seconds into realspace and the depth of Thrawn's brilliance became undeniable. The New Republic's forces had been brought out of hyperspace by two Interdictor cruisers, which even now started to fade back toward the Imperial lines. This left the New Republic's ships well shy of the Bilbringi shipyards and facing an Imperial fleet arrayed for battle. The two Interdictors that had dragged them from hyperspace were a small part of a larger force scattered around to make sure the New Republic's ships were not going to be able to retreat.

"Battle alert!" Captain Tycho Celchu's voice crackled over the comm unit. "TIE Interceptors coming in—bearing two-nine-three, mark twenty."

Corran keyed his comm unit. "Three Flight, on me. Hold it together and nail some squints."

The cant-winged Interceptors rolled in and down on the Rogues. Corran kicked his X-wing up on its port S-foil and flicked his lasers over to quad-fire mode. While that would slow his rate of fire, each burst had a better chance of killing a squint outright. *And there are plenty that need killing here.*

Corran nudged his stick right and dropped the cross-hairs onto an Interceptor making a run at Admiral Ackbar's flagship. He hit the firing switch, sending four red laser bolts burning out at the target. They hit on the starboard side, with two of them piercing the cockpit and the other two vaporizing the strut supporting the right wing. The bent hexagonal wing sheered off in a shower of sparks, while the rest of the craft started a long, lazy spiral toward the outer edges of the system.

"Break port, Nine."

As the Gand's high-pitched voice poured through the comm unit, Corran snaprolled his X-wing to the left, then chopped his throttle back and hauled hard on the stick to take him into a loop. An Interceptor flashed through where he had been, and Ooryl Qyrgg's X-wing came fast on its tail. Ooryl's lasers blazed in sequence, stippling the Interceptor with red energy darts. One hit each wing, melting great furrows through them, while the other two lanced through the cockpit right above the twin ion engines. The engines themselves tore free of their support structure and blew out through the front of the squint, then exploded in a silver fireball that consumed the rest of the Imperial fighter.

"Thanks, Ten."

"My pleasure, Nine."

Whistler, the green and white R2 unit slotted in behind Corran, hooted, and data started pouring up over the fighter's main monitor. It told him in exact detail what he was seeing unfold in space around him. The New Republic's forces had come into the system in the standard conical formation that allowed them to maximize firepower.

THE COURTSHIP OF
PRINCESS LEIA
by Dave Wolverton
Setting: Four years after *Return of the Jedi*

One of the most interesting developments in Bantam's STAR WARS novels is that in their storyline, Han Solo and Princess Leia start a family. This tale reveals how the couple originally got together. Wishing to strengthen the fledgling New Republic by bringing in powerful allies, Leia opens talks with the Hapes consortium of more than sixty worlds. But the consortium is ruled by the Queen Mother, who, to Han's dismay, wants Leia to marry her son, Prince Isolder. Before this action-packed story is over, Luke will join forces with Isolder against a group of Force-trained "witches" and face a deadly foe.

HEIR TO THE EMPIRE
DARK FORCE RISING
THE LAST COMMAND
by Timothy Zahn
Setting: Five years after *Return of the Jedi*

This #1 bestselling trilogy introduces two legendary forces of evil into the STAR WARS literary pantheon. Grand Admiral Thrawn has taken control of the Imperial fleet in the years since the destruction of the Death Star, and the mysterious Joruus C'baoth is a fearsome Jedi Master who has been seduced by the dark side. Han and Leia have now been married for about a year, and as the story begins, she is pregnant with twins. Thrawn's plan is to crush the Rebellion and resurrect the Empire's New Order with C'baoth's help—and in return, the Dark Master will get Han and Leia's Jedi children to mold as he wishes. For as readers of this magnificent trilogy will see, Luke Skywalker is not the last of the old Jedi. He is the first of the new.

The Jedi Academy Trilogy:
JEDI SEARCH
DARK APPRENTICE
CHAMPIONS OF THE FORCE
by Kevin J. Anderson
Setting: Seven years after *Return of the Jedi*

In order to assure the continuation of the Jedi Knights, Luke Skywalker has decided to start a training facility: a Jedi Academy. He will gather Force-sensitive students who show potential as prospective Jedi and serve as their mentor, as Jedi Masters Obi-Wan Kenobi and Yoda did for him. Han and Leia's twins are now toddlers, and there is a third Jedi child: the infant Anakin, named after Luke and Leia's father. In this trilogy, we discover the existence of a powerful Imperial doomsday weapon, the horrifying Sun Crusher—which will soon become the centerpiece of a titanic struggle between Luke Skywalker and his most brilliant Jedi Academy student, who is delving dangerously into the dark side.

I, JEDI
by Michael A. Stackpole
Setting: *During that time*

Another grand tale of the exploits of the most feared and fearless fighting force in the galaxy, as Corran Horn faces a dark unnatural power that only his mastery of the Jedi powers could destroy. This great novel gives us an in-depth look at Jedi powers and brings us inside the minds of the special warriors learning to use the Force:

I switched to proton torpedoes, got a quick tone-lock from Whistler and pulled the trigger. The missile shot from my X-wing and sprinted straight for her ship. As good as she was, the clutch pilot knew there was no dodging it. She fired with both lasers, but they missed. Then, at the last moment, she shot an ion blast that hit the missile. Blue lightning played over it, burning out every circuit that allowed the torpedo to track and close on her ship.

I'm fairly certain, just for a second, she thought she had won.

The problem with a projectile is that even if its sophisticated circuitry fails, it still has a lot of kinetic energy built up. Even if it never senses the proximity of its target and detonates, that much mass moving that fast treats a clutch cockpit much the way a needle treats a bubble. The torpedo drove the ion engines out the back of the clutch, where they exploded. The fighter's hollow remains slowly spun off through space and would eventually burn through the atmosphere and give resort guests a thrill.

CHILDREN OF THE JEDI
by Barbara Hambly
Setting: Eight years after *Return of the Jedi*

The STAR WARS characters face a menace from the glory days of the Empire when a thirty-year-old automated Imperial Dread-naught comes to life and begins its grim mission: to gather forces and annihilate a long-forgotten stronghold of Jedi children. When Luke is whisked aboard, he begins to communicate with the brave Jedi Knight who paralyzed the ship decades ago, and gave her life in the process. Now she is part of the vessel, existing in its artificial intelligence core, and guiding Luke through one of the most unusual adventures he has ever had.

DARKSABER by Kevin J. Anderson
Setting: Immediately thereafter

Not long after Children of the Jedi, *Luke and Han learn that evil Hutts are building a reconstruction of the original Death Star—and that the Empire is still alive, in the form of Daala, who has joined forces with Pellaeon, former second-in-command to the feared Grand Admiral Thrawn.*

PLANET OF TWILIGHT
by Barbara Hambly
Setting: Nine years after *Return of the Jedi*

Concluding the epic tale begun in her own novel Children of the Jedi *and continued by Kevin Anderson in* Darksaber, *Barbara Hambly tells the story of a ruthless enemy of the New Republic operating out of a backwater world with vast mineral deposits. The first step in his campaign is to kidnap Princess Leia. Meanwhile, as Luke Skywalker searches the planet for his long-lost love Callista, the planet begins to reveal its unspeakable secret—a secret that threatens the New Republic, the Empire, and the entire galaxy:*

The first to die was a midshipman named Koth Barak. One of his fellow crewmembers on the New Republic escort cruiser *Adamantine* found him slumped across the table in the deck-nine break room where he'd repaired half an hour previously for a cup of coffeine. Twenty minutes after Barak should have been back to post, Gunnery Sergeant Gallie Wover went looking for him.

When she entered the deck-nine break room, Sergeant Wover's first sight was of the palely flickering blue on blue of the infolog screen. "Blast it, Koth, I told you . . ."

Then she saw the young man stretched unmoving on the far side of the screen, head on the break table, eyes shut. Even at a distance of three meters Wover didn't like the way he was breathing.

"Koth!" She rounded the table in two strides, sending the other chairs clattering into a corner. She thought his eyelids moved a little when she yelled his name. "Koth!"

Wover hit the emergency call almost without conscious decision. In the few minutes before the med droids arrived she sniffed the coffeine in the gray plastene cup a few centimeters from his limp fingers. It wasn't even cold.

THE CRYSTAL STAR
by Vonda N. McIntyre
Setting: Ten years after *Return of the Jedi*

Leia's three children have been kidnapped. That horrible fact is made worse by Leia's realization that she can no longer sense her children through the Force! While she, Artoo-Detoo, and Chewbacca trail the kidnappers, Luke and Han discover a planet that is suffering strange quantum effects from a nearby star. Slowly freezing into a perfect crystal and disrupting the Force, the star is blunting Luke's power and crippling the Millennium Falcon. *These strands converge in an apocalyptic threat not only to the fate of the New Republic, but to the universe itself.*

The Black Fleet Crisis
BEFORE THE STORM
SHIELD OF LIES
TYRANT'S TEST
by Michael P. Kube-McDowell
Setting: Twelve years after *Return of the Jedi*

*Long after setting up the hard-won New Republic, yesterday's
Rebels have become today's administrators and diplomats. But
the peace is not to last for long. A restless Luke must journey to
his mother's homeworld in a desperate quest to find her people;
Lando seizes a mysterious spacecraft with unimaginable weapons
of destruction; and waiting in the wings is a horrific battle fleet
under the control of a ruthless leader bent on a genocidal war.*

THE NEW REBELLION
by Kristine Kathryn Rusch
Setting: Thirteen years after *Return of the Jedi*

*Victorious though the New Republic may be, there is still no end
to the threats to its continuing existence—this novel explores the
price of keeping the peace. First, somewhere in the galaxy, mil-
lions suddenly perish in a blinding instant of pain. Then, as Leia
prepares to address the Senate on Coruscant, a horrifying event
changes the governmental equation in a flash.*

The Corellian Trilogy:
AMBUSH AT CORELLIA
ASSAULT AT SELONIA
SHOWDOWN AT CENTERPOINT
by Roger MacBride Allen
Setting: Fourteen years after *Return of the Jedi*

*This trilogy takes us to Corellia, Han Solo's homeworld, which
Han has not visited in quite some time. A trade summit brings
Han, Leia, and the children—now developing their own clear per-
sonalities and instinctively learning more about their innate skills
in the Force—into the middle of a situation that most closely
resembles a burning fuse. The Corellian system is on the brink of
civil war, there are New Republic intelligence agents on a mysterious mission which even Han does not understand, and worst of
all, a fanatical rebel leader has his hands on a superweapon of*

unimaginable power—and just wait until you find out who that leader is!

The Hand of Thrawn
SPECTER OF THE PAST
VISION OF THE FUTURE
by Timothy Zahn
Setting: Nineteen years after
Star Wars: A New Hope

The two-book series by the undisputed master of the STAR WARS novel. Once the supreme master of countless star systems, the Empire is tottering on the brink of total collapse. Day by day, neutral systems are rushing to join the New Republic coalition. But with the end of the war in sight, the New Republic has fallen victim to its own success. An unwieldy alliance of races and traditions, the confederation now finds itself riven by age-old animosities. Princess Leia struggles against all odds to hold the New Republic together. But she has powerful enemies. An ambitious Moff Disra leads a conspiracy to divide the uneasy coalition with an ingenious plot to blame the Bothans for a heinous crime that could lead to genocide and civil war. At the same time, Luke Skywalker, along with Lando Calrissian and Talon Karrde, pursues a mysterious group of pirate ships whose crew consists of clones. And then comes the worst news of all: the most cunning and ruthless warlord in Imperial history has returned to lead the Empire to triumph. Here's an exciting scene from Timothy Zahn's spectacular STAR WARS novel:

"I don't think you fully understand the political situation the New Republic finds itself in these days. A flash point like Caamas—especially with Bothan involvement—will bring the whole thing to a boil. Particularly if we can give it the proper nudge."

"The situation among the Rebels is not the issue," Tierce countered coldly. "It's the state of the Empire *you* don't seem to understand. Simply tearing the Rebellion apart isn't going to rebuild the Emperor's New Order. We need a focal point, a leader around whom the Imperial forces can rally."

Disra said, "Suppose I could provide such a leader. Would you be willing to join us?"

Tierce eyed him. "Who is this 'us' you refer to?"

"If you join, there would be three of us," Disra said. "Three who would share the secret I'm prepared to offer you. A secret that will bring the entire Fleet onto our side."

Tierce smiled cynically. "You'll forgive me, Your Excellency, if I suggest you couldn't inspire blind loyalty in a drugged bantha."

Disra felt a flash of anger. How dare this common soldier—?

"No," he agreed, practically choking out the word from between clenched teeth. Tierce was hardly a common soldier, after all. More importantly, Disra desperately needed a man of his skills and training. "I would merely be the political power behind the throne. Plus the supplier of military men and matériel, of course."

"From the Braxant Sector Fleet?"

"And other sources," Disra said. "You, should you choose to join us, would serve as the architect of our overall strategy."

"I see." If Tierce was bothered by the word "serve," he didn't show it. "And the third person?"

"Are you with us?"

Tierce studied him. "First tell me more."

"I'll do better than tell you." Disra pushed his chair back and stood up. "I'll show you."

Disra led the way down the rightmost corridor. It ended in a dusty metal door with a wheel set into its center. Gripping the edges of the wheel, Disra turned it; and with a creak that echoed eerily in the confined space the door swung open.

The previous owner would hardly have recognized his one-time torture chamber. The instruments of pain and terror had been taken out, the walls and floor cleaned and carpet-insulated, and the furnishings of a fully functional modern apartment installed.

But for the moment Disra had no interest in the chamber itself. All his attention was on Tierce as the former Guardsman stepped into the room.

Stepped into the room . . . and caught sight of the room's single occupant, seated in the center in a duplicate of a Star Destroyer's captain's chair.

Tierce froze, his eyes widening with shock, his entire body stiffening as if a power current had jolted through him. His eyes darted to Disra, back to the captain's chair, flicked around the room as if seeking evidence of a trap or hallucination or perhaps his own insanity, back again to the chair. Disra held his breath. . . .

STAR WARS®

THE FORCE IS WITH YOU

whenever you open a *Star Wars* novel
from Bantam Spectra Books!

*The novels of the incomparable
Timothy Zahn*

___29612-4 HEIR TO THE EMPIRE $5.99/$6.99 Canada

___56071-9 DARK FORCE RISING $5.99/$6.99

___56492-7 THE LAST COMMAND $5.99/$6.99

___29804-6 SPECTER OF THE PAST $5.99/$7.99

___10035-1 VISION OF THE FUTURE $24.95/$34.95

The original Star Wars *anthologies
edited by Kevin J. Anderson...*

___56468-4 TALES FROM THE MOS EISLEY CANTINA $5.99/$7.99

___56815-9 TALES FROM JABBA'S PALACE $5.99/$7.99

___56816-7 TALES OF THE BOUNTY HUNTERS $5.99/$7.99

...and by Peter Schweighofer...

___57876-6 TALES FROM THE EMPIRE $5.99/$7.99

Please send me the books I have checked above. I am enclosing $_____ (add $2.50 to
cover postage and handling). Send check or money order, no cash or C.O.D.'s, please.

Name _____

Address _____

City/State/Zip _____

Send order to: Bantam Books, Dept. SF 11, 2451 S. Wolf Rd., Des Plaines, IL 60018.
Allow four to six weeks for delivery.
Prices and availability subject to change without notice.   SF 11 1/99
®, ™, and © 1997 Lucasfilm Ltd. All rights reserved. Used under authorization.